By Lee Pini

The Boyfriend Fix
Good at People
Six Places to Fall in Love
Strangers to Husbands

CAMP LAKE BAY HOLIDAY
As Long As You Love Me So
When We Finally Kiss Goodnight

Published by DREAMSPINNER PRESS
www.dreamspinnerpress.com

Six Places TO FALL IN LOVE

LEE PINI

Published by

DREAMSPINNER PRESS

8219 Woodville Hwy #1245
Woodville, FL 32362 USA
www.dreamspinnerpress.com

Six Places to Fall in Love
© 2025 Lee Pini.

Cover Art
© 2025 Reece Notley
reece@vitaenoir.com
Cover content is for illustrative purposes only and any person depicted on the cover is a model.

Trade Paperback ISBN: 9781641087667
Digital ISBN: 9781641087650
Trade Paperback published January 2025
v. 1.0

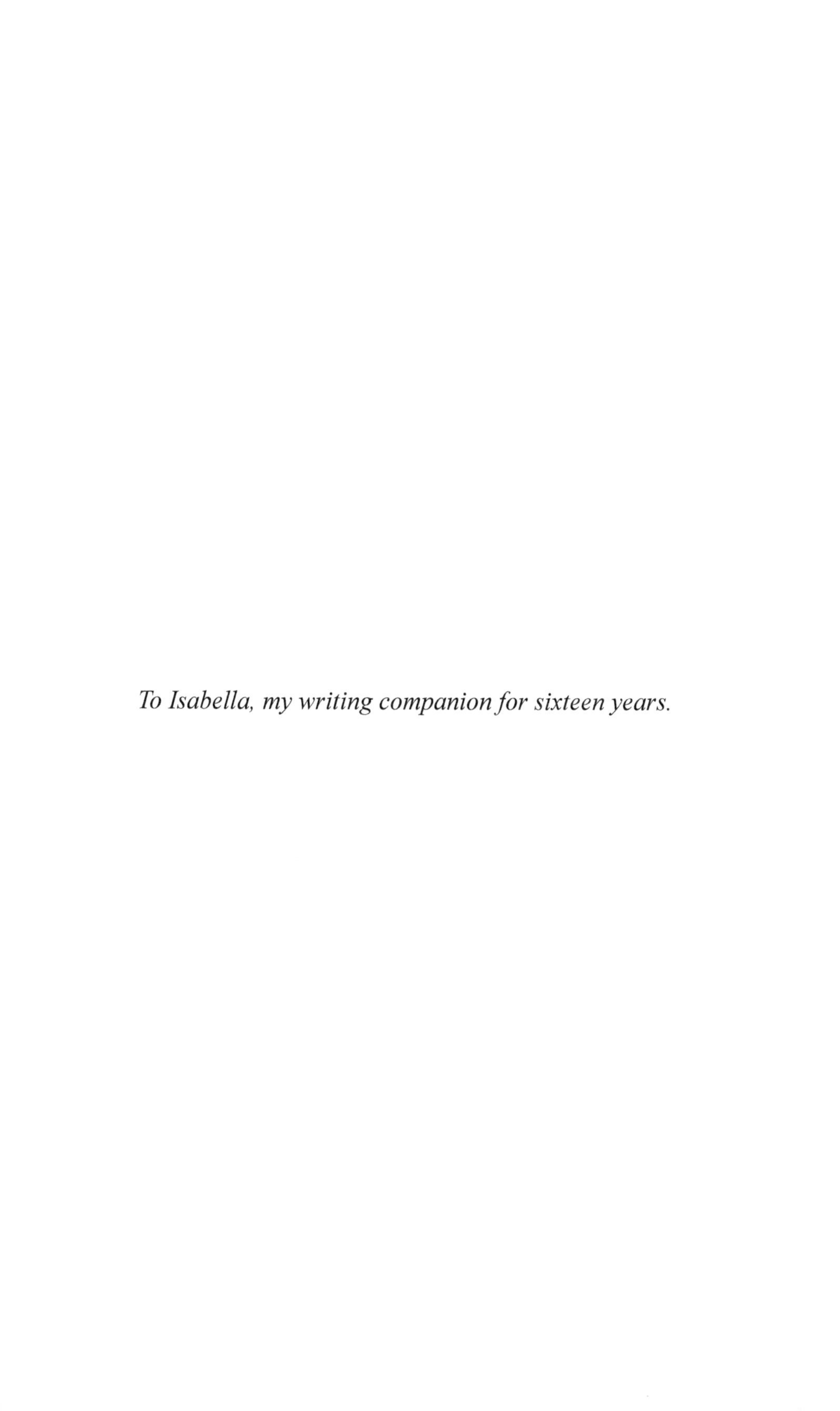

To Isabella, my writing companion for sixteen years.

Part One: The Bush

Chapter One

June

THE RED of the sand against the blue of the reflected sky is so stark and bright it sears Percy's eyes. His camera shutter snaps as he takes a picture. It won't sell—who wants a picture of a puddle?—but it captures something about this place. The sky, the earth, the colors— maybe it's because he's from here, but there's nothing like an African sky to make him feel connected to everything. Everything that matters, at least.

The hum of an engine drifts in on the cool breeze. Percy's knees pop as he stands from his crouch in front of the puddle. He's feeling every one of his thirty-two years lately. It's going to be hell when he's actually old, but he'll keep coming to the bush until he literally can't. They'll have to drag him away.

No, scratch that—just let the hyenas and the jackals have him. Back to the land, or something. When he tells his friends he'd rather be eaten by scavengers, they either laugh like he's joking or look horrified. But if he says he wants to be part of the landscape he loves, that lives inside his soul, for eternity, then they look at him like he's mad. Maybe a bit happy clappy.

A Land Cruiser comes into view, bumping along the rutted road. Less road, more track. This is the part of the reserve set aside for conservation, so the roads are nearly nonexistent.

Percy shifts his camera and his rifle on his shoulder and watches the vehicle's approach. Its occupants resolve into two figures, driver and passenger. He hooks his fingers into his water bottle, pulls it out of his backpack, and twists the cap off to take a long drink.

The Land Cruiser pulls up in a cloud of dust and a man jumps out. It's one of those quintessential safari moments. Percy thinks about snapping a photo but doesn't. The man lifts out a pack and swings it onto his back, thumps the side of the Land Cruiser, and heads Percy's way.

Percy lifts his hand in a wave to the driver—it's Rhys, who cheerfully offers to sleep with Percy every time Percy's here (and just as cheerfully accepts the rejection)—then turns it to a thumbs-up. The Land Cruiser reverses, turns around, and is gone, leaving dust and the sound of its engine behind. Both settle to nothing as the man jogs across a gully with a trickle of water at the bottom.

Percy shoves his water bottle back into its pocket, considers smiling, and decides against it. Smiling doesn't come easily these days, and he's awkward enough without his weird hostage-situation rictus.

Midday sun glints off the silver in the man's hair. The contrast between the silver and the black of the rest of it is as stark as the sky against the ground. It would make a nice photo. The silver is premature—this man is surely around Percy's own age, maybe even a year or two younger. It's odd having seen someone's CV and knowing when they finished university, and by extension how old they are, but not having met the person yet.

As the man gets close, he extends a hand. "Hey there. I'm Rob. You must be Percy de Villiers."

Rob Hale's—he pronounces it Ha-lay, which is something Percy is determined to get right—easy grin makes it difficult not to like him immediately. The grin, plus the shadow of stubble on his jaw, plus his golden skin and the beachy wave to his salt-and-pepper hair, also makes it difficult not to find him attractive, which is sort of the last thing Percy needs.

"Yeah," Percy says, shaking Rob's hand. He watches for the flicker of reaction at his limp handshake. The bush is for the man's man, and Percy has been around enough men overflowing with misplaced machismo to last a lifetime.

Rob doesn't react. "It's great to finally meet you," he says in some indeterminate American drawl that might be Southern. There's a little gravel to his voice. He's shorter than Percy, but most people are. Some sort of Dutch gene for height was hiding in his mixed-up family tree and came out of hiding when he hit puberty. Rob is solid, too, almost stocky. Muscular. With a beard, he'd make a great bear. He's dressed appropriately for South Africa in late fall: brown khakis, gray T-shirt, green hoodie tied around his waist.

Percy casts a critical eye over Rob's pack, but it looks good. Compact, with the bedroll secured at the bottom. Percy has the tent—only one—strapped on his own pack. For safety's sake, he wanted them sleeping in the same tent, because that way Percy will wake up if Rob decides he wants to go on a late-night bush walk.

Hint: this is a bad idea.

"Listen," Rob says, "I want to start out by thanking you for letting me come with you. I know you had a lot of journalists submit applications, so it's really an honor to be selected."

God, Percy *hates* this sort of fawning. But Rob is right that a load of journos wanted this tag-along. What Rob doesn't know is that he only got the gig by the skin of his teeth. Percy's agent, Eunice, lobbied hard for a big-shot French nature writer, but Percy dug his heels in. He wanted Rob, and he's not sure he could even tell you why. His credentials aren't anything special, and he's never had a piece blow up. His blog does middling numbers. On the surface of things, he's an entirely average travel writer.

"Thank you for accepting the offer," Percy says. Can't go wrong with platitudes, yeah? "How was the trip in?"

"We had to stop and wait for elephants to cross the road!" The pure glee in Rob's voice makes Percy smile.

"Ellies are still hanging round the main fence, then, yeah?" The camera bumps against Percy's hip. "They were there when I drove up the other day too."

Percy could never be in the hospitality industry—and safari camps are a whole other level of hospitality. But the wonder on Rob's face gives Percy an inkling of why people do it. And he can tell that Rob is the kind of person who makes it worth it.

Something eases in his chest. This whole thing has been so stressful, even though it was his idea in the first place. The endless second-guessing about his choice has plagued Percy ever since Rob signed the contract. He hasn't had a solid six hours of sleep in months. Then again, he's got plenty to lose sleep over, so.

"I love it here already," Rob says.

"Your first time in Africa?"

"I went to Morocco once to write a piece on Moroccan leatherwork," he offers. "But sub-Saharan Africa, yeah. First time."

"You like it so far?"

Rob rakes his fingers through his shaggy black hair. "Honestly, I went straight from the airport to my hotel, and my transfer picked me up this morning and drove me up here. So I kind of feel like I've barely seen any of it so far."

Yeah, Americans don't tend to stop and play tourist in Joburg. Percy's usually torn between pride in his country and complete and total agreement on that score.

"Well," Percy says, "hopefully you got to stop at the lodge for some lunch before Rhys brought you out here."

Rob's eyes light up again—and again, Percy is struck by how good-looking he is. Obviously, Percy did some light online stalking of all the serious candidates, but he doesn't remember thinking Rob was anything special. Turns out he was very, very wrong about that, because Rob is dead fit.

"Yeah!" Rob replies. "Wow. It's gorgeous, isn't it? Have you stayed there?"

Percy nods. "The camp manager is a friend." Sort of an understatement. Katlego is the reason Percy made it out of childhood with his sanity intact. Intact-ish. She was his governess's daughter, and they were basically raised together. Katli is more like a sister than a friend. "You're staying a few nights after we're back from the bush, right?"

There's that easy grin again. "Are you kidding? That's definitely not the kind of place I can afford normally. I'm taking the chance to stay in the lap of luxury."

Percy's bankrolling this whole thing. He sees it as an excellent use of family funds. Doubtless his father would disagree, but his father has rather worn through his credibility when it comes to the proper use of money.

"Good," Percy says. He's itching to get out into the bush. His camera is loaded up with two blank memory cards, he has his other lenses snugged in the custom pocket in his pack, and he can tell the light's going to get better and better as the day goes on.

He clears his throat. "So. I know you signed all the waivers and release forms—"

"Yeah, if a lion eats me, my family won't sue."

With a snort, Percy goes on, "We have to go over some rules, though. Mainly one, really—the rest are all sub-rules of that." He pauses to make sure he has Rob's attention. "You must, at all times, do what I say. If I say stop, you stop. If I say go, you go. If I say climb that tree, you climb the tree. If I say run—and you better hope I don't say run—then you run. Also, my rifle is off-limits."

Rob nods. "Understood. You're the expert."

Sometimes people say that and they're patronizing him. It doesn't matter how many awards he's won, how many back country or bush or mountain treks he goes on. Some people hear de Villiers, and all they can see is a pampered, rich Cape Coloured kid. Never mind that he's got an Apprentice Field Guide qualification, and that includes the four hundred required hours. To plenty of South Africans, Percy is always going to be rooftop infinity pools, manicured gardens, eight beds/eight baths, and so far removed from the way most South Africans live that it's a joke.

Not that having the NQF2 is exactly a window into how most South Africans live, but, well—he did that on his own, and no amount of money or family connections could buy it. It's one of his proudest achievements.

It's also the only reason he can be out here in the bush with, as far as insurance is concerned, a tourist.

"My job isn't just taking nature photos this week." Percy gives Rob a serious look. "It's keeping you safe. Just because your family won't sue me if a lion eats you doesn't mean it's a good look."

Rob holds his hands up. "Sure. You have a reputation to consider. I get it."

Percy's shoulders tighten and he can't help the twitch of tension. "Yeah, right. My reputation. That's the idea behind all of this—get the focus back on my work, instead of"—he grimaces—"my personal life."

There's a sympathetic light in Rob's eyes, but Percy seriously doubts he has any real idea of what Percy's gone through the past few months. Which—ugh—sounds so whinging, so poor little rich boy. Other people have it worse. Obviously. So much worse. In fact, Percy feels responsible for a lot of that so-much-worse.

"I'm here to focus on your work," Rob says, before adding with a half smile, "And to not get eaten by a lion."

Oh *no*. He's this good-looking and he has a sense of humor?

Percy shifts his pack on his shoulders and steadies his camera and rifle. "Any questions before we start? Concerns I can alleviate?"

"Isn't bringing a healthy level of concern into the bush the right way to approach this?" That half smile flits across Rob's face again, a flash of crooked front teeth that Percy didn't think Americans were allowed to have.

It's impossible—literally impossible—not to return the smile. And that's red flags across the board, alarms and red alerts, all-hands-on-deck level *do not get this way with the journo you handpicked for this excursion.*

"I think we're going to get along," Percy says. He swigs from his water bottle and offers it to Rob, who takes it without any hesitation and drinks. "We walk single file. Keep your voice down and stay close to me so we don't look like something big and easy to pounce on."

Rob nods. Percy surveys their surroundings once more. There's nothing but birdsong and the occasional buzz of the insects that survive South Africa's fall and winter.

With a quick hand signal to indicate the direction they'll start off in, Percy takes the first long stride that will take them into the bush.

This had better all be worth it.

Chapter Two

ROB TOOK too many caffeine pills this morning.

He misjudged how it would feel to fly from Atlanta, Georgia, to Johannesburg, South Africa. It's a fifteen-hour flight, sure, but South Africa's only six hours ahead of Atlanta. It's like going to Europe! It's like the return trip back from Oahu.

Except, lol, no. It's not at all. It's the longest flight he's ever been on, fifteen hours outside of time in a dark tube hurtling from afternoon, through night and morning, and straight to afternoon again. It's weird to lose a whole entire day—weird to grab his pack from the luggage carousel and step outside into afternoon, same as he put behind him as he walked into good old ATL.

So when he woke up this morning, thankfully not still feeling like he was on a plane (are air legs a thing?), he combated the jet leg, general exhaustion, and yucky feeling with two caffeine pills. And then a third in the SUV that picked him up.

The last thing he wanted to do was look like a jittery mess when he met Percy de Villiers.

And okay, like. Y'all. Rob was not *prepared* for Percy. So maybe he has a hero worship thing going on with the man—what travel writer wouldn't? Percy's photos aren't just pictures of places, they're windows. When Rob looks at them, he feels himself not only knowing the place Percy shot the photo, but also knowing something in himself that he didn't realize was there.

Back in college, at UW Madison, all Rob knew was he wanted to go into journalism. He wanted to be one of those journalists who got embedded for a story, who spent weeks living with the people he'd be writing about and teasing out something essential about the human spirit. Flipping through a *National Geographic* one day, Rob came upon the most arresting photograph he'd ever seen. It made him freeze and just—stare.

It was a photo of the reddest sand dunes Rob had ever seen and the bluest sky. Floating in between was a band of purplish mist, flowing down the dunes like a river, or a glacier. To this day, he remembers how it made him feel both small and huge simultaneously—like he was completely insignificant in the face of a place like that, but also like he was part of the planet, that he was connected to that place and to everyone on Earth, because this place existed.

The caption identified the place as Namib-Naukluft National Park, Namibia. The photo credit belonged to Percy de Villiers. That photo was what made Rob want to become a travel writer. It made him want to do with words what Percy de Villiers was able to do with a camera.

So, yeah. Rob's been following Percy's work for, like, kind of a while. And now he's *here*. In Africa. With him. Somehow, out of all the people that must have applied for this week in the bush with Percy de Villiers, Rob is the one following him through dry, crunchy yellow grass. He'd pinch himself, except the three caffeine pills are enough assurance that he's awake.

Today is all about observation. He wants to get a feel for how Percy works—does he look for the perfect photo? Does he camp out in one place all day until that one moment when the cheetah breaks cover? Does he set up his shot, maneuvering pieces of the landscape so they balance the way he wants them to? Or does he just see something and know it's going to make an amazing picture?

From a purely aesthetic—and admittedly unprofessional—standpoint, observing Percy is a delight. He's tall and lean and moves with fluid grace. His skin is light brown, beautifully warm in the sun, while his hair is black. It's done up in twists, then pulled back into a bun on top of his head. Gold rings, cuffs, and beads glint where they're nestled in the twists, and several of the twists have gold threads wound around or within them. He has a gold nose ring and a line of three tiny gold studs on the helix of one ear.

He's *very* good-looking, with the kind of dark, fathomless eyes and bone structure that Rob has been falling for since he and Joey Nakamura got locked in together during Seven Minutes in Heaven in seventh grade and decided to kiss "because it would be funny." Haha, yeah, very funny, especially since it was Rob's gay awakening and he ended up pining for beautiful Joey Nakamura with the Cheekbones until his dad got a new job and relocated them all to Atlanta from Honolulu.

But. Rob is a professional, and he's on this project because he's good at his job. So does he think Percy is extremely sexy? Yes, he has eyes. Is he going to give Percy even the tiniest hint of that fact? No! He's not a creep.

They walk for about twenty minutes before Percy stops for the first time. He adjusts the settings on his camera and aims it toward the mountain looming over the landscape. After taking a few shots, he glances at Rob and asks, "Am I supposed to be describing my process?"

Oh good, they can talk now. Rob didn't want to break the silence first. Since they began walking back at the road, Percy hasn't said a word, so Rob wasn't sure if maybe "keep your voice down" actually meant "don't talk." "Just do what you'd normally do. Pretend I'm not here."

"Well, it's a bit hard to do that," Percy replies. His eyes widen fractionally, and he adds quickly, "Because I'm responsible for keeping you in one piece, that is."

Would it be big-headed of Rob to take that to mean Percy finds him attractive? It's no secret that Percy's queer, so it's not impossible.

"I just want to watch you work today," Rob says. "But I'd like it if later—maybe when we stop for the night?—we go through some ground rules for when you're on the record."

"Ground rules," Percy repeats. He has an interesting accent—it's part South Africa, but there's also the crisp, cut glass of middle-class English. "Good idea."

While he takes a few more pictures, Rob sips from his water bottle. "Remind me what those mountains are called?" he says during a lull in Percy's photographing.

"The Waterberg." Percy snaps one more picture and turns to face Rob. Clipping the lens cap back on, he adds, "Thaba Meetse in Northern Sotho. The language spoken around here. One of them, at least."

"There are eleven official languages in South Africa, right?" Rob knows he's right, because he's boned up on his South Africa knowledge since he got accepted for this project three weeks ago.

"Yeah." Percy cocks his head, and the sun catches on one of the bright gold cuffs in his hair. "Now let's hear you name them."

Shit. "Uh—"

Percy smiles, not in a mean way. "Don't worry," Percy says. "There are plenty of South Africans who couldn't name them, either."

It goes without saying that Percy de Villiers isn't one of those South Africans. Rob makes a mental note to hop on Wikipedia the minute he's back on Wi-Fi so he can memorize all eleven languages. English, Afrikaans, Zulu…? Shit!

The expression on Percy's face gets wryer. There's warmth in it, though. "C'mon. We have a fair bit of ground to cover. I want to camp on high ground tonight." He points at a mountain in the distance. "That's just over three kilometers. Good camping spots on the slopes if we can get there."

Rob looks around. The grass is tall and tawny, perfect for any lion that wants to sneak up on them. Trees dot the landscape, rising over the grass and spreading their branches wide. Rob doesn't know the names of any of them.

They continue onward, dry grass crunching under their feet. There are some places where grass isn't growing and fine, red sand clings to Rob's hiking boots as he slogs across it. The feeling is familiar—Oahu has the same kind of fine sand that makes you feel the way you dream about running, slow as molasses and ten times as hard as it should be.

For the first couple hours, they don't see any animals. Rob doesn't let it get to him. At least, he doesn't let it get to him too much. They're out here for a week, and he has a couple days at the camp, which will include game drives. He's going to see animals. It's just, the elephants on the way in kind of set the tone. And he's totally going to be *that* tourist, at least in his head. He's in Africa!

And sure, he's a thirty-year-old travel writer who's been all over the world. But. *Africa.* He wasn't immune to humming Lebo M quietly to himself on the car ride to the reserve this morning.

They see evidence of animals. There are small brown pellets covering the ground in some places, which Percy informs him is impala dung.

"There's a lot of it," Rob says, weirdly impressed.

Percy smiles slightly. "There's no shortage of impala here."

"Is that good or bad?"

For a moment, Percy stares at the ground. Then he scuffs the toe of his brown leather boot in the impala dung. A few of the pellets bounce away. "Mm. They need to have their population controlled some years."

Oh god, he doesn't want to hear about Bambi's mother being shot.

That exact thought must be showing on Rob's face, which isn't a surprise, because he's no good at hiding what he's feeling. "They're live-trapped sometimes," Percy says. "And brought places that need them."

They keep walking. Percy points out other evidence of animals—a rhino midden, giraffe dung, and hyena scat. When they stop for a snack in a wide-open space, Percy says, deadpan, "I seem to be giving you a shitty experience so far."

Rob, of course, lets out his dumb, loud bay of a laugh, the one which multiple boyfriends have said sounds like a seal. Clapping a hand over his mouth, he says in a muffled voice, "Sorry, I'm going to scare the wildlife."

Percy heads for a sun-bleached dead tree. Its gnarled roots twist toward the sky, bare of soil and probably long uprooted. As he rests his pack on the ground, his eyes flash with delight. "Oh, this has been the rarest sighting of all, though—someone who laughs at my terrible jokes."

"I thought it was a good joke," Rob says fairly. "I guess you have to be a fan of puns."

"My friends are all sophisticated gays who wouldn't dream of even acknowledging a pun." Percy smiles and sits, patting the spot next to him. "C'mon. You've got to be knackered. I've got biltong and dried fruit for snacks, if you want to share?"

Gratefully, Rob takes a seat. He *is* knackered. He's in pretty good shape, but this is still a lot of walking with a heavy pack, especially when he's jet lagged and sleep-deprived.

He only vaguely knows what biltong is, but Percy produces a paper bag from a small pocket on his pack and offers it to him first. Whatever it is, it's probably not the weirdest thing he's tried (that honor goes to Tamilok woodworms, or maybe penis fish). When he reaches into the bag, his fingers encounter what feels like jerky. So he pulls it out, and… it looks like jerky.

He bites into it. Yep. Tastes like jerky too.

While Rob takes his biltong journey, Percy has already chewed and swallowed a couple pieces of it. "This is kudu, I think?" He makes a face. "I can never tell. It all tastes the same to me."

"It's good."

"You think so? I personally find it sort of revolting, but"—he shrugs—"good source of protein, yeah?"

Rob fishes another piece of biltong from the bag. "I did this piece on Colombian food once, and my hosts spent one night feeding me all the weirdest stuff, trying to gross me out. They were sure the hormiga culona would do it, but I scooped up a handful of those and ate them like peanuts."

Scrunching his nose, Percy asks, "That's some kind of bug, isn't it? Ants or something?"

"Yeah, exactly. They're tasty."

"I've never had them." Percy sounds wistful. "I like to try new things, even if I end up hating them."

There's a spark of electricity in Rob's chest, the sort of thing that happens every time he meets a kindred spirit. This one feels supercharged. "Me too."

Percy pulls another paper bag from his pack and peeks inside. "Oooh, it's mango! Good. I owe you, Katli."

They eat in silence for a few minutes and rehydrate. Rob's second water bottle is almost empty. He has one more full, so he's hoping they come across a water source in the next few hours. Percy's agent assured him over email that water would be plentiful on the reserve, he just needed to bring purifying supplies.

Just as he's feeling revitalized, a loud, nasal cry comes from behind him. "KWEH!" some—thing? One?—cries. "KWEHHHHHHHH."

Percy lets out a snort of laughter and swivels at the waist. "Grey go-away," he says, pointing at a tree behind them.

Rob follows the direction of his finger and quickly locates the source of the sound. It's a gray bird about the size of a crow, with a long tail and a crest on its head. It cocks its head at them and calls again, "KWEH!"

"What's it saying?" Rob asks.

Percy looks at him. A smile twitches at his lips. "Go away, of course." His camera's strap pulls taut over his chest and digs into the fabric of his shirt as he hauls it around and takes several rapid photos of the bird. The bird preens, unconcerned about their presence, though you wouldn't know it from the noise it makes.

Swinging a leg over the dead tree so he's straddling it, Percy fiddles with his camera and glowers at the view screen. "Mmph. Want to try it with my six hundred millimeter…."

With one hand, he reaches for his pack, finger-walking his way to a pocket on the front, which he unzips quietly. By feel alone, he selects a huge telephoto lens and eases it from his pack.

The bird is still preening, and considering how quiet Percy is, Rob isn't surprised. He moves like a cat, slinky and fluid, and even in Rob's head it sounds trite. But it's true.

Still. He's probably not going to put it in his piece.

There's a very quiet click as Percy detaches one lens and locks the other into place, but he muffles both sounds in his clothing.

With the telephoto, he takes a few more pictures. The grey go-away obliges by remaining on its perch for another few minutes. Then it shakes its feathers out and launches itself into the air, flying so slowly that it looks like it might fall out of the sky.

Rob watches it wing away, but he looks to Percy as the other man says, "No one will want those pictures."

There's a prickly note in his voice, like maybe he thinks Rob is going to agree—but the look on his face is thinly veiled resignation.

Another frisson of electricity goes through Rob's chest, this one fainter than the earlier spark. Like an echo of it.

"Why not?" Rob asks.

Percy shrugs. "Grey go-aways are really common. And they're not colorful. Have you ever seen a green turaco?" When Rob shakes his head, Percy goes on, "Similar bird, but green. There's the great blue turaco, as well." He shrugs again. "People like pictures of colorful birds. They're prettier."

"I thought the grey go-away was pretty," Rob says, feeling a weird kinship with the bird. He's a brown gay man—he knows what it's like to be considered not the ideal.

"Yeah?" Percy flashes him a smile. "I like them too."

They sit for a few more minutes as Percy puts his telephoto lens away (who can blame him—the thing probably costs more than Rob's car). Then Percy meets Rob's eyes and asks, "Ready to keep going?"

"Let me get one more piece of biltong," Rob says. A smile twitches at Percy's mouth again as he waits for Rob to snag one last bite, and then he folds the bag up again and stows it in his pack.

As they stand, a flock of small birds alights in the nearest tree, twittering and cheeping. Other bird calls begin to sound—or maybe they were there the whole time, and Rob just wasn't tuned into them?

They walk on, the landscape alive with birdsong.

Chapter Three

THEY MAKE better time than Percy expects. Maybe he had expected Rob to gawk. Or not be fit enough to walk all day. Nothing in his prior work or credentials suggested he spends much time roughing it.

Which Eunice pointed out to Percy. Repeatedly. Ad nauseam. "He's going to cry for mama the minute he hears the hyenas," she predicted. "Why do you want a glorified blogger who writes listicles about the best clubs to visit while you're abroad?"

Because, Percy wanted to say, but didn't, *because he writes about gay clubs. Because he's queer, and if I'm going to talk about myself—if I'm going to let someone* in—*I want to know I can trust him on at least one thing.*

Anyway. They're starting up the slope of the mountain now, and the sun's still comfortably above the horizon. This has been, Percy is tentatively willing to declare, a good first day.

Though Rob hasn't started asking questions yet.

Just the thought makes Percy's shoulders tighten. No matter how much he doesn't want to talk about… *things*, they're bound to come up. Of course they're bound to come up—the whole point of Rob being here is to deflect the attention glaring Percy's way toward his work.

A francolin alarms in the distance. Percy stops and holds up a hand. Rob stops too, so that's good. He also doesn't speak—even better. Percy's been on game drives with journos who don't get that this isn't a zoo, that the bush is real and unpredictable and sometimes dangerous. The fact that Rob understands is nice.

They stand in silence for a minute, then two. Percy listens and turns slowly in a circle, making sure to pay special attention to anything in his peripheral vision. It's better at picking up movement.

The francolin stays quiet, though, and it doesn't flush. Percy lowers his hand but remains still. Better to be sure, even though the francolin was behind them. They're more trustworthy than impala for alerting their fellow prey animals to danger. Out here, Percy and Rob are very much prey animals.

The minutes tick past with no further warnings from the francolin. Percy nods to Rob. He looks nervous, so Percy explains, "That was a francolin alarming—what animals do when they see something that might be trouble. They're—"

"Oh, I know francolins!" Rob's voice comes out loud, and he cringes, then whispers, "Sorry."

He is... *so* good-looking. And cute too. Bloody lethal combination.

In a more circumspect tone of voice, Rob says, "We have francolins in Hawai'i."

"Yeah?"

"Yeah! I mean, they were introduced, so." Rob makes a face. "Can't love them or anything, because of our native birds being in so much trouble from all the invasives, but. I still kind of love them. I didn't know they lived here too!"

"The ones here are endemic. I'm pretty certain, at least?" Damn, he'll have to google that. He's not as good a birder as he could be—which is why he hasn't gotten his NQF4 yet. The specialized bird knowledge section is murder.

Every time Rob gets excited about the wildlife, something warm and fizzy bubbles in Percy's chest. Rob's whole face lights up when he's interested in something, and his smile seems like the easiest thing in the world. Percy wonders if he realizes that about himself.

He wants to ask about Hawai'i. The way Rob said, *We have francolins in Hawai'i,* makes it sound like he's from there, but Percy thought he was from Atlanta.

Percy is, however, terrible at small talk. It's so much easier to say nothing than to worry about saying the right thing and not being too... whatever. Passionate, knowledgeable, boring. The good thing about the bush is you've got to be quiet as you can while you're moving, so that's a good excuse to not ask about Hawai'i.

Even though he really does want to know.

They keep walking, but it's only another five minutes or so before tracks catch his eye.

He kneels to look more closely. "Cheetah came this way recently." Was that what had made the francolin alarm?

Rob breathes in sharply. "How do you know?"

With the side of his hand, Percy cuts a line in the dust at the front and back of the paw print. "Here. Cheetah can seem tricky because—" He stops when he realizes Rob is standing back a little. "Um, you can get closer to see if you want."

Sheepishly, Rob says, "I didn't want to wreck it. It's so clear."

A smile blindsides Percy—his *real* smile, which feels creaky on his face because it sees so little action these days. "It's all right. Plenty more where this came from, yeah? But here." He takes a picture. "It's a nice clear track, you're right."

Rob crouches next to him, his gaze lingering on Percy's real smile. Probably as shocked to see it as Percy is to display it.

Now that Rob can see better, Percy points at the front of the track. "Most of the time it's easy to tell the difference between dog and cat tracks because cats have retractable claws and dogs don't." As Rob nods, Percy goes on, "But cheetah don't have retractable claws, so you can see the claws—they're here, see?—and maybe think, ah, this is a canine."

"I would totally do that," Rob says.

The real smile thinks about making another appearance, and Percy isn't sure what's happening. "Second easiest way to tell the difference between feline and canine tracks: look at the palm. This part, see?"

He taps his finger in the center of the track. Rob delightedly asks, "It's called a palm on animals too?"

"It is, yeah. On cats, the leading edge has two lobes. On a dog, it would be like"—next to the track, he draws an example of a canine track in the dirt—"just one lobe, yeah? And if you look at the back edge of the palm, there are three lobes. Dogs just have two. So. Cheetah."

Suddenly feeling a little flustered and stupid, he sits back on his heels. This wasn't billed as a safari—it was billed as a chance to have exclusive access to a famous and elusive wildlife photographer. Going into field guide mode is probably something he should curb.

But Rob is looking back and forth between the real cheetah track and Percy's example canine one. "That's so cool," he murmurs.

Responses flit through Percy's mind, ranging from *Thanks* to *It's really not* to *I think cheetah are cool too*. The urge to say it's nothing and deflect the praise seethes under his skin, and then too much time has gone by to say anything and not sound weird.

He rises to his feet, still staring at the ground. "It's just one. Might be the female that had a few sub-adults last time I was here, but it looks like she's on her own now. Or it could be one of the males, but they mainly stick together in coalitions here." He scratches at his chin. Stubble scrapes against his fingertips. "I'd like to see if I can find her, if you don't mind. Tomorrow. Not tonight."

The excitement on Rob's face is answer enough. "Yeah! Of course! I mean, no, I don't mind. I was hoping I'd get to see you track some animals."

"You know I can do that?" Something hollow and achy forms at the pit of Percy's stomach.

Rob looks confused. "Yeah? I assume everyone who applied for this knew that. Didn't they?"

"I don't know," Percy answers honestly. Rob's giving him a baffled look, but honestly, if he had to say, he would've said no, they didn't. He's used to people caring about a few key points about him: his photography, his very rich and very troubled family, the color of his skin, and who he sleeps with. The rest of it hasn't traditionally mattered. And maybe—probably—he thought most of the people who sent in their CVs to spend this week with him were mainly interested in his family, and the scandal, and the trial, and the prison sentence—

It gets hard to breathe before he registers the pressure on his lungs, and he grabs his camera and grips it hard. The rifle is a grounding weight on his shoulder. Birds call all around them. Something moves in the distance and Percy focuses on that, focuses on letting the winter sun warm his head and the back of his neck.

"Giraffe," he manages to get out, sounding sort of normal, and Rob's head whips round to look where Percy's pointing. They're so far away, it's not a great sighting—just their heads visible between some trees—but Percy's grateful to them for giving him a moment to get himself under control. At home, in his flat in the Green Point district of Cape Town, he goes into his office/greenhouse and curls into his papasan chair, watching the play of light and shadow on the wall from the glass mobiles and plants waving in the breeze. And then, eventually, he can breathe again.

Thing is, in the bush, you don't get to curl into the fetal position and wait for it to pass. The bush is his sanctuary, his therapy. But now the grasping realities of who he is and who he's not and who he never wants to be are finding their way to him here.

Wind hisses through a nearby umbrella thorn and the grass wavers. The air smells dusty and sharp. It will be cold tonight. They'll be cozy in their tent, though.

The tightness in his chest eases just as Rob turns to him, looking thrilled about the giraffes. But his expression falters, like he's seen something on Percy's face that troubles him.

"Everything okay?" Rob asks.

"Yeah, fine." Percy gestures for Rob to follow as he keeps walking.

There are animal trails going up the mountain. Percy keeps to one that's clearly been well used by antelope. There's impala, bushbuck, kudu, and reedbuck dung. There are even—aardwolf tracks?

He stops to study those. Yes, aardwolf. His pulse patters. He'd love to see an aardwolf. That would be nice for Rob too. They're not common; that would be really exciting for a safari first timer. Even Percy's only seen an aardwolf once, and he didn't get a photo.

"Something cool?" Rob asks.

"Aardwolf," Percy says. "Oh! And look, genet, here. The aardwolf's been by more recently."

But, hm, probably at least twenty-four hours ago. Maybe it's still hanging around. Hopefully it's still hanging around.

The climb gets steeper from there. They startle a reedbuck, which leaps away, white tail flashing. Rob looks disappointed, and Percy wants to tell him it's okay, they'll see more animals.

Or maybe he's disappointed because Percy didn't know it was there. So much for that field guide qualification, he's probably thinking.

The sun gets low and the sky turns watercolor, blue bleeding into orange. Time to stop, because Percy never misses a sunset in the bush.

There's a spot he remembers being around here, fairly level and without any big trees for leopards to climb up and drop down on them from. Last time he camped here he made a little fire ring, so if things look different, that should make it easy to spot. Another couple minutes brings them to it, just like he remembered.

"We'll stop here," he announces, swinging his pack onto the ground. His fire ring is a little askew, like something's pushed the rocks around. A quick inspection of the area doesn't turn up any predator tracks, and he didn't see any on the way up. Good. This should be safe.

The lingering pull in his chest fades completely at that thought. The bush keeps him from going to pieces because he has to keep himself safe, but keeping Rob safe is on an entirely different level. It makes him steadier, thinking about that responsibility. Maybe that's odd. It probably is. Everyone thinks he's odd once they get to know him.

"Oh man, it feels good to put that thing down."

Percy looks over at Rob as he speaks, catching him in the process of leaning back, hands on his hips, to crack his spine. When he stretches both arms over his head, hooking his hands together and standing on his toes, his shirt rides up and exposes his stomach. His pants sag between the bones of his hips and Percy is—staring. Nothing else to call it. He's staring at a soft tummy covered in dark fur, a thicker line of it trailing down, and he feels hot.

Fuck, well. *That* is not the reason Rob's here. And it's not professional. And it's creepy. The whole point of this week is to deflect scandal away from him, not to create an entirely new scandal. *Photographer Lures Journalist to Bush to Sexually Harass Him.* Or wait, no, they'll make sure to mention the color of his skin and his sexual orientation to make it both lurid and wink-wink-nudge-nudge-what-can-you-expect.

He turns away fast, rubbing a hand over his elbow, picking at the skin there before he can stop himself. He rips off a chunk of skin and realizes what he's doing, then grabs his camera to distract his hands.

The sunset is getting to Impressionist painting stages now. Percy goes to the edge of their campsite, where the mountain drops off in a steeper slope. "Come look?" he says to Rob, who looks a little like a puppy who's just been allowed to come for a ride in the car.

"It's beautiful," Rob says as he stops next to Percy.

Percy nods. His hands are on his camera, but he doesn't raise it to his face. Sometimes it's good to just look. The sun is behind the mountains now and the sky glows red and violet, fading to indigo, like the color of your favorite pair of jeans, worn and washed out. When Percy's in the bush, sunset makes him ache with want for something he can't name. He feels expansive, but he's still just… himself. Himself, stuck in his body, when he wants to be everything. He wants to be part of that color. He wants that purity.

They watch the sky shift from warm spectrum to cool, red and violet dimming to purples and the deep blue of the night sky. Should he say something? Being out here like this has always been a solitary experience for him. Practically spiritual.

"I always watch sunsets," he finally settles on, which makes him sound like an idiot. *Fucking good for you, de Villiers. Because sunsets are such an uncommon thing to watch.* God, he sounds like he's about to tell Rob to Live Laugh Love.

"This is a good one," Rob says, apparently insensate to Percy self-immolating with shame and despair. "I love sunsets too."

He looks over at Rob, who looks back and smiles at him. It doesn't seem to occur to him that Percy's making himself look like a twat.

They both turn back to the sky. After a minute, Rob says, "Hawai'i has good sunsets too."

Perfect opening—didn't Percy want to ask him about Hawai'i before? He rehearses it in his head a few times, then says, "Do you visit Hawai'i a lot?"

"Oh, I'm from there!" Even out of the corner of his eye, Percy can see the way he grins. "Yeah, I guess that's not really on my CV. I try to get back once a year at least. Still got lots of family there."

Light fades from the sky quickly now that the sun is gone. Percy loves this part too—watching the stars come out one by one, and then all at once in a thick spray of light.

"That's cool," Percy says. It feels extremely inadequate. He's genuinely interested in this. Genuinely interested in *Rob*. He clears his throat. "Why—um, why did you leave in the first place?"

Venus is the first visible thing in the night sky, shining bright white overhead. Mars will make an appearance once it's darker, and then the Milky Way.

Next to him, Rob puts his hands in his pockets. There's a chill in the air now that the sun's gone—nearly time to put on a jacket. Hawai'i and Atlanta are both warm, so Rob is probably going to feel the cold more than Percy does.

"We moved when I was fourteen," Rob says. "My dad's a pilot and he ended up getting a job with Delta. He always says they gave him a choice of where he wanted to be based, Atlanta, Detroit, or Minneapolis, and he told them, 'You think I'm lolo? I'm not going anywhere with all that snow!'"

Percy can't help laughing along with Rob. "That must have been a big change," he says and wants to kick himself immediately. This is why he takes photos—he doesn't know how to talk to people. *That must have been a big change?* Great, yeah, bang-up job at conversing. Perhaps next he'll observe that water is wet.

"Ugh, I was so mad when my parents said we were moving." Rob makes a noise and Percy looks at him. He looks sheepish. "I yelled and slammed a lot of doors and locked myself in my room and listened to—oh my god, this is embarrassing—My Chemical Romance. And probably some Fall Out Boy. Like, for three days straight, that was all I did. Blast MCR as loud as I could and post emo shit on MySpace. *Yes*, I still used MySpace in 2007."

Percy tries to hide a smile and fails. "Well, I suppose, just being fair, life's quite hard when you're fourteen." Hurrah! A complete sentence! Clauses, even!

"Life has never been as hard for anyone as it is for you when you're fourteen," Rob agrees with a grin. It fades, and his expression becomes more thoughtful. "And, you know. I was just figuring out who I was. I had my first crush on a boy, and suddenly my parents were taking me away from him and everything else I knew. I didn't get it. And I didn't want to. I didn't get why my dad couldn't just keep flying for Hawaiian."

"Did you ever ask?"

Rob laughs. "Oh, repeatedly. Usually at the top of my lungs. It was good in the end, though. We got to travel to more places since Delta flies to a lot more destinations."

It's hard to look away from Rob's face—from his gorgeous smile and those dark eyes. Percy realizes he's squinting to continue staring at Rob, because—fuck—it's nearly dark.

He jerks away to look at their campsite, which is currently a flat patch of dirt and rocks with a cold fire ring and two packs. No fire, no tent, certainly no dinner out and ready to be prepared. God, a beautiful man smiles at him in the bush and he goes to pieces? "Fuck, I'm being a chop," he mutters, striding to his pack. He puts his camera away and pulls out a torch and battery-powered lantern.

"Rob, can you pitch the tent?" he asks. At least having to get things done banishes his shyness.

Rob coughs and Percy looks at him, but he seems fine, just—

Oh.

"Pitch the tent," Rob giggles.

Percy hovers in a nebulous space between mortified, appalled, and frustrated with himself. His mouth opens to—maybe apologize? But what comes out instead is a loud, unfiltered snort of laughter. Rob laughs louder, the same joyful bark he let out earlier. Somehow, it fills Percy with joy, too, because it's the laugh of a person who loves what he loves and doesn't let anyone make him feel bad for it.

And ag sies man, it's enough to make Percy fall half in love with him.

He clutches the torch tight, flips it on, and goes to gather firewood before he can develop any other inconvenient feelings.

Chapter Four

THE FIRE is burning lower and Rob is pleasantly full of de-, then re-hydrated curry. There's a bite in the air, which he was prepared for. Still, he wasn't prepared for how cozy his hoodie would feel. He wants to snuggle inside it, slouch in front of the dancing orange flames, and drift off to sleep. This is the life—sitting at a campfire in the South African bush, listening to the crack and spit of flames and all the sounds of the nighttime.

A raspy screech sounds from somewhere below them and Rob jumps. Okay, *that* wasn't an idyllic nighttime sound.

Percy gives him that slow, shy smile that's starting to give Rob heart palpitations. That smile is a weapon of mass destruction, and Percy doesn't seem to have any idea. "That's an African grass owl," Percy says.

"They don't eat people, right?" Rob says, smiling to show he's joking.

He's rewarded with Percy's smile brightening. A *weapon.* Christ.

"Rodents," Percy says. "So we're safe."

"Whew."

The firelight glints on the gold of Percy's piercings and the beads and charms in his hair. The play of light on the gold thread twined through his twists almost makes it look like they're moving, and Rob thinks again of the fluidity of everything Percy does. It's been probably harder than it should be (in keeping with the tent pitching—that's what he said) to keep his focus on his incredible surroundings and not on his subject/guide.

But Percy *is* his subject. They enjoy the fire for another minute, and then Rob sighs. As much as he hates to bring up business right now, he knows they need to have a conversation about boundaries. Rob isn't going to stomp all over Percy's tender spots with his questions, but he has to know what they are if he's going to avoid them.

With a throat-clear to telegraph his intentions to Bring Up Something Awkward, Rob straightens and says, "Can we talk about the piece I'll be writing?"

The change in Percy's demeanor is immediate. Once they ate dinner, he got all loose-limbed, sprawling in front of the fire with his legs splayed and his hands flat on the ground behind him to prop himself up. At Rob's words, he draws inward, his legs curling up and his arms coming forward, until his shoulders are tensed and rounded.

A lump forms in Rob's throat, because he recognizes that kind of reaction. People do that when they want to make themselves harder to see. It's the reaction of someone who's used to being hurt when attention is focused on them. Rob hates seeing that in anyone. He really hates seeing it from another queer person, especially a queer person of color. And he really, really hates seeing it from Percy specifically, who he's only known for nine hours but likes so much.

He holds out a hand like he's soothing a frightened cat. "I want to talk about it because I want to respect all your boundaries. If there's anything you're not comfortable telling me or discussing with me, please say. I'm not here to put you on the spot." When Percy just watches him, a wary look flickering in his eyes in time with the flames of the campfire, the lump in Rob's throat gets bigger.

He forces himself to speak past it. "Did you think I came here to ask you questions that would make you uncomfortable?"

Percy's eyes drop to his lap, and he rubs a hand along his forearm. The fabric of his sweatshirt bunches up under his palm. "I assumed you'd ask me questions about my family."

"But…." Rob tries, but he can't make sense of that. "Isn't the whole point of me being here with you so that we can talk about your work, and *not* your family?"

The way Percy's eyes shoot back up to meet his makes Rob's heart thud against his sternum. "I never said that. Nothing about the job said this is to distract from… my family troubles."

"Well, no," Rob says slowly. "But I read between the lines. Or at least, I thought I was reading between the lines? The timing, and the stuff about how you've always defined yourself by your work and not relied on your family's name." Percy looks increasingly flabbergasted. "I just thought it was obvious," Rob finishes, which sounds somehow insufficient.

When Percy doesn't say anything, Rob tries not to feel faint. God, did he fly all the way out to South Africa with completely the wrong idea? *Is* he here to get the exclusive interview with Percy de Villiers about his father's government corruption trial?

"Um, sorry," he manages to stutter out. "Did I mess something up somewhere? Like, get my wires crossed, or…."

"No," Percy says forcefully. "No, you got it exactly right. I just didn't think…."

He trails off, and Rob fills in a little sadly, "That anyone would actually just want to hear about your work?"

Percy's fingers close around the fabric of his sleeve, gripping it hard. "Yes. No? I thought anyone who did this with me would want a story." Softly, he adds, "People are angry. My father…. What he's done. Well, it would be normal for someone to want to hear from me. The famous prodigal son of the corrupt South African official."

"But you don't want to talk about that?" Rob says, just to be clear. Because everything in Percy's demeanor screams he doesn't. He looks like he's just been told he has to have half his teeth pulled without any anesthetic. Like this is probably necessary, so he'll soldier through it, but he's not going to pretend he's not making himself ill with fear.

"I don't," Percy says, quiet but steady.

"I don't want to talk about it either," Rob says.

Percy meets Rob's eyes again. "Really?"

"Really." Rob doesn't blink. "I sent my resume because the chance to spend a week with you, learning about where you're from and what inspires you, and how you see the world, how you get the photos you do, that sounded like a dream. Like winning the lottery." *Wow, okay, get a grip, brah.* "Um, I think I mentioned in my cover letter that I've been following your work for a while. This is a huge opportunity for me. I can't stress how much I'm *not* here to paparazzi you."

That gets a little smile. "I'm not interesting enough for paparazzi. Just the South African press."

"South Africa doesn't have paparazzi?"

"We don't!" That actually makes Percy laugh. "So I suppose it could be worse, yeah?"

The tension breaks. Rob doesn't know where the urge comes from, but he extends his hand. It's an offering of—trust? Friendship? If Percy doesn't take it, Rob won't be surprised.

But Percy does. His palm slides over Rob's and neither of them moves—their hands just stay clasped. Percy's skin is warm and dry and there are calluses in interesting places. Maybe from his camera? Maybe from carrying bags on all his traveling? Maybe Rob's overthinking this? Maybe his brain is beach-balling because Percy leaned forward when he took Rob's hand, and Rob's noticing for the first time how there's a thick spray of freckles across his cheekbones and the bridge of his nose.

"Okay," Percy says. His Adam's apple bobs with a swallow, and Rob tries hard to ignore the crackle of electricity the sight sends to that spot low in his belly. Percy hesitates, then repeats, "Okay. Then—ground rules? Things I don't want you to ask me about. Definitely my father's trial. I have nothing to do with it and I… I'm so ashamed."

Their hands are still clasped. They don't need to be, but Rob can't bring himself to let go. And he's glad, because now he can squeeze Percy's hand for reassurance as he says, "Done. I won't bring it up. Anything else?"

"My father in general." Finally, Percy's fingers slide away from Rob's. "Though I imagine he'll come up if we start talking about my childhood."

"We don't have to talk about your childhood if you don't want to," Rob says. It makes him sad that Percy's already knocking down his own boundaries because he expects them to be trampled.

Percy catches his bottom lip with his front teeth. "I had such a good feeling about you when I saw your CV," he says. "I'm a bit shocked to've been right."

"You don't even want to know how hard I worked on getting my resume perfect before I sent it," Rob admits. "This was a really, really big deal to me. Seriously."

"I believe you. I just don't really understand."

"Maybe by the end of this week you will," Rob says with a smile.

"Or maybe you'll regret everything," Percy points out.

"I'll regret nothing. Hand to God." Rob says it in a jokey way, but he means it. It may have only been nine hours, but Rob knows deep in his bones that whatever happens out here, he's not going to regret coming.

Chapter Five

THE SOUND of lions roaring in the distance wakes Percy at fuck-off o'clock. You'd think with the life he leads, he'd be used to getting up long before sunrise. But no—give him a lie-in until noon any day over getting up early. Mossie-poep wake-up calls are his least favorite part of nature photography.

He rubs a hand over his face and pushes his sleeve up to check his watch, cupping his hand around it so the brief glow doesn't disturb Rob. It's not quite half four, and the sun won't come up until nearly seven. There's no point in Rob getting up.

Percy pulls his sleeve back down, covering his watch, though he clutches his hand around it for a second. Ma gave it to him on his eighteenth birthday, and even though the sight of it fills his stomach with a sick, twisted knot of anger, guilt, and grief, he can't take it off. Ma has stood by his father through all of this, and the last time they spoke, they had a massive row.

Since then, Percy hasn't been able to look at her number on his phone. He leaves her on read every time she texts, and then he deletes the conversation. Not that it matters, since it just pops up with their whole history the next time she texts to try to initiate contact. Blocking her number would put a stop to that, but he can't bring himself to go through with it. His relationship with his father has been strained for a long time, but Ma meant everything to him.

Lying there in the dark, listening to the lions—they're miles away, so he's not concerned—he can't help playing a highlight reel of the past few months. More of a lowlight reel. All the awful moments that felt like the worst it could get, only for something else to come along, some other revelation of his father's depravity and the depth of corruption in his department in South Africa's government.

There was the day he came for lunch with Ma, having recently returned from a weeks-long shoot in Rwanda. There were men with his father carrying papers to the braai, which was in the courtyard, not the ocean-view patio where it usually was. Smoke was rising from it and flames leapt up from the grate. As Percy watched, a blazing shred of paper caught on the updraft, sailing into the sky before winking out.

There was Ma's brittle smile and his father doing something with the house's personal server.

There was the day his father was arrested on corruption charges. Percy found out what they were along with the rest of the country. Embezzling funds from aid money for health initiatives in South Africa. Money that was meant to help with HIV/AIDS, malaria, covid. Money for women, the LGBTQ+ community. His father was being charged with stealing millions and hiding it in offshore accounts. Tax shelters or whatever it is that people use to get away with this kind of thing.

There was the day of the protests, when he hadn't slept and still couldn't sit in one place. Jittery and nauseated, he left his flat, knowing he should stay away from the crowd on Adderly Street. He wore a hoodie in a nod toward anonymity, but someone recognized him anyway. He's the local boy made good, a photographer of South Africa who's actually South African. A Coloured man, and a queer one, who's never forgotten where he comes from.

That day, no one cared. He got grabbed and shoved and someone called him a moffie, then someone else yelled a slur about the color of his skin, and Percy just... went away. His body curled up like a touch-me-not plant and—

Well, he was lucky. His friend Sipho pushed through the crowd, and no one messes with Sipho. He's big and muscular and he protects his friends like a lioness protecting her cubs, even though he's the kind of person who catches spiders in cups and releases them outside.

On cue, the lions roar again, calling to each other over the dark plain. Next to him, Rob grunts in his sleep and shifts. It's too dark to see him, but they're so close Percy can feel his body heat and every time he moves. And that's....

Percy takes a deep, slow breath, filling his lungs. It's stirring feelings in him that shouldn't be there. He's not immune to a gorgeous man, but listening to Rob sleeping makes something twang in his chest. It's the kind of feeling that urges commitment, and Percy isn't built for commitment. He's damaged goods, not in any big traumatic way, but in a thousand small hurts he can't seem to get past. And then there's the travel. He's always traveling! No one wants to date a man who's halfway across the world every few weeks.

It's probably not *Rob* who's making Percy feel this way. It's just everything he's been through. That makes sense. Doesn't it?

When hazy light begins to show through the tent, Percy gently shakes Rob awake. Rob snorts, mumbles something unintelligible, then opens his eyes stickily. "Ung," he says.

"Morning," Percy replies.

"You sure?"

Percy smiles, and it's really starting to feel natural to do that around Rob. "D'you fancy some coffee?"

"Oh my god, I fancy some coffee *so* hard." Rob's eyes roll back, and he puts a hand over his heart. "*Coffee*! Take me, I'm yours."

It's a joke, it's obviously a joke, but Percy still feels heat flood his cheeks. "I'll get a fire started and boil some water."

Propping himself up on an elbow, Rob asks, "Want some help?"

The way Rob's hair is sticking out in different directions is destroying Percy a little bit. The photo of Rob that appears at the end of his blog posts does *not* do this man justice. "I'll take care of it."

If he doesn't, he might just sit here staring at Rob like a twat.

The embers from last night's fire are still smoldering beneath the mound of charred wood and ashes. Quickly, he builds it up again, getting his camp pot from his pack while it gets going. He fills the pot with enough water for two cups of coffee and nestles it near the flames, sitting back on his heels to wait.

The sky is a smoky gray, a shade lighter above the mountains. Percy shivers as the warmth of the fire glows over his body. Rob is probably cold now that he's in the tent alone.

Maybe that's why he crawls out of the tent a few minutes later, looking rumpled and tired. Yawning, he opens his pack and pulls out a jacket. It takes him a few tries to get his arms inside. Percy has to look away to hide his smile.

They don't speak as the fire heats the water. Birds begin to call through the predawn, emerald spotted doves cooing—*coo coo-cooooo coo-cooooo coo-cooooo*. With a shiver, Rob hugs his arms around himself. "It gets cold at night," Percy says. Idiotically. Rob is obviously fully aware it's cold. He was dressed appropriately, wasn't he? He has a good, warm sleeping bag. Why is Percy so incapable of making conversation like a normal human being? Why does he insist on pointing out stupid things? Is he going to inform Rob that the sky is blue next?

"That tent was so cozy," Rob says, as though Percy doesn't sound like a prat. He glances at Percy, opens his mouth, and then shuts it, looking embarrassed.

Oh god. Oh *fuck.* Did Percy do something? Did he talk in his sleep? Or cry? It wouldn't be the first time, but usually his face is damp when he wakes up. Or if he's dreaming about the day he nearly got beat up, he'll wake up slicked in cold sweat.

"What?" Percy asks.

Rob looks startled. "Huh?"

"You looked like… I dunno. Like you wanted to say something." Percy bites his lip. "Did I do something strange? While I was asleep?"

Now Rob looks horrified. "What? No! No. Oh my god. I was just going to say something stupid. But then I realized it was too stupid to say. And inappropriate? I'm pretty sure—yeah. Definitely. Inappropriate." He winces. "This isn't making it better."

"It's not," Percy agrees. "I think you may actually be making it worse."

It comes out so easily—the way he'd banter with his friends. It feels right. And good. And like he just removed a load-bearing piece of the wall that makes him so awkward around strangers.

Rob laughs—his loud bark of a laugh that Percy finds *more* charming this morning—and rubs his face. "I was going to make a dumb joke about how it would be really easy for me to cuddle you in my sleep. But like, that's not true! I mean, I'm not going to do that. Because for one thing, we're both in sleeping bags. So it actually wouldn't be easy for me to cuddle you in my sleep, the logistics are actually kind of tricky, like, I'd have to get out of my sleeping bag and unzip yours—or maybe I'd just wrap my arms around your entire sleeping bag? It's dumb! Wow, oh my god, please don't abandon me to be eaten by those lions I can hear roaring. At least I'm pretty sure they're lions. Are those lions?"

For a second, all Percy can do is look at Rob. He giggles. "They're lions." His face aches with a smile because he's so out of practice. "And I'd honestly take it as a compliment if you sleep-cuddled me."

Rob looks surprised. The more important thing is that he's smiling. "Well, I'm warning you, it might happen. I've done it before. You can wake me up if I do it to you."

He could, but maybe he wouldn't. It might be nice to be cuddled, even if it was unintentional.

The water finally boils, and Percy makes a cup of coffee for each of them with his little portable coffee maker. It's not winning any taste tests, but it's passable. Most importantly, it's full of caffeine. By the time they've drained their cups and had a quick breakfast, the sky has lightened to a gray the color of a dove's wing. The bush is waking up, birds singing and beginning to move around in the trees.

It will take a while for the sun to rise, since it has to come up over the mountains—but the sky is turning a clean, pale blue that promises daylight soon. Percy splashes water in the coffee cups and his coffee maker and sets everything on a rock to dry while he takes down the tent. Rob rolls up the bedrolls without being asked and puts out the fire. By the time the tent is rolled up and strapped to Percy's pack, there's nothing but a thin twist of smoke rising from the ashes.

Percy wipes the cups, coffee maker, and kettle dry with a clean T-shirt and puts them away. His stomach jumps uncomfortably. Now that they're ready to start the day, it means Rob's questions will start too. He reminds himself that Rob reiterated his commitment to respecting Percy's boundaries several times. And also that this whole thing was his idea in the first place. If he isn't comfortable giving a writer unfettered access to ask him questions for a week, well then, he shouldn't have invited a writer to come out here to have unfettered access to him for a week.

"Where to today?" Rob asks.

"Is that your first question?"

"I think my first question was something about if it was actually morning." Rob's lopsided smile and crooked teeth make the jumpy feeling in Percy's stomach settle. Something about him puts Percy at ease. He might've missed his calling by going into travel writing. Certainly, he's not being used to his full potential. Percy is the most closed-off, shy person he knows—and Rob makes him want to open up.

Picking up his pack and swinging it over a shoulder, Percy says, "You're still all right to track that cheetah?"

A flicker of trepidation crosses Rob's face but disappears quickly. "I'm game."

Percy thinks about saying something reassuring but decides against it. Having a healthy respect for the bush is good. If Rob is nervous about tracking a predator, it means he'll be more aware of his surroundings.

With a nod, Percy says, "We can walk for a bit and then you can—" He waves a hand in the air. It feels big-headed to say, *You can interview me*. People think Percy is purposefully cultivating a mystique by hardly ever doing interviews, but the truth is that they make him horrifically uncomfortable. He never liked talking about his family, even before the arrest. He doesn't like talking about his privileged upbringing. It makes him feel like none of his achievements are his, or like they aren't real. Katli says that's imposter syndrome and he should stop listening to it; Percy thinks his imposter syndrome might make some valid points.

Rob shrugs his pack over his shoulders. "Talk about your photography?" he suggests.

His throat tight, Percy nods. The tightness isn't nerves the way it normally it would be. It's… something else. Something that makes him think, with hope that's pale but growing, like the light over the mountains, that talking to Rob won't just be not so bad. He's starting to think that maybe it will be good.

Chapter Six

WHEN THEY stop for their first break, Rob pulls out his recorder. "Are you okay with me asking you some questions now?"

Percy surveys their surroundings. They're in a clearing with good sight lines. Off to one side are some umbrella thorns and tall grass, but there aren't any signs of predators—no recent scat or tracks, and no birds or antelope are alarming. The cheetah he's tracking came this way, but it's been hours. Not that he worries about a cheetah attacking them, but seeing one up close would probably make Rob nervous.

When he's satisfied nothing is stalking them, he scuffs the toe of his boot in the dry, yellow grass. "Yeah. That's fine. Better get started, I suppose."

Rob starts his recorder in an exaggerated way that seems designed to make sure Percy sees him doing it and sticks it in his front pocket. "We'll start out easy. What made you want to be a photographer?"

Percy laughs a little. "Really?"

"Like I said, softball."

A bird flies overhead and Percy squints up at it. "That was a lilac roller," he says, pointing. "They're really beautiful," he adds, feeling weirdly apologetic that it's already winging out of sight. It's not like he could get it to stop and show off for them. Then again, with the gem tones of their feathers—blues and purples and greens catching the sun and taking your breath away—they don't really need to do much more than exist to show off.

Rob smiles—but gently. "Are you maybe stalling a little?"

"I'm *completely* stalling," Percy says. With a little huff of air, he adds, "I'm sure you know this. I've been asked this question before." In the very few interviews he's done, yeah.

"Humor me."

Percy looks up at the sky, down at the ground, and finally to a point somewhere on Rob's right cheekbone. "I got into wildlife photography probably the same way most people do. Used to? Maybe they don't anymore. Anyway, *National Geographic*. All those close-up shots of big cats staring into your soul; who wouldn't want to take something like that?" His eyes drop to Rob's shoulder. "I used to steal my ma's old Kodak and use up the whole roll, then put it back on her desk."

Rob chuckles. "Bet she loved that."

"There were a few Christmases and birthdays where she used colorful language when she discovered there weren't any pictures left on the film." The memories, soft-edged and warm, make him smile. *O fok, die verdome kamera is vol!* "But she never scolded me. She encouraged me, actually."

His eyes sting. Maybe he should have said he didn't want to talk about his ma.

"What does she think of how successful you've been?" Rob asks.

It's like someone is scraping a dull razor blade across all Percy's tenderest spots. And he can't blame anyone but himself. Of course Rob would ask about how he got interested in photography, and of course Percy would say without thinking how he stole Ma's camera. It's always been a nice story. Ma tells it proudly at dinner parties. At least she used to. Dinner parties probably aren't on the docket currently, what with the imminent trial.

And considering how he cut off contact with her for supporting his father, her first emotion when she thinks of him probably isn't pride.

"I think she's pleased," Percy says. Anodyne and meaningless, just the way he's always been in public. If he never says anything personal about himself, no one can ever attack him for it. Being Coloured and queer make him a target, of course, but that weirdly makes him feel like he's part of a community. He's far from the only person dealing with the shit that comes his way for being a queer person of color.

The stuff with his family? He's entirely alone. Not a lot of people can say their father stole millions from aid money earmarked for healthcare.

Rob looks surprised. "You only think she is? You don't know?"

"Look, can we—" Percy clenches his fists. "Sorry. I'm just…. Talking about my family isn't easy at the minute."

Now Rob looks guilty. "Sorry. You're right."

"Don't apologize." Percy swigs from his water bottle. They'll have to refill today. Luckily, with the reserve butting up against the Waterberg, water flows through it year-round, not just during the wet season. "I'm the one who brought my ma up."

A suffocating feeling balloons in his chest—but for once, it's not the need to shove everything down as far as it will go. It's the opposite. It's a desperate need to talk to someone about what happened. About how he feels. About the fact that Ma has always been his best friend, his constant, cheering him on and helping him up when he stumbles. She's always been his role model. Her generosity, her passion for helping others, for lifting people up, has always made him want to be better. He never questioned that her moral compass was true and unwavering.

And then she had to go and stand by his father.

It terrifies him, because if she could support someone who's so thoroughly rotted, what does that say about the fact that she's always supported *him*?

Deep down, is Percy as rotten as his father is?

Then comes a very strange and jarring realization. It's not that he wants to talk to someone about all of it. It's that he wants to talk to Rob. Rob who he doesn't even know. Rob who's here to get a story about him. Rob who has a recorder running in his pocket right now.

Impala bark nearby. Rob jumps and draws closer, his eyes wary. He probably doesn't realize impala are making that sound. Well, of course he doesn't. Rob hasn't ever been in the bush, and they hardly saw any animals yesterday, not even any impala. Their bark sort of sounds like a cat hissing, and if you've never heard it, and especially if the person you're with looks watchful, you might think it's a leopard or something.

"It's okay," Percy says. "Just impala. Their own shadows startle them sometimes."

The tense set to Rob's shoulders eases. "Impala—antelope, right?"

"Right." Percy cocks his head and listens. Grass crunches nearby. They're close, just behind the thicket of umbrella thorn and tall grass.

Motioning for Rob to follow him, Percy crosses toward the thicket, making sure to stay upwind of the impala so they'll smell the two of them coming. Impala aren't dangerous, but anything can be dangerous if you startle it. Accidents happen. An impala bowling you over will hurt even if it has no intention of eating you.

There's another bark, then several more, and the impala come into view. It's a smallish group, a male with—Percy counts—nine females and a few nearly adult calves. They're all still and staring, heads up, ears swiveled forward.

"Wow," Rob breathes.

Which is adorable. In a few days, Rob probably won't care about seeing impala, since they're everywhere. But it's magical right now, and that makes it sort of magical for Percy too.

Of course, he likes impala the same way he likes grey go-aways. They're an animal everyone takes for granted, but they're beautiful, really. They're built to outrun everything that wants to eat them, which is kind of everything. The sleekness of their bodies and the grace of their movement is hard to look away from, from the points of the males' horns to the way their tails flick.

Rob stands stock-still without being told. The impala watch, staying nearly as still themselves. They won't get completely comfortable with people standing there, but some of them might go back to eating, especially the young ones. As long as the male keeps watching—and he's definitely keeping an eye on them. One of his horns is missing the tip. Probably broken off in a dominance display with another male. Maybe that's why his herd is so small. Or maybe he's just old. Making it to old age as an impala is no mean feat.

The ram's ears flick and some of the ewes and calves do, indeed, go back to grazing, even though they look jumpy. Next to Percy, Rob seems to barely be breathing. Percy wishes he could take a picture without scaring the impala, and not of the animals. No, he wants to take a picture of Rob, who's radiating so much joy and excitement at seeing nature's most plentiful snack that Percy's chest is doing something funny.

One of the nearly grown calves takes a step and lands on some dry wood, which snaps loudly. The impala scatter, barking and leaping away.

"Oh no." Rob looks devastated. Something else happens in Percy's chest—something he still doesn't know how to describe, other than *funny*, even though it's distinct from the other funny thing. Or maybe it's just more of it, and Percy's so unused to it that he can't distinguish what's a separate emotion and what's just a stronger version of an emotion he should know.

All things he won't be sharing with Rob, incidentally. If word gets around how much of an emotional wreck he is, visas might be more difficult to come by.

Rob turns to Percy. "I didn't mean to scare them."

An insane urge to grab Rob's hand seizes Percy. He fights it off—barely. "You didn't scare them," Percy says. There's a soothing note in his voice that he didn't mean to be there. "Like I said, they get scared of their own shadows."

Once he no longer wants to take Rob's hand, he says, "Ready to keep moving?"

With a nod, Rob says, "Thanks for the impala sighting."

"Well. You're welcome." Shyness and pleasure twine around each other in Percy's spine. "Hopefully we'll see other animals. Shame, I didn't even ask if there was something you wanted to see?"

"Whatever we see is what I want to see." Somehow, Rob looks and sounds absolutely genuine about this. "And, you know. Whatever you think is important enough to photograph."

That makes Percy chew on his cheek, considering. Should he say this? Rob's here to write about him, right? "I don't always photograph things because I think they're important, or more worth seeing than other things."

"Yeah?"

Did he just…? Percy manages to suppress the urge to harrumph at being maneuvered into answering a question that wasn't asked—even though his suspicion that Rob would be that kind of writer was one of the reasons he chose Rob in the first place. "I think most things are worth photographing. The reason I don't photograph everything is… well, you've got to live your life, yeah? You can't go round with a camera stuck to your face."

"You need to experience stuff."

"Yeah." Percy waves a hand vaguely. "When I choose to take a picture, it's loads of things going into that choice."

Now Rob looks thrilled. The expression makes him look like an excited puppy. It tugs at the messy knot of feelings in Percy's chest. When he chose Rob, he had no idea that he'd be so enthusiastic. But it's good. It's good. Percy loves his work—has never stopped finding joy in it—but joy has been in short supply in his life lately. Even Thaba Boroko Reserve hasn't brought him the same euphoria it usually does. Rob, though. Rob's joy is helping Percy find his again.

Rob points to the recorder in his shirt pocket. "Care to elaborate?"

He considers saying not until the next stop, then relents. "Lighting, framing, overall composition. My own position relative to whatever I'm photographing, and if I could get a better shot from a different place. My mood." Too honest? "Sometimes if it's going to be a difficult shot and I'm short on time, I have to consider if I'll be able to sell the photo."

"Ah." If Rob expected him to be a pure artist, Percy just obliterated that idea. It will probably disappoint him.

But Rob goes on, "I know that feeling. With writing, not photography." He looks thoughtful. Wistful? Maybe sad. The morning sun glints on the silver in his hair. That would make a lovely photo. Rob, back to the pale autumn light, the golden brown of his skin flaring against the silvery backdrop of the bush.

Rob sweeps a hand through his hair. Instead of pushing it back, it falls back across his forehead, a soft sweep of black threaded with quicksilver.

Percy's heart clutches and flails.

"What else do you write?" he asks, even though he already said they should get moving. Even though probably no good can come of learning more about Rob Hale, because they've barely known each other for twenty-four hours and Percy already likes him so much.

It's a shame he can't be like all his friends and flirt with a cute guy, then let it go nowhere. No, he has to be *shy*, and when he wants to get to know someone, it's a deeper want that he can't put aside. It's not helpful to catch feelings for Rob. He's a travel writer who lives in a different hemisphere. Two different hemispheres. And Percy travels a ridiculous amount for his career. There's no future there. There's not even a possibility of a future.

Percy has two settings: anonymous hookup and we-might-be-soul-mates monogamy. Rob is already far past the point where he could be an anonymous hookup, so Percy needs to hold the line. There's no point in feeling anything for Rob because they're not going to be in a relationship.

Not that it stops him from wanting to know what else Rob writes.

Bashfully, Rob sticks his hands in his pockets. His crooked smile is horrifically charming. "Well, I really want to write something more long-form. The listicles and best-of pieces pay the bills, but I would love to go somewhere and really live there. I guess my dream is to write a book about a place I'm in love with. You know, make other people see what's so special about it."

Curious despite every single clearly laid-out reason he shouldn't be, Percy asks, "What would the book be about? I mean, what's the place?"

"Oh, um." Rob's cheeks darken a little. "I don't… uh… know. I haven't found it. I'm just… waiting for someplace to grab on to me and refuse to let go."

He looks thoughtful. Percy thinks, unhelpfully, that it would be nice if South Africa was that place for Rob.

"You'll find it," Percy says.

"Yeah. I guess maybe I feel like I've been so many amazing places, I should have already?" Rob shakes his head. "First-world problems."

With a small smile, Percy says, "Maybe it's because you grew up somewhere really amazing. Isn't Hawai'i supposed to be paradise?"

"Try sitting on the H1 at rush hour." But Rob chuckles. "Nah, it is. You might be onto something. I miss Oahu like crazy."

Silence catches like a breath, like both of them are feeling a sense of say-something-else. Neither of them does, though. Say something else, that is. But their eyes meet and hold, and Percy feels just a bit breathless.

He turns away because it feels like the only way to fill his lungs. "Ready to keep going?" he asks.

"Yep!" Rob sounds as cheerful as ever. Maybe he didn't notice what just happened. Maybe nothing *did* happen. Maybe Percy is being as dysfunctional as he always is, getting a crush on a man he's never going to get involved with.

On one hand it's a benefit that they have to stay silent as they walk, because it doesn't give Percy the chance to talk more to Rob and realize how much he likes talking to Rob. On the other, it gives him time to think about how much he likes Rob. And how much he wants to talk to him and how there are a million things he wants to say, which—where has *that* come from? He's definitely Like That (his dearest friends say they sometimes have to remind themselves that he's shy, because he isn't around people he's close to), but usually it takes much longer than twenty-four hours.

As the morning goes on, they see several more herds of impala, a group of shy kudu, squirrels and mongoose, and loads of birds. By midday, they're approaching one of the tributaries that flows into the larger river that cuts through the reserve. Percy's used it to refill his water supply on previous trips—it looks clean and there's a nice, flat rock that juts into the water where you can get a good three-sixty of your surroundings.

Percy leads the way, following the same track the animals do. There are rhino tracks that look fresh, so he's hoping there will be something really good to show Rob. Every time they've seen animals since the impala, Rob's entire face lit up, and Percy's fast becoming addicted to seeing it. Not just seeing it—being the one to make it happen.

Even if it's not really him making it happen, it's the fact that they're seeing wildlife. But since Percy's the one pointing out the wildlife and talking about it in a hushed voice, it kind of feels like he's the one responsible.

They reach the banks of the stream, and Percy slows to check for danger or anything interesting.

Yes. His heart leaps. There, thirty meters downstream, a white rhino is standing, head lowered, to drink from the water.

He puts a hand out to stop Rob, and Rob's midsection bumps against his arm. The warmth zings through him, making his blood feel fizzy. And it's not the time for that, because a large animal that can be genuinely dangerous is very near.

Not that Percy's afraid the rhino will come for them. They're downwind—purposefully, because Percy knows animals come here to get water too. It's a good spot. But the rhino won't smell them. It probably won't really be able to see them, either, though it will hear them. Probably already did.

Percy turns to say something to Rob, like *Be very still and very quiet,* but Rob's face arrests him. Rob's eyes are wide, catching the sun and looking like moss in a sun-dappled clearing. For a second, Percy can't breathe, because they're so beautiful and *god,* he wants a picture.

Reality reasserts itself quickly as Rob mouths *Oh my god.* Slowly, Percy moves forward, holding out a hand palm-out so Rob knows to wait. The soles of his Courteneys grip the dirt bank as he inches into a better position to view—and photograph—the rhino.

The rhino's head comes up, ears flicking, and that allows Percy to see the other rhino behind her: a calf, not a year old yet.

Only years of experience keep him from shouting or awwing or otherwise making a sound that would either scare the rhino or make her charge. Instead, he takes a moment to put a hand on his chest and feel his heart beat, to feel his lungs fill with air. Then he turns to Rob and motions to him.

With anyone else, Percy wouldn't have trusted them to make the approach quietly. But when Rob joins him, Percy realizes he never even thought about it. He just knew Rob would do the right thing.

The female rhino is blocking the calf again. Rob still doesn't know it's there. Leaning so close that Rob's hair tickles Percy's nose, he breathes, "There's a baby rhino behind this one. Definitely born during the last rainy season."

Rob's chest hitches. Percy is close enough to see goose bumps rise on his neck. The mother rhino shuffles back and the baby comes into full view. It splashes in the water, playing. This sort of thing always turns Percy into a sodden mess of gooey, melty feelings, and one look at Rob is enough to prove it's having the same effect on him.

Even though Percy wanted photos, he doesn't turn his camera on. Neither of them moves as the female rhino drinks her fill and her calf gambols around her. The sun glints on the spray the baby kicks up, and the mother flicks her ears each time a drop of water lands on her head.

Soon, the adult rhino turns to leave. As she faces Percy and Rob, she stops, seeming to catch sight of them. Maybe she smells them—the wind's shifted round a bit, and it might be carrying their scent to her. She freezes. Percy stays still and Rob follows his lead without being told, even though adrenaline's probably spiking through him the same as it is for Percy. An adult rhinoceros turning her attention on you should activate anyone's fight-or-flight response—and since you don't fight a rhino and win, that means the only thing you really want to do is run.

Percy will if she gives any sign she's turning aggressive. Right now, she's only looking at them, ears pricked forward, her body between them and her calf. Percy can hear Rob's breathing—fast. The tips of the rhino's eyelashes catch the sun.

With a snort, she turns away from them and leaves the stream bank. She disappears into the tall grass and scrub, her calf following her. Her exit is silent, and the only sign they were there are wet footprints on the stone and a rustle of grass that could be nothing but the wind.

Percy gives it a few minutes to make sure she isn't going to come back. The real worry is startling her, since rhinos don't see well and charge when they feel threatened. When she doesn't reappear, he relaxes, shaking out the stiffness in his muscles from standing frozen.

"I don't think she's coming back," Percy says, because Rob's still not moving a muscle.

Clearly, he was waiting for Percy's permission to move, because he lets out a huge breath. "*Wow.* Holy shit. I mean—holy *shit*. She was—she was right *there*. Wow. Oh my god. I've never—that was amazing."

Something warm and sparkling fills Percy's chest. It's seeing the rhino and her calf, yeah. But more than that, much more than that, it's Rob's reaction. It's seeing that wonder on his face and hearing it in his voice.

Percy grins. "Yeah, it was."

"Do you see stuff like that all the time?" Rob's eyes are still wide with awe. The two of them are standing—close. Close enough to pick out all the individual colors that make up Rob's eyes. Rich loamy earth, ink, chocolate, the darkest of dark burgundy wine. They're too pretty. Percy has always been helpless against pretty eyes.

Percy makes himself stop getting lost in the endless depths of Rob's gorgeous fucking eyes. "No. That was a really good sighting. I think you've got first-time safari luck."

"Did you just call me a good luck charm?"

That pulls a laugh out of Percy. "Maybe?"

Rob holds his gaze. Percy lets him, because. Well. Pretty eyes and well-documented helplessness. "I'll take it. Sounds like a great credential. *Percy de Villiers's good luck charm.*"

Is this—is Rob—are they flirting? Percy's very bad at flirting. Percy's very bad at *telling* when someone is flirting with him. His friends tease him about it, and they tell him when they think someone's flirting with him, and he inevitably refuses to believe them, but it's rather a moot point since none of his friends are here right now to tell him whether they think Rob is flirting with him.

Percy swings his camera around, flicks it on, and takes a photo of the stream, because he has to do something to distract from the sudden railway clatter of his heart pounding against his ribs.

He doesn't actually need his friends there to tell him if they think Rob's flirting with him. For once, Percy's pretty sure he can tell.

Chapter Seven

ONE OF Rob's favorite things that he's learned about Percy is how watchful he is. That vigilance is definitely something Rob's going to write about. It goes beyond watching for danger. It's something else, a stillness and a wariness that seems to be part of Percy, as much as his dark eyes and brown skin and freckles are.

But the fact that he wants to write about it undersells it, somehow. Rob wants to…. He doesn't even know. Doesn't have the words. Pretty sad—a writer who can't find the words. He wants that watchfulness turned on him. He wants to be worthy of being studied and contemplated the way Percy does their surroundings.

Sunlight catches on the gold woven in Percy's hair as they stop for their last break of the afternoon. After this, they'll head for tonight's camping spot—same mountain, different face. They're still tracking the cheetah.

The winking gold beads in Percy's hair are pretty. *Percy* is pretty. Way too pretty to ever look twice at Rob, who's stout, with a gut he can't seem to plank or crunch away. If he hadn't been selected for this story, Percy de Villiers wouldn't ever notice him.

Which should be entirely beside the point of anything—but Rob can't quite convince himself to put it aside. Because Percy is like no one he's ever met, and like no one, Rob's positive, that he'll ever meet again.

Today has been really good. Rob's gotten good material for the piece he'll write. They stopped for an hour or so and waited for photo opportunities and wildlife to come to them. Percy talked in that low, careful way he has about the magic of being still in the bush, how you notice smaller and smaller things that would never enter your awareness any other time.

They're trying it again now, sitting in one spot on an old, dead tree. The big things are easy to notice—impala browsing nearby, a few blue wildebeest farther on. Rob even spots a couple monkeys in a tree, scampering along the branches.

Percy snaps a few photos. Even though Rob wants to know everything about why he chooses his subjects, what about this shot was interesting, he also doesn't want to shatter the moment. For every minute he lets himself sink into the landscape and become part of it, the landscape gives back and shows him something he might not have noticed, just like Percy said. Tiny blue and brown songbirds in a nearby bush. A beetle crawling along the ground. A fox with huge ears poking its head from a hole and looking around before ducking back down.

Percy switches to a longer lens and gets down on the ground, stretching out on his stomach and holding his camera ready at his eye. "That's a bat-eared fox," he says.

"It's really cute."

"Yeah, they are. And they can be shy, so it's quite cool to see one at its den. Ah! Look—" The camera shutter clicks a number of times in rapid succession as the fox pops its head up again. "The light is *perfect*," Percy murmurs.

Rob probably could have figured that out if there'd been a pop quiz or something. Golden hour is approaching, and the light is already taking on a honeyed quality. South Africa—or maybe it's just this part of South Africa—is tugging at something in him. He's afraid he isn't taking it in enough. He wants it imprinted on his brain, because just seeing it doesn't feel like enough. Every time he blinks, he's closing his eyes and missing out on part of this place.

But the way the day moves through the color spectrum—the way the light and the angle of the sun changes everything—is something else here. Silver and amethyst in the predawn, sunshiney yellow in the morning, deep sapphire blue and burnt ochre orange at midday, rich gold as afternoon sinks into evening. Garnet and ruby as the sun goes down, then inky skies and stars strewn from horizon to horizon.

Is this the place that finally hooks Rob and won't let him go?

Another head pokes out of the ground as a second fox joins the first one. Percy makes a delighted noise and takes a bunch more pictures. Rob can't help grinning at the foxes. Their ears are bigger than their faces, pricked straight up above the black masks across their eyes.

Apparently, they decide that Rob and Percy aren't a threat, because they venture out of the den. A third fox emerges after them, looks around, and trots away. The first two stay near their burrow, staring intently at the ground.

Percy spends another few minutes taking photos, still sprawled on his front. His shoulder blades move under his shirt as he shifts his arms, and suddenly Rob's noticing the way Percy's shirt pulls taut across his shoulders and how the cords of his neck move. That kind of lean, rangy strength is solidly Rob's type. He loves guys that can hold him down even though they look like they should be too skinny to.

And *wow*, okay bless his heart, but that is *not* an image that should be in his head. Percy on top of him is—delicious, actually—but *no*. He should *not* be thinking this when the man is lying in front of him.

Er, for photos. Of animals.

To distract himself, he watches the foxes. One of them leaps on something, which results in a few more photos. Rob tries really, really hard to not look at how Percy's muscles flex in his arms and back. Oh. And oh god. And in his ass.

None of this is going in his story, obviously.

Finally, with a quiet *oof*, Percy shuffles to his knees and rocks himself back to take a seat next to Rob again. "They eat termites and beetles, mostly," he says. "And they'll have more than one entrance to their den throughout their territory."

"So we could see the same ones come out a totally different door tomorrow?" Rob asks.

"Mm-hm." Percy fiddles with his camera for a second. "They'll hunt most of the night. Speaking of—we should keep moving. Get to our camping site before sundown."

Rob climbs to his feet. "Gotta get a good view of the sunset for you."

That sunlight smile flashes across Percy's face and Rob dies a little. He's going to remember every single time he makes Percy smile like that. He's going to preserve each and every instance of it like a diorama at a museum.

"You remembered I said that?" Percy asks.

Yeah—he's remembered most, if not all, the things that Percy has said. If South Africa has a grip on Rob, so does Percy de Villiers. "Sure," he says casually, even though he doesn't feel casual at the moment. "That's my job."

The smile on Percy's face dims a little. Rob wants to take back what he said immediately. "S'pose it is," Percy says, picking his pack and rifle up.

Wordlessly, they continue on their way.

THEIR CAMPSITE has another glorious view of the sunset. It's another of those I-don't-want-to-blink times as the sun paints the mountains unreal colors. Rob's never seen the sun turn gray rock into such deep reds and purples. They don't stay one color, either, shifting by the minute to richer shades or different hues entirely. Coral turns to scarlet turns to burgundy, and Rob wonders how he'll ever put this into words.

At least Percy's photos will be part of the story. Rob's never been able to adequately photograph sunsets on Oahu, but if there's anyone he trusts to get a good picture of a spectacular sunset, it's Percy.

When the light starts to fade, Percy sighs, "It makes me wish I could paint."

"That wouldn't be fair," Rob says. "You've gotta leave some talent for the rest of us."

Percy flashes that smile at him again. Rob returns it. He wants Percy to know he's joking, but he also wants Percy to know what that smile does to him. Just a little bit. Not the full impact it's having on his heart.

They pick their way back to the fire. Tonight's campsite is rockier than last night's—more pieces of mountain jutting up through the dirt, AKA more tripping hazards if Rob has to get up in the middle of the night to pee. Not that he *would* get up in the middle of the night to pee. Whenever one of them has to, as Percy says, use the bush toilet, he always makes sure there's no danger of anything sneaking up on them. The second to last thing Rob's going to do is leave the tent on his own at night to pee. The *last* thing he's going to do is wake Percy up to supervise him while he leaves the tent in the middle of the night to pee.

Last night he stashed an empty bottle next to his sleeping bag. If he wakes up in the middle of the night and has to go, he'll be using that.

They eat another delicious dinner of freeze-dried camp food and sit together companionably. At least Rob thinks it's companionable. It is for him.

Percy pokes the fire with a stick. "I thought you'd grill me more than you have."

"Grilling doesn't seem like it would make you comfortable."

"Would it make anyone comfortable?"

With a chuckle, Rob says, "Guess not. Want to talk more?"

Percy fiddles with the stick he's holding, peeling at a shred of bark. "I guess, yeah." His eyes flick toward Rob's and he adds, sounding the tiniest bit playful, "We've barely scratched the surface of my childhood."

"Well, let's do it." Rob pulls out his recorder, starts it, and puts it on the ground between them. "Percy's childhood, here we go."

Percy looks thoughtful. "I mean, it was privileged. I'm an only child and my parents…. Well, there wasn't anything they wouldn't give me if I wanted it. I didn't really have friends, though."

Oh no, this is sad. It doesn't feel right to record this, not when this piece is supposed to be about Percy's work. Before he can pick up the recorder, though, Percy waves him off. "Don't. I mean, do. I mean—it's okay. Recording this."

"You sure?"

The tentative smile on Percy's face sure does some things to Rob's insides. "Yeah."

"Well, okay." Rob settles back into place. The fire makes his front toasty warm, but his back is chilled from the cool air on the mountainside. "So, uh, you didn't have friends?"

"Except Katli." Percy's smile gets surer. "Kat was my governess's daughter, but we were sort of raised together. At least until I went to school."

Something about the name Katli sounds familiar, and it hits Rob. "Katli—she's the camp manager, isn't she?"

"Yeah. She's kwaai."

"Okay, I'm gonna need a translation on that."

With a grin, Percy says, "It means really cool. Yeah. She's brilliant. Ah, I missed her during the school terms."

The fire spits. Rob watches sparks wink out in the air. "You went to a boarding school or something? How far from Cape Town was it?"

"Mm, about ten thousand kilometers."

Uh, Rob's not great at the miles to kilometers conversion, but he's pretty sure that's a whole lot of miles. Like, probably the length of South Africa several times over. "I'm sorry, ten *thousand* kilometers?"

There's an unhappy smile on Percy's face now. "I went to Eton."

"Eton, like, *England* Eton."

"As a graduate of Eton, I believe I'm required to point out there *is* no other Eton." Percy's tone is withering.

Rob's shook. "Well, okay. Wow. I didn't know that."

The corners of Percy's lips turn down. "Oh, please don't look at me like that."

"Like what?"

Percy makes a flicking motion with his hand, which has the not-helpful side effect of drawing Rob's attention to how graceful and fine-boned he is. "Like," Percy says, "I'm different from you. Fundamentally. Like there's… space between us. And like I'm not someone you can…."

When he trails off, Rob prompts gently, "Someone you can what?"

For a second, Rob's positive Percy isn't going to answer. But, softly, Percy finishes, "Someone you can spend time with."

This time, Rob shuts the recorder off. It doesn't feel right to make a permanent record of this conversation. All he can see is a skinny young boy, his best friend the staff's kid, sent to the other side of the world. Percy's eyebrows shoot up when Rob stuffs the recorder back in his pocket.

Only then does it sink in—it's important to Percy that Rob feels they can spend time together like two normal people. It's important to Percy that… Rob likes him?

"Don't worry, I'm not going to fawn because you went to a fancy school."

"Posh school," Percy corrects him, but his smile is back, and he looks like a weight just fell from his shoulders. "And good. Um, you really don't have to stop recording."

Rob shrugs. "I know. I just—maybe this is more of a like, friend conversation. Or maybe that's being really presumptuous."

"No, I…." Percy looks at a loss. He pulls his knees up to his chest and hugs his arms around them. Firelight collects in the hollow of his cheekbone and gilds the tips of his eyelashes. "Normally it takes much longer for people to want to be friends with me."

"Well, you're forgetting, I kind of hero worship you for your amazing photography."

That gets a laugh out of Percy. "As a friend, then, you can't want to hear about Eton, surely?"

Taking a chance, Rob gives him a tiny nudge with his elbow. "I mean, I just went to Alpharetta High School, so I probably can't really relate, but yeah, man. Of course."

Percy rests his cheek on his arm and smiles—a soft, happy smile that feels like seeing a rare, beautiful bird. "Will you tell me about Alpharetta High School?"

"Sure." Maybe on the surface, their school experiences had nothing in common. But possibly, at a deeper level, they were depressingly similar. They were both far from home, in a new place with a bunch of kids they didn't know. They both would have struggled to fit into a place where the language was the same in the place you left, but the culture was completely different.

With a quiet sigh, Percy says, "I was sent when I was thirteen. I didn't want to go, but, well. My father wanted me to, and that was that. My parents moved me in, at least. I remember being absolutely terrified I was going to have to make my own way there. For months beforehand, I had nightmares about running after a double-decker bus and trying to carry my suitcase."

Rob winces. "At least they went with you."

"Yeah." Percy looks like he can't decide if he's happy about it or not, all these years later. "I decided after one particularly unhappy phone call where I begged to come home that my father didn't care about seeing me safely to school so much as he cared about being *seen* seeing me safely to school."

The fire spits again. Sparks fly into the air and spew across the ground, scattering at their feet. One by one they go out, except one that pulses brighter right at Percy's toe. He rubs it with his toe to extinguish it. "There you go, I'm talking about my father even though I told you not to ask about him."

"It's hard not to talk about parents," Rob says quietly.

"Ugh. True. But I try not to be that poor little rich boy who can't stop flogging his daddy issues."

With a chuckle, Rob says, "Well, cheers to that, I guess."

Percy shoots him a tiny smile. "You promised you'd tell me about Alpharetta. I've a very specific vision of American high schools, and I've got to tell you, I'll be devastated if you shatter any of my dearly held ideas."

Rob slowly unscrews the cap of his water bottle to buy himself time before he answers. The treated water doesn't have the best taste, and Rob's never been able to figure out if it comes from the treatment or if that's just how non-city water tastes. "Give me your biggest one. The one you totally can't live with me disabusing you of."

"Oh." Percy wrinkles his nose and stares into the distance. "Prom. *Everyone* goes to prom, and it's always incredibly lavish. And the average American high schooler's fortunes rise and fall depending on who they go to prom with."

Laughing, Rob says, "Yeah, movies gave me unrealistic expectations for prom too. Mine was in the ballroom of a Hilton. There was some kind of insurance event going on at one of the other ballrooms. My date's mom was at that, I remember. All the like, insurance salespeople wanted pictures at the prom photo op things."

Percy takes a swig from his water bottle. "So you went to prom. Thanks for not bursting that particular bubble."

"Yeah, when you move from Hawai'i to Georgia, you kinda try to fit in as much as you can." Rob sweeps a hand from his head to his feet. "Especially when you look like this."

The way Percy's eyes follow the motion makes Rob feel warm. He doesn't look unappreciative. "I know about not looking the same as everyone else," Percy says.

Yeah. A South African kid at Eton—it's not hard to imagine. "It wasn't just being kanaka." At Percy's furrowed brow, he clarifies, "Native Hawaiian. It was the trifecta—Native Hawaiian, gay, and... on the heavy side."

Some of the weight dropped off when he went to college, and the gym helped him turn some of the fat to muscle—but it's fucking *hard* to be a brown, husky gay man. Grindr's a hellscape, like the freeway in a post-apocalyptic wasteland, hazards everywhere for him to avoid when he's just trying to meet a nice guy. Between the dick pics, the casual racism ("White only"), and the obsession with the lowest possible ratio of body fat to lean tissue, Rob practically has to schedule a telephonic therapy session every time he scrolls through Grindr.

With a sad twist of his mouth, Percy says, "Did you, like me, tell yourself teenagers were cruel, and it would get better?"

"How'd you guess?"

Percy sweeps his hand from head to feet, echoing Rob's gesture. "I was the only South African boy at Eton. There were other children of rich foreigners, but mostly Saudi and Chinese. And Eton's one of those places where, despite boys getting each other off at a much higher rate than the general population, it's still not popular to be openly gay." He makes a face. "And I'm still talking about it. I want to hear about prom. Please tell me you had a live band and a Ferris wheel, and you and your date kissed at the top of it."

"I think that's *Love, Simon*?" Rob laughs. "I *don't* want to ruin your image of American proms, so I'm not going to tell you about it. But I did go with a guy—he was my boyfriend—and we danced and kissed and got those cringey, awkward Lifetouch photos taken."

He wonders how Mason's doing. They keep in touch but haven't seen each other for a few years. Between Rob's traveling and Mason moving to LA, it's hard.

Even though it's just the Standard Prom Experience™, Percy looks charmed and a little wistful. "You fit in by the end of high school, then?"

"I tried really hard to fit in." Rob shrugs. "I hated standing out and auwe, man, did I stand out. There's pretty much no one of Pacific Islander descent in Atlanta and, like, less than pretty much no one in Alpharetta. I got a lot of people assuming I was Latinx or Asian. Which was actually better than them knowing I was Hawaiian, because they'd either say something stupid, like did we have luaus at home, or they'd tell me all about their Hawaiian vacation."

Percy laughs. Another one for the mind palace. "Is it nice otherwise? Alpharetta."

The way he says the word is sexy. Woof, a guy saying *Alpharetta* has never done it for Rob before, but there's a first time for everything, he guesses. And just generally, the accent is doing it for him. Now that he knows Percy went to Eton, he can hear the blend of South Africa and England. His consonants curl around Rob's ears and those broad vowels settle somewhere low in his stomach.

"Alpharetta's… fine. No, I don't know. It's nice. It has its charms. Cute downtown, good restaurants, nice parks. It's like half an hour from downtown Atlanta, so you're close enough to go downtown but far enough away that you're not in the city. It's a suburb, you know? We lived in a suburby part of Oahu, too, but Hawai'i's… different." Rob has that crawling feeling you get when you've talked too long about something intensely mundane. "But, uh, yeah. Atlanta's a pretty cool city. That's why I still live there. There's a decent queer scene in Midtown."

Percy fingers the studs in his ear, his fingernail clicking along them. There's a thoughtful look in his dark eyes, but he pokes at the fire for a moment before speaking. "I'd like to go to Atlanta someday." His eyes flit to Rob's. "I'd like to go to a load of places in the States I've never seen. It's so… big. I feel as though I've hardly scratched the surface."

Clasping his hands around his knee, Rob says, "If you come to Atlanta, you gotta let me play tour guide. Or hell, not just Atlanta, anywhere in the southeast." Shit, was he too enthusiastic about that? He's been told he can be a lot when he gets excited about an idea. The idea of Percy visiting Atlanta or like, a two-hundred-mile radius around Atlanta is definitely exciting.

A small, shy smile is flirting with the corners of Percy's lips, though. "I'd like that," he says quietly.

Nebulous we-should-hang-out-sometime style promises of seeing Percy during some unspecified future visit to Atlanta shouldn't make Rob's heart canter and leap the way it does—but here they are, and it definitely is.

The fire crackles. There's a spooky noise off in the distant dark, but Percy looks entirely at ease, loose-limbed and relaxed, and Rob trusts him. If there's something to be concerned about out here, Percy will be aware, and Percy will keep him safe.

Chapter Eight

THEY GET distracted from Project Cheetah Tracking in the morning when Percy finds lion tracks. Percy gets all excited, crouching on his haunches and peering at them, following them a little ways before stopping again, looking at broken and trampled grass. He tastes some dirt? Which Rob is *desperate* to ask about, but Percy is so fixated on the tracks that Rob doesn't want to interrupt him. There's like, clearly some tracker juju going on, and Rob's here for it, even if it looks like magic to him at the moment.

After a good thirty minutes of walking a few feet, pausing to study the tracks, walking another few feet and pausing again, they've covered about three hundred feet. But Percy straightens, his eyes gleaming, and says, "There's a mating pair of lion nearby."

Lion and *nearby* are two words that send a primordial shiver up Rob's spine. The hairs on the back of his neck stand on end. There might be a predator watching him right now, and he'd never know it. Out here, he's nothing but prey, isn't he?

His eyes dart to Percy, who's thrumming with excitement. There's no fear or concern on his face. Seeing that, Rob takes a deep breath and calms down. His faith in Percy to not put him in a dangerous situation hasn't wavered.

Well, an intentionally dangerous situation. Rob made himself actually read all the waivers he had to click through and sign in Adobesign. Obviously, this trip isn't without risk. But he's absolutely sure that Percy won't let him become dinner for a lion.

Since Percy's talking, Rob starts his recorder. "Okay, you sound excited about mating lions. Are we just stoked to perv on them?"

Percy laughs, a beautiful, bright, golden starburst of a thing. The phrase "head over heels" has always struck Rob as metaphor, but when Percy lets out that laugh, Rob's knees feel weak, like they might buckle and send him tumbling ass over kettle.

Head over heels sounds nicer, that's for sure.

"It's just a cool thing to see," Percy elucidates, charming in his totally uninformative excitement. "When a female lion goes into estrus—heat—she and the male whose territory she's in won't do anything but copulate for the entire time. They don't even eat! And then at the end, they'll hunt together and share their kill."

"Romantic," Rob says.

"Like a man insisting on buying dinner for his date," Percy says.

Rob chuckles. "If a guy takes me to dinner, he definitely expects to get laid, so I'll give it to the lion for being gentlemanly even after sex. Gentlelionly?" Percy giggles, which is more than the joke deserves. Rob should actually ask some intelligent questions. "How long is the female in estrus?"

"Five days, give or take."

"And they don't eat that entire time?"

"Nope."

"All they do is…?"

"Yep."

Rob just barely stops himself from massaging his junk in sympathy. "Brah, I wouldn't have the stamina. Imagine how sore you'd be."

Percy makes a funny, panicked kind of face, but he recovers quickly. "It's actually very painful for lion. The, um, act. Males have barbs on their penises—"

"They *what?*" It takes Rob a second to realize he has both hands clapped tight over his mouth.

"Yeah, actually all cats do. Domestic cats too! So when the male ejaculates and pulls out, the spines scrape the female." Percy winces, *finally*. He delivered all that with a straight face. "She gets pissed at the end. You'll see, hopefully!"

"I just…. Why? *Why*, evolution?"

Percy laughs, but Rob's serious. He's rubbing his ass without thinking. Barbs! On a penis! If human men had that, Rob wouldn't let a dick inside any of his orifices ever again. Still smiling, Percy says, "The theory is it stimulates ovulation, or maybe scrapes out semen from other males."

With a shudder, Rob says, "Thank god that adaptation didn't pop up in apes."

Percy seems to notice that Rob's got his hand on his own ass for the first time. He goes a little red, splotches of rose across his cheekbones. "Um, yeah. That would definitely… er… yeah. Not be nice."

Rob shudders again. "I guess some people would like it. BDSM's a thing. God, I went on this date once, and the guy—" At Percy's absolutely appalled expression, Rob shuts up. He's oversharing already and they've only known each other for a few days. When is he going to learn no one likes that? "Um, never mind. You don't want to hear my dating horror stories. Anyway, lions, freaky BDSM dicks. Nature's crazy."

At least the aghast look isn't on Percy's face anymore. He's studying the lion tracks again. Rob stares down at them intently, too, like he has any idea what he's looking at. He quizzes himself on what makes it a feline track and is pretty sure he gets everything right.

"This is sort of weird," Percy says. When Rob makes an interrogative noise, Percy points to two tracks. "This is two individual lion, see? But they're both really… big." His brow furrows and he tilts his head at the tracks, like seeing them from a different angle will help him solve the puzzle. "They're so close in size, I can't really tell which one is the female."

He straightens out of the crouch. "Well, let's find them. Stay close—"

"Single file and no talking." Rob shoots him a smile.

They walk for hours, following the tracks, without a lion sighting. There aren't many other animals, either. Maybe they're worried because the lions are close. Just lots of birds, which Rob likes watching too. They stop for a minute to discuss if they should skip the morning break. Well, Percy asks Rob if he wants to stop and rest or keep going, and since Rob can tell Percy really, really wants to keep going to better their chances of catching up with the lions, he says he's fine.

Which he is. The day isn't hot. It's way more important to make Percy happy and lit up with a sighting of the mating lions.

When they come upon the pair of lions at last, Rob's lizard brain reminds him that he is PREY and maybe he should RUN. Adrenaline floods him so fast and hard at the sight of the two lions sprawled in the grass that it feels like someone kicked the bottom of his spine and tried to yank his brain out through the base of his skull.

His heart is going a hundred miles an hour, and his breath is coming in short pants. Can lions smell fear? Probably, right? Rob's gotta be giving fear off in waves.

Something touches him and he starts. It's Percy. He rests a hand on Rob's shoulder and squeezes, then moves his palm to the center of Rob's back and rubs gently up and down.

Percy doesn't look scared at all. Percy looks—excited. Excited but tempered with concern for Rob. Aw damn, that's too sweet, and Rob wants Percy to have this moment. His mantra is that he trusts Percy not to lead him into danger, right? So he trusts Percy right now.

After a few deep breaths, he nods and makes the A-okay symbol. Hopefully South Africa's not one of the places where that means "asshole"—Rob technically knows all of them, but his brain is extremely smooth at the minute.

The lions aren't actually that close. As terror ebbs from Rob's brain, he calculates the distance roughly at two hundred feet. They're hard to even see that well, beyond the fact that they're definitely lions.

Percy leads Rob to some deadfall, keeping the same distance between them and the lions. They climb a little ways off the ground, Percy graceful and assured and Rob… not so much. He gladly accepts Percy's help. When they're settled on what seems to have been the roots of a tree before it fell, Percy whispers, "Do you have binos?"

It takes Rob a second to figure out what he means, but then he nods and carefully gets his binoculars out of his pack. Percy's changing lenses on his camera to the long telephoto one, and while he does that, Rob looks through the binoculars.

After some fiddling with the focus, he brings the lions into crisp view. His brows furrow against the eyecups. Lowering them, he leans close to Percy. "Are we sure these are the mating lions?"

Percy gives him a funny look, so Rob offers him the binoculars. After a minute, Percy hisses something in Afrikaans that sounds distinctly like profanity. "That doesn't make sense! You could see where they matted the grass down, and the tracks moving on…."

He looks despairingly at Rob like Rob can confirm that he was right, and the lions have pulled a bait and switch. "Um, yeah, you pointed that stuff out to me," Rob agrees. Anything to get that heartbroken expression off Percy's face. "So, those are… definitely two male lions?"

The heartbroken expression goes nowhere. "Yeah. *Fuck.* How did I fuck that up so badly?" He thrusts the binoculars back at Rob. "*Dammit.* Bloody fucking hell, I wasted half the day tracking a couple of male lion...."

"They're cool, though!" Rob says. "I've never seen lions! It's still a good picture, right? I mean, with the mountain in the background? And the clouds are kind of cool?"

Percy still looks dejected, but Rob's attempt to appeal to his photographer's eye at least brings an assessing crook to his mouth. "The clouds are definitely cool," he murmurs, raising his camera. "Unusual too."

Rob feels extremely proud of himself for correctly identifying that the scene would make a good photo.

After snapping a few close-ups of the lions, Percy pulls out his wide-angle lens. At that moment, one of the lions stands up with a huge yawn and a stretch. "Biiiiiig stretch," Rob says. Percy side-eyes him, smiling a little, and Rob's face gets hot. His parents have a big, floofy Maine Coon who stretches the exact same way. What is Rob supposed to do, *not* narrate a big stretch?

The lion shakes his mane and pads over to the other lion. They nuzzle each other. Aw. And then one of the lions... mounts the other?

"Um," Rob says.

The wide-angle lens falls from Percy's fingers back into his pack. "Eish!" He fumbles for his camera, still sporting the telephoto lens, and glues his face to it. "Rob, Rob, get your binos out! Look, look—this is mad!"

Rob doesn't need to be told twice to look through the binoculars. A better view confirms what he thought he saw without them—it's definitely two male lions, and one of them is *definitely* doing the nasty with the other one. "Diversity win," Rob says vaguely. "Your safari has gay lions."

Percy lets out a mildly hysterical laugh, the shutter on the lens clicking a mile a minute. "Milly," he says. "Absolutely fucking milly. Do you know if—no you probably wouldn't know—damn I wish I got bars out here—ah! Look look, he's pissed off from the barbs, see!"

The—er, bottom?—whips his head around, teeth bared, and lashes out. The mounter leaps away to a safe distance and flops onto his side for a rest. After a second, the other lion lies back down too.

Percy spends another few minutes taking photos while Rob leans back on his perch. His heart, he realizes, is pounding. Even though most of his knowledge of lions comes from *The Lion King*, it was impossible not to get caught up in Percy's excitement. His glee was infectious.

Also, just like, kind of selfishly, Rob's really happy to see Percy's big, excited smile. His heart might be going so fast a little bit because of that too.

Satisfied with the photos he's gotten, Percy drops his camera to his lap and looks at Rob. His face is wide open, eyes bright, smile completely devastating. Oof, Rob could fall in love with this guy so easily.

"Wow," Rob says.

Somehow, Percy's smile gets bigger. "That was an amazing thing we just saw. I just—wow! Wow."

Rob laughs and wraps an arm around Percy, giving him half a hug. Percy leans into it and turns his head, bringing their faces inches from each other's. Rob's heart stutters as Percy's smile takes on a different quality, which he should be able to describe since he's, you know, a *writer.*

All he knows is it gets smaller, but not dimmer. It grows softer and takes on a luminous quality.

And—oh shit. Rob really, really wants to kiss him.

He squeezes Percy's shoulders and drops his arm, as much as it pains him. Kissing Percy is a bad idea. For one thing, he has no idea if Percy wants to kiss him. For another, Percy's the one who chose him to come out here. So just… no. Bad move all around.

"So that wasn't a normal sighting in the bush?" Rob asks playfully.

"Um, *no,*" Percy replies. He flops back against the slope of the root behind them, both hands on his face. His joy is adorable. "I've never seen homosexual behavior in animals in the wild! I mean, it's not that uncommon, but being in the right place at the right time—I never dreamed I'd get to see something like that." He looks up at Rob and nudges him with a knee. "Told you. First time safari luck."

Rob nudges him back. "Happy to help."

Percy laces his hands behind his head and lets out a long, satisfied sigh. "See, that's what I love about it out here. You can come to a place over and over again, but it's never the same. You'll always see different things. Different animals, animals behaving differently, clouds changing the light or even the way the animals act on a given day…."

There's such a contented look on his face that Rob doesn't want to break the spell. He remembers yesterday when they sat and just watched, and Rob saw all the tiny details that he wouldn't have if they'd been moving. Now Rob's taking in Percy the same way: the thicker cluster of freckles under his right eye, the spread of his long eyelashes over his cheek every time he blinks, the shape of his elbows and the way his sleeves pull taut over his triceps, the long and graceful curve of his neck and the jut of his Adam's apple. Light glints on his jewelry and the beads in his hair. With the sun shining on them, his eyes are the color of barrel-aged bourbon.

He realizes he's staring and quickly looks away. *Don't be a creep, Hale.*

Which means he probably does have to break the spell. "I definitely see why people say it's such an experience to come here," he says. It sounded stupid in his head, but it sounds even more stupid coming out of his mouth.

But Percy looks at him upside down and smiles. "Yeah? You like it so far?"

Rob nods. Their eyes lock. Percy's throat bobs, Adam's apple tracking the motion of a long swallow, and Rob feels the first edge of panic. What if he can't stop wanting to kiss Percy?

He clears his throat and fiddles with one of the shoulder straps of his pack. "We're not giving up on the cheetah, right?"

"No." Percy straightens. "Are you ready to go back to that?"

Is *Rob* ready? "It's your shoot," Rob says. "I'm just along to document it."

Percy's eyebrows draw together and he opens his mouth, looking like he's going to disagree. Nothing comes out, though, and the quiet is broken by a grey go-away calling. With a wry smile, Percy says, "Well, then we'll get back to cheetah tracking."

Chapter Nine

THE AFTERNOON is getting on by the time they return to the intersection of the cheetah tracks and the lion pair's tracks. The cheetah is hanging close to the mountains, which is good for Percy and Rob. Percy's camped on the plain before, but he doesn't want to take any chances with Rob.

At first that was just normal common sense. "You're doing this to get your name in the media for *good* reasons, Perce, so don't go and get an American killed," Eunice said the last time they spoke. It was the day before Rob arrived, and Percy was at the lodge, relaxing before the week in the bush.

Now he wants to keep Rob safe because… well, because keeping *Rob* safe, specifically, has become very important.

They set up camp on the next mountain over. Rob says he'll help collect firewood, but Percy decides he has to supervise after Rob brings the first armful back. "That'll poison us if we burn it," he says gently. "Smoke inhalation."

Rob looks horrified and lets the branches fall to the ground with a clatter. "There's poison trees?" he asks, stretching his arms out and studying them in panic, then looking at his hands.

Before he thinks what he's doing, Percy wraps his hands around Rob's. "You don't have to worry about touching it," he says. "See?"

He's asking Rob if *he* sees—but what Percy sees right now is their hands fitted together like they were made to be that way.

Percy lets go. "It's tamboti. Spirostachys. If you break open the leaves, they'll ooze latex. They poison the soil around the roots, too, so nothing else can grow. If we breathed in the smoke, we'd spend all night vomiting."

There's a miserable expression on Rob's face. "I almost poisoned us."

That's the moment it becomes very, very clear that Percy's commitment to Rob not getting hurt extends to his feelings. "You didn't," Percy says, fighting the urge not to take his hands again. Rob's big, strong hands, which feel warm and vital, and which felt perfect fitted into Percy's. "I always check what I'm burning, even when I'm the one gathering it. Here, I'll show you what to look for while we collect firewood."

Within fifteen minutes, they've got enough for the night. Then it's time for their tradition of watching the sunset. It's going to be hard to go back to watching sunsets out here alone.

He cuts his eyes toward Rob and his breath catches. Something about the exact angle of the sun as it sinks for the horizon is making Rob's hair glow, black turning to mahogany and the gray becoming threads of silver. He looks like he's crowned with silver vines and copper.

The photographer takes over and he swings his camera up to his eye.

When the shutter clicks, Rob starts and looks over, wide-eyed. "Um, not sure how I should feel about a wildlife photographer taking a picture of me?"

Heat creeps up Percy's neck. What was he thinking? He didn't even ask. "Sorry," he says. "You just…." He waves a hand, then explains inadequately, "The light. You just… you looked"—his hand flaps again, somehow more ineffectually—"I wasn't—um. I can delete it. Sorry."

"Can I see?" Rob asks.

Percy's first reaction is to shy away and refuse. It was a violation to take the photo; he just wants it gone.

Even though Rob looks beautiful, and Percy wanted to capture that.

"Please?" Rob doesn't sound upset that Percy took the picture.

The sun is still crowning Rob in copper and silver. "It might not be any good," Percy mumbles. Instinct took over when he snapped it. He hardly ever takes photos of people, and when he does, he has to fiddle with all his settings to get it just right.

"If it's no good, that's on me, isn't it?" Rob says, an easy grin on his face.

Percy wrinkles his nose. "*No*, of course not! You're—"

Just in time, he shuts his mouth. His teeth click together. *You're beautiful*, he almost said.

To distract from that, he pulls up the picture on the camera's display and hands it to Rob. "The light," Percy says. "It was just… nice. And you looked… er, yeah."

Before he handed the camera to Rob, he got a look at the photo. It *is* good. It's very good. Rob in profile, chin tilted up, gazing into the distance. Every color of the sunset is reflected on his skin—reds and oranges and pinks—and his eyelashes look like they were dipped in gold. His silver and copper crown of hair glows.

The photo is breathtaking, but not because of anything Percy did. It's breathtaking because *Rob* is breathtaking. Somehow Percy captured how his insides have started feeling about Rob in that photo.

Rob stares at the camera before his eyes flicker up to Percy's. "This is nice." His voice is quiet, which Percy doesn't quite know how to take.

"I can delete it," he repeats, his mouth weirdly dry.

"Don't," Rob says firmly. Uncertainty flashes over his face. "Unless you don't think it's any good."

"No, I—I do." This is quickly becoming the most awkward picture Percy's ever taken. "I can send it to you, if you want. If you'd like?"

A sweet, surprised smile creeps over Rob's face. "Yeah?"

"Yeah."

"Okay. Sure."

They get a fire going, cook dinner, and talk about what led them to this point in both of their careers. When Percy set all of this up, he imagined whoever he chose would have a list of questions to ask him, and it would be like an interview. He would be wooden, because he always is in interviews. He'd come off stilted and odd, but definitely devoted to his work.

Instead, Rob makes it into a conversation. He starts his recorder, and he asks a question, but then they just… talk, and pretty soon Percy forgets the recorder is on. Which could be scary, because what if he says something really bad or embarrassing? Except every time that fear nibbles around the edges of his consciousness, he remembers Rob shutting the recorder off when Percy talked about Eton.

His father would call him too naïve and trusting, but Percy can't help how much he trusts Rob.

Percy talks about being accepted at Oxford, where his father expected him to read law—but then fucking off to Amsterdam to Gerrit Rietveld Academie to study photography. He talks about his time in Amsterdam, so different from Eton. "And funny Afrikaans!" he says aggrievedly. "I could just about understand Dutch, but it was like listening to Afrikaans all garbled."

It makes Rob laugh. "I kinda felt the same way about Dutch. Funny English."

There are loads of salacious stories Percy could recount about Amsterdam—wild nights spent high as a kite, waking up with men he'd never seen before in his life, fucking in bathrooms and under bridges.

Instead, he tells Rob about how he started cycling round the city during his second year, once the rebellious urge to smoke and fuck his way through Amsterdam had burned itself out. He'd take his camera, a notebook, and a sketchbook, and he'd ride all weekend. By the end of his photography program, he knew every inch of the city and had photographed most of it too. For his final project, he put together an exhibition on natural spaces within Amsterdam.

"A gallery owner saw my project and got me my own show at her gallery," he says, imposter syndrome niggling at him to this day.

Rob rubs a hand through his hair, making it stick in all different directions. "I remember that show."

If Rob had just said he was a time traveler, actually, Percy would be slightly less surprised. "You… what? I don't think so…."

"Sanne Hendriks was the gallery owner, right? And your show was called *Wilde Amsterdam*?"

Percy's mouth is hanging open. Good thing it's not summer or he'd be getting a mouthful of flies. "You… what?"

Rob winces and his shoulders hunch. "That's creepy, isn't it? Sorry, I swear I'm not a crazy fanboy or something. I've just always really admired your work."

Shaking his head slowly, Percy says, "It's not creepy. I just…. It wasn't anything special."

Rob gapes at him. "Um, are you being serious right now?"

"Yes? It was my final project for university."

"A *gallery owner* literally set you up with your own show *in her gallery*. And it was the real deal, it wasn't like, 'I'm doing a favor for the academy and here's a little student show; aren't I a great person?'" Rob pauses. His eyes widen, and then he covers his face with his hands. "Ohmygoddd I just made myself sound so much creepier."

"Were you *there*?" Percy asks.

"Um. Yes?" Rob peeks out through his fingers. "I was in Amsterdam and I kinda knew you had a show, so I badgered my boyfriend into going."

Percy's heart is rabbiting. "Did we meet?" What a horrifying thought—that he met Rob Hale and *forgot* him. How could he have done that? How could he look into Rob's eyes and forget him?

"No." Rob looks both regretful and relieved. "I was hoping I'd get to meet you, but you weren't there." He shrugs. "It's a good thing, actually. Me and the boyfriend got in a huge fight. Would've been weird if you'd seen that."

"Oh. I'm, um, sorry?" Percy's not sorry that ten-years-ago Rob got in a fight with his boyfriend, because hearing Rob say *my boyfriend* makes unhappiness and jealousy prickle at Percy's skin. It's a very stupid reaction to have, which is why Percy is obviously not going to let on that it's happening, but—yeah. He doesn't like the idea of Rob having a boyfriend.

He's an absolute twat, probably. Percy, not the boyfriend. Though Percy's willing to assume that all of Rob's boyfriends have been twats.

With a chuckle, Rob says, "It's fine, I'm over it. We broke up when we got home."

Good. "Oh."

"Plus that was a long time ago."

"I can't believe you saw my show." Now that it's sunk in, it's filling Percy with a warm, burbly feeling.

"You don't think I'm a stalker?" When Percy shakes his head, Rob lets out a whooshing breath of relief. "Somewhere out there on the internet, the article I wrote for my college newspaper about that trip is still preserved."

The burbly feeling is still there, sitting in Percy's chest. "I want to see it."

"You really don't. If I'm remembering right, there was a lot of purple prose about canals, tulips, and windmills."

Percy ducks his head to hide his smile, then wonders why he's trying to hide. "Remind me where you went to university again?" It was on Rob's CV, but Percy doesn't like to put much stock in where someone gets their education. The most prestigious uni in the world won't guarantee you a good education. You have to work for it, and you have to have the right instructors. People can get that at community college, even if people like Percy's father look down on community colleges. Katli went to a community college, and now she's managing a five-star safari camp.

"University of Wisconsin, Madison."

"Wisconsin…. It's cold there, right?"

"Very cold," Rob confirms. "Imagine a Hawaiian kid by way of Georgia voluntarily choosing to spend four years in a place where winter lasts like six months. And I'm talking *winter* winter. Multiple feet of snow winter." When Percy tilts his head, Rob goes on, "There's a really good journalism program there. And Madison's a great city, actually. Really pretty when there's not five feet of snow on the ground. Quirky, too. It was a good place for me."

That's a rather alien feeling for Percy—going somewhere else and feeling at home. For all that his career is travel, he only feels *right* when he's home. "Cape Town is good for me," he says vaguely.

Would Rob like Cape Town? Percy likes to think he would. Cape Town is hard not to like.

"And here is good for you," Rob says. His gaze seems fonder than it should after only a few days, but Percy wants to pull it around himself like a blanket.

"Here too," Percy agrees.

They meet each other's eyes and smile. The fire tries to bring out all the same colors in Rob's hair that the sunset did, but it can't compete.

Chapter Ten

THEY HAVE an amazing experience the next day. Percy's beginning to seriously think Rob *is* a good luck charm, but he knows better than to make a joke that Rob should always come on shoots with him. For one thing, he doesn't want to use the word "come" and "shoot" that close in a sentence together, because he will *definitely* turn bright red. More importantly, telling a man you've developed quite the thing for over just a handful of days that you'd like to travel with him sounds like an emphatically terrible idea.

Percy knows elephants are around. Their tracks and dung are impossible to miss. When Rob says they can't be too close, since they can't hear them walking, Percy tells him how quiet they are. He can tell Rob wants to believe him, but doesn't.

Well, he does now.

They're sitting in a grove of umbrella thorn having a bite to eat when the first elephant brushes through the trees. Rob's mouth drops open. Percy raises a finger to his lips, but Rob, as usual, is doing exactly what Percy asked him to on the first day.

The elephant looks right at them. Her skin is saggy and dusty. Percy recognizes her. She's the matriarch of Thaba Boroko's elephants, the oldest and most dominant female. Her dark, limpid eyes take them in, and Percy keeps his hands where she can see them. A glance at Rob assures Percy he's doing the same thing.

After regarding them for another moment, her ears flap. Dust and insects fly off her in a cloud, and she continues into the grove.

Behind her comes the rest of the herd.

Their footfalls are nearly soundless. There's the barest crunch of grass, but as the huge animals thread through the trees, the loudest sound is branches snapping as the elephants use their trunks to break them and put them in their mouths.

Soon, they're surrounded as the elephants spread out through the grove to find the tastiest leaves. Percy's ribs hurt and his eyes sting. Every time he sees them. *Every* time. They're beautiful, magnificent animals, and it's an honor to be in their presence.

There are calves with the herd, sticking close to their mothers for the most part. Percy has no doubt some of that has to do with the humans in their midst. The matriarch may have judged them nonthreatening, but elephants are smart. It's easy to believe they know that as small as people are, they're killers.

That makes Percy's ribs hurt too.

One of the calves approaches them curiously. His mother keeps a close eye on him as he edges closer and closer. When he's close enough that either of them could reach out a hand to touch him, he bleats loudly and rushes back to mama—but then dances close to them again.

Percy presses his lips tight to keep from bursting out laughing, but when he hears a snort from Rob, he can't stop his own guffaw from escaping. A few of the elephants look at them. Mama wiggles her ears, and the baby looks delighted with itself in that way that all young children do when they're hamming it up and getting exactly the response they want.

They sit like that, surrounded by elephants, for an hour. Profound peace settles through Percy, right down to his marrow. His mind quiets, his breathing steadies. Elephant watching is the best stress relief.

Gradually, the elephants trickle out of the grove, moving on to feed elsewhere. The matriarch is the last one to leave. She comes close to them, close enough that Percy can see Rob and him reflected in her eye. She blinks, her thick fringe of eyelashes brushing her dusty skin. The intelligence looking out of that eye isn't human, but it's undeniably intelligence.

Percy wishes he could tell her he's humbled she trusted her family around Rob and him. Maybe she already knows. He tilts his chin down anyway, hoping he's communicating something. Some kind of exchange, from one intelligent being to another.

Then she's gone, melting through the trees like she was never there.

THE WEIRD clouds from yesterday are still there today. They make for a breathtaking sunset. All those reds and oranges and pinks and purples linger in the sky long after the sun is gone, reflecting off the undersides of the bubbly clouds. The colors of the sunset seep into the mountains, too, turning their faces a deep carmine that Percy hasn't ever seen.

That's probably why he does something stupid, which he most definitely knows better than to do. But the light is so beautiful, so different to anything he's seen here before. It would be incorrect to say he *wants* to get photos. He *needs* to get photos. It's not something he can control. And because they've already got the fire going, and the colors keep painting the clouds and the mountains after the sun is gone, Percy needs to get away from the light.

He tells Rob to stay at the fire. Then he takes a torch, his camera, and a couple lenses, and he slips through the purple gloaming until he's far enough from the fire not to catch any of its light. He braces his camera on a branch. Not ideal, but his tripod is back at the camp. Anyway, he's got steady hands—he should be able to get wide shots of the mountains without motion blur, even with the low light.

He falls into the rhythm of shooting photos—a few practice ones to tweak his settings, then lining up shot after shot and taking it, shutter click-click-clicking away. He loves that sound. It makes him feel like he's doing something worthwhile.

By the fourth time he adjusts the exposure, he realizes it's very dark. Almost completely dark. Shit—he got caught up. And he left Rob by the fire alone. How long has it been?

He flips his torch on to make sure he's got everything. That's when he hears it.

Something is coming through the trees. It's headed straight for him.

Adrenaline and fear floods him. Rob. Is Rob safe? Rob has the fire, and they've talked about how to escape from various animals. Up here, there shouldn't be any big predators. *Shouldn't be* are the key words.

If Percy gets hurt or killed by whatever's coming through the trees, he won't be able to do anything for Rob. As much as it kills him, his first priority has to be his own safety. Like on planes when they tell you to put your own oxygen mask on before helping anyone else—as though Percy would actually do that. If he was sitting next to Rob on a plane and the masks came down, he'd definitely help Rob with his first.

The crashing in the trees gets closer. He left his rifle at the fire, so Percy uses the best defense he's got—his torch. He turns it to its brightest setting and shines it directly into the path of whatever's coming toward him.

"AHH!"

Percy startles, fear ripping up his spine, and drops the torch. In the careening light, he catches sight of a body falling toward him.

Instinct takes over and makes him stick out his arms. Rob tumbles into them.

Thick arms wrap around Percy and Rob shudders. Percy's arms are around Rob, too. When did that happen? "What are you doing?" Percy demands. "You were supposed to stay at the fire where it's safe!"

Rob's face is turned into the crook of Percy's neck. He hasn't let go yet. In fact, he squeezes Percy tighter, like he doesn't quite believe he's real. "Got worried about you," Rob says in a muffled voice.

Percy's heart gives a painful twang. "I'm fine."

"Well, yeah. I know that *now*."

With their chests pressed together, Percy can feel how hard Rob's heart is hammering. He wishes he knew how to comfort people. This is yet another reason he's not a guide. Sometimes jarring, even scary, things happen in the bush, and Percy doesn't know how to make people feel safe again.

So he just hugs Rob, because that seems to be working. At least Rob isn't letting go, so Percy hopes it's working.

Up close like this, Percy can smell him. They're both ripe, which is no mystery, what with sharing a tent. But this is different; more intimate. This is hair and skin and *Rob*. He smells like salt, like the sea, and like something vital and alive. Percy's heart is still pounding, but now it's not entirely from fright.

Finally, Rob lets out a shuddery breath and loosens his grip. The space that gaps between them allows Percy to pick his torch up, which is skewed at an angle that looks appropriate for a horror film. Clutching it, Percy says guiltily, "I'm sorry. I lost track of time. Are you all right? Nothing came into the campsite?"

"No, no, I just—you were gone awhile, and then your light came on, but you didn't come back, and...." Rob rakes his fingers through his hair. It's so dirty that it sticks up. With a sheepish laugh, he says, "I got worried you fell or something, and you were trying to signal me with the flashlight."

"If I fell, I would have just yelled for you to come help me," Percy points out.

There's a beat of silence. "Um. Yeah. I guess… that makes a lot more sense. Okay, well, all good! I'm cold, are you cold? I'm gonna head back to the fire."

Before Percy can stop him, Rob darts away through the trees toward the faint glow of the campfire that Percy's dark-adjusted eyes can make out.

He makes his way back. Rob is near the fire, his shoulders bowed. Percy stands at the edge of the flickering light. Something is chewing at his sternum that takes him a second to put a name to. Disappointment. Up until now, Rob's always listened to him. Trusted him.

"I could have shot you," Percy says quietly.

Rob's spine goes ramrod straight and he swivels to look at Percy with wide eyes. "You left your gun here, though. You have another?"

He doesn't, and if he was doing what he's been trained to do, he wouldn't have walked off and left his rifle behind. He's supposed to have his rifle on him when he walks around in the bush, and that's the only thing beating right under the surface of his skin right now. If Percy did what he was supposed to, Rob could be dead.

Sick what-might-have-beens crawl over Percy's skin like insects. He sits down at the fire opposite Rob. It was nicer the previous nights when they sat next to each other, but Percy's—rattled. Angry at himself for being rattled too. Angry at Rob for rattling him, even though Rob doesn't really know better, so it's not fair to be upset at him.

"I was just worried," comes Rob's low rumble from the other side of the fire. Percy stares into the flames without blinking until the brightness inverts and flares negative across his eyes. He shuts them but still sees the fire dancing on the backs of his eyelids. Dirt and rocks crunch as Rob shifts. "I fucked up," Rob says. "I'm sorry, okay?"

Percy wishes he could explain, except explaining means getting a handle on what he's feeling right now. That's always been the crux of the problem. His feelings are too big and confusing, and he can't wrestle them into order.

One thing he's sure of? Lines have somehow been crossed between them, because Rob shouldn't be apologizing to them like they're lovers having a fight.

"Don't." His eyes are still closed. "Keeping you safe is my job. I didn't do my job."

"I'm safe."

"Something bad could've happened."

"Perce."

Percy's eyes snap open. Rob isn't on the other side of the fire anymore. That crunchy gravel noise was the sound of him shuffling closer. Now he's kneeling near Percy, firelight flickering on his skin. Something gets caught in Percy's throat. There are only a few people on this planet allowed to call him *Perce*.

Rob looks like he's rewinding something in his brain. He grimaces a little. "Can I call you that? Maybe you hate that nickname."

His throat still won't work, but Percy swallows once, twice, then a third time, and finally makes his voice work. "I don't hate it."

There's hesitation on Rob's face, like he wants to point out, maybe, that *I don't hate it* isn't the same as *It's okay if you call me that.* "I'm safe. Nothing bad happened. But I shouldn't've left the fire. I should've done what you told me to do. You're the one who knows what he's doing."

Percy can't make the image of Rob with a bullet in his gut go away. It's there in his head like it really happened—the blood seeping across his shirt, the shocked expression on his face, the way the life goes out of his eyes.

His breath shudders like he's going to cry. He digs the heels of his hands into his eyes, which makes him look like a berk, but at least Rob won't see the tears leaking out.

"Hey." Rob thumps down next to him. "Hey. Percy. What's wrong? Did I hurt you? Did something happen?"

Percy folds his knees up to his chest and drops his forehead onto them. "Please don't put this in your article" is what comes out of his mouth.

A warm, steady hand presses into his back, rubbing up and down his spine. "I won't. I wouldn't."

What Percy would like, more than anything right now, is for Rob to put his arm around his shoulders and hold him. That's not going to happen, though, and nor should it. Clearly. This is happening because Percy's got attached to this man. "I have—I imagine terrible things happening. It's like they really happened. Even when they didn't. Intrusive thoughts. That's what they're called." Just another fun part of his anxiety. Usually he's safe from them in the bush.

"Oh." It's one exhaled syllable of understanding. "Okay." Rob's hand keeps up its slow rhythm on Percy's back. "And—me getting…. Okay. Perce, that didn't happen. It's not going to happen."

"It could."

"You left your gun here with me. And I definitely didn't touch it."

Percy presses his forehead into his knees harder, the pressure and pain distracting him from the images in his mind. They're fading now, but he has to be careful, or they'll come back. He has to skirt around their edges and not look at them head-on.

Rob scoots closer and settles into a more comfortable position. His warmth at Percy's side does the same thing that the pain does. "I've never done anything like this in my life. Trekking through the wilderness for a week? Getting close up and personal with animals that could end me without even thinking about it? *Camping?*"

The incredulity on that last one gets a snotty, sputtery laugh from Percy. At last, he turns his head to look at Rob. The care on Rob's face almost undoes Percy all over again. They've only known each other for a few days, but there are only a few people who have ever looked at Percy like that.

Coincidentally, they're the people allowed to call him *Perce.*

Rob gives him a warm smile. "I was kind of nervous about all of it when I was getting ready to fly over. Maybe really nervous. I was meeting you and doing this kind of legit scary thing. But you've made me feel so totally safe. You always know exactly what to do. So every time I get nervous or scared, I just look at you and I feel better. Because I know you wouldn't ever put either of us in a situation that wasn't safe."

Something's stuck in Percy's throat again, but it's different this time. No one has ever said anything like that to him. No one's ever described him that way.

He drops his gaze to the ground, where shadows dance from the fire. There's a chill in the air tonight and a stiff breeze that keeps rustling the leaves above them. The flames gutter and Percy shifts the wood around to keep them lower.

He wishes he could say the right thing to Rob—but he doesn't know what that thing is. He doesn't know if he should apologize for snapping or thank Rob for trusting him so much.

Wouldn't it be nice if they could skip ahead to a time when Percy understands what he can say and what he can't? If they already had the kind of relationship where Percy could make a joke now, and Rob would laugh, and they'd both know everything was fine?

Already. Like it's inevitable that they'll have that kind of relationship someday.

He should say something, even if it's not the right thing. But Rob seems to be okay with the silence. So Percy lets his knees fall open, nudging Rob ever-so-slightly with one. Rob cuts a look over at him, that same warm smile on his face. It's gone softer now.

Who could blame Percy for wanting Rob in his life past this week?

Chapter Eleven

ROB THINKS everything's okay again by the time they crawl into the tent to sack out. The smell of two men who've been hiking for days, not showering, and crammed into a two-person tent should be hella nasty by now. Rob, though, is the opposite of grossed out by it. The smell of Percy's body is nice.

Okay, fine. Smelling Percy's sweat and musk is turning him on.

It's comforting, too, though. And like, totally not the kind of thing he'd be able to explain to any of his friends. But they're out here, and it's just them, and Percy's smell is the smell of safety and his… person? Even if Percy isn't his person anywhere besides here.

So yeah, falling asleep is easy, his sleeping bag rucked up to his chin and Percy's presence a faint buzz of awareness through Rob's body.

A crack of thunder wakes him. His body jerks and his eyes snap open as his heart slams against his ribs.

He flops onto his back again, heart pounding crazily. Jesus.

"Storm just hit." Percy's voice is low, almost too low to be heard over the roll of thunder.

He turns and props himself on an elbow. Flashes of lightning shine on Percy's eyes. "Are we okay in here?" Rob asks.

There's a slightly too long beat of silence from Percy. At least, slightly too long for Rob's complete and total comfort. A flash of lightning makes grasping fingers of the branches, clawing across the canvas of the tent.

"We'll be fine." Despite the time it took Percy to answer, he sounds sure of himself. That's enough to make Rob relax.

Lightning flashes again, a one-two-three flicker flash of blinding white on the canvas. The wind gusts and the tent billows.

"Didn't you say the clouds looked weird?" Rob asks.

The lightning is coming so often now that Rob can see Percy's face, including the look of surprise. "Er, yeah, I did." A hard gust of wind catches the sides of the tent and moans through the canvas. Rob shivers at the creepy-as-fuck sound, and Percy yanks his sleeping bag up around his chin.

Something smacks the top of the tent. Rob jumps. "Was that a rock?"

There's another smack, then another, and in the flash of lightning, dark patches of wet canvas dance. "Rain!" Percy's voice gets a little high. "It's *raining*. It's not supposed to rain at this time of year!"

The clouds open the fuck up, and it's pouring. The sound is deafening, almost enough to drown out the rumble of thunder. Almost. Rob can still hear it rolling, a constant grumble punctuated by harder, sharper cracks.

They're not going to get struck by lightning, right?

Rob decides you can only worry about so much, and getting struck by lightning is going to have to take a number. The tent blowing over or springing a leak both seem way more likely.

There's a flash of lightning so blinding bright that it illuminates the inside of the tent like daylight. An earsplitting crack tears across the mountain, so loud that all of Rob's worries are taken over by a tree falling on their tent.

Something smacks into him and he yells, adrenaline flooding him. He'll lift the fucking tree off them if he has to, he—

His flailing hand comes in contact with Percy, who is quite suddenly pressed up against him, hands twisted into the collar of Rob's sweatshirt.

No tree falls on them, which is when Rob realizes the sound was thunder from a close lightning strike. But their tent is still standing, and he can't see any flames from burning trees.

"I think we're okay," he says, though he's not complaining about having Percy pressed up against him. Not that there's anything erotic about it—they're both wearing warm clothes and in their own sleeping bags. But the backs of Percy's fingers are resting against Rob's collarbone, and he likes it.

There's another loud crack of thunder and Percy jerks again, moving closer. Rob nudges him. "Hey, you have to take me to dinner first."

A surprised snort comes from Percy. His grip on Rob's shirt loosens. "What do you call the last few nights? I brought all the food."

Rob wiggles a little, happy his scheme to make Percy laugh worked. "Okay. I'll admit it, I'm pretty easy. You just have to buy me a drink first."

Percy laughs more easily this time. God, Rob would kill to put an arm around him. He wants to pull Percy close and hold him until the storm passes, so every time there's a loud boom of thunder, he's already there in the circle of Rob's arms. Because thunderstorms apparently freak Percy out! Who knew?

"I'm being stupid, I know," Percy says. "Never meet your heroes, right? You might find out they piss themselves over a stupid storm."

"Nah," Rob says. "You wanna hear a dumb fear?"

"Okay."

Thunder rolls again, its jagged edges not as sonically defined as the last few cracks have been. Percy is warm in Rob's arms. "I can't look at the plane wings when I fly. *Terrified* to look at them. I try to never, ever have a seat over one of the wings, and if I get stuck sitting there, I keep the window shade closed for the entire flight. First thing I do when I sit down, and I don't put it back up when the plane lands."

Percy gives his chest the tiniest push. "Stop. That's not true."

"Hand to god!" Rob fights the urge to rest his face against Percy's. Percy's hair smells nice—sweet and maybe a little bit coconut-y. His twists have gotten progressively frizzier as the days have gone by, but Rob just wants to feel that frizz against his face, same way he wants to feel Percy's stubble on his skin.

Rain keeps pounding on the tent. The low moan of the wind on the canvas sighs again, bringing a chill puff of air over the top of Rob's head. The tension in Percy's body loosens. He doesn't move away, though, and Rob doesn't want to move a muscle in case Percy's forgotten they're cuddled up together.

"Why are you afraid of sitting over the wing of the plane?" Percy asks in a tone that suggests he knows Rob is trying to distract him, he knows he's supposed to ask this question, and he doesn't mind. That, in fact, he may be grateful.

Something hits the tent with a wet, flapping thud. Percy startles, and Rob unthinkingly puts an arm around his back, fitting them snug against each other.

And then he forgets to breathe for a second. Oh. Oh no. It feels really, really good to hold Percy. But what are the chances Percy thinks it feels really, really good for Rob to hold him?

Percy doesn't move, though. So Rob unfists his own fingers and lays them flat against Percy's body, curling them around his side. His arm is outside Percy's sleeping bag, so it's not even like he can feel much of anything.

"Rob?" Percy's voice is soft. "Why does it scare you?"

Okay, shake it off, brah. Rob grounds himself in the sound of the rain and the fact that whatever just hit their tent didn't cause any damage. Probably just a small branch. "You ever watch *The Twilight Zone*? The old one with Rod Serling?"

Percy shakes his head, which Rob can feel more than see. "I watched the Jordan Peele one."

"Oh, yeah, that one was good too. But okay, so in the old show, there's this episode with William Shatner in it. He's flying for the first time since getting out of a mental institution, and he's supposed to be fine, right? Only every time he looks out the window, he sees this like, creepy-as-fuck gremlin thing. And he's losing it, right? And no one else sees the thing! Every time anyone else looks—his wife or the flight attendants or whatever, there's nothing there." Rob shudders just thinking about it. "Anyway, he sees the thing sabotaging parts of the wing, and he ends up stealing a gun and opening the emergency exit to shoot it. At the end he's being taken away in a straitjacket. Ugh." Another shudder. "It's so creepy."

There's a softness to Percy's body that wasn't there before. His muscles are loosening as he relaxes. Maybe it's Rob telling him about this ancient episode of television—or maybe it's just the fact that the thunder is tapering off, rolling quietly into the distance like the background rumble of traffic.

"Is the gremlin real?" Percy asks.

"Yeah. At the very end you see the damage to the plane's wing."

Percy's silent for a moment. "Are you afraid of flying?"

"No! That's the thing! It's just this dumb fear of like… I don't even know. Seeing a monster on the wing? It doesn't even make any sense." He mulls over it. Usually this is one of his deepest, darkest secrets, but telling Percy felt nice. "I think maybe it's the idea of something being wrong and being the one responsible for making someone listen to me. You know? Like, I'm not out here to be the hero."

Neither of them speaks for a minute. Finally, Rob says, "It's dumb."

"Thank you for telling me," Percy says nearly at the same time, so their words overlap. Then: "I don't think it's dumb."

Finally, Percy moves away, shuffling back to his side of the tent. It's not very far away, but it feels like miles. The empty space against Rob's chest has weight that it shouldn't. Rob smiles into the darkness, fake-it-till-you-make-it style, even though Percy can't see him. "Most planes don't even crash because of a problem on the wing."

There's such a long silence that Rob wonders if Percy fell asleep. Or maybe he's just done talking about this. When Percy's voice floats through the dark, it does something to fill that cold, empty space pressing up against Rob's chest. "That's not really the point, though."

"I guess not."

The pounding of the rain eases off slowly, going from hammering to pattering to the slow drip of water falling from the trees overhead. The wind eases, too, growing soothing instead of howling. Rob floats between sleeping and waking, a half-somnolent insistence from his brain that he should stay alert in case the storm gets bad again and Percy needs him.

Dumb thought. Percy needing him. Even half asleep, he knows that's not the case.

The soft gray of sleep is just starting to fold over him when he hears a quiet, "Rob?"

"Mm?"

Warm, callused fingers find his where they're resting over his sleeping bag. "I'm really glad I chose you to come on this trip. And I'm really glad you came."

Fuzzily, still mostly asleep, Rob brushes his thumb over Percy's hand. "Me too."

Chapter Twelve

OVER THE next few days, Rob gets tons of great material for the piece he'll write about Percy. They spend most of one day walking, still tracking the cheetah, and another day sitting in one spot, waiting for the cheetah—or anything else—to wander past.

That day, Percy sets up a temporary photo blind, which Rob helps him construct. It's just branches and leaves for them to hide behind while Percy props his camera on something stable. He rarely uses a tripod; that's a thing that Rob learns. Also, he's intensely patient, can maintain incredible stillness for hours, and has probably forgotten more about the South African bush than Rob could ever learn.

He's happy to tell Rob about the techniques he uses to photograph his subjects, be they animals, landscapes, or sunsets. At first, he cuts himself off when he starts to get enthusiastic, but Rob encourages him to keep talking, and then he's off. Rob's initial impression of Percy de Villiers was that he's very smart, very gifted, and very shy. After spending nearly a week with him, Rob knows that he's even smarter, even more gifted, and yes, shy. Shy, but opening to Rob in a way that feels as precious as blown glass.

He knows that Percy is passionate about not just his photography, but about the landscapes he works in. They have a number of conversations about conservation and the things Percy wants to do to help—the ways he envisions getting involved to save South Africa's wildlife and unique environments. He knows Percy is bitingly funny and clever. Rob hasn't laughed to the point of wheezing for ages, but Percy manages to make him several times over a few days with a well-timed remark or the perfect delivery.

He knows that Percy wants to do more, that he gets fierce and teary when he talks about queer rights in Africa and around the world. He knows that Percy has a small but close group of friends in Cape Town. He knows Percy loves his hometown but hates it, too, in ways that he doesn't articulate, but which Rob can hear threaded into the subtext of what he says.

Maybe everyone hates their hometown a little bit, though, especially when they also love it. When you know how amazing it can be, it hurts that much more when it falls short.

So, yeah. Rob's main concern re: the article is how he can possibly capture this interesting, talented, complicated man in a couple thousand words.

Oh, and also? Rob's, like. Totally gone for him. He has it bad for Percy, and he suspects that Percy's into him too.

Their last full day in the bush dawns bright and chilly. Their breath fogs as they pack up their campsite for the penultimate time. Frost rimes the grass and leaves, sparkling delicately, before it burns off with the rising sun. They make little progress until then, because Percy takes a million pictures. Rob can't blame him. It's beautiful.

Their cheetah has been leading them in circles. Percy's convinced it's nearby, but they haven't managed to catch sight of it yet. Since they head back to the safari camp tomorrow morning, this is their last chance to get a glimpse of it.

Rob will be bummed if they don't, since it's been, like, their quest for this entire week. But even if they don't, he's seen things this week he never imagined. And he got to spend a week with Percy, who…. Well, yeah.

If he's not bummed about not seeing the cheetah, it's because his sadness is all used up on the fact that this is the last full day with Percy. They both have rooms at the Thaba Boroko safari camp for a couple days, but Rob isn't letting himself hope that Percy will want to spend time with him there. The deal was one week together in the bush. It wasn't one week together in the bush, and then maybe a romantic candlelit dinner with a nice bottle of South African red in the safari lodge.

At midday, they stop for lunch in a clearing. There are cheetah tracks and scat around, but no cheetah. As Percy breaks into a protein bar, he says, "I sort of feel like I led you on about this cheetah. Feel free to put that in your article: makes big promises about big cat viewing, doesn't deliver."

"Cheetah-baiting." Rob salutes him with his own protein bar. "*Sherlock* did that, right?"

Percy offers him a bright, crooked grin, eyes crinkling in amusement. Rob dies a little bit.

"I *am* sorry." Percy makes a face. "The ones around here are shy. With it all being reclaimed farmland, most of the wildlife is still wary of people."

"Hard to blame them."

They've talked poaching, of course. You don't go on an African safari without having a conversation about poaching at some point. The entire reserve is fenced in, and Percy told him about how the guides for the safari camp don't talk about heavily poached animals over the radio, just in case poachers have zonked the channel.

Percy gazes into the distance as he chews. Rob could watch him think forever. He gets this faraway expression in his eyes, like he's only tethered to this world by a cable he could cut any time.

His eyes cut back to Rob suddenly, though. "It's funny to think that tomorrow we'll be"—he gestures vaguely—"back in civilization. I always struggle remembering how to talk to people."

"You've been talking totally normally to me," Rob says with a smile.

Percy opens his mouth, his eyes gleaming with a little mischief, but then he closes it and snorts air through his nose. "It would have been too easy to make that into a joke at your expense."

"Aw, and you held back! You can, though. I'm a big boy. I can take it."

Percy's eyebrows creep upward and his face gets that rosy flush to it. Rob reexamines what he said. Yeah, that might have been a little innuendo-y. Sorry not sorry.

A flash of motion catches Rob's eye. He shifts his gaze—

And freezes. There's a cheetah. There's a cheetah right there. Right. Fucking. There.

Rob's hand shoots out to grab Percy's. "Perce." His voice is strangled. Percy swings his head around and stills.

Oh god. The cheetah's looking at them. Its muzzle is red. Is that *blood*? Oh shit oh no there's a predator, cheetahs are *predators*; god Rob was lulled into utterly false complacency by memories of YouTube videos with adorable titles like "Cheetah And Dog Are Best Friends" or "Cute Cheetah Purring And Cuddling."

This cheetah is not purring. It's staring unblinkingly, its amber eyes locked on them. And it's *covered in blood*.

They're going to die. This is how Rob's going to die.

"Rob," Percy says, his voice low. "It's okay."

Which is when Rob realizes he's squeezing Percy's hand hard enough to break bones. His breath is coming too fast. He wants to respond, but he's not sure he can actually make his voice come out.

The first couple attempts produce nothing but a hiss of air, but finally he swallows a few times and manages, "Is this like *Jurassic Park?*"

"What?" Percy asks quietly.

Okay, now Rob wants to laugh. That would be the hysteria. "When Muldoon tells Ellie they're being hunted and she has to run—"

"We're not going to run."

Rob squeezes Percy's hand harder and Percy squeezes back with the same bone-crunching force.

The cheetah watches them for another moment. Then it yawns and flops to the ground, sprawling in a lanky jumble of legs and curled tail. Its belly is white and looks soft. The rest of its fur is ruffled tawny gold and black spots, and Rob never imagined seeing a big cat in the wild no more than ten feet away. It looks fake, and it looks way too scarily real.

The two of them don't move. You couldn't pay Rob to let go of Percy's hand. It feels like that's the only thing holding him down. He'd bolt otherwise, and the cheetah would chase him, and then that would be *his* blood all over its face.

"She has a kill nearby," Percy murmurs. He sounds happy about it. Maybe it's a good thing—if the cheetah just ate, it won't want to eat *them.*

The black tip of the cheetah's tail twitches. Rob might shit himself.

"Rob?" Percy squeezes his hand. "It's fine. *You're* fine. She won't hurt us."

Voice shaking, Rob asks, "How do you know?"

Slowly, Percy aligns his body with Rob's, so they're sitting side by side, shoulders touching, both facing the cheetah. "Because cheetahs don't attack people."

"But—"

"Rob." Suddenly Percy's big, warm hand is on Rob's face, palm pressed against Rob's week's worth of scruff, fingers brushing the hair at his temples. His ink-dark eyes hold Rob's. "They don't. She won't hurt you. You trust me, right?"

"Yeah," Rob whispers.

Percy nods. His thumb swipes slowly across Rob's cheekbone and he smiles, squeezes Rob's hand again, and tilts his head in the direction of the cheetah. Rob gets it. He should look at the animal they've been tracking all week, but Percy's going to hold Rob's gaze until Rob manages to stop pissing himself and do that.

When he turns to look at the cheetah again, he half expects it to have moved closer. But it—she—is still sprawled in the shade of a scrubby tree, watching them with a total lack of concern.

"She really won't hurt us?" Rob asks.

"Really. Bet we could pet her."

A wave of icy heat crawls over Rob's skin from his wrists to the back of his neck. "That's okay."

"I wouldn't really do that."

Rob wishes he could say he recognized the comment as irreverent, but he has too much adrenaline coursing through his veins to distinguish jokes from real suggestions.

In that moment, he can't imagine relaxing while this large, very fast, very pointy-teethed predator lolls on the ground ten feet away from them.

But that's the secret to homo sapiens' success, right? They can adapt to anything. And maybe Percy's right that none of their distant ancestors ate it at the hands—paws—of a cheetah, because all she does is lie there.

After she ascertains that they aren't going to approach her, she doesn't even bother keeping an eye on them. With another yawn, she raises a paw and starts licking it, using it to wash her face clean of blood.

Slowly, the adrenaline and fear drain from Rob. The cheetah is totally unconcerned with their presence. Watching her is like watching a house cat clean itself. She has all the same moves—crane your neck to get your back, clean between your toes, lick a paw and use it to wash behind your ears and get your fur all adorably ruffled. When she's done washing herself, she goes back to her relaxed sprawl. Her eyes droop to slits and she lets her head drop back into a more relaxed position.

When Percy quietly gets his camera out, her eyes open up again and her ears prick forward, but she doesn't get up. Percy takes a few pictures, and she watches him closely. Huh. She's trying to determine if they're going to hurt her. Rob would say in a revelatory tone that she's just as afraid of them as he was of her, except that's clearly not true, because he was practically hyperventilating while she was content to chill in the shade as long as they weren't making any move toward her.

She settles back down and Percy's able to photograph her to his heart's content. The whole thing starts to feel very zen—the warmth of the afternoon, the ground soaking up the heat, the birdsong around them. The click of Percy's camera shutter, the rhythm of him shooting and checking what he captured, shooting and checking what he captured. The way the cheetah trusts them, and they trust her, and they're just here, coexisting.

He sounds like a stoner. Yeah, man, we're all just, like, here on this Earth together.

God, except that's how it feels. A deep well of connection to everything floods him. The sky and the ground, the smell of grass and dirt, the way the breeze puffs against his neck every now and then.

Percy, whose intensity and quiet concentration make his heart flutter. Their sides are pressed together, shoulders knocking when Percy shifts for a different camera angle. Rob likes that he's so focused on taking photos that he doesn't even seem to notice. There's no apology Rob has to pretend to find reasonable, because the truth is he's hoarding every case of incidental contact between them.

The sun arcs across the sky and the shadows lengthen as afternoon sinks toward evening. The cheetah dozes on and off. Percy gets snacks out, which makes the cheetah perk up. She quickly decides whatever they have is of no interest (it's dried mango) and relaxes again.

Rob and Percy don't speak. A week ago, before coming on this trip with Percy, Rob would have struggled not to talk a mile a minute if something like this happened. Sitting silently hasn't ever been one of his strengths, and if something crazy happens? Yeah, forget it.

Maybe it's Africa, maybe it's the bush, maybe it's just Percy. But hours pass and Rob doesn't say a word. He's not even tempted to. It's the three of them—Percy, Rob, and the cheetah—and the bush. Sky and earth and all the life in between.

When the light turns golden, the cheetah climbs to her feet. She stretches, front paws out, butt in the air, and then reverses the pose— back legs stretched behind her, one, then another. A huge yawn gives the light a chance to shine glinting white on her mouthful of extremely sharp teeth, but Rob isn't even worried anymore.

At least, he's not worried for more than like, half a second.

The cheetah stands there looking at them. The fluid, graceful line of her spine and the trim taper her body comes to at her hips reminds Rob of Percy. Her amber eyes meet Rob's. Slowly, she blinks. Rob's been around enough cats to know what that means—some measure of trust, an understanding that hey, you're okay.

Rob slow blinks back. Silently, the cheetah turns and walks away, her lanky body casting an even longer shadow.

When she disappears into some scrubby bushes, Rob puts his hand on Percy's knee. Percy's hand rests on top of Rob's.

Chapter Thirteen

THEY'RE QUIET as they make camp for the last time. Percy's head is full of images from the past week—all the things he captured with his camera, and all the things he knows no collection of pixels can ever do justice to. That's the thing with photography. Sometimes it gives the illusion of intimacy, a good telephoto lens standing in for proximity. But sometimes there's intimacy so intense that a lens can't ever do it justice.

At least Percy can't. He feels his limitations as a photographer keenly when days like today happen. The afternoon with the cheetah was more like a session with a human subject, and he doubts he captured even half of what it felt like to sit there with her.

And then there's Rob. Since that sunset photo, Percy hasn't taken any pictures of Rob. It's not that he hasn't wanted to. Bloody fucking hell, he wants to. He wants to be able to pull them up and look at them when Rob's back in America and Percy's in Cape Town, and they're not threaded together by days and nights in the bush.

If he asked, he's sure Rob would be fine with being photographed. It's just that Percy doesn't trust himself to get a picture that contains the full spectrum of him. He doubts he can get even half of what makes Rob so… Rob. Which he really means as a synonym for "wonderful." Percy's memory may not be as accurate as a picture, but his memory gives Rob a glow that the real world only allows to manifest at sundown.

By the time they crawl into the tent to sleep, Percy's chest hurts. He doesn't want this week to end. He doesn't want to go back to the real world, and his father, and the press calling him and emailing him and sometimes showing up outside his flat.

He wants Rob. Maybe it's not appropriate or professional, but god. Percy wants him.

By all rights, Percy should be exhausted, but the combination of last night's melancholy and Rob's nearness keeps him wide-awake. Outside, the fire crackles. It's one of Percy's favorite sounds. Sometimes on his last night in the bush, he sits by the fire all night, letting the bush as deep into him as he can. Tonight, there was no chance he'd pass up one final opportunity to sleep next to Rob, even if it's not really *next to* Rob.

Rob's sleeping bag rustles. "You awake?"

Percy smiles in the darkness. "Yeah. Can you hear me being sad about going back to civilization?"

"I can't hear anything over my own feels." There's another slither of fabric, and Percy opens his eyes. A dim orange glow lights the sides of the tent. It's enough light for Rob to find the little camp lantern. He turns it on and props himself on an elbow. His eyes rest on Percy.

Percy stares back. Rob looks grubby. They both clean up as best they can, but you don't spend a week outside without getting grimy. His hair is dull with dust and oil, and he has scruff all over his chin, cheeks, and upper lip. Percy's in exactly the same state. The difference is, seeing Rob like this ignites something low and biting in Percy's body. Seeing himself in this state just makes him grateful he's going to get to take a shower soon.

Rob, though. Rob looks....

Masculine. Sexy. Like something Percy wants to swallow whole and drink until every last drop is gone.

If Percy didn't know Rob by now, he'd probably just think he looks like a man who's not bathed in a week. But Percy *does* know Rob, and he knows how he's grown to feel about him.

They look at each other. Percy wants to say something. Anything. Whatever will make it so Rob will put those strong arms around him again, like he did the night of the storm. Whatever will make it so that they stop dancing around their attraction to each other and do something about it.

He'd settle for being able to articulate even a tiny bit of how wonderful this past week has been because of Rob specifically.

"Hey, Perce." Rob's voice is soft. Every time he says *Perce*, something in Percy vibrates with happiness.

Percy props himself up on an elbow, mirroring Rob's position. "Yeah?"

There's a visible flutter on Rob's neck—his pulse thrumming at the surface of his skin. Percy wonders what he'd taste if he put his mouth right on that spot. Dust and salt and Rob, whatever Rob tastes like. Percy wants to know.

The tent feels small suddenly, the space between them buzzing with something that's been between them for a while. There's a little part of Percy reminding him that Rob's yet to write the article about this week and that letting that crackling, electric attraction have its way is exactly as bad an idea as it's always been. Unprofessional, and a bad idea, besides.

Rob lives in America. Percy lives in South Africa.

Slowly, Rob extends a hand across the crackling space between them. Like a magnet, Percy's hand meets his. Rob's warm, dry fingers slide against Percy's and he brings Percy's hand to his mouth. He kisses the back of it gently. "Thank you. Today was… amazing. I'm never, ever going to forget it."

The brush of Rob's lips against his skin makes Percy dry-mouthed and hummingbird-hearted. This man is funny and warm and kind, and *courtly*, apparently, and Percy hasn't felt his heart and lungs and stomach fill with beating wings for a man for a long time. "I won't either," Percy says.

In the lantern's tepid light, Rob's face is a landscape of shadows. But his eyes are bright, amber and rust and beautiful. They hold Percy's gaze and Percy hangs on them, the beat of blood loud in his ears and hot in his fingertips. Rob doesn't let go of Percy's hand. Slowly, he kisses each knuckle.

The hot stir of desire pools like liquid gold low in Percy's gut. His mouth and throat go dry, and he desperately wants to speak but is afraid if he tries, all that will come out is an inarticulate rasp.

He licks his lips. They feel overly sensitized, almost but not quite aching. It's possible he's never wanted to kiss someone this much in his entire life.

"Are these thank-you-for-the-amazing-day kisses?" he manages to ask, voice hoarse.

Rob's lips skim the back of Percy's hand. They're soft, unbelievably soft, and it's impossible not to imagine how they'd feel pressed against Percy's mouth. Or against his throat. Or elsewhere. Places he doesn't let just anyone put their mouth. The hairs on Percy's arm stand straight up in a shiver of need.

Against Percy's skin, each one of Rob's words puffs like another kiss. "These are I-want-you kisses." Gold. Rob's eyes look gold. "And I-hope-you-want-me-too kisses."

Percy nearly sobs. "Rob. Rob, of course I want you too."

The jump in Rob's throat nearly makes Percy groan. "Yeah?" Rob asks, sounding breathless.

Their faces are so close, both of them propped on one elbow, drawn together like planetary bodies. If they were, Percy would be the planet and Rob would be the star that captured him in his gravity.

Percy swallows hard. "Yeah. And I really, really need you to kiss me first because otherwise I'm going to feel like I lured you out here to seduce you."

The laugh Rob lets out is rich and low and devastatingly sexy. "Yeah. I can do that."

His hand cups Percy's cheek, thumb sliding up his jaw and rasping along his stubble. His eyes drop to Percy's lips, and Percy can't stand it any longer, no matter what he said. He leans across the space separating them and presses his lips to Rob's.

Rob makes a noise, nearly a moan, and curls his fingers around the back of Percy's head. He pulls Percy closer and his mouth opens, hot, wet warmth and shared breath. Soft lips. The shock of intimacy when their tongues slide together. The swoop of lust careening through Percy's gut as Rob chases Percy's tongue into his mouth so Percy can suck on it.

It's a first kiss that leaves you unable to feel your hands and feet. Which is possibly why Percy's got a hand under Rob's shirt, palm to the warm bare ledge of Rob's hip, without remembering putting it there.

He draws back with a ragged "Sorry—" but Rob shuffles closer to press their bodies together, capturing Percy's mouth again with his own as he breathes, "Don't be sorry—put it back. Please." His heart is hammering. Maybe that's Percy's. "Please just touch me."

"Twist my arm," Percy groans, and slides his hand back under Rob's shirt. His fingers trace up Rob's rib cage, smooth skin and the divot of muscle and bone, to hard, solid pec.

Rob echoes the groan, and the sound goes straight to Percy's balls and his erection. His hips move, and there's Rob, just as hard. Percy dances his fingertips along the line of Rob's pec, through the pelt of his chest hair, teasing a nipple but not touching. Some men aren't sensitive there.

But Rob shudders and locks his arm around Percy's back, crushing their mouths together.

It makes Percy go mad with need. Ah fuck, he's gagging for it, isn't he? He gets a good hold on Rob's clothes and rolls onto his back, hauling Rob on top of him, pushing his shirt up to his armpits, and getting his hands all over Rob's gorgeous, thick body.

Rob makes a helpless sound and pushes Percy's chin up. His teeth rake a line across Percy's throat until he finds a spot he wants to suck on—which he does. *Hard.* Percy's hips roll up as he gasps at the sharp sting of Rob's mouth on his neck, the harsh rasp of stubble on his Adam's apple.

When Rob's nipples pebble and harden under Percy's touch, Rob cries out and bites the cord of Percy's neck. "Fuck, Percy," he gasps. "*Fuck.*"

"You like that." Percy circles both Rob's nipples with his thumbs, then squeezes them hard. Rob moans and grabs his ass, shoving their cocks together.

The heat is nearly unbearable, and there's still layers of trousers and underwear between them. Rob's weight on top of him is the best thing Percy's felt in—a long time. Ever. God he's beautiful and solid and *there*, too much for Percy to resist.

"What do you like?" Rob asks, hands exploring, fingers finding their way under clothes and making Percy arch into Rob's body.

Their mouths find each other again, kissing messily, and Percy manages, "Anything. Won't take much. Rob—fuck—"

He fumbles at someone's trousers; it doesn't matter whose, and he's past the ability to work it out. Then Rob's hand is there too, and there's fingers and fumbling and slick wet pre-cum and Percy would laugh if he wasn't breathless, because he feels like he's back at Eton, clumsily jerking off Peter Abney behind the boathouse. His desire is a wild, teenage first-time conflagration.

Rob gets his hand around both their cocks and holds them pressed tight, jacking them together in long, hard strokes. They're kissing—Percy's got a leg up around Rob's back and his hands down the back of his trousers, grabbing that fantastic fucking ass hard enough to bruise, and Rob's free hand is jammed between them so he can roll Percy's balls in his blazing hot palm.

"Rob," Percy sobs. "I won't last. I can't—"

Each pull of Rob's hand on his cock brings him impossibly closer to the edge. His orgasm is gathering, pushed and pulled by Rob's hand and Rob's cock and the way Rob's massaging and tugging on his balls, and—

With a guttural, filthy moan, Rob pulls back enough to look at Percy. His pupils are blown wide and sweat darkens his hairline. "God, I wanna see you come, Perce. Show me that. Let me see you come, baby."

The singularity of impossibly dense pleasure surges, rushing Percy in a blackout, annihilating wave of ecstasy.

He's shuddering, coming, hips pumping as heat pours over him and out of him and ropes of hot cum splatter his belly. Rob yells and there's more, and Rob's fucking against Percy and oh it's good, it's amazing, it's a honey sweet drowning that leaves him gasping and trembling.

Gradually, his brain puts itself back together and the world rearranges into something that makes sense. Little camp lantern making giants of their shadows on the sides of the tent. Hard, cold ground under Percy's back. Warm, soft Rob on top of him. Night sounds outside—wind soughing over the mountainside, hissing through the umbrella thorn and the dry grass. The mournful hoot of an eagle-owl. Jackals yipping far away. Rob breathing hard, Percy doing the same.

Rob finally breaks the silence. "Wow."

Percy can't help it. He laughs, and then he puts a hand to the back of Rob's neck and pulls him close for a kiss. "Yeah," he agrees.

Rob's kiss is soft and slow, embers glowing in the remains of a fire. It might be the best kiss Percy's ever had.

When they draw apart, Rob runs his thumb along Percy's cheekbone. An impish grin dimples one cheek. "Confession: I really wanted to suck you off."

Percy groans a little. "It's a nice thought, but god, it's not pretty down there at the moment."

"Oh yeah? I'll be the judge of that." The dimple gets deeper as Rob reaches for the camp lantern and rolls off Percy enough to shine its weak light in the general vicinity of Percy's hips. "Yeah, just as I expected. Gorgeous."

Laughing helplessly, Percy bats at the lantern. "I couldn't live with myself! I know full well I'm ripe."

Rob swipes a finger across Percy's belly, right through the thickest pool of cum. As Percy watches, Rob sticks it in his mouth and sucks.

Obviously, Percy feels *that* right in his balls.

"We'll be back at the safari camp tomorrow," Percy says breathlessly. "Yeah?"

"Yeah, I mean, if… if you want to…?"

What is he asking? For a repeat of this? Or for… more?

"I want to," Rob says definitively. There's no room for Percy to doubt how much Rob wants him, not in the way he's gazing at Percy or how he keeps tracing the line of Percy's cheekbone to his jaw, down his neck to his collarbone. He's good at doubting, but Rob's looking at him like he wants to devour him and worship him at the same time.

"I do too." Percy gives him a shy smile. Absurd, after the week they've spent together and what they just did.

"Good," Rob murmurs before he brushes his lips over Percy's again.

Rob kisses the same way he's done everything this week—confidence over a deep care for Percy's well-being. It's—fuck, it's nice. Maybe the nicest Percy's ever had, kissing just for the sake of it. One of Rob's hands cradles Percy's jaw as the other strokes down his side, down his back, up his front. He's not trying to get anywhere, just touching Percy, and Percy arches into his touch, holding Rob's hips, feeling the shift of muscle and bone in his strong body.

"We could share a tent," Percy gets out breathlessly.

Rob kisses behind his ear, the angle of his jaw, where his chin curves down to his throat. "Been sharing a tent, haven't we?"

"Tomorrow, I mean. And the day after—however long you're staying at the lodge. We could share a tent there."

Such a bad idea, but Percy can't stop himself. The question leaves him feeling like he's just sprinted a mile, but he doesn't regret asking.

Rob pulls back a little to look Percy in the eyes. His thumb smoothes over the frizz of baby hairs along Percy's hairline that have escaped from his twists. "You haven't had enough of sharing space with me yet?"

A smile tugs at one corner of Percy's mouth. It wants to turn into a sun-bright beam, but his muscles need to relearn how to smile like that. "Recent evidence would suggest I haven't."

Rob gathers him in his arms. "Recent evidence."

"Yeah. You're getting it all over yourself."

"Mm." Another slow kiss. Then: "I'd love that."

Percy makes a happy noise.

Sounding entirely too amused with himself, Rob says, "And yeah, sharing a tent at the camp would be good too."

The laugh that startles from Percy makes him bury his face in Rob's neck. He smells like dust and sweat and salt, and he smells like sex, and like something clean and perfect. Percy hasn't felt like anything he's touched has been clean and perfect in too long.

He cuddles up to Rob and holds on, looking forward to leaving the field for the first time ever.

Part Two: Thaba Boroko

Chapter Fourteen

A DISTANT ENGINE rumble, then a cloud of dust, herald the Land Cruiser's approach long before they can see it. Percy thinks about snatching his hand back from Rob, who's holding it, rubbing his thumb gently over Percy's knuckles. It makes them look like teenagers.

Since Percy feels a bit like a teenager, though, he doesn't pull his hand back. Which means the guide driving, Magriet, aims a knowing wink his way when she parks the truck. "Hoe was dit?" she calls.

Percy hauls his pack over his shoulder with a groan. The time roughing it always catches up with him all at once at the end, and his body complains about every indignity he's put it through and rock he's slept on. "It was good," he tells her. "Always is."

"Good pictures?" she asks, grabbing both of their packs from them as they approach the truck. "You get caught in that storm? Shame, man, that was something."

The camp has full occupancy until the afternoon, so instead of bringing them back there to sit around in their week's worth of backpacking grunge, Magriet drives to the staff dorms, where they're able to shower. It's not luxurious, but Percy doesn't care. He uses too much water, scrubbing at his skin until he feels raw and clean. He washes his twists, which are going to need maintenance. That can wait till tomorrow—anyway, his twist cream is in the bag he left in the camp office.

He also spends extra time cleaning, well. Certain areas of interest. Rob's sex-blitzed admission that he wanted to suck Percy off last night has been taking up more space in Percy's brain than it probably should. And if Rob wants to suck Percy's cock, maybe he wants to do other things.

Anyway, Percy gets everything spick-and-span down there.

They dress in some extra clothes Magriet set on the corner of one of the bathroom sinks. Possibly she nicked them from one of the other guides, but Percy's not going to question it. He'll wash and return them tomorrow—it's shorts and the polos the guides wear, so nothing too special.

Though when Percy sees Rob's legs in shorts, it feels distinctly more special.

They catch a ride over to the main lodge with a guide who's bringing guests out for an afternoon game drive. At the lodge, Percy heads straight for the office, gesturing for Rob to follow him.

His favorite person in the world is sitting at the desk, typing furiously. Percy knows that deep furrow between her eyebrows and the speed with which her fingers are flying over the keys. Internet's spotty some days, and that means you do as much online work as fast as possible. He feels bad interrupting and starts to duck out.

Too late, though. Her brown eyes flick up and she squeals in happy surprise as she launches herself out of the chair and into his arms. "You're back!"

"Always so surprised," he teases.

Katlego thumps him on the shoulder. She has to reach up to do it, because she's nearly a foot shorter than him. Even with her hair in a high puff, he can still see over her head. "You know I'd never let you out there alone if I thought you weren't going to come back." She hugs him again. "Everything was okay with that storm? I was worried about you. I *know* you don't want me to worry but it's not actually possible for me not to worry about you."

Percy ducks his head as they step apart. "I survived the night and remain in one piece."

She scrunches her nose at him and sticks her tongue out. "And how was your journali—oh!" She catches sight of Rob standing behind Percy. "Rob! How did you like being out on the reserve with this one?"

Percy steps into the office so Rob can fit through the door too. With a smile and a glance toward Percy, Rob says, "It was amazing. Once in a lifetime. I think I'm spoiled forever—what's going to measure up to this place?"

Even though Percy wasn't planning on pawing at Rob in front of Katli, he knows exactly how he's looking at him right now. Big, soppy doe eyes. There may as well be hearts popping out of them. And just in case Katli misses that, Percy brushes a hand over Rob's elbow.

The contact makes Rob meet his eyes. "I got spoiled forever for company on a trip too."

Katli is quite clearly cataloging their words, their goopy gazing at each other, and that elbow touch, adding it all together, and coming to exactly the conclusion anyone with eyes would.

Clearing his throat and shuffling his feet, Percy says, "So, um. I know you two met before, but Rob, Katli's my best friend in the world. She's tops. She's—" It hits him that he's nervous. He can't remember the last time he introduced Katli to someone he was…. Well, to a man he's this interested in. Years ago, probs. Their schedules don't match up. When she's in Cape Town, he's traveling; when he's in Cape Town, she's here. And he never brings his boyfriends here.

He clears his throat again. "She's the best. And also the best camp manager ever—"

"Oh god, stop," she says, putting her hands to her cheeks and batting her eyes. When Percy pauses, she flashes him a grin. "Never mind, don't stop."

Rob laughs. "Every time I had to get comfortable on a rock last week, I thought about how amazing this camp looked when I got here."

"Well, we're going to take great care of you for the next couple days." Katli motions for them to leave the office. She leads them through the lodge's open, airy main breezeway. "Rob, I just need a few signatures from you. You know the drill, Perce. And I'll get you some iced tea, if you want to have a seat here."

The entire back of the lodge is devoted to a deck that faces a lawn. Impala are grazing and birds trill from the shade trees. Chairs all along the deck face toward the mountains, which rise over the lodge and are currently gray-white in the midday sun.

Rob plops down in a comfy-looking deck chair and sinks back into the cushion. With a gusty sigh, he closes his eyes and says, "Yep, I like the bush, but this is pretty great too."

He's left all the buttons of his borrowed polo undone and as he sprawls, the fabric pulls tight over his shoulders and makes the V gap wide. Dark hair peeks out. His collarbone is sharp and defined. The polo's sleeves are cutting into his biceps, which are. Nnnng.

Really, the shirt's a bit too small for him. Percy's not complaining. This view is making his brain short-circuit. He's *felt* Rob's body, but he hasn't *seen* it—both of them had layers and sensible clothing on in the bush—and now that he's getting to take it in, he's revising his opinion of the nicest thing he's seen this week.

Katli leaves to get the tea and paperwork, but Percy darts after her. "Kat! Kat, wait." She stops, smirking at him, and discomfort worms into his chest. Which is bollocks. This is Kat and he can say pretty much anything to her.

Still, he's blushing as he says, "Um, Rob and I—you can… er, you can put us in the same tent."

She looks completely unsurprised—but also completely gleeful. "Oh, can I? You need to take care of that Erica you were getting from eye-fucking him?"

"Shut *up*, I do not have—" He has to adjust himself because actually, yeah all right, he *was* getting a bit of a hard-on. "Anyway, can you? I'll get his things—you don't have to ask Emmanuel or Kwame."

"You just don't want them to tease you."

"I wouldn't want them to take away any opportunities from you."

She laughs as she disappears to the staff offices in the back. Percy waits in the middle of the breezeway, awkwardly fiddling with a Sotho pot on one of the long tables. Outside, water trickles from a fountain into a small, recirculated stream. It's relaxing, but Percy always feels on edge when he first comes back to the lodge after being in the bush. Everything's fine with Katli, but he has to remember how to interact with other people. Guides and lodge staff he doesn't know as well, and other guests. The bush is easier.

On the other hand, he's really, *really* looking forward to the big bed he knows is waiting for them in their tent.

Katli reappears from the office. She's got a leather folio tucked under one arm and a tray bearing two glasses and a pitcher of iced tea. "The housekeeping ladies will bring his bag over to your tent. And they won't even tease you." She waggles her eyebrows. "Which means no competition for me."

Percy blushes again, and she bumps him with her hip on her way back out to the deck.

Most of the paperwork is for Percy, since he's the one paying for everything. Rob's is just a liability waiver for the game drives. Once they've guzzled more than their share of iced tea (honestly, it's the most delicious tea Percy's ever had, and he's never been able to reproduce it at home despite knowing the secret formula), they head down the crushed quartz path to their tent.

They're in the very last one, a good seven-minute walk from the lodge. It's Percy's favorite tent. Katli really is the best, making sure he got it even though the camp's busy. Compared to the bush, it's not isolated. But having no one to one side and the neighboring tent hidden by trees gives the illusion of isolation. Percy needs to ease back into regular life.

"Hooooly shit" is Rob's reaction to stepping inside the tent.

Percy slides the screen door shut behind them and latches it. One time a monkey opened the door and strolled right inside while he was going through photos, so he's always on monkey-guard now.

He got a good picture of it, though. Didn't sell that one—too much of his life is on display, even though this isn't home. He doesn't need anyone knowing what his swimming trunks look like, and they're in the picture.

Rob's mouth is hanging open. "Okay, I knew this place was nice, but this is like…." He fingers the wire-and-string curtain separating the bath from the main area. Beads strung along it click. He runs his hand along it and wanders toward the back of the tent.

The whole thing is semipermanent, built on a deck with a brick wall in the center. Wood beams support the canvas—an inner closed tent and an outer one for further protection from the elements. The bed abuts one side of the brick wall, and around the back is the minibar and closet space. Their packs will be back there, having been brought by the porters… or apparently the housekeeping staff. There's a concrete counter along the back wall, where the sinks are. The tent has a WC with a door, and for all one's bathing needs, there's a massive stone tub, an indoor rain shower, and an outdoor shower.

Rob appears around the other side of the wall, nearly bumping into the desk on the opposite side of the tent as he continues to gaze around, openmouthed and wide-eyed.

"Do you like it?" Percy asks shyly.

"Um, *yeah.*"

"Yeah? Good." Warmth floods Percy, even though he can't take credit for anything about this place. It's nothing to do with him; he just likes it. Katli and the staff get all the credit, and the far-off owner, who Percy met once during an excruciating white-tie fundraising dinner in Cape Town. Not that he wasn't a perfectly nice person, and the dinner was to raise money for conservation efforts. Percy's just terrible in those sorts of situations.

"Is this crazy expensive?" Rob asks.

"Um, it depends?" Percy doesn't like the way coming back to the real world has made him so unsure of how to speak to Rob. Out in the bush, he's in his element. His authority gives him confidence, and he can talk sort of like a human being. But now he's back at a fancy safari camp, and there are going to be other people competing for Rob's attention. Maybe Rob will realize how awkward he is.

"So… yeah, it's crazy expensive." Rob sits on the bed. "Should I pay for myself?"

Percy shuffles where he's standing. "No. Of course not. I have the money. One of the perks for you is having a nice stay."

After studying Percy for a second, Rob scoots over on the bed. Once he's within reach of Percy, he takes his hand and draws him closer, encouraging Percy to sit next to him on the bed. "That was before."

"I've already paid for both of us." His fingers tighten in Rob's. He really, really doesn't want Rob to turn out to be the typical macho chauvinist Percy's so used to dealing with in South Africa. Paying Rob's way is no financial hardship, and he's so not interested in manly pride over money.

Rob looks at him in consternation. "Okay, but isn't that some kind of, I don't know, conflict of interest?"

"What? Why?"

"I mean, we had sex, we're sharing a tent… with one bed… which kind of implies more sex—"

"Yes," Percy says quickly. His trousers get a little tighter.

Rob looks momentarily thrilled, but then his face falls back to uncertainty. "Right, but I'm writing the article, and you're paying my way. Wasn't there something in the contract?"

"No?" Quite contrary to his normal awkwardness—and honestly the awkward weirdness of this conversation—Percy smiles. "Did you read the contract?"

"Um."

Right, Percy will take that as a no, then. He nudges Rob with a shoulder. "You really should read contracts."

"I trusted you not to screw me over." Rob opens his mouth, then closes it and gives Percy a sidelong look. "Didn't think you'd be interested in screwing me any way, actually."

There's a little gravel in Rob's tone, and that doesn't help how tight Percy's trousers are. He clears his throat. "I don't really think the, um, sex changes anything. You were already supposed to write a favorable piece about me."

"Was that in the contract that I skimmed?"

"Rob, you really, *really* should read contracts."

There's a flash of a grin on Rob's face, and then he leans in and kisses Percy quickly and softly. Percy has to stop himself from touching his fingertips to his lips. It was such an easy kiss, like they do it all the time, like it's completely natural.

This thing between them isn't even twenty-four hours old. Or it's just under a week old? Either way, Percy hasn't had the time or inclination to think about where it might lead. For that matter, he hasn't had the time or inclination to think about whether it's going to lead *anywhere*.

But that little peck of a kiss from Rob. Percy could see himself not wanting to give that up. Possibly ever.

So apparently he's thinking about it now. He'd like to try to work it out properly. He looks down at their intertwined fingers and says, "The camp is doing their braai tonight."

The subject change doesn't throw Rob. If their positions were reversed, Percy would be picking apart why they're suddenly talking about dinner instead of what they were talking about before. Looking excited, Rob says, "Oh nice, I really wanted to do a braai while I was here! Is there going to be game? Man, that feels kind of bad to hope I'm gonna eat some adorable impala, but like… I kind of hope I get to eat impala."

"There's kudu usually too."

"Oh my god, I'm going to be such an American." Rob looks halfway to ecstatic just at the thought.

He could leave it at that. They're going to eat dinner together. They're going to have sex later. This is good. Normal people can leave it at this. But not Percy! No, Percy twists uncomfortably and feels his armpits get damp. "I was wondering… if you'd like to… um, go with me?"

Rob looks at him. A line appears between his eyebrows. "Oh, I thought… I just assumed we were going together."

"No—I mean, yes! Yes, we were. Are." Fuck, why is he like this? It could not be easier to ask a man out, considering they're sitting on a bed together, holding hands, and already going to the same place for dinner. To the same *table* for dinner. "I meant do you want to go… er, *together*."

Realization smooths Rob's forehead. "Like, together together." Percy nods and tries not to cling too hard to Rob's hand. "Like go with you as a date."

"Yes!" Percy says, his voice a combination of misery and hope. Maybe this was too much. Maybe he shouldn't have done this—this feeling out if they want to make this more than what it is, which is having some fun together. And now Percy's made it awkward, because he asked Rob on a date. Gay men still date, right? They haven't abolished dating in favor of hookup apps, have they? Is it different in America? Percy's had his share of anonymous hookups, but he's *sure* he's seen people on actual dates. *He* has been on actual dates. Hasn't he?

Oh no, now he's not sure he's ever been on a date before. Maybe he just fell into long-term relationships with his past boyfriends because the hookups stopped being anonymous?

Rob's arms slip around Percy's neck. "Yeah." His lips curve into a smile. They're so plump and soft, and Percy's seized with a desperate need to lick them, which he restrains. "I totally want to go on a date with you."

There are loads of things they can do now—have lunch, explore the camp, relax on the deck, even go on the afternoon game drive if they want to. Instead, Rob pulls Percy down to the bed and closes those soft lips over Percy's.

Chapter Fifteen

BRAAI IS maybe the best thing ever. Why hasn't anyone made this a thing in America? Rob can't stop making inappropriate moaning sounds. Every time he does it, Percy's face flushes. Which honestly, isn't any incentive to stop. Percy blushing is adorable.

His lips tingle from the spices in the food—and from their lengthy make-out sesh earlier. Mm. There's more where that came from later too. Rob's had to devote a pretty substantial amount of brainpower to not drifting off into fantasies about all the stuff he wants to do to Percy once they're back in their tent for the night.

Also to not getting a boner. But that's not as important because they're sitting at a table, and they're eating outside, and it's dark. Boners can be hidden.

Genuinely, though, he wants to take in this moment and enjoy it, and his dick is doing its best to take him to sexual fantasy island. The atmosphere is really cool—the dark all around them, torches surrounding the tables, and the braais going. The air smells like green and smoke, spices and meat. Stars sweep across the sky like someone took a handful of diamonds and spread them out.

The Milky Way is something else in the Southern Hemisphere. Rob's seen it. He knows how bright and defined it is. But every time he comes south of the equator, it takes his breath away all over again.

Even with that celestial stunner in full view, Rob's attention is drawn constantly back to Percy. He's gotten used to seeing Percy's face in firelight. At least, he thought he was used to it. Now it's almost more romantic than he can stand.

"You like the food?" Percy asks. That shy note is back in his voice. It's like he's afraid Rob's going to throw a tantrum because something isn't up to his standards. Thaba Boroko is so far above his standards that *that* would never happen. More importantly, Rob doesn't throw tantrums. He loves to travel, and he's stayed in seedy motels, bare-bones hostels, even a convent once.

"The food is amazing." Rob shovels another forkful of chakalaka into his mouth. The spicy vegetable and bean dish burns his tongue, so he follows it up with pap, which reminds him of grits.

Percy looks happy. "I can't believe how much bobotie you ate."

"Why didn't anyone ever tell me South African food is the shit?"

Percy's happiness tips over into so much pleasure he actually squirms in his seat. "The food is really good here. But, yeah. I'm biased, I suppose, but it's definitely the shit."

"You must have missed this when you were living in England."

A melodramatic expression of long-suffering settles on Percy's face. "God, you have *no* idea. Have you ever seen what they call barbecue in the UK?"

Rob laughs. "I try to stick to the UK's culinary strengths when I've been there."

"Country pubs, chippies, and curry houses?" Percy's lips quirk into a little smirk, and lord have mercy, Rob's gone for him.

The smile flickers and fades from Percy's face as his gaze finds something over Rob's shoulder. "What's up?" Rob asks, turning in his seat to see what caught Percy's attention.

All he sees are other guests, many of whom are mingling with each other, excitedly sharing stories about what they saw on their game drives earlier today.

The things Rob and Percy saw this week would blow all their sightings out of the water. It's tempting to go over there and brag a little. But that's not fair—seriously, this experience has been so jaw-dropping that if he shared it with the other guests, they just wouldn't be able to enjoy their safaris. He's such a good guy.

When he looks at Percy again, Percy just shakes his head. "I thought...." His eyes are troubled.

Which gets Rob right in the chest. Percy should never look troubled. Percy should always have that little smile on his face, the one that means he's about to say something dry and funny. Or he should be beaming, which Rob now realizes might be the rarest sighting of all in the bush.

Or. You know. His face could be contorted in ecstasy, mouth open as he comes. That's a good look too.

Rob leans across the table and touches Percy's wrist, running a finger down to his hand. Percy's wrists are weirdly sexy. They're bony and delicate, but the way the veins stand out gives them a ropey strength.

It's one of those things where Rob feels like he understands the Victorian mindset of women's ankles and wrists needing to be covered. Turns out those body parts *can* turn a dude on!

As Rob's finger traces the back of Percy's hand, Percy flips his hand over and captures it. "I'm not doing a very good job of making this our first date."

"You're doing a perfect job of making this our first date." Rob brings Percy's hand to his mouth and kisses the back of it. Percy's sharp intake of breath is like music. What Rob *really* wants to do is whisper dirtily in Percy's ear, *You like that?* while he drops kisses on Percy's palm, the inside of his wrist, and all the way up his arm.

Rob reminds his dick to settle down. But he kisses Percy's hand again, because he likes the way Percy looks at him when he does it—like he's starving, and Rob's the first solid meal he's seen for days.

Their fingers intertwine, and Percy takes a healthy swallow of his wine. His throat bobs on the wine's way down, which isn't helping Rob's boner situation. "I keep feeling like everyone's watching me. Because of…."

In the quiet at the edge of his words, the murmur of conversation and the crackle of the torches and braais rush in. Rob squeezes his hand. "Because of the whole"—vague hand wave—"thing?"

He's going to keep his promise not to talk about Percy's dad.

And Percy looks relieved, so Rob knows he did the right thing. "Yeah. Because of… all of that." Percy's shoulders hunch and his eyes flick to whatever keeps catching his attention behind Rob.

Rob looks again. This time, he sees a man at a nearby table who quickly turns in the other direction. Meeting Percy's eyes, Rob asks, "Is that guy staring at you?"

"Um." Percy fidgets. "I don't know. I…. Well, I mean, I think he might be? But sometimes I'm paranoid… I've been really paranoid lately. So maybe he's not. Maybe I'm just. You know."

"Huh." Trying to be sneaky about it, Rob stretches and drapes an arm over the back of his chair so he can get a look again at the man. A spark of anger sputters to life in his chest at the thought that anyone might be staring at Percy. The guy's phone is in his hand, but he seems to be reading something on it, not taking pictures or anything.

At the thought of someone taking photos of Percy without his consent or knowledge, Rob's little match-flame of anger gets bigger. But what's he going to do? He didn't see the guy staring, much less catch him taking pictures on his phone. What he *can* do is squeeze Percy's hand again and ask, "Want to go back to the tent?"

"No! I want you to enjoy this." He gives himself a shake. "I'm all right. I'll stop fixating on people imaginary-staring at me."

Yeah, except Rob's not sure Percy's imagining it.

Rob pushes his chair back. Gravel crunches beneath it. Very conscious of sightlines in a way he normally isn't, he goes to stand in front of Percy, blocking him from the man's view. He leans a hip against the table. "I enjoyed it. This is so cool, and the food was unbelievable." He nudges Percy's foot with his toe. "I normally don't put out on first dates, but I think I could maybe be convinced to break some rules tonight…."

"You're being nice to me," Percy says, ducking his head.

"Um, yeah, I'm being nice to you. I like you." When Percy's eyes flick up to meet his, Rob adds, his voice softer, "I really like you. Seriously, like… so much, Perce. So let's get out of here."

A smile, one of Percy's bright, beaming ones, flickers up on his face for a second. It's fast, but it's there, and Rob stamps it on his memory and tells it to stay. Percy stands, and then he leans down and kisses Rob right there.

Rob's stomach swoops. Percy's lips are so warm and soft. He tastes smoky and spicy, hints of cinnamon and turmeric on his lips. Rob leans closer and slips a hand over Percy's hip, and Percy responds by pressing up against him, his gentle kiss turning molten as he opens his mouth. Rob chases the taste of him, and when their tongues slide together, he lets out a quiet noise.

"There," Percy says, breaking the kiss. He looks bright and defiant, and more than a little turned on. "I don't care if anyone gawked at me."

Rob grins. "Wait, do you get off on being watched?"

"No!"

"Just a little? Exhibitionism kinda your thing, huh?"

Even in the dim firelight, Rob can see Percy turning red. But he's laughing, so Rob tugs him down for another quick kiss. "Pretty sure I mentioned some things I wanted to do to you last night," he says against Percy's lips. "That's still my plan, in case you're wondering."

"Oh," Percy breathes. One of his hands wanders to Rob's front and hooks into the waistband of his jeans. Probably not appropriate for the setting, but hey. It's dark. No one can see.

And it's definitely hot.

He pushes up onto his toes so he can whisper into Percy's ear, "Take me back to our tent so I can suck your cock, baby."

Percy makes a strangled little sound and steps back. His fingers lock around Rob's. "C'mon."

Oh yeah. His come-wreck-me voice never fails. Thank god, because his pants are seriously tight through the crotch right now.

On their way out of dinner, Katlego waves to them from where she's chatting with some other guests. She directs a wink at Percy, and as they pass her, she reaches out and punches him lightly on the arm. "Go get 'em, tiger."

"Planning on it," Percy shoots right back, and Rob wants to jump him right there. Shy Percy is cute, but Percy comfortable and out of his shell is a fucking delight.

Speaking of fucking delight…. Percy flicks on a flashlight and tugs Rob down the path. Their tent and that massive, comfortable bed await.

Chapter Sixteen

THE TENT zips open and closed, which is too much of a process for Rob.

"There might be animals!" Percy laughs as Rob traps him in the circle of his arms. His hard dick is pressed against Percy's very nice ass, and his fingers are in an excellent place to start unbuttoning Percy's shirt, which he does.

"*I'm* feeling like an animal right now," Rob growls. Cringey, but Percy lets out a little pant that zings straight to Rob's balls.

He gets Percy's shirt unbuttoned and pulls it part of the way down his arms, leaving it mid-bicep to trap Percy's arms at his sides. The friction of Percy's undershirt on Rob's palm is almost too much. He's going to lose it when it's just skin-on-skin.

Percy's fingers scrabble at Rob's sides. "You're not playing fair."

"Oh, totally not playing fair," Rob agrees as he holds Percy in place with an arm across his chest. With his other hand, he finds one of Percy's nipples. Under his attention, it hardens quickly to a point. Rob gives it a flick and Percy grunts, his head dipping back.

That's such a good reaction that Rob transfers his attention to the other nipple. Percy's hard chest moves under his palm, pecs flexing as he tries—unconvincingly—to get free from Rob's hold on him.

"I think"—Percy hooks a finger into one of Rob's pockets—"you should turn around."

Burying his face in the crook of Percy's neck, Rob inhales. Percy smells like woodsmoke and aftershave. It's a bright, woodsy smell. And Rob gets the best of both worlds, because Percy left some stubble when he shaved. All the better for Rob to feel scraping across his body once they lose some clothes.

"Rob." Percy's voice has a needy edge to it.

"Mm?" Rob's hand creeps lower and Percy's stomach moves under his touch.

The way Percy squirms into him makes it impossible for Rob to hide his arousal. That's okay, because when his fingers skate lower, there's a hard answering bulge at Percy's front.

"I was expecting animalistic."

"I can be animalistic and slow." Rob licks a stripe up Percy's neck.

With another wriggle, Percy says, "Animals don't fuck slow."

God, now *that's* a dirty thought. Like those lions, rutting and biting, one mounting the other and just taking fast and hard. Thing is, in that scenario, Rob doesn't know which he'd rather be.

"I bet some do." Rob rolls his hips languidly. The friction and press of Percy's ass against his cock makes his head light. "Sloths. I bet sloths make slow, tender love to each other."

Percy laughs. How can a sound make him so happy and turn him on so much at the same time? Seven days ago, he had no concept of the things he'd do to make Percy laugh, or what the sound does to his insides. "I'm googling it," Percy huffs.

"Now? I thought you wanted to fuck."

"Well, you're teasing, so maybe a little light animal-fact googling is what this needs."

Rob palms Percy's dick through his pants. The way it fills his hand is almost enough to make him weep. Maybe the threat of animal facts was warranted since they're both still fully clothed.

So Rob pulls Percy's button-up off his arms, then yanks his T-shirt over his head. With Percy's gorgeous shoulders exposed, it's impossible not to take a moment to nuzzle across them, to plant kisses on both shoulder blades and bite at the base of his neck. He multitasks and gets Percy's pants off too.

"Progress." Percy spins and goes to work on Rob's clothes, stripping him mercilessly. Or maybe mercifully? When Rob's pants hit the floor, Percy kisses him, fingers digging into his hips hard enough to bruise before he explores.

His touch everywhere else is light, teasing across nipples and chest, tracing Rob's collarbone down along his ribs, over thighs and ass. Goddamn, it feels good, but it would feel better if he'd stop avoiding Rob's cock.

"You were on *my* case for teasing?" Rob groans, pressing chest-to-chest against Percy. His skin is so warm, soft and hard in all the right places. Rob wraps Percy up in his arms and pulls them tight together, his body demanding more closeness, more skin, more heat.

And oh, does he ever have a good idea of how to get closer.

Rob pushes Percy toward the beautifully turned-down bed. Percy doesn't need any encouragement, falling onto his back and spreading his legs wide. With a groan, Rob crawls over him, kissing his way up Percy's chest. The drag of his cock on Percy's thigh, sparsely fuzzed with hair, makes pleasure crackle along every nerve in his body.

Fingers twist in Rob's hair and Percy arches against him, moaning. Fuck, if he keeps that up, there's no way Rob will last. He'll come just from rubbing off against Percy's perfect skin. Which wouldn't really be a *problem*, per se, since Rob plans on blowing Percy's mind with his mouth. It would just be kind of embarrassing. Very horny-teenager-making-out-with-another-boy-for-the-first-time.

"How do you feel so amazing?" Percy's hand slides down to curve over the back of Rob's neck. "Not fair. Absolutely not fair. You must drive all the American boys crazy."

With Percy's miles of warm brown skin underneath him, Rob really couldn't give less of a damn about American boys. "Only care about driving you crazy right now."

His thumbs trace Percy's ribs, then down his sides to the smooth curve of his ass. When he looks up at Percy's face, all he can see is the long column of his neck and the jut of his Adam's apple. He slides the tip of his tongue over to Percy's nipple just to watch the clench of Percy's jaw and the way his throat works. Of course, the way it feels against his lips, pebbled and hard and just perfect for fitting his teeth around, is good too.

Percy's reactions and noises as Rob works his nipples with teeth and tongue are so fucking hot. God, he loves a guy with sensitive tits, loves to make that teasing promise of his mouth working other body parts to rigid hardness. He loves how Percy's already writhing beneath him, hands grabbing and squeezing, and Rob hasn't even gotten to the main event yet.

Why wait? He flicks his tongue a final time against Percy's nipple and works his way down, down, down, until Percy's gorgeous, swollen cock is right in his face.

He's cut, the smooth, blunt head of his dick looking like the perfect mouthful. The thatch of dark, tightly coiled hair around his cock is wild and overgrown, which needles Rob in some tender spot behind his ribs. Everyone's about the dick pic these days, selling yourself so you don't get summarily blocked on Grindr because there's plenty of dick out there to be had—no reason to go for a jungle when you can have an English garden.

Or… something, weird mixed metaphor there. The point is, Rob likes that Percy isn't tending to the landscaping. He likes it so much that he buries his face in all that dark, curly hair, breathing deep and getting soap and musk and man.

He lets out a noise without meaning to and runs his lips up Percy's hard dick, which gets a grunt and a hiss of pleasure from Percy. Mm, yeah, good, but Rob can do way better. When he finds himself back at the tip of Percy's cock, he uses his lips there too. Lips and tongue, and when he takes it in his mouth, just the head, Percy cries out and fists the sheets.

Okay, damn. This is going to be fun.

Teasingly, Rob pops off with a wet sucking sound, then runs the tip of his tongue around Percy's slit. Salty, bitter pre-cum pulses out and Rob laps it up languidly.

"Oh my god, *Rob*, would you just—"

"Just?" Rob asks, trailing fingers up the insides of Percy's thighs and around the base of his dick.

"Just"—Percy's voice gets strangled as Rob tongues the underside of his shaft—"just stop being an *arse*—"

Rob laughs. "Aw, sweetheart, you had no idea what you were getting into. I like to take my *time*."

Percy moans and sinks his fingers into Rob's hair. Some guys want to take control back right about now, want to fuck Rob's mouth. Which Rob can definitely be down with, as long as he gets a heads-up. Gagging and choking can be really damn hot, but it's nice to be on the same page about that beforehand. Percy doesn't do that, though. Rob may be the one taking it, but the control is all his, and Percy's well on his way to coming apart in Rob's hands. And mouth. Definitely mouth.

The way Percy is trembling beneath Rob's hands and lips makes him show mercy. In one long, smooth slide, he swallows Percy's cock down.

And Rob would be lying if he said he doesn't almost come from the way Percy's body spasms and the low, filthy groan he lets out.

Rob makes a noise too, totally against his will. Percy's too fucking sexy, naked and writhing. Rob prides himself on his cock-sucking abilities—never had any complaints, only breathless praise—and he's always loved giving head. But Percy's elevating the act to a whole new level. How the hell is Rob supposed to blow anyone else after this?

When Percy's hips arch off the bed, Rob shifts, getting a shoulder under one of Percy's legs and lifting it up so he can get better access to everything. Slowly drawing off Percy's dick, Rob licks his way back to his balls, deliciously ungroomed, and laps eagerly before taking them in his mouth. Percy's heel digs into Rob's back as he hooks his leg tighter over Rob's shoulder.

The more Rob kisses and licks and teases with his fingers, the noisier Percy gets—wanton, desperate sounds, incoherent begging, occasional swearing, which makes Rob laugh and slow down. By the time he fucks his tongue into Percy's hole, Percy's a mess.

And Rob is so hard it hurts. It would be so, *so* easy to get off getting Percy off. A few strokes and he'd be done; Percy's got him that worked up.

He squeezes the base of his cock to back himself off the edge. With the other hand, he traces circles around Percy's rim.

"*Yes*," Percy chokes. "Yes, *that*."

"That, huh?" Rob sticks his fingers in his own mouth, slicking them up. Percy's already relaxed enough that two slide right in, no problem. Rob crooks them against his prostate and Percy swears.

The time for going slow has officially passed. Rob sucks Percy's cock and finger fucks him fast and hard, surfacing only to pant, "Get there, baby… want you to come all over me."

Percy moans and Rob's entire world narrows to the thick cock in his mouth, the slickness of Percy's balls, the hot, tight heat of his ass clenching around Rob's fingers. "Fuck—Rob, I'm—god I can't stop—"

Rob dives down on Percy's dick again, swallowing it whole, choking back a gag as it hits the back of his throat. He palms Percy's balls with one hand, rolling them as they tighten, while he keeps up a steady rhythm with his fingers, fucking Percy, rubbing his prostate, drawing out the most delicious noises with each thrust.

"You wanna come on my face, don't you?" Rob asks as he comes up for air. "Wanna shoot all over me—"

The strangled cry Percy lets out is pretty much the best sound Rob's ever heard in his entire life. Percy's cock gets impossibly more rigid, his balls draw up, and then he's coming on Rob's face, shot after shot painting Rob's eyelids and cheeks and chin.

While Percy's still shuddering, Rob clambers to his knees between Percy's legs. He keeps a hand on Percy's cock, working him through the aftershocks, and grabs his own dick. He jerks himself quick and hard, three times—and he's done. With a gasp, he shoots across Percy's stomach, stripes of white cum on brown skin his new favorite color contrast.

Boneless, Rob flops on his side to stretch out next to Percy, whose eyes are closed in apparent rapture. He uses the runner on the bed to wipe his face off, mentally apologizing to the housekeeping staff.

Percy's head rolls limply to one side and his eyes open. His pupils still look blown wide. There's a lazy, sated smile on his face. "Next time, I'm getting you off." Percy groans. "God. That was amazing."

"Honey, if you think that didn't get me off, we're making a video next time." Rob lets out a whoosh of air and a laugh. "*Fuck* that was hot. You're something else."

Percy opens his mouth, then shuts it. And then he hauls Rob in for a slow, deep kiss. Eventually, he pulls back, but not far. His lips keep brushing Rob's in tiny, fluttering kisses. "A video. That could be interesting."

"I just like the idea of next time," Rob murmurs, capturing Percy's lips again with his own.

Even though they're both sticky with sweat and cum, they come together, legs and arms tangling as they kiss. *Next time* is vague as hell, but Rob will take it. He doesn't know if they're just having fun or what, but this thing between Percy and him is great, and he wants to keep it going as long as Percy's into it.

Their kissing turns to snuggling, Percy tracing lines up and down Rob's body. The tent is warm and cozy between the heater turned up full blast and the blaze of Percy's body, and Rob's eyelids droop in post-orgasmic relaxation.

"Are you flying home in a couple days?" Percy asks, bringing Rob back to awareness. "Once you leave Thaba Boroko, I mean?"

Weird to think they haven't talked about anything past this time together. Maybe that says something? Something like, *This was fun, but it was a fling.* Shit, it really *is* going to be awkward when it comes time to write the article about Percy. Obviously he's going to keep the sex stuff far, far away from his writing.

He opens his eyes to find Percy watching him. There's a guarded expression in Percy's eyes, though not guarded enough—Rob's pretty sure it's hope. "No, I'm hanging around for another week to do tourist stuff. Guess I should ask if you have any suggestions."

"Come back to Cape Town with me," Percy says in a rush, the words running together. When Rob's mouth opens soundlessly, Percy looks mortified. "Ohmygod ignore that. Me. Forget it. I just—sorry. Sorry."

Rob tucks his arm around Percy's back and pulls him close, so they're body-to-body again, chests and hips and skin. It feels hella right, like they're adjacent puzzle pieces, made to fit together. "I'd fucking love to come to Cape Town with you."

The mortification on Percy's face recedes. "Really?"

"Um, yeah." Rob's hand drifts down to Percy's backside and squeezes. "All other good reasons aside, how else am I going to get more of this sweet ass?"

Every time Percy blushes, Rob falls a little further. Which is a thought that he didn't give his brain permission to have. Falling? Come on. He can't fall for Percy. That would be stupid.

Still. Percy blushing, it definitely does stuff to Rob's insides. Planting a kiss on Percy's cheek, Rob asks, "How's the hotel situation this time of year? Any recommendations?" Obviously, he wants to stay with Percy at his place. Sweet ass notwithstanding, he's gotten used to waking up next to the guy. Waking up next to him with cuddling and sex on the table is definitely a level up.

The mortification comes back, and Percy blushes harder. "Oh. Um." There's heat actually radiating off his face. "I thought. I mean, you obviously don't have to, but. My flat…."

"Yes," Rob interrupts. "Your flat. Perfect."

"I only have one bed." Percy's still flushed, but there's a sly tilt to his smile as he says this.

"Oh no," Rob says, completely unconvincingly. "And here I am, an incorrigible sleep cuddler."

"Never mind being a sleep cuddler—you're apparently a person who says 'incorrigible' in normal conversation."

"Those are both points in my favor, right?"

Percy gets a soft look on his face. "Yeah." His fingers comb through Rob's hair. "So you'll stay with me? And I can show you around? And we can keep doing…."

"This," Rob finishes for him. "Yes, yes, and yes." Like he could say anything else to Percy.

Part Three: Cape Town

Chapter Seventeen

PERCY TORTURED himself over whether to drive or fly to Thaba Boroko, weighing if it would be worse to be stuck on flight with people who might gawk and jeer at him, or to take the risk at each petrol and hotel stop of the same thing happening. In the end, he chose flying.

Now that Rob's coming back to Cape Town with him, Percy's relieved it's a couple flights back instead of an eighteen-plus-hour drive in his Toyota Hilux. He loves his bakkie, but the single cab isn't exactly the height of comfort for that length of time. Not something he particularly wants to inflict on someone he wants to… impress? A person he wants to like him? Someone he wants to keep comfortable, at least.

After their week in the bush and their two nights at Thaba Boroko, Percy knows he's getting in too deep. His friends will tease him. Katli already *did* tease him, right after she gave him some banana-flavored condoms she found being given out for free in a petrol station toilet.

To be fair, his friends, Sipho especially, will then do exactly what Katli did, which was take his hands and ask if he's being careful with his heart, because they all know him. It's anonymous hookup or the love of his life, and they've all seen it before.

"We're just enjoying ourselves," Percy told her. And it's true. It's not like he's expecting anything long-term from Rob. Even if Percy were in a good place for it, there are too many barriers. Their careers require a lot of travel. They live so far away from each other. Percy's father is a criminal and is going to be put on trial. Just normal things that any two people might have to deal with when deciding to give a relationship a try.

The trip from Cape Town International Airport to Percy's flat is a much more reasonable distance in his bakkie. Their plane lands as the sun is setting, another glorious South African sunset. Percy isn't too proud to take photos from the plane window.

Langa Township is dark as they drive into the city on the N2. Shit, Percy forgot to check the load shedding schedule, and while his building has an inverter to keep some of the lights on, he won't be able to run the heater or the electric kettle.

"Is that a township?" Rob asks as they pass the neighborhood. He sounds horrified. "They don't have *electricity*, even?"

"Ah—no, they do." Percy winces. "It's load shedding. I think you call it rolling blackouts in the States?"

"Oh! Like a power supply issue. Yeah." Rob's silent for a second. "Wait, is that, like, a normal thing here?"

"Mm." Not an answer, Percy. "It's been worse. We usually just have one a day in Cape Town. Two, sometimes. It's sometimes five or six a day in Joburg."

Rob makes a contemplative noise. "Was it not going on the last few days? I didn't notice any power outages at Thaba Boroko."

"Thaba Boroko's got generators." Percy taps the steering wheel. This conversation has the potential to veer perilously close to the thing he doesn't want to talk about with Rob: government corruption, of which his father is the current and most obvious example.

That's another good reason to just keep this thing light and fun between them. Percy won't have any reason to talk about his father. If they got serious....

But why would he even think something like *if they got serious*? They've known each other for a week. This is exactly why his friends tease him. A week is long enough to know if the sex is good, not enough to know if you're going to introduce a guy to your parents.

Fuck, what a horrifying thought. Introducing a boyfriend to his parents. He should stop dating just to prevent that.

He and Rob aren't *dating*. Percy reminds himself of that, then reminds himself again for good measure. They're not dating. He's not going to do that thing he always does. He's going to just have fun.

They've not had any trouble talking on the trip from Thaba Boroko. Conversation's been so easy. Percy naturally prefers to do less talking, but Rob doesn't use that as an excuse to dominate what they talk about. Somehow he has a way of drawing Percy into speaking without Percy noticing he's doing it. Well, until he did, and then it made something warm flicker in his chest.

Now, though, the easy conversation sputters to a halt. Not a surprise. Americans, if they can afford the plane ticket to get to South Africa, never know how to react to South Africa's issues. There will certainly be a moment when horror washes over Rob's face when he gets a decent look at the townships.

It's a double-edged sword, because Percy *wants* people to know, he wants people to care, he wants money flowing into townships to get people out of poverty. On the other hand, he bristles at the pity, despises the inescapable flash of, *I thought I was in one of the* good *African countries.*

And also, what right does he have to feel any way at all, because he's filthy rich, and his father was stealing money from South Africa's most vulnerable.

"Is it disruptive?" Rob asks. "The power outages?" He doesn't sound horrified or pitying, but like he's genuinely curious.

"For me, not too much. My building has a power inverter and solar panels, so we still have some lights. But mainly it's there so we can run our refrigerators. Oh, and Wi-Fi."

"Obviously Wi-Fi."

Percy takes the final freeway exit into the Cape Town city center. "There's places selling dry ice now if you don't have any power at all during load shedding."

Rob lets out a surprised laugh, that startled, barky sound that Percy thinks is adorable. "Really?"

"Oh yeah. There's this one company always advertising on the radio." The red lights blare on Buitengracht Street, brighter for all the street lights being dark. "That's South Africa—an advert for Land Rovers followed by an advert for dry ice to keep your perishables from spoiling."

"Wild." Rob leans forward in the passenger seat. Percy can't help sneaking a glance over, though he should be watching the road. The red glow of the traffic signal limns him like a saturated sunset—strong, broad nose and ledged cheekbones, bushy brows raised in curiosity and interest. Percy decides then and there that he needs to keep seeing that expression on Rob's face for as long as Rob's here. Maybe if Rob is endlessly delighted by all the Mother City has to offer, it'll be easier to keep what's between them light and fun.

When the glow goes green, Percy needs a second to process grassy light instead of fire before he turns his attention back to driving. As he takes another turn, he says, "This is De Waterkant. Most of the gay scene is here." *More* of the gay scene was there pre-pandemic, but who wants to talk about that? Percy's first, second, and third favorite bars all went belly-up between lockdowns and alcohol bans.

Rob cranes his head, probably looking for something neon or glittery. The clubs are down side streets, though, and they use generators more on their interior electric needs than the exterior ones. "Is it always this quiet on Friday nights?"

"It's busier in the summer."

They cross the invisible line that separates De Waterkant from Green Point and Percy's shoulders loosen a little. Home. "I live in this neighborhood," he says proudly. His father's voice hisses at him that it's not a prestigious enough address for a de Villiers, and hasn't he proved his point with his worthless art school degree?

As always, Percy shakes the voice away. Shame no one can arrest the bitter, petty shadow of his father that lives in his head, but it will be waiting to berate him again soon.

"It's nice when you can see it, promise." Percy makes the left onto his road. Up the hill, which the engine roars for. Good bakkie. It needs the exercise after sitting in the airport carpark. His building is at the very end of the road, butting up against the pedestrian staircase leading up to High Level Road.

He has to jump out to open the garage door manually with the power out. There was a time it had been annoying—now he's used to it. He pays for two parking spaces inside because his truck doesn't fit comfortably in one. It's luxurious at times like this, when he gets home from a trip and he doesn't have to worry about scratching his neighbors' doors as he unfolds his limbs and stumbles, joints cracking, out of the bakkie.

They both grab their bags from the back of the truck cab and Percy leads them into the building and to his flat, which is on the ground floor. Only a few of the lights come on when he flips the switches. Before he leaves for a project, he always cleans out his refrigerator, so nothing to worry about there.

"Huh." Rob lowers his rucksack to the floor and shifts his duffel on his shoulder. "Don't take this the wrong way, but I figured you'd be in the penthouse."

"Everyone says that." Percy takes Rob's duffel and brings it, along with his, to the bedroom. It's a three-bedroom flat, but it's still not big, so he's only gone for a second. Rob's already poking around his bookshelf, which is a mishmash of photography, nature, and history books—plus odds and ends he's picked up in his travels. "I'll show you in the morning why I wanted this flat."

Turning and flashing a smile at Percy, Rob says, "It's not because you don't want to walk up all those stairs?"

That smile could take Percy apart if he lets it. "Maybe a little."

It always makes him nervous having new people in his space. What are they going to think of it? Are they judging him? Are they finding him lacking somehow? Is he too much of something, or not enough of something else? Is he less interesting than they thought he'd be? Too pretentious?

And it's especially acute with Rob. He really, very much doesn't want Rob to think he's too much or not enough of anything.

"Can I have a tour, or are we skipping straight to the bedroom?" Rob's still smiling, like he knows Percy's getting a bit lost in his head. He shouldn't be able to tell that already. They've only known each other a week.

"Oh! Um." Percy makes a dumb, gangly, flapping motion with his hands and immediately feels like a twat. "We can…. Did you want to? Go straight to the bedroom?"

Rob laughs again, but it's kind and affectionate. He sweeps his hair off his forehead with a hand. "Actually, I kind of got hooked on that whole shower thing. If you don't mind?"

"No, of course not." Something twisty and sparkling winds through Percy's gut, and he wants to kiss Rob right now. Not for any particular reason. He just… does. Rob's floppy hair and his easy smile and the kind, warm crinkles at the corners of his eyes—it all just makes Percy happy. It's been a while since a man made him feel that way.

So he does. Two long steps to cross the room to where Rob's standing by the bookshelf, and Percy leans down to kiss him lightly. Rob's head tips up and meets the kiss like he was waiting for the chance.

"Would you be interested in saving water?" Percy asks, his nose brushing Rob's.

"I think it's very important to conserve as much water as possible." Rob's eyes are very serious, but the huskiness of his tone maybe undercuts his environmental convictions. Just a bit.

"I'll give you the tour first?" Percy slides his hand into Rob's, feeling giddy. His heart shouldn't be thundering the way it is, but Rob's big, strong hand around his, and the images flickering through Percy's brain—slick, hot bodies in the shower, then straight to bed—are sending blood rushing downward.

"Yeah. Guess I requested it." Rob slips a hand round the back of Percy's neck and brushes his lips over Percy's jaw, ending with a kiss behind his ear. "The anticipation will make it better?"

"Are you asking me or telling me?" When Rob hesitates before making a frustrated little noise, Percy makes himself pull back, though he keeps his hand in Rob's. "Look, main room. Kitchen's there. And down here"—he tugs Rob with him down the hall and flicks a light switch on—"is the bathroom, which we'll come back to."

"I approve of the size of your shower." Rob's eyes look dark and a shiver goes up Percy's spine. It's a bit hard to remember how many days he spent *not* fucking Rob, when now it's all he wants to do.

His office garners more exploration. Corkboard covers most of the walls, and photos cover them. Many of the photos are his own, not because he's that self-important, but because he wants the reminders of where he could have done better.

Yeah—most of the photos are his *least* favorites. It motivates him. And also occasionally focuses his bouts of self-loathing to something he can actually change, instead of just… who he is. Pinned over his obscenely large Mac are some of his very favorite photographs, all taken by other people. Plants sit on most of the flat surfaces and hang in baskets from the ceiling alongside glass mobiles. His de-stressing papasan chair is in one corner.

Next is the bedroom. The wooden birds hanging from the ceiling draw Rob's eye and make him smile. "This is *so* much more whimsical than I expected from you."

"I know. You're not the first person I've disappointed with it."

Spinning to face him, Rob asks, "Did I say I was disappointed?"

Percy's mouth opens, but nothing comes out. He knows better than to answer a rhetorical question, and Rob looks puzzled. As though he can't imagine why Percy's mind would skip straight to how he's lacking.

It tells Percy so much about Rob's life—about his family and his friends, all the people who surrounded him because of accidents of fate and nature, and the people he chose to surround himself with.

And for one awful moment, Percy is absurdly, horribly envious of him.

Then he's envious of the man who Rob will meet sometime in the future, a man who doesn't live on the other side of the world and who doesn't have an airplane cargo hold's worth of baggage—the man who will get to keep Rob, because whoever he is will be someone who gets to have nice things without mucking them up.

Rob puts his hands on Percy's face and kisses him softly. "I'm disappointed we're not getting naked right now."

Percy's eyes flutter shut and he savors the brush of full lips over his, along with a hint of wintergreen on Rob's breath. Eyes still closed, he points out, "You asked for the tour."

"Total miscalculation. I can't enjoy your gorgeous, fancy apartment when I want to suck you off this bad."

Electricity zings from the base of Percy's spine to ding off his skull and ricochet straight back down, skipping along a path from his ass to his prostate to his balls to his dick. "Well, I want you to get as much enjoyment as possible from your stay here, so…." With a smile that he hopes is sultry and not shy, he hooks his fingers into the waistband of Rob's jeans, brushing his thumb over the growing bulge just below.

This is just fun for now, but Percy's going to enjoy it. He may not be the man who gets to keep Rob Hale, but he's the man who's got him right now, and *that*, he's reasonably sure, is not something he's going to muck up.

Chapter Eighteen

ROB DOES a thing when he wakes up in a new place where he tries to remember all the details about the room he's in without opening his eyes. He tries to remember spatially where he is. Like, how far away are the windows? How is the bed placed against the wall? Is he facing toward the door or away from it?

Usually he's pretty good at it, but sometimes he opens his eyes and he gets that rollercoaster drop stomach swoop of disorientation, because he's completely wrong. The door isn't on the opposite wall, it's behind him. Or there's half the space between the bed and the window that he thought there was.

This morning, the lurch comes from a related misconception: he reaches toward the warmth of Percy's body next to him in the bed, and he gets nothing but sheets. Sort of warm sheets, but still. Just sheets.

He opens his eyes and stretches, joints cracking and the sheet slipping down over his chest. The bed is hella comfortable, so he luxuriates for a moment. The luxuriating would be way better if Percy was here next to him.

It doesn't take much imagining Percy luxuriating in bed with him before Rob's body starts to get ideas. The bed smells like Percy, too— and it smells like Rob, and the two of them together, and the excellent sex they had last night before they fell asleep tangled together.

Closing his eyes, Rob gives himself an indulgent stroke. Hell, maybe he gives himself two or three. But his right hand can't hold a candle to Percy, who, in theory, is nearby, so Rob rolls out of bed, pulls yesterday's boxer briefs on, and pads out to the main room and kitchen that he barely looked at last night.

It's very modern and fancy, lots of blond wood and minimalist copper hardware. An electric kettle sits on the counter, full of water. Next to it is a navy-blue mug, a jar of instant Nespresso coffee, and an open wooden box filled with tea—those fancy pyramidal bags made of clothy stuff, not the standard paper sachets that plebs like him are used to.

Obviously, Rob has to take a minute to riffle through the tea and see what flavors Percy has. There are like three different kinds of rooibos (no points for calling it), a bunch of herbal stuff that would be trendy even for Whole Foods, and the standards like Earl Grey, Lady Grey, Jasmine, and English Breakfast. Rob deliberates, feeling like he should be classy and go for tea, but he's a coffee guy, so he just makes himself a cup of Nespresso.

Inspection of a couple ceramic jars nearby yields sugar and powdered milk, both of which he uses liberally. Just as he picks the mug up, Percy appears, his head poking through diaphanous curtains. "You're awake!"

"Missed you next to me," Rob says, cupping his hand around the bottom of the mug and crossing the room to Percy. Cool, fresh-smelling air wafts in, making the curtains billow slowly.

The expression on Percy's face is everything. He looks surprised and thrilled and *happy*, and making someone get that look on their face is like a drug for Rob.

Percy's wearing boxer briefs and a charcoal drop armhole tank in a soft-looking material. It's showing off his lean chest and muscled arms to an extent that he might as well not be wearing anything, but the fact that it moves and hides parts of his body makes it sexier than him just wearing no shirt at all.

For the first time, Percy's twists are out of the knot on top of his head, flowing loose around his shoulders. The charms, beads, and wires glint gold in the early-morning sun. As a writer, Rob isn't supposed to go for clichés like *it took his breath away*. Thing is, sometimes they're clichés for a reason, and for a second, Rob really does forget to breathe because Percy looks so beautiful.

"I was thinking about the pictures I took," Percy says. "I got excited. Would you, um. Would you want to see some of them?"

"Perce. You don't even have to ask."

Percy's face lights up further. "Okay! Here, come outside—" He steps back and stretches an arm out at the same time, sweeping the curtain aside to allow Rob to duck under it.

For the first time, Rob sees what's outside Percy's flat. "Whoa." He stops dead. Coffee almost sloshes over the sides of his mug. "I guess this is why you live on the ground floor, huh?"

"Yeah." There's a shy but pleased note to Percy's voice. Rob glances at him, and his face looks the same way. Obviously, he wants people to like this—not that it's hard to. The sliding-glass door in Percy's main room leads into an oasis—a fenced-in green space tucked between stone walls and buildings. There's an area with big paving stones, where a wooden table sits surrounded by several chairs. A laptop is open on the table, a steaming mug next to it.

The paving stones give way to lush grass, trees, and vines. There's a trickling water feature under one of the trees that turns to a small stream picked out of stones, including some of the pink quartz used at Thaba Boroko. The stream empties into a small pool. Next to the pool is a hanging swing chair with a sky-blue cushion.

And all over the space are bird feeders. There are all different kinds for, Rob can only assume, every bird imaginable. He recognizes suet feeders and what look sort of like hummingbird feeders, and there are tubes of varying sizes hung from branches and hooks.

As Rob watches, several songbirds descend on the garden, squabbling over space at one of the feeders until they work it out.

Rob turns to face Percy. "I didn't know you were a birder!"

Still looking happy, Percy replies, "I don't think I am, really. I just like watching them."

"This is so cool." Rob spins around and cranes his neck to look up at the rest of Percy's building. There are decks sticking out, but none on this side. It's not totally private—there are windows in both Percy's building and the neighboring ones that overlook the garden—but it feels private. Which is good, since Rob is still in his underwear.

More birds arrive, choosing feeders, settling on branches, or heading for the water feature to have a drink or take a bath.

"I just sort of finished it last summer." There's pride in Percy's voice, and Rob doesn't blame him. This is a beautiful, peaceful space. Rob wishes he had something like this at home, where he could take his laptop and get his zen on as he worked.

Then something dark shutters over Percy's features. He doesn't say why or what's bothering him, but some of his contentment with his garden drains away in front of Rob's eyes. Rob almost, *almost* asks what's wrong—and then he remembers he and Percy barely know each other. And that this is a fling. Right? What else could it be?

It's just, there's this feeling Rob gets when he looks at Percy—this feeling in his chest and his stomach, and like… it hurts, but it's a good pain. The pain of possibility, like when you ache from a good workout and you know good things will come from it. And there's a feeling, too, when he sees that darkness on Percy's face, like maybe he'd do anything to take it away.

Rob's never felt that way about a fling.

But he's sure Percy sees them that way, because he's never given any indication that he plans on this lasting beyond Rob's time in South Africa. If their thing has an expiration date, Rob's just going to concentrate on enjoying Percy's company.

"Bet your friends always want to come over to your place," Rob says. "If I knew anyone with an awesome space like this, you'd never get me to leave."

Percy looks startled for a second, and then one corner of his mouth quirks up. "You do know someone with a space like this. Does that mean you're not leaving?"

Rubbing a hand over his face, Rob says, "No, sorry, I just meant— you know what I meant. Right?" But Percy just smiles a little bigger, and Rob likes it. It's teasing, it's a little bit of that easy comfort Percy had with his friend Katli, and shit, Rob might have just discovered he's a total slut for it.

"You can stay if you want." Percy's crooked little smile is still on his face, but the smile doesn't quite reach his eyes. Or, it does, but it turns sad on its way there, so his eyes don't have the same teasing glint his mouth does.

There's a weird, fraught energy to the moment suddenly, so Rob sits down in one of the chairs at the table. He angles it so he can see Percy's laptop screen but doesn't actually look at it. He's a writer; he knows how annoying it is for someone to look at your screen when you're working on your craft.

Granted, a lot of times, Rob's not working on his craft so much as trying to earn a paycheck.

"Show me what you got," he says, patting the other chair. Percy's been out here long enough for the wood to have soaked up his body heat, which transfers to Rob's palm.

Percy slides into the chair and gulps down some tea before tapping the trackpad. "I can't help feeling like you're going to lose your artistic respect for me once you see my photos in their natural state?"

"Oh, shut up, you know I'm not." Playfully, Rob bumps his elbow into Percy's arm. "I already saw some, remember? And that was just on your teeny camera screen."

"Hides the imperfections," Percy mumbles. He gathers his twists in his hands and tucks them over one shoulder, where he leaves one hand so he can play with the ends. "And we were in the bush. It's easy to think everything's better than what it is."

Rob leans over and drops a kiss on Percy's bare shoulder. His skin pebbles under Rob's lips, so Rob leaves them there for a second. He likes making Percy get goose bumps, and he also can't get enough of how warm his skin is. Taking a chance, he says, "Okay, imposter syndrome. Now that that's out of your system, pics or the safari didn't happen."

With a laugh, Percy says, "You were there!"

"Nope, pretty sure we never saw that cheetah. Damn, if only there was some photographic evidence to prove me wrong…."

Percy laughs again and mouses around his computer. Whatever photo editing software he has looks expensive, and he moves through it so fast that Rob can barely follow. Geez, and sometimes he struggles with freaking Microsoft Word.

A photo pops up of the cheetah they saw on their final day. Rob's breath catches. It's like she's in front of him again, like they're face-to-face over this table. She's staring right into the camera, amber eyes relaxed, ears pricked forward. Percy's camera picked out such fine detail that you could count her individual furs if you wanted to. The picture has *texture*, from the cheetah's short, dense fur, to her wet nose, to the liquid quality of her eyes. For a fraction of a second, Rob's convinced that if he reached out, he'd be able to feel her fur against his fingers.

"This one's pretty good." Percy's voice snaps Rob out of his mesmerized state. "My agent will want to see it. She says pictures where predators are staring into your soul are the easiest to sell." He studies it for another moment. "It's good, but it's not my favorite."

It's super tempting to make some kind of sarcastic comment. Not like, in a mean way, but in a like, *Oh, right, this absolutely gorgeous, amazing photo isn't your favorite, because you're just that good* way. "Can I see your favorite?"

"Um, yeah." Color rises up Percy's neck, which is both adorable and sexy. Adorable in that, well, Percy's cute with his dichotomy of knowing exactly how good he is but also being modest. And sexy in that it reminds Rob of all the skin under Percy's tank and how easy it would be for him to touch it. Just slide a hand through that dropped armhole and lay it on Percy's chest, maybe play with his nipples a little before trailing down and getting those boxer briefs out of the way—

The thought makes him hard, and he's supposed to be looking at photos. Funny how two weeks ago, if you'd told him he'd be sitting in Percy de Villiers's garden looking at brand-new photos before anyone else had seen them, he would have considered it to be one of the best things that could happen to him. He just never considered that that picture could include the two of them not wearing pants.

And he's only a man. Put a gorgeous guy in minimal clothing next to him at a table, and he'll happily compromise all his intellectual and artistic integrity.

Percy pulls up another photo and turns the laptop so Rob can see it better. As soon as he sees it, Rob gets it—why this is Percy's favorite, not the money shot he showed before. In this photo, the cheetah is flopped back on her side, lolling on the ground, with her mouth wide open in a yawn while her tongue spills out of her mouth in a way that's totally feline and completely undignified. Even the way the sun gilds her whiskers doesn't make her look less like a happy house cat in a sunny patch.

Rob laughs. "I love it."

"Yeah?"

"Yeah. It's perfect. It captures her personality."

His words seem to make Percy practically vibrate with happiness. "Yes! It does! That's completely what I thought!" Quickly, he grabs Rob's hand and squeezes. "I'm glad you think the same."

The warm, firm heat of Percy's fingers around his makes Rob's heart skip. "It's your photography. You're so good at capturing stuff like that."

"No, but—" Percy knocks his knee into Rob's. "But that was what I saw in her, and I just… I'm happy you did too. I'm happy you liked the bush. I think… I think you got it. Or I'm just making a fool of myself and you were counting down the minutes until you could take a hot shower?"

That skip to Rob's heartbeat doesn't seem to be getting better. "I loved it. I couldn't have asked for a better first safari experience." He pauses. "But I also wanted a hot shower."

Percy laughs and squeezes Rob's hand again. "Do you want to see more? I haven't even looked at most of these. They might be really bad."

"I want to see everything," Rob says.

Chapter Nineteen

THE REAL reason Percy had to get up before Rob was because he kept catastrophizing about something terrible happening to his memory cards. Usually the first thing he does when he gets home from a shoot is to pull the photos off the card and back them up. Usually, though, he doesn't have a man with him. Good digital habits were just not happening once Rob kissed him.

Luckily, and not at all surprisingly, a boulder hadn't somehow crushed his camera in the night. No one had broken in to steal it, nor had Percy chucked it out the window on the way home from the airport last night in a fit of insanity that he somehow forgot about until this morning. Stupid brain—he can imagine in vivid detail all these awful things, but when he went away to Eton, sometimes he couldn't remember Ma's voice.

Now, though, he's nearly frantic to show Rob around Cape Town. There's so *much* to show him, and it seems desperately important for him to love the Mother City. Maybe he won't love it as much as Percy does, but even just loving it half as much would be good. Because he wants Rob to have a nice time, obviously. And Percy needs to be the one to show him how wonderful Cape Town is, because, also obviously.

On the trip here, a whole week in Cape Town with Rob stretched in front of him, glorious and endless. Now that they're here, the days are ticking down, and it makes Percy feel sick. It would be nice if when Rob goes, Percy has memories of him as vivid as a South African sunset, so when the anxiety and intrusive thoughts assault him, he can try to combat them with something good.

After showering, Percy encourages them out the door. "Is there anything you refuse to leave Cape Town without seeing?" he asks as they walk down the hill toward the waterfront.

"Table Mountain? I feel like I have to do Table Mountain. Is that like, embarrassingly touristy? I won't make you go up there with me."

Percy laughs and doesn't answer at first, and Rob looks scandalized. "Oh my god! You seriously are too embarrassed to be seen at Table Mountain with me! *Perce!*"

It's the kind of teasing he only feels comfortable doing with his closest friends—people like Katli and Sipho. But here's Rob making his chest light and making him feel like he can relax. Rob makes him feel like he can be a bit silly, when all he's felt since his father's arrest is that he's not allowed to be light and happy, especially not where anyone can see him.

The first place Percy brings Rob is Oranjezicht Market, right on the edge of the Victoria & Alfred Waterfront. Coming here is practically a ritual. Saturdays are for shopping and Sundays are for brunch with his friends, which they do once a month. It's still early enough that the market isn't too busy, which makes it easier to walk around the food court and decide what coffee to get.

Rob bounces from stall to stall, oohing and ahhing over the chalkboard menus, and finally wails, "I want *everything*!" Percy's favorite coffee place overhears and insists on giving him samples, after which Rob settles on which roast he wants to buy.

That means within fifteen minutes, Rob is hopped-up on caffeine, and it's one of the most charming things Percy's ever been treated to. Everything is exciting to him, like he's a puppy going on a walk for the first time. He's just as indecisive and thrilled by the food options, so Percy suggests the pastry stall he always goes to. They get too much to eat and weave through the growing crowd to find a table outside.

The seating area overlooks the V&A Waterfront and Table Bay, which is calm and deep blue today. Rob takes a load of photos on his phone, holding it over his head to get shots over the chain link fence surrounding the market. Percy almost tells him there are better places for pictures but stops himself at the last second. The point isn't that there are better photos somewhere else. Not everything has to be about the perfect shot. The point is to take a photo at *this* moment, to remember when he sat in the sun and put away two croissants (one chocolate, one almond), a flapjack, a muffin, and half a slice of banana bread.

Which. How. Percy feels guilty for starving the man while they were in the bush.

When the banana bread defeats Rob, Percy finishes it off. Rob flops back into his chair with a happy groan. "Christ on a bike. Please tell me you eat here every day."

Percy laughs. "It's only open on weekends. But I do my best."

Looking just short of comatose, Rob says, "I'll have to work all of that food off somehow."

And how, honestly, *how* is Percy supposed to stop the way he raises an eyebrow or the sly smile that creeps over his face? He'll have to *work it off*? He might as well say, *We're going to fuck like rabbits*—and Percy is very much not objecting.

Rob grins and nudges Percy's foot under the table. "Glad we're on the same page."

"Absolutely." Percy leans forward over the table with his very best come-hither expression. "Needlepoint."

When Rob lets out his loud, exuberant seal-bark of a laugh, Percy feels a hard knot loosen in his chest. It's probably only one of many hard knots in his chest, but it's another one dissolved. That seems to be happening a lot in Rob's presence.

Rob grabs his phone and holds it up. Percy doesn't even realize he's taking a picture until he slides the phone across the table and asks, "Is it okay if I keep this?"

The photo Rob just took makes a knot form in Percy's chest again—but it's a different kind of knot. In the photo he looks… happy. Happy and light and free, like he isn't the son of a corrupt businessman turned politician. Like his father isn't going to stand trial. Like he isn't going about his life worried at every moment that someone will post his picture on the internet to scold him for smiling every now and then.

Rob did that. Rob *does* that.

It's only a mildly terrifying thought.

"Yeah." Percy's South African accent comes out stronger than it usually does, turning *yeah* into *ja*. Yes, he'd like Rob to remember him like this—this smiling, happy version of Percy de Villiers that somehow he's made a safe space for.

The thought of Rob only remembering him makes him sad. But it's best not to get his hopes up and spin a fantasy relationship in his mind when Rob's going back to America at the end of the week.

All it takes is Percy's *yeah* to bring back Rob the excited puppy. "Sweet, thanks!" He takes their empty plates and chucks them in a nearby bin. "Can we see the rest of the market?"

Percy laughs and stands. Somehow, he's catching Rob's hand without thinking about it or meaning to and squeezing it before he lets Rob lead him back inside.

They look at the shoes and clothes, where Rob seems genuinely enchanted to see wooden birds strung from the ceiling just like the ones in Percy's bedroom. They're by the same artist, and yes, Percy saw them here for the first time and fell in love with them. Rob tries on a pair of kudu leather boots, is completely and rightfully enamored with how they look, and spends ten minutes fretting about whether they'll fit in his luggage until Percy says, "Rob. They're obviously too sexy for you to not buy them. Worry about how you're going to get them home later."

Which is quite rich, coming from him. Worry about it later? Right. As though he's ever not worried about something the moment it occurred to him to do so.

"Speaking as the child of an airline pilot, that's the devil talking." Rob holds his legs straight out in front of him from and angles his feet back and forth. "Uggghhh, but they *are* really sexy, right? Okay, yeah, I'll take them."

The woman running the stall winks. "Good choice."

All in all, they spend a couple hours poking around the market, even though it's not very big. But Rob wants to look at everything, and watching him enjoy himself makes Percy happy. It's that same knot in his chest that formed when Rob showed him the picture of himself. Only, it's not a knot at all, it's… a bloom? A tightly furled little fynbos bud poking into the stiff prevailing winds.

The metaphor is almost embarrassing, considering the last thing he always does before he leaves the market on Saturday is to buy fresh flowers for his flat. It's peaceful picking flowers for a posy, controlling the play of colors and textures and knowing the only person he needs to make happy with it is himself.

When they leave, he's got an armful of lavender, eucalyptus, tea roses and regular roses, statice, and a few proteas just because he likes them. They cross the street, but Rob abruptly asks him to wait while he runs back for something he wanted to buy but forgot to.

Percy smiles and waits as Rob jogs back across the street and slips through the market's gate, shifting from foot to foot. A couple women pass him on the pavement, looking over their shoulders and giggling. Percy's smile fades. Did they recognize him? Are they whispering about how he's out having a nice time at a bougie farmer's market when there are people dying because the money for their health care ran out?

His brain jitters, scurrying down all the worst-case scenario roads this can take. They'll post on Twitter. They're making a TikTok right now. They're—

"Hey! I'm back!" Rob's bright, smiling face suddenly fills Percy's vision.

Percy snaps out of his spiral and takes a deep breath. "Hi," he exhales. "Did you get what you wanted?"

"Yeah." His smile getting bigger, Rob pulls an arm from behind his back. He's holding a single pink rose, which he proffers to Percy. "I know roses are kind of basic, but, um…."

"But?" Percy prompts.

Rob's mouth hangs open for a second before he closes it and shrugs sheepishly. "I didn't really have a way to finish that."

At uni, all of Percy's friends would have torn a romantic prospect to shreds if they'd bought roses, and Percy would have joined right in. Now, he takes the rose, buries his nose in the soft petals, and breathes in deeply. The smell of roses transports him to—somewhere, sometime in the past, though he's not sure if it's a real memory or imagined nostalgia. The cool sweetness of roses feels like it should be from his childhood, even if he can't remember anything specific.

"Thank you," Percy says into the rose. The petals tickle his nose and lips, a gentle kiss from the bloom. His eyes tick up to Rob and he takes a step forward, hooking an arm around Rob's neck to pull him into a kiss as soft as the rose's petals.

"Not too basic?"

Percy shakes his head and kisses Rob again a little harder. Rob grips his hips, a steadying, grounding grasp. It would be so nice, and so easy in a way, to let himself be held in place by a grip like that.

For the first time, he allows himself to consider the possibility of Rob being in his life as more than a contact in WhatsApp whom he chats with every now and then. Past the moment his plane takes off for America in six days. Maybe it's not the first time he's considered it. Maybe it's been a bit of a fantasy since they kissed on their last night in the bush, but he just hasn't let himself think about it.

Because it's mad, it's absurd, and Percy, despite the fact that his life is to all appearances completely and utterly charmed, is still in possession of a modicum of sense. Long-distance relationships are very, very difficult. They're difficult when you live in the same country, they're even more difficult when you live on the same continent, and they're almost impossible when you don't. And South Africa is so far from *everything*. He acts like he's used to twelve-plus-hour flights, but no one ever gets used to that. It's just not something he's going to complain about.

The posy rustles between their chests, and Percy breaks the kiss slowly before leaning back. "You're so sweet." He carefully tucks the pink rose into the flowers he's already holding. "So sweet."

Rob's hands are still on his hips. "Gotta buy you flowers while I can."

Right. Because in six days, he's leaving. Rob's so sweet it hurts, but he understands the score. Percy's the one who's deluding himself that this relationship's shelf life is longer than a jug of maas.

It's nice that he hasn't moved his hands, though. Percy could go a good long time with the imprint of Rob's hands fitting into the grooves of his hips, fingers edging toward the curve of his ass, and thumbs settled along his hip flexors.

"We have to bring everything back before we go anywhere else," Percy says. If he doesn't say something, he'll stand here all day watching how the sun gleams on the silver in Rob's hair and brings out faint copper tones in the black, and how when the light hits them just right, his eyes are a deep, rich umber brown.

"Oh, yeah good point." Rob's arms drop. The canvas tote holding all his purchases thumps against his shin. "Where are we going next?"

Percy starts walking toward home. "It's a surprise." It is—he hasn't decided yet, so it will be a surprise for him too.

Rob fixes a knowing look on him, but he looks amused and affectionate instead of exasperated. "You're still thinking about it, right? Trying to figure out the best place to showcase your hometown?"

Percy makes a noise.

There's a growing smile on Rob's face. "Ta-ble Moun-tain," he chants softly. Percy pretends not to hear him. He's not at all opposed to doing Table Mountain with Rob, but it seems like it might be sort of a thing between them now? Percy pretends he's too cool for Table Mountain and Rob keeps insisting they do it?

"Table Mountain," Rob chants again, louder. "Table Mountain, Table Moun—"

"Okay!" Percy laughs, bumping his arm against Rob's. "You've worn me down! We'll go to the *extremely* touristy geologic centerpiece of this city."

Looking a little guilty, Rob says, "Wait, you're cool with it, right? I'm messing around, you don't have to go. I mean, I definitely want you to come, like—I'd love it if you came with, but if you don't want to—"

Or maybe it's not a thing and Percy saw a fun, flirty inside joke where there wasn't one. "No, I want to bring you. I'm only—sorry. I was joking. I like Table Mountain. I haven't been there in ages, either. It'll be good. I want to show you."

For a second as they walk, Rob looks at him. Then he breathes, "Perce." And he kisses Percy again, right there and for no reason, as they're passing the walls of the Cape Medical Museum. "Perce, don't worry."

God, that's what Percy wants—to not worry. He kisses Rob back. "You worried first."

Rob leans in and kisses one corner of Percy's mouth before catching his bottom lip again. "Uh," Rob mumbles, which isn't an answer. It is, actually, very difficult to worry when Rob's lips take him apart so gently and thoroughly. It's also wreaking absolute havoc on his plans to not want more from this.

"I'll make a deal with you." Rob runs his thumb along Percy's hairline, then combs his fingers through his hair. Percy's been trying not to wince when he sees the state his twists are in—he really needs to go to his salon—but the way Rob's looking at him makes him feel gorgeous. "I won't worry if you won't worry. Sound fair?"

Fair but almost certainly impossible. Worrying is what Percy does best, with the possible exception of photography. But Rob doesn't need to know what a head case he can be, not when their time together is so short. So, he says, "Deal," and interlaces their fingers.

Chapter Twenty

TABLE MOUNTAIN is breathtaking, not that Rob expected anything less. It would take a lot to ruin the view from over 3,000 feet (3,563 feet to be exact, the internet informs him). Cape Town tumbles down the sides of the mountain until it hits the ocean, sparkling and almost cerulean as the winter sun's rays slant across it. The curve of South Africa's coast is a sharp enough line to trace, cutting to the south until it reaches the Cape of Good Hope.

And yeah, it's touristy, of course. But it's a mountain, and there's plenty of room to get away from the hordes. Plenty of room for Percy to lead him off the graded, gravel route and onto the hiking path, where he points out the big things (Cape Town Stadium, built when Cape Town hosted the World Cup, Signal Hill, Lions Head, Robben Island, hazy in the distance) and the small ones (crows and ravens catching thermals, an outcropping of rock, the way clouds still cling to the sheer sides of the mountain like scraps of lace).

When Percy gets going on the plants, every bit of his shyness and reservation disappears. He gets a passionate light in his eyes and the barely constrained catch in his voice that Rob's come to associate with Percy's brain running so fast that his mouth can barely keep up. His passions are a runaway horse, and Rob's never been more exhilarated trying to catch up.

It's kind of embarrassing to admit, even to himself, but when he applied to accompany Percy into the bush, his imagination wasn't inventive enough to conceive of something more interesting than Percy working. Joke's on him. Percy talking about the things he loves is pure joy, and Rob feels like he has a slowly inflating balloon in his chest, crowding out everything but how he feels about Percy. It aches, but it's all he wants.

Also, it's not germane to the piece he'll write about Percy's work, but man, he wants to mention how much Percy knows about the Western

Cape's biosphere. Fynbos, which Rob's never even heard of. He can't even google it because he keeps hearing "fain-boss." Percy has to spell it for him.

Also also, Rob would be hard pressed to think of a more dramatic make-out spot. As in, a more dramatic spot *to* make out, as well as a more dramatic spot that he *has* made out. Unfortunately, the fynbos doesn't provide enough cover to do anything but kiss until their lips are swollen and sore.

That's just day one.

Real talk, Rob could stay in Percy's apartment for the entirety of his stay in Cape Town, and he'd be happy. In fact, as the days go on and his time in South Africa draws closer to being over, he finds himself *wanting* to just stay in Percy's apartment.

They tick off the tourist attractions, which are great. The penguins? Adorable. Cape of Good Hope? Suitably impressive. Wine country? Delicious and intoxicating. They do the aquarium at the V&A Waterfront and take a Marine Big 5 boat tour from Hermanus (they don't see great white sharks or southern right whales, but they see tons of dolphins, plus seals and penguins, so Rob's happy). They spend an afternoon in Kalk Bay browsing the quirky hipster shops, prompting Rob to comment he's in his natural environment. They do the Cape Wheel and walk Sea Point Promenade, eat ice cream and Cape Malay food and African specialties. Rob feeds seagulls despite the disapproving looks he gets and laughs every time they let out their aggrieved squawks. Er, the seagulls, not the people giving him the aggrieved looks, though he'd maybe laugh at them too.

But. At the end of each day they get to do his very favorite thing, which is go back to Percy's apartment. The sex is crazy good. Mind-blowing, forgive the cliché. Percy's body deserves poetry way better than anything Rob could ever come up with, and the things he can do with his fingers and mouth—poetry might not even capture it. That might require sonatas. Maybe symphonies.

So yeah, he's having a great time in Cape Town seeing the sights. But the thing he really wants? He wants to stay in bed, their legs tangled together as they wake up slowly. He wants to have breakfast out in Percy's garden and press their bare feet together as they while away the morning talking.

Rob the travel writer, Rob who doesn't know the meaning of the words *relaxing vacation*, wants to spend his time in South Africa doing nothing.

Except it wouldn't be doing nothing. He'd be with Percy, free of distractions, free to slip a hand under his shirt or kiss him, or just be uncomplicatedly together.

He wants this to not end.

That's the long and short of it. He likes Percy. A lot. A *lot* a lot. And for all that he can second-guess romance with the best of them, everything about how Percy acts tells Rob that Percy likes him too. So… all that's left is to bring it up. Rob likes Percy, Percy likes him—ergo, maybe this doesn't end when Rob leaves Cape Town?

As they have dinner over candlelight at the V&A Waterfront, one day before Rob's departure, Rob decides it's do or die time. If he doesn't say anything before he leaves, he's going to lose his chance.

He should do it tonight. In this restaurant. Over dinner. The only thing stopping him is his own self-doubt. Insert sports metaphor here, or something.

"You look thoughtful," Percy says, which brings Rob firmly back to the moment. Almost as stupid as not shooting his shot with Percy before he leaves would be wasting their remaining time together dwelling on what-ifs and might-have-beens. Might-bes?

"I just can't believe I'm leaving tomorrow." That fifteen-hour flight's going to be rough. He's going to spend all of it missing Percy and he's already dreading it.

"Well." Percy's smile is sad as he sips at his wine. "Your flight's not until the evening, right? So at least we have most of the day."

"Yeah." Rob nudges Percy's foot under the table. "Think we can come up with some good ways to occupy ourselves?"

"We haven't done the Zeitz Museum…."

"Perce. I'm sure it's very cultural, but I do not want to spend tomorrow at an art museum."

The spark of mischief in Percy's eyes sends a tingle of desire down Rob's spine to his hips. "I'll just have to think of another experience you can't get anywhere but here," Percy says. He sounds real innocent, but the way his eyelids lower to half-mast and he looks very unsubtly at his lap makes it clear he's not talking about "here" as in Cape Town.

And obviously the blatant innuendo gets Rob half-hard. Man, now he just wants to get back to Percy's place. But they don't have their mains yet, and Rob hasn't taken the plunge and asked Percy what he thinks about making this thing between them more permanent.

There's a pause in the conversation. Percy's brow furrows. Shit. This is the moment, isn't it? He's gonna say something right now. He hasn't even thought about how he's going to say it, but… that's okay. It'll be okay.

His heart is jackrabbiting. He nudges Percy's foot with his again and Percy's toe nudges him back. "So, um, hey," Rob says. Inspiring start. "You know how I'm leaving tomorrow?"

"I do, yes. Isn't that literally what we were just talking about?" Percy sounds amused, but also sad.

"No, yeah, we were." God. "No, so, I was thinking. I've been thinking, like, for a few days now. Maybe, um…."

Percy's face looks gray. "Shit," he breathes, and covers his eyes. "I had a feeling this was coming."

Oh. *Oh.* What happened to Rob's jackrabbiting heart? Oh, ha, okay, yeah—it stopped beating. Cool cool cool.

Why did he decide to do this tonight again? He could have kept his mouth shut and they'd have the rest of the day and tomorrow. Now everything will just be awkward, because apparently Percy's been dreading Rob asking him this question—dreading it so much that he doesn't even want to let Rob get the words out.

Percy takes a deep breath and sets his shoulders. He reaches across the table to grab Rob's hand. Oh god, he's going to do the gentle breakup thing. The *it's not you, it's me* line. Like Rob's never heard *that* before.

Well, actually most of his exes haven't had much problem telling him that it was him. Not that Percy will even be an ex. What they have— had—doesn't even rise to that level, because Rob couldn't get his ass in gear and ask.

"I know my agent's going to give me shit," Percy says. "But I'll talk her around."

Wait. What?

"I trust you to be objective. And I mean, honestly, the call wasn't really for objectivity? But, er. I also trust your integrity. And Rob, really, I don't… I can't imagine doing this again with someone else. You know, who's not…." Finally, Percy breaks their eye contact. He runs his finger along the table, disturbing a droplet of water from the condensation on his sparkling water. "I don't want to do this again with someone who's not you."

Okay, wait. What?

"Sorry," Rob says. "What are you talking about?"

Percy blinks and lets go of Rob's hand. "You were going to say you don't feel right doing the article since we've been sleeping together." His face goes from gray to flushed impressively quickly. "Weren't you?"

That thrum and thump in Rob's chest is his heart finally restarting. "No." He wants to laugh with relief. "I haven't been worrying about that since we talked it out at Thaba Boroko. Have *you*?"

"Oh god." Percy sinks down in his chair.

Seeing Percy look so mortified isn't a great feeling, so Rob pushes on as quickly as possible. Though maybe Percy will be mortified by trying to let Rob down gently too. Oh well. You miss 100 percent of the shots you don't take, or something?

"I was going to ask if you want to keep seeing each other," Rob says. "After I leave. Like, dating. I'm—Christ, this shouldn't be so hard." He takes a breath. It's not hard. It's just important. It's really important. Rob isn't ready to say goodbye to Percy, and words are his thing, and he feels like he should have asked this better. "Do you want to give being boyfriends a shot? That's what I'm trying to say."

He thinks about that for a second. "Wait, would it be a conflict of interest if your boyfriend wrote a glowing piece about how you're the most fascinating, talented, and just overall best photographer working today? Or possibly ever?"

Percy has straightened up. "Do you mean that?"

"Uh… which part?" Wait, wrong answer. "Yeah. Yeah, I mean all of that. Especially the part about how I want to date you."

The flush in Percy's face is deeper than Rob's ever seen it. But his eyes are bright and hopeful, and there's a smile waiting to bloom across his face. His pulse is visible in his neck, beating strong and fast. Rob can imagine exactly how it would feel under his lips, because they've spent a lot of time in that spot over the past week.

And it seems like… maybe, *maybe*, it's something he'll get to keep doing?

Rob puts his hands in his lap and rubs his palms on his thighs. They're sweaty. "So, uh, just curious how long you're going to leave me hanging?"

"Oh," Percy breathes. "Did I not answer?" Before Rob can say anything, Percy grabs his hand and pulls it toward his chest. But that doesn't seem to be quite what he wants, because he makes a frustrated growl and stands. His chair scrapes loudly on the floor and before Rob processes what's happening, Percy's hands are cupped around his jaw and he's leaning close.

Their foreheads touch. Rob doesn't breathe. He can feel Percy's pulse in the fingertips cradling his face.

Softly, Percy kisses him. "We should try that, yeah."

Rob lets out a loud, squeal-y, stupidly excited sound. Right in Percy's face. Percy starts but Rob catches him around his forearms and keeps him from tumbling backward.

Side note: man, Percy has sexy forearms.

"Sorry!" Rob reels Percy back in. Would it be really inappropriate if he just pulled Percy right into his lap and kissed him until neither of them could stay upright?

He glances around. People are looking at them. Someone has their phone up like they're recording, and shit, that's not good. Hopefully Percy hasn't noticed, but now that Rob has, he can't just not do anything about it. What a shitty first act as Percy de Villiers's boyfriend that would be, huh?

When he gets to his feet, still holding Percy's arms (still so fucking sexy, he has his sleeves rolled up to just below his elbows and the cuffs strain around the muscle), Percy looks confused. "Be right back," Rob assures him, before walking over to the table with the raised phone.

It's a trio of young people, and the one with the phone finally puts it down at his approach. "Hey," he says, doing his best Friendly, Easygoing Southerner Drawl. "You wouldn't happen to have been recording us, were you?"

"Umm." The young woman darts a glance at her friend across the table.

"You can follow her TikTok if you want a copy," the guy next to her says.

She smacks his leg. "I'm not going to make him follow me just to get a copy of his proposal." Her hopeful gaze turns to Rob again. "Unless you want to?"

"Can you delete it, please?" Rob says, still all smiles. *Don't say you were livestreaming, don't say you were livestreaming.* He's not going to touch whether it was a proposal or not. Don't get bogged down by details—he definitely had a professor scrawl that across a paper once.

"Umm," she repeats. "I was streaming, so...."

Shit.

He waits, hoping his smile hasn't cracked. He can't actually feel it on his face anymore. She doesn't volunteer a course of action. He waits another second, willing his voice to come out normal. "You can still delete it, right?"

There's a sullen expression on her face. "Ja."

God, hopefully the smile's still there. "Okay, then. Delete it."

Finally, she does. When he walks away, he hears her mutter, "Doos." Presumably that's offensive, but he doesn't care.

Right after he slides back into his chair, their mains get delivered. Rob can't even remember what he ordered. It sounded delicious at the time. Now he's not even hungry. He's—he doesn't know what he is. He was really happy two minutes ago. The moment feels flattened now. Something really good happened and a random stranger stole it away from them just to get views on the internet.

"They were recording us, weren't they," Percy says quietly. There's no question in his voice, because it was completely obvious.

"I made her delete it." They feel like the most ineffectual words ever.

"Yeah." Percy picks up his fork but only pushes food around his plate. With a wan smile, he looks up at Rob. "Thanks. Chivalry's not dead."

The table who recorded them is whispering together now and occasionally glancing over. If this is what the rest of dinner's going to be like, it's going to be impossible to enjoy. And this is Rob's last night here. His last night, and Percy just said he wanted to date.

Rob stands. "Let's get out of here."

For a second, Percy just looks at him, eyes wide, liquid, and ink-black. There's so much in Percy's eyes right now, different emotions faceting with each gutter of the candle flame on their table. None of them are positive. Fear, weariness, anxiety, resignation. Some sadness.

Rob knows his own expression is swinging between anger and heartbreak. Percy looks the way he does because he's used to this. He's used to people holding up their phones to film him, used to them whispering as they dart glances at him.

A badly tattered curtain shushes over Percy's face, hiding some of the rawness. He stands and takes Rob's hand firmly, long fingers curling into a tight grip. Rob can feel his heartbeat pounding in his fingers. "I'm in the mood for something less posh, suddenly," he says in a tone that's brighter and harder than Rob expected.

That's good, probably. It's good Percy is able to keep this stuff from getting to him. Maybe being hard is just the way he has to do it.

Chapter Twenty-One

PERCY IS afraid for the first ten minutes of the walk that he's going to have a heart attack. His heart isn't so much racing as careening down the side of a mountain toward a cliff. He's having to think much harder about breathing than he normally does, and his chest is as tight as it gets when he's in the throes of his worst intrusive thoughts.

It's been more than a decade since he's had a panic attack—he was still at Eton last time—but the alarms are blaring. He's headed straight into one now if he can't rein it in.

Rob's grip on his hand is a lifeline, something to focus on, but it's not enough. What he needs is to break his brain and body out of the feedback loop it's rocketing into, and—"Ice cream!" he yelps, tugging Rob toward the cheerful little shop right on the outskirts of the Waterfront. The cloying scent of sugar and pastries floats out the door.

Inside the smell is overwhelming. Percy feels like it's wrapping him in a weighted blanket. He breathes deep and closes his eyes. His heart is pounding and his chest is still tight, but something about the sugary, creamy smell and the bright clapboard interior of the shop is calming him.

He realizes it's been a good ten minutes since he looked at Rob—since they left the restaurant. No, since Percy took Rob's hand. The minutes between that and walking out the door are a hole in his memory. Rob must have paid. Maybe Percy paid? Either way, he can't remember.

Percy takes another deep breath and turns to Rob. "What are you having?"

Rob looks spooked. It makes Percy's gut twist unpleasantly, even though it's not a surprise. Not really. Who wouldn't be unnerved by Percy's behavior over the past fifteen minutes?

"I bet no one even saw her video of us," Rob says, his voice soothing and quiet.

There's a weird rushing feeling in Percy's head, like dizziness or lightheadedness from standing up too quickly, only he's been on his feet for a quarter of an hour. "Can we—I just want to get some ice cream." Percy hates how choked his voice sounds. "It'll… I don't know. Help. Somehow. I'll pay. I wanted to buy you dinner."

The spooked expression on Rob's face trickles away, which is a relief. That makes a little of the tightness in Percy's chest ease too. Bad enough to have a panic attack about his happiness being blasted all over TikTok—the last thing he needs is Rob thinking he's a freak.

Percy knows he's not a freak. He just has issues. Everyone has issues. His are just sort of terrible right now. And his mental health isn't the greatest. It's a rough patch. It will get better once Rob writes his article and any bad news about him can be countered with links to that. If there's negative coverage, he'll have Eunice throw the article at them.

It will help everything. It will definitely help everything.

For the first time since he conceived of this plan, doubt chews at Percy. This *will* help everything, won't it?

They get their ice cream—a mint chocolate chip waffle cone for Rob and sweet cream in a cup for Percy—and sit down in a corner of the patio. It's a little darker over here and Percy purposefully chooses his chair so he's facing into the corner. There's probably some sort of joke here about being backed into a corner or how you're supposed to make sure there are walls at your back so you can see what's coming. Or maybe it's not a joke at all. Maybe it's just a sad commentary on his psyche.

The ice cream helps with the building panic attack. When he was young, before he was shipped away to school on the other side of the world, Mama would give him ice cream whenever he had one of his spells. She told him the sugar and the cold tricked your brain into thinking everything was safe, and you wouldn't be scared anymore. He doesn't remember how old he was when he realized she just made it up and was giving him ice cream because children like ice cream. Too old, probably.

Now, it just helps because of the memories of it helping. Which makes his head hurt a bit. Or maybe that's brain freeze?

The pain gets stabbing and he scrunches his face. Yeah, definitely brain freeze.

Reaching with his spoon to steal some of Percy's ice cream, Rob says, "Sorry that happened."

"It's not your fault."

There's a silence. Because, Percy assumes, Rob knows it's not his fault, and he was just being kind, and Percy kicked it back in his face. His tone, if he thinks about it, was clipped.

Rob's next words take him by surprise. "It was kind of my fault." When Percy furrows his forehead, Rob drops his eyes to his ice cream.

Under normal circumstances, Percy would find his slow licks across the mounded surface of the ice cream to be incredibly suggestive. Especially since it's Rob's last night. And because Percy's been thinking he'd like to ask Rob to fuck him. They haven't done that together yet. The sex has been amazing, so if Rob's not interested in fucking, that's fine, but Percy's got to ask, because he wants it.

At least, Percy was *going* to ask until the restaurant happened. Now he can't feel a whisper of desire. Something else ripped away from him for clicks.

"It really wasn't your fault." This time, Percy's careful to keep the snappishness from his tone.

Rob looks miserable as he stares at his ice cream cone. "If I hadn't asked you about dating there, they never would have noticed us. I made us into something interesting."

"People have been taking pictures and video of me since the news about my father broke." Why can't he make his voice stop coming out so sharp?

But Rob's shaking his head. "I don't think they even know who you were. They thought I was proposing to you." His full lips twist in an unhappy smile. "They tried to get me to follow the woman videoing so I could see our big moment."

Even though Percy doesn't want people knowing who he is, the fact that the people in the restaurant had no idea and filmed them anyway makes him feel cold. So they were just a couple of strangers whose privacy didn't matter. If his privacy doesn't matter when he's a nobody, how can he ever hope things will go back to normal when he's who he is?

"Oh" is all he can say. Rob winces, which makes Percy feel further like shit. It's absolutely not Rob's fault. But he's beginning to feel like a broken record saying so.

The cool, damp air penetrates Percy's sweater and jeans, and the cold of the metal chair is seeping through his clothing too. Eating ice cream is making him colder. At least they can take their time. It's not melting.

"That happens to you a lot?" Rob's voice sounds small. Percy hates it. Nothing about Rob is small. Rob sounding like this makes Percy want to curl up, pangolin-esque, and wait for the danger to go away.

Percy nods. Then he nods again. Then he says, "When I left for the bush, I didn't want to come back. But you weren't what I expected, and I… did. I wanted to be around you when I'd showered and put on cologne."

"You do smell really good." Rob cracks a small smile and eats some ice cream. "I didn't know things were that bad with people invading your privacy."

Grimly, Percy spoons ice cream into his mouth. "You haven't googled me since everything happened?"

"Not really. I mean, I already knew a lot about you." Rob winces again. "Wow, that sounds stalkerish. I just mean, I don't know, I didn't really want to read about you if it was just going to be in the context of who your dad is. You know? I don't care about any of that."

That makes Percy want to cry. He stretches his leg until he can nudge Rob's toe. "I know."

The pressure against his toe from Rob nudging back makes the achy about-to-cry feeling in Percy's throat even worse. He swallows convulsively several times and gets it under control.

They finish their ice cream in silence. Percy drops his rubbish in the bin as they leave. It's still early, and if Percy was a good host, he'd ask Rob if there's anything he wants to do on his last night. But he's not feeling like a good host right now, so he doesn't. He just wants to go home.

The streetlights are off in Green Park from load shedding, which Percy's perversely glad of. No one will know who he is in the dark. Rob's knuckles brush his as they walk, and Percy can't decide if he wants to yank his hand back or cling tight.

Rob hooks a finger around one of Percy's, not insistent but wondering. Offering. Percy's throat hurts. After a second, he slides his hand into Rob's.

They stay hand-in-hand until they reach Percy's building. When they walk inside, Percy flips on the lights. Only half of them come on, and there's something empty and depressing about the thin, washed-out illumination of the low-wattage lights that run off the power inverter.

Rob puts his hands on Percy's shoulders and steers him toward the office with all its plants. Something ugly twists through Percy at the fact that Rob knows this about him—that the office is his sanctuary, where he can hide behind plants when the world's grasping fingers become too intrusive. Worse than the metal tang of resentment is the gratitude.

None of the lights in the office work during load shedding, so Percy folds himself into a huddle on the papasan chair in the dark. Rob kneels in front of him. Light shines on his eyes. "Can I make you some tea?"

Percy laughs and then, mortifyingly, sniffles. "The kettle won't work."

"Dammit." Rubbing a hand over the back of his head, Rob says, "I'll get you some water, then."

As he stands, Percy grabs his hand. "I'm fine. I'm fine. Just"—he gestures helplessly, ridiculously, at the papasan chair—"sit. Please."

He almost says *stay*. But Rob is leaving tomorrow, and Percy will be alone again. The thought shouldn't scare him so much. He's been alone forever. A couple weeks with a wonderful, warm man doesn't, *can't*, wipe away a lifetime of coping and survival mechanisms. Will it matter that they'll be together in spirit, if not in actuality? That they can plan when they'll next see each other?

Now Percy's worried. What if it doesn't help? What if it makes everything worse?

The chair isn't big enough for two grown men, but Rob squeezes himself onto it anyway, the warm, solid bulk of him right there, and his arms come around Percy. And no, no, Rob could never make anything worse. Percy can't fathom it. Rob only makes things better. Really, he's too good for Percy's messed-up, clingy affection.

"I've got you, baby," Rob murmurs into Percy's temple.

Squirming closer, Percy closes his eyes. "I'm not even having a panic attack right now."

"Before, though. Were you?"

His heart gives a painful pound at revealing this part of himself. But Rob wasn't frightened off by the intrusive thoughts, so maybe the panic attacks won't scare him. "Close. Sorry you had to see it."

"Don't apologize." Rob kisses his forehead gently. "Don't ever apologize for that stuff." His arms tighten around Percy. "I hate that those people made you feel like this. And it's my last night, and I just...."

The light in the hall buzzes in the silence. Rob's last night, and this is how he's going to spend it, comforting Percy through an almost-panic attack. He sits up. "It's your last night," Percy agrees. "We should…."

What? Of course he had plans. He was going to pin Rob to the bed and make him see stars. He was going to ask Rob to fuck him, because he wanted that ache tomorrow when he has to watch Rob walk away.

One of Rob's big hands comes up to cup the back of Percy's neck, warm and steady. His thumb rubs circles in the cords of Percy's neck. "We don't have to do anything."

"No, but we don't know when we'll see each other again. We should fuck."

It's perhaps the least sexy thing Percy's ever said in his entire life. Certainly it's the most tepid, sad request for sex he's ever made. It's not a request, even. The way he said it, it sounds more like a chore.

The way Rob tenses tells Percy that he thinks so too. And now Percy feels like shit for that. An hour into this relationship and he's already fucking it up.

He leans back, pushing against Rob's hold, but Rob doesn't let him go. "Sorry," Percy mumbles. "Sorry, that was shit of me." He scrubs a hand over his face. "What do you want to do?"

"Make you tea," Rob says. There's a hesitant smile in his voice. When Percy risks a glance up at him, it's there on his face, too. Cautious, wary, but there, ready to come out when Percy stops being such a bellend. Rob leans forward and his forehead bumps against Percy's. "I like you so much, Perce. I just want to do whatever's going to make you smile again tonight."

That heart attack Percy felt like he might be having earlier might as well have struck him down, because Rob's sincerity makes him hurt all over. He sags against Rob and twines his arms around him, pressing the side of his head to Rob's chest. It's not a comfortable position at all, but Percy can hear Rob's heart beating, and it makes him breathe easier.

"Do you want to watch stupid South African soap operas once the power comes back on?" Percy asks, his voice muffled by Rob's shirt.

"That's a thing?"

"*Such* a thing." Percy's neck already hurts from the awful angle he's got it at, but he likes how cozy and protected he feels nestled against Rob. "We can stream them."

Rob chuckles. "I love when you talk dirty to me, baby."

Percy winces. "Unless you'd rather go to bed and—"

"Perce." Rob drops another kiss on his forehead. "The sex is amazing. I always want to have sex with you. But I want to do other stuff with you too. And we don't have to have sex just because it's my last night."

"You wanted to."

Rob wiggles backward so he can look Percy in the eyes. "So did you, right?"

"Yeah."

"And now you don't. So I don't, either."

It's not even quite that Percy doesn't. Obviously, he's not in the mood right now. But tomorrow will come, and Rob will go, and Percy knows he'll regret not taking this chance while they had it. But he's also exhausted and wrung out, and if he's really honest, the idea of cuddling with Rob sounds more appealing than anything else.

Except tea. He really *would* like some tea.

Leaning into Rob again, Percy says, "If you don't mind getting cozy, we can watch soap operas on my laptop. The power will come back on soon."

"*Mind.*" Rob kisses Percy's forehead. "That's a prerequisite."

Can Percy hug him and never let him go? It's not fair that Rob's so sweet, and it's baffling he's here with Percy. "Let's go to bed," Percy murmurs.

Rob gets out of the chair first, offering Percy a hand, which he doesn't need but takes anyway. Few people have thought to ever offer him that kind of help—poor little rich boy, independent and off on his own as a boy. Percy de Villiers can take care of himself.

It's just nice for someone to know that and to think that sometimes, just maybe, he could use a hand anyway.

Chapter Twenty-Two

OKAY. LOOK. Obviously Rob wanted to fuck Percy last night. After the restaurant, after Percy turned that washed-out color and his pulse kept jumping in his throat, Rob didn't know what to do. He figured he should be kind to Percy. Kind and undemanding, and follow Percy's lead.

They cozied into Percy's bed and watched a few hours of soap operas, which Rob can only describe as B-A-N-A-N-A-S. Halfway through the third episode, Percy confesses to watching *Coronation Street* religiously while he was at Eton. They fell asleep together with the laptop still playing and people screaming at each other in Afrikaans.

In the morning, Rob woke to a hand stroking his cock. Now Rob's got Percy flat on his back while he kneels above him. Percy's hands grip Rob's hips, guiding his thrusts as he fucks into Percy's mouth.

So sure, they didn't fuck last night, but this works too.

When they're lying tangled together, sticky, sweaty, and spent, Rob idly traces the cords of Percy's neck, down his shoulder and along his arm. He's been trying not to think about how he's leaving today. There's nothing he can do to stop time from passing, but he wants to sink his fingernails into these remaining hours and yank them back, make them slow down.

"What do you want to do today?" Percy asks lazily. His voice is a little hoarse, and that makes Rob turn his face into Percy's neck and grin. He's not above feeling proud of his sexual prowess now and then.

"You."

"You just did."

"Lotta hours in the day, baby."

Percy laughs, hoarse again, and Rob props himself on an elbow to kiss him soundly. He tastes like sex, which makes Rob's balls feel heavy, even if he can't get it up again quite yet.

For a moment, Rob just gazes down at Percy. He wants to etch Percy into his skin. Into his bones. He doesn't want to go home and not get to see Percy's twists glinting with gold, his inky eyes and their deep well of emotion, his scruff and his piercings and his bony wrists. His floral button-up shirts and his skinny jeans and his Courteney boots he wears everywhere. The way he'll get lost in his head, but he'll come back and always have a smile for Rob.

Yeah. Rob's going to miss that smile most of all.

"Seriously," Rob says, smoothing some of Percy's baby hairs down. "I don't need to do anything today except be with you. Nothing fancy."

Percy pulls him down into a kiss, and they do that for… a while. Rob's really going to miss the way Percy kisses too. Is it too early to buy plane tickets to come back to Cape Town?

Eventually, they get up. Coffee and breakfast in the garden has become their routine, and while they sit under a robin's-egg-blue sky, ankles brushing, Rob concedes that he'd like to go out for at least a short walk to pick up some souvenirs.

"Wine," he specifies. "My family just wants wine. My friend Jaxon wanted biltong, but I can't bring that back, so he's getting wine too."

Percy remains silent, looking some flavor of thoughtful. Eventually, he says, "I'm jealous of Jaxon."

"Oh god, don't be. He dresses like a dad, for one thing." When Percy laughs, Rob adds, "I don't let him see me naked, either."

"It will just be odd, won't it? We've been together every second of the day for weeks now, and…."

Rob stands up and tugs Percy to his feet as well. "C'mon, let's go out for a bit. I'll satisfy all my souvenir needs and it will take our minds off of later."

Later, when he leaves, and who the hell knows when he'll next see his boyfriend.

They shower and get dressed. Since they're only going to De Waterkant to shop, they don't bother with Percy's truck in the parking garage. It's an easily walkable distance. As they leave through the side door of the building and walk past the garage, Percy jerks to a stop. At first, Rob doesn't realize, and he keeps walking, only to have his arm yanked from where his hand is joined with Percy's.

Rob turns. An ugly scrawl of black spray paint is slashed across the building's garage door. DE VILLIERS EAT SHIT, it says. Long black drips of paint trail from the words down the door.

A sick, heavy feeling settles in Rob's stomach. Traffic whooshes by on the road just above them. A truck beeps somewhere down the hill. And Percy stands, completely still except for his pulse thrumming in his neck.

Is it coincidence that the video of them went up last night? But it was only for a minute; who could possibly have seen it, saved it, and dispersed it so fast?

"Perce?" Rob asks hesitantly.

The bob of Percy's throat is jagged and labored. "Let's go!" he says, his tone way too bright, way too hard. Rob hates it immediately. It makes Percy sound like a stranger.

"We don't have to…." Rob trails off when Percy turns around, his eyes flat, his pulse still jumping in his throat.

"It's fine, this is what we planned." Percy gets his phone out of his pocket, his wrist snapping in jumpy movements. His hands are trembling as he unlocks it. "I have to call the building manager. They'll get someone out here to clean that off."

"Percy, do you want to… I don't know, talk about it?" Rob tries, but Percy jerks his head no, putting the phone to his ear and starting down the hill.

Queasiness bites at Rob's gut. As he follows Percy, he gets out his phone and does a quick google for Percy de Villiers, already cringing at whatever he's going to find. Hopefully it's all old stuff, articles from when the news broke about his dad's arrest, and this is just bad timing.

He stumbles when the results load. Right there at the top, screaming in all caps, is a clickbaity hit piece from last night.

PLAYBOY SON OF CORRUPT MINISTER FLAUNTS LAVISH LIFESTYLE AND SPLASHES THE CASH AS ELECTRICITY SHORTAGES DESTROY FAMILIES.

He shouldn't click on it, but he does. And—oh no. Oh no no no. Up pops a blurry, but still entirely identifiable photo, of Percy.

And Rob.

They're at Thaba Boroko, eating braai surrounded by torches and hanging lanterns. Half empty glasses of wine sit on the table, and both of them have plates piled high with food. Rob's back is to the photographer, but Percy is on full display. Rob's immediate, damage-control thought is that maybe Percy can put out that this photo wasn't taken where it says it was—but there's no mistaking that where they are is very, very nice and very, very expensive.

He thinks back to that night but can't remember a photographer, let alone media. The photo almost certainly was taken on a phone, though. It has that look. Anyone could have taken a picture on a phone. *Rob* was taking pictures on his phone. It was probably just another guest. They recognized Percy and figured they could get a small payday with a sneaky photo of him.

Percy's voice floats back, still unnaturally bright. "Right! Thanks loads!"

Rob shoves his phone back in his pocket. The graffiti on the garage door is bad enough, but at least hardly anyone will see that. Quiet street, building right at the end? Only the people in the neighboring buildings will spot it. It'll be gone by the end of the day.

The internet, though—that's forever.

Hustling to catch up with Percy, Rob touches his shoulder and asks, "Are they going to take care of it?"

"They're sending someone to clean it off right now." Percy's voice is the bright, brittle sunshine of one of those bitter cold January days in Wisconsin. The world sparkles, but the cold snaps so hard it hurts to draw a breath, and it might as well not be sunny at all.

Rob finds Percy's hand, half expecting him to pull away. He lets Rob interlace their fingers, though. Percy's fingers are cold, but his palm is clammy and moist with sweat. "It's just some asshole," Rob says, trying to sound upbeat.

Letting out a shaky, unhappy laugh, Percy replies, "Right. Right. I know. Just some asshole. They saw me on that video those people took. Didn't you say they took it down?"

"Yeah. I watched her do it. She deleted it."

They reach the end of Percy's road where it intersects with a larger thoroughfare. Traffic speeds by, and Percy shrinks back against a building, his head bowed like he's terrified a driver will stop their car to accost him. He scrubs a hand over his face and leaves it there, covering his eyes.

Rob's stomach hurts. He feels sick and helpless and just—he's not good at stuff like this. He's good at not paying attention to the bullshit, at waving aside the tea and all the mean things people say about others, and looking for the person underneath all that. Now, though? With the tea swirling like toxic sludge around their feet? He has no damn idea what to do.

He puts his arms around Percy. It's awkward as hell. Percy's entire body is rigid, his breathing fast and his heart rabbiting. Rob rubs his back. "Someone must've seen it before it got deleted."

The words are out of his mouth before his brain has a chance to hit the brakes. That's not what happened. Rob *knows* that's not what happened. And all it will take for Percy to know that's not what happened is a simple google search.

But Percy won't know that Rob knew, and Rob just wants to salvage some of this day.

"It'll be fine," Rob murmurs, guilt gnawing at his stomach. "Let's get wine for ourselves too. Wine makes everything better."

Some of the rigidness goes out of Percy. His shoulders are still like granite, but he leans into Rob a little and loops one arm around Rob's waist. He's still trembling.

"It's okay," Rob murmurs, kissing Percy's face. He doesn't care who's watching or who sees. "It's just some dickhead with too much time on their hands."

"They know where I live." Percy's voice is small and choked, and Rob can't decide if this is better or worse than the fake brightness. "They know where I live, and you're in the video, and what if someone comes after you, what if you get caught up in this, and you're leaving today and I won't know—"

"Percy." Rob's chest feels tight. "Baby, that's not going to happen."

"It could."

"It won't." Rob's talking out his ass. What does he know? Maybe there's some nut out there who hates Percy's family enough to be violent. Coming after him in Atlanta seems a little farfetched, though. He rubs Percy's back. "We'll talk every day, texting or Skype or whatever. Okay? So you'll know I'm alive."

Possibly not the best choice of words. Percy shudders. A pair of women walk past, and Percy turns his face away so they won't see it.

And Rob thinks, shit. Percy's way more messed up than he realized. The thought unnerves him a little. All the guys he's been with have had their issues. Everyone does…not like this.

But the thought also makes him feel kind of proud. Because here he is, sticking with his man through something hard. And it's only been a week, which means it would be really easy for him to bail. He's not going to. He's going to be there for Percy, because it's clear Percy needs someone.

It's going to be good when his dad's scandal and trial are over, though. Things will be so much better for Percy.

"Are people looking at me?" Percy asks, his voice muffled.

"No," Rob replies honestly. There are plenty of people around, a mix of locals and tourists, but most of them hardly glance at Rob and Percy.

Taking a deep breath, Rob says, "Hey, let's go shopping, okay? Get your mind off this stuff. I need your expertise on South African wine. Otherwise I'll just buy whatever has the prettiest label."

That gets a weak laugh from Percy. After another moment, Percy detaches himself from Rob. He glances around furtively, but people continue to pay them no attention.

What does Percy see when he looks at these people? In his eyes, do they all have the potential to turn on him? Is he thinking that any one of them could have defaced his building last night?

That's a hard way to live. And like, Rob's brown and queer, so he gets it—that feeling that anyone might hate you for who you generically are. But right now, every time Percy goes out in public, he must wonder if everyone hates him for who he *specifically* is: Percy de Villiers, son of Pieter de Villiers, disgraced Minister of Health.

Rob takes Percy's hand tightly, determined to still have a good day. There's a timer in his head, ticking down to when he has to arrive to the airport. He wants these hours to be good. He'll *make* them good.

Chapter Twenty-Three

Percy puts on his best show, but inside, he's crumbling. They found him. They found him at his *home*. All because of some video on the internet showing him happy, that was only up for a few minutes. The people have spoken. He's not allowed to be happy. He's as culpable for his father's crimes as his father is.

It's not much of a change. When has he ever deserved to be happy in public? That's always been a losing proposition, all the way back to Eton, where he was tormented for any obvious displays of queerness—never mind that Eton's pupils still engaged in the rich English boarding school tradition of being extremely gay.

This is why he loves being in the field. The only observers of his happiness are the trees and the sky and the animals. He doesn't have to worry about turning off his phone and keeping it off, because he's cut off from the world there.

Shopping distracts him, but it's over too soon. The intrusive thoughts return on the slow walk back to Green Point: Rob being confronted. Rob getting in a fight. Rob held up, or beat up, or hurt because of his association with Percy.

And yes, of course, *of course*, there's the voice in his brain telling him it's all so unlikely. The little logical voice of reason pointing out that Percy's father's crimes probably haven't even made the news in America, so no American will care, certainly not to the extent that they'd ever be aware of Rob's extremely tangential role in it. *Tangential* is too strong a word, even.

If Rob were identified in South Africa, what South African would get on a plane, fly to America, and hunt him down? They'd have to be crazy. The problem is, Percy feels like he might be crazy, so imagining that someone else might be isn't so difficult.

But but but. What if Rob is identified. What if there's someone whose life was destroyed by Minister de Villiers's corruption and theft. What if they want to hurt Percy's father, so they hurt Percy, and to do that they hurt Rob. What if their phones get hacked and all the emails and texts they haven't exchanged yet get leaked. What if their lives are splashed all over clickbait media and Rob knows what it's like to be Percy, always wondering if people are staring and hating you.

What if Rob blames Percy for all of it, which he would, because it's Percy's fault. Percy's fault for not being careful, Percy's fault for getting caught.

When they get home, a crew is scrubbing off the graffiti from the garage door. EAT SHIT is still there, but at least his name is gone.

Percy freezes, paralyzed by indecision. Should he thank them? Tip them? Or if he does, will they know who he is and put the graffiti back? They'll get a good look at Rob too.

Before he can decide which is the least bad option, Rob approaches them and thanks them, then proceeds to have a perfectly normal conversation with a few of the men. Percy folds himself back into the shadows. He's never been brilliant at that kind of easy social interaction, but he used to be better at it. Now, he feels like he can barely fake it—and when he's trying, he comes across manic and hard and not quite right.

Hands shaking, he pulls out his keys, unlocking the door as Rob rejoins him. "Nice guys," Rob says. Percy just nods jerkily.

His flat isn't the safe haven it was when they left this morning. He feels jittery, paranoid, like people are watching him through the windows. He nearly draws all the curtains, but part of him recognizes how that would look. Things aren't that bad yet. Are they?

"If my flight leaves at nine tonight, what time should I get to the airport? Six? Earlier?" Rob asks.

"Seven is fine," Percy says, latching on to something solid that he can plan. It's already past three in the afternoon, which means he has to say goodbye to Rob in less than four hours. "It's a small airport. Yours might be the only flight leaving at that time."

"That'll be a nice change from Atlanta." Rob stretches, then grimaces. "I guess I should pack, huh?"

"I'll help!" This time, Percy grimaces. It's probably obvious how desperate Percy is to think of something, *anything* besides his own problems, but showing that kind enthusiasm for Rob preparing to leave is a shit move, even for him. "I didn't mean it like that," he blurts. "I don't—it's not that I want you gone, I just—"

Rob hesitates before taking Percy's hands. "I'd love the help. And I know you're not excited to get rid of me."

Mouth dry, Percy nods, and the two of them go to his bedroom. Rob's suitcase needs to be hauled out of the closet, because somehow, in a week, his belongings all found homes in Percy's home. His toiletries mingle with Percy's in the bathroom, his clothes are hung up with Percy's, and the books he brought along sit in a stack on the bedside table.

A lump rises in his throat. It felt natural to interlace their lives for this week. It wasn't real life, exactly, but could it have been? Could they have this sometime in the future, the two of them in one place for good, no suitcase being filled at the end of vacation?

Only if Rob can stand being with him when he's like this. Days like today aren't the exception, not since his father was arrested. They've become the rule, the horrible norm, and that was without people posting videos of him online and his home being defaced with profanity. He's under no illusion that he's easy or fun to be with in this state.

He's a fucking mess, and he's sure Rob's having second thoughts about wanting to be with him.

A hard blaze of anger and longing for his father's conviction burns through him. If they send him to jail, this can all go away. Percy's life can go back to normal, or as normal as he's ever been.

"What's your next job?" Rob asks.

His voice snaps Percy out of his own brain. "I don't know yet. Eunice—my agent—has some possibilities lined up, but I haven't chosen yet." Carefully, he folds one of Rob's shirts and lays it in the suitcase. "I have a meeting with her next week."

He should turn his phone back on, because he knows Eunice has probably been trying to text and call him all day about the video being online.

"I'll keep my eye out for any possibilities in north Georgia." Though Rob's tone is joking, there's a desperate sadness on his face.

God, Percy's really been a cunt. *Do you want to try a long-distance relationship? Sure, just let me have a breakdown and ignore the fact that you're probably quite sad about having to leave, but I'll make your last hours in Cape Town completely about me! What an absolutely tops boyfriend I am!*

"When can I visit you?" Percy asks, so loudly and suddenly that Rob looks startled. "I mean—well, that's what I mean. I'll come to America."

"Won't that depend on your next job?" Rob looks unsure. "And… anything else you might have going on?"

Will you need to be at your father's trial, he means, and it hits Percy right in the solar plexus. They've successfully not talked about any of that while Rob's been here, but considering what's happened today, it was stupid of Percy to think that would last.

"I'll choose my next job around when it works to see you," Percy says, trying to sound chipper.

For a second, he's afraid he's grossly misstepped. The look on Rob's face is unsure, but then it gets tender. "Perce, I don't want you to do anything like that." The soft drawl in his voice comes out a little more. "We'll make it work around your schedule."

"But I want to know when I'm seeing you again." Percy sounds pathetic. Needy and weak, the boy weeping as his parents walked away from him at Eton.

Instead of telling him to stop crying and be a man—not that Rob ever would, but the fear lives in Percy, so ingrained he doubts it will ever leave him—Rob pulls out his phone. He sits on Percy's bed and pats the spot next to him. "C'mon, let's look at my calendar."

When Percy sits, Rob's already got his calendar open. He's slowly thumbing from July to August to September. "Not that long," Percy says. "September's too far from now."

Rob looks relieved. "I was hoping you'd say that."

Percy looks at all the days in Rob's calendar marked with something and wonders what they are. Reminders, birthdays, appointments? Drinks with friends, dinners with family? There's a whole life scheduled here that Percy hardly knows anything about. It's a bit terrifying. What if Rob's feelings fade once he gets back to his normal life?

There's a silence, and Percy realizes Rob is looking at him and waiting. Percy glances at him, eyebrows drawn together in question. "Are you too busy in July and August?" he asks, trying his best not to sound miserable.

"Huh?" Rob glances at his phone. "Oh, ignore all that. I mean, I think I have some friend nights in here, but they'll want to meet you. No, I figured your schedule wasn't as flexible." Rob balances the phone on his leg, cups his hands around Percy's jaw, and kisses him.

The taut energy coiled in Percy's muscles loosens as he kisses Rob back. Rob's sure, strong hands make him feel grounded and like everything will be okay.

When Rob pulls back, he says softly, "Tell me what days you want to come, and I'm all yours. Whenever."

Percy takes a moment to breathe slowly, trying to memorize Rob's warm smell for the coming months. No, weeks. Definitely weeks, because he'll lose his mind if he can't see Rob again for months.

Hoping he doesn't come across as pathetic and clingy, he taps a day at the end of July on Rob's phone. Rob types in "Percy."

And everything seems brighter. Even with the graffiti still being cleaned off the garage door, even not knowing how far the video from last night spread. He's got something to look forward to. It's not that long until he'll be visiting Rob, who makes him feel safe.

Evening ticks closer as they pack Rob's suitcase. They order in an early dinner. Percy does it from his computer, because he can't handle turning his phone on yet. Not when he's found this bubble of stability.

Far too soon, it's time to leave for the airport. It doesn't feel real. How can Rob be leaving when Rob's sitting in the truck next to him, his hand resting on the back of Percy's neck while Percy drives?

When he pulls the bakkie alongside the curb at Departures, he shuts off the engine. "Do you want me to come inside with you?" he asks.

Rob looks torn, but he shakes his head. "I think it'll make it harder. Unless it would make it easier for you?"

"Nothing's going to make this easier," Percy says, trying not to sound too tragic about it. Only having those plane tickets for the end of July could soothe the hole opening in his chest.

Why doesn't he just buy them now? It might make Rob feel better too.

He'll have to turn his phone on sometime and face all his missed notifications—maybe it's better to do it while Rob is next to him and when he can distract himself with airfare.

As he gets out his phone, he says, "I'm going to buy a ticket for my trip to see you in July."

Rob grins, though it looks more pained than usual. He's clearly putting on a cheery face for Percy's benefit. "Send me a screenshot. I might make it my lock screen."

Percy grabs Rob's hand as his phone powers on. The minute it connects to the network, notifications start rolling in. He ignores most of them, only taking note of Eunice's many, many texts. The most recent says, *Read my email for details. Tl;dr piece is removed from site. Thaba Boroko trying to determine who took photo to ban them from all properties.*

Thaba Boroko? What does Thaba Boroko have to do with anything?

His eyebrows draw together as he stares at his phone. It's such a confusing message that all his emotions have stuttered to a halt. He can't even be happy about the piece getting pulled. Rob squeezes his hand and asks, "What's wrong?"

Wordlessly, Percy turns the phone so Rob can read the message—not that it will make any more sense to him.

But Rob makes a satisfied noise. "Good for Thaba Boroko. I didn't think they'd be okay with one of their guests taking a picture of you and selling it to the first trashy site that offered them money."

The confusion deepens. Even more baffling, Rob looks horrified, like he didn't mean to say what he just did. Percy looks from Eunice's message back to Rob, then at Eunice's message again.

Like he's feeling his way through thick fog, an explanation fits itself together in Percy's mind. He remembers now—at the braai. There was a man who Percy thought was watching him, maybe taking pictures of him. It was added incentive to get back to the tent.

That, not the video of Rob and him in the restaurant last night, was what was posted online. A guest at Thaba Boroko took photos of him at a luxury safari camp and sold them, and someone came to Percy's home and scrawled *eat shit* across his building.

And Rob knew.

Percy's chest feels like it's being excavated. Hollowed out. He keeps staring at his phone, pressing his fingers tighter against the screen. "You knew the graffiti wasn't about the video?" he asks, trying to keep his voice from shaking. It doesn't entirely work.

There's silence from the other side of the bakkie. Percy doesn't want to look at Rob, doesn't want to see the truth on his face.

He makes himself. Rob looks stricken. "I didn't want to make things worse," Rob says. "That's why I didn't say anything."

"You knew." There's no hiding the tremor in his voice. "You *knew.* You—googled it?" Rob's guilty expression is all the answer Percy needs. "You didn't tell me."

"I just thought you were dealing with enough already." Rob's tone is apologetic—the apologetic of someone who's sorry they got caught, but not really sorry for what they did in the first place.

"So you kept it from me. You let me think something completely wrong." Percy's mind is going from frozen to whirling. "You *knew* it had nothing to do with the video, but you let me walk around today thinking everyone was staring at me and despising me."

"No! Oh my god, Perce, no, that wasn't—I didn't think about it like that—"

"You knew I did, though." Clenching his fingers around the door handle, Percy says, "You knew I thought everyone was looking at me and judging every move I made. And you still didn't tell me the truth."

Rob's mouth opens and closes soundlessly a few times. Finally, he says, "I thought it would be worse if you knew it was from Thaba Boroko."

He's trembling, he realizes. His heart is pounding, and it's getting harder and harder to breathe. He can't—this is—why would Rob think this was okay? Ever since Percy met him, Rob has been sneaking through his defenses, making him feel like maybe he didn't need them, at least not with this person. This wonderful person who seemed to understand him and what he needed, and who made him feel safe. Protected. Seen, and not scared by it.

It was a mistake to let his guard down. The tightness in his chest is getting worse. His heart is jumping, racing, banging painfully against his rib cage. The panic attack is creeping up behind him, hooking claws around Percy's throat.

Was it only earlier today that Rob made Percy feel better? Now Percy doesn't know if he can trust him. He *can't* trust him. Rob kept the truth from him. Rob *lied*, because Percy said what he thought happened, and Rob agreed, but he already knew. That's lying.

Percy can't breathe. At all.

"Are you okay? Perce, you don't look good, should I get some help?" Something heavy lands on Percy's shoulder and sends pins and needles prickling through his entire body. It's Rob's hand, and it feels leaden and out of place and *wrong*.

Percy jerks away. His lungs are concrete, incapable of doing their job. No air in, no air out, and his heart is straining. Sweat sticks his shirt to his back.

"You should go," Percy manages. Why did he think he could trust a man he just met two weeks ago? He's so stupid. Stupid stupid stupid, and if he's going to die in this car, he doesn't want Rob witnessing it.

That might ruin Rob's day.

The bitterness is an emotion besides sick panic and the acid bite of betrayal, and Percy grabs for it. "Your flight." His throat spasms and he funnels that bitterness into making his voice come out steady. It doesn't work, not really, but it's better than what it could be. "Just—go."

Rob's hand snaps back like Percy tried to bite him. "Oh," he says. His eyes are big and brown and wounded, but they're also confused, and how can he not get it? How can he not understand how fragile Percy is right now and how much he needs someone he can trust?

It was stupid to think he could be romantically involved with someone right now. Stupid to think he could handle it, stupid to think the other person could give him what he needs when he barely knows what he needs.

"What about your trip to Atlanta?" Rob asks in a small voice.

"I don't...." Percy feels like his voice is coming from a long way off. "Maybe we should put that on hold."

"Oh," Rob says again. He reaches for Percy again, but Percy shoves himself up against his door. The bakkie cab is closing in on him.

"Please just go," Percy says.

There's a teary shine to Rob's eyes, a sheen of sweat on his forehead. His pulse is beating in his throat. "Percy," he whispers.

If Rob doesn't get out of this truck right now, Percy will have to. He needs space, he needs *air*, he needs to be back at his flat by himself, alone where no one can mess him about or fuck with his head.

Percy looks away. There's a silence, long and choked, tightening like a noose around his windpipe.

"I'm sorry," Rob says again. Percy doesn't respond. Even if he wanted to, he can't. He's seconds from hyperventilating, holding it down through sheer force of quickly depleting will. He doesn't want Rob to sit here and try to help.

The door clicks as it opens on Rob's side. The bakkie dinging its alert is the best thing Percy's ever heard. Fabric rustles as Rob slides out of his seat. The bakkie keeps dinging as Rob opens the back and pulls out his backpack and suitcase.

Percy's heart beats twice for every ding, at least. Maybe three. Maybe it's going to give out.

"I'll, um. I'll be in touch about the article, I guess."

Email it to Eunice, Percy wants to say. He can't speak, though. The words won't come out. He's starting to gasp.

Fumbling for the keys, Percy starts the engine. Out of the corner of his eye, he sees Rob start backward from the open passenger door. His mouth drops open soundlessly again, endless seconds where Percy could be driving away before he suffocates.

Finally, Rob's shoulders slump, his head drops, and he shuts the door.

Percy drives away without watching him leave.

Part Four: Atlanta

Chapter Twenty-Four

July

Percy,

I'm not sure if you'll read this. You probably won't. I don't know if I would, if the situation was reversed. But I wanted to write to you anyway, because, well, the article's all done and posted. Eunice okayed it—I didn't know if that meant you read it and signed off, or if she just has a list of things that are all right to say in an article. I'd like to think you read it. I hope you read it. But, again, if the situation was reversed....

I'm sorry I broke your trust that day in Cape Town. I had a lot of time to think about it on that sixteen-hour flight home, and I haven't really stopped thinking about it since I got back to Atlanta. It was selfish of me, because I wanted one more day with you, and I didn't want anything ruining it even more. What I realized on the flight home, though, is that nothing was ruined. You weren't a vacation, you were—are—important to me. I should have been there for you however you needed me, whatever was going on. I should have trusted you and your reaction to bad news instead of trying to put it off so I didn't have to deal with it.

You don't have to write back. If you even read this far. People say you can apologize, but you have to be prepared for the other person to not accept your apology. I'm being selfish again and hoping you do, but I know I hurt you, and you might not be ready to, if you ever are.

Those weeks with you in South Africa were the sort of a thing a writer struggles to put words to. It was beautiful. I'll never forget it. I miss you.

Yours,
Rob

Percy closes his laptop and stares into the distance, gaze unfocused. Doves coo in the trees edging his garden and seagulls cry in the distance. He pulls his cardigan tighter around him, trying to ward off the chill in the air.

Yeah, he's read Rob's article about their week together in the bush. Sort of. He's read the first paragraph thirty or forty times: *The first thing you notice about Percy de Villiers is his focus. It's that focus that allows him to capture the kind of incredible wild moments that look staged: two African fish eagles in a dramatic dive, talons locked. A leopard lounging in a dead tree, silhouetted against a riotous sunset. A cheetah with a bloodied muzzle stretching like a house cat.*

That's roughly the point where his vision goes blurry and he has to stop reading. After their breakup—which seems a silly thing to call it when they'd only been official for a day—Percy thought Rob might write something awful about him. Something that hewed to the letter of what he was supposed to write, but snuck in digs that close reading would reveal.

After he had his panic attack along the hard shoulder just beyond the Departures drop-off at Cape Town International (until the police came along and knocked on his window to tell him to move along), after he white-knuckled his way home, after he locked himself in his flat for three days straight, after crying and freaking out and crying some more and ignoring texts, then calls, from his friends....

After all of that, he realized that Rob wasn't that sort of person.

After that, he started regretting how things ended. He started regretting that things ended at all.

When he burst into tears at his meeting with Eunice, she announced, "That's it! I'm calling my therapist and we're getting you seen."

Eunice takes no prisoners. She's from a family of nine, raised in Khayelitsha Township in Cape Town, where she still lives and serves on boards of multiple social organizations. She represents artists and writers across South Africa, and Percy counts himself unbelievably lucky that he's one of her clients.

Obviously, he goes to see her therapist.

It's been a few weeks of that, and medication, with his most recent appointment this morning over video chat. The email from Rob was sitting in his inbox, unopened, but Doctor Mente worked with him on whether he wanted to read it or delete it. He ended the appointment by vowing to read it.

A couple swee waxbills land on a feeder and he watches them pick out seeds to eat. Something is slowly crystallizing in him, all the regrets and longing he's been struggling through for the past month. It's all pulling itself into a semblance of decision.

Well, *decision*'s a bit strong. It's probably closer to an admission: an admission that he made a mistake, that he's not over Rob, and that he desperately wants to apologize.

If Rob's email can be believed, he'd accept an apology, even though every time Percy thinks about what an absolute fuckwad he's been, it's a bit dizzying. What Rob did wasn't right, but the way Percy behaved toward him was reprehensible. *Yes, what you did was very upsetting, and not how a person in a relationship should behave toward his boyfriend, so I'll do the completely adult thing and toss you out of my car and my life.*

What it comes down to is that Percy regrets, nearly every minute of the day, that he ended things between Rob and him. He misses him. Knowing Rob misses him too, even after everything, knots his stomach with nerves and excitement.

His phone pings with a text from Eunice. *Meeting before you moved to tomorrow. Want to meet for lunch at Marco's in 30?*

Say no more, he texts back.

The waxbills call softly to each other and Percy stretches his arms over his head, letting his spine slouch and curve into the chair. His brain feels quieter these past few weeks than it has in far too long. His father's crimes and the increased scrutiny on Percy brought his panic attacks back, but if he's honest, he was on a downward mental slide long before that. After uni he took meds. Probably never should have stopped. The difference it makes now that he's back on them makes him want to cry sometimes.

It's about a mile to Marco's, an African restaurant/institution in Bo-Kaap, so Percy laces up his Courteneys and walks over there. Eunice is outside, typing furiously on her phone, but she looks up at his approach and gives him a big smile, her teeth white against her dark brown skin. Her flat twists are in a mohawk updo and she's wearing a chunky-rimmed pair of glasses.

"Whakind, sunno!" she greets him, giving him a tight hug. "You look even better than last week. That therapist is good, right."

"Do you need more thank-you flowers, or should I send a box of chocolates this week?" Percy asks, smiling back. Smiling has been coming more easily these days too.

"Gift cards," she says, tapping him on the chest. "American Swiss, but as long as it's luxury, I'm not picky."

Percy laughs and they go inside. Once they've chatted and ordered lunch, Eunice plants her elbows on the table and leans forward, fixing Percy with a stare and a crooked little smile. "You asked me to look for opportunities in the States. I've got a list put together, if you want to have a look?"

"Oh my god, Eunice, you're amazing."

Airily, she replies, "I know. That's why you pay me so much." She pulls out her tablet from her bag and folds out its stand so she can use the keyboard. "There are several organizations in New York City who were thrilled when I contacted them, so those are yours for the taking. One of them couldn't stop talking to me about your show in Amsterdam and how they would love to see someone of your talent put together something similar for each borough."

"Hm." Percy sips his water. "What else?"

One of Eunice's eyebrows goes up, but she doesn't press him on New York. "Washington, D.C.—an installation in low-income neighborhoods featuring artists of color from around the world. Your focus would be nature reserves around the city."

How far is Washington, D.C. From Atlanta? God, that's a good project. He'll consider it. It's definitely closer to Atlanta than New York, isn't it? "Maybe. I like the sound of it."

She types something on her tablet and continues through her shortlist. There are museums, galleries, city councils, and organizations that want to hire him from Boston to Miami, and there's something about every single one of them that isn't quite right.

Namely, they aren't in Atlanta, Georgia.

"Is that all?" he asks when her pause between projects lasts longer.

Pursing her lips, she says, "There's one more, but it seems…."

"What?"

"Small-time. For you."

"I haven't got a problem with small-time."

"Small-time and not very interesting," she amends. "Explore Georgia wants to revamp their website and all their materials on the

Northeast Georgia Mountains region with new photography. The photographer they'd signed with had to pull at the last minute, so they're looking for someone, like, immediately."

Butterflies whirl in a fluttery storm in his stomach. "Explore Georgia?" he asks, trying to sound casual, knowing he doesn't. "Where are they based?"

Her brows draw together as she checks her notes. "Atlanta, I think. It's part of the Department of Economic Development and Tourism." Giving him a curious look, she asks, "You're interested in this one, really?"

He makes a noncommittal noise and shrugs. "Do you know where my lodgings would be?"

"They forwarded all the accommodation info to me that they booked for their no-show. I'm sure it could be changed, though—I know you prefer to isolate yourself during nature shoots—" She taps around on her tablet. "Atlanta, Ellijay, and Clayton."

Atlanta.

"When would I need to leave?" he asks.

Eunice looks confused and like she's trying hard to work out why this project caught his fancy. Then her face clears. "Rob Hale was from Atlanta, wasn't he?" When Percy just makes a noise between a throat-clear and assent, she leans over the table. "You fucked him, didn't you?"

Their food arrives at that moment. Percy takes the opportunity presented and stuffs his face, assuring he can't answer Eunice's question.

Unfortunately but predictably, his oxtail curry runs out. When it does, Eunice is still waiting. Before he can confirm or deny, she waves a hand. "I can tell you did. Percy, *please* tell me you didn't fall apart over a man, or that you're making career decisions to win him back."

"I fell apart because tabloid nonsense was posted about me, which put my private life on display, and someone vandalized my building," Percy says sharply. "And because, I'm sure you recall, my father is awaiting a trial date for funneling international aid money into a bank account in Singapore."

Eunice looks like she wants to say something else, but she sighs and shakes her head. Reaching for his hand with both of hers, she says, "I'm your agent, so it's my job to help you make the best decisions for your career. But I'm also your friend, and I don't want to see you make decisions that aren't good for *you*."

She squeezes his hand tighter and tighter, her favorite thing to do when he tries to get away with not keeping up his side of these sorts of conversations. When the pressure reaches the point of possibly causing bone fractures, Percy says, "It was more than fucking."

Her grip slackens, but she keeps holding his hand. It will still be a moment before he can feel his fingertips. "Do you really want to work for the Georgia Department of Tourism, or is this just an excuse to see him again?"

"Both."

"Percy, if he ended things…."

"He didn't." Percy's throat jumps, and he looks down at the table. Rob's email has been woven through his thoughts since he read it. *I miss you.* Meeting Eunice's eyes again, he says, "I'll look up the area to make sure I can do it justice. Does that make you feel better? I'll let you know just now."

She huffs out an exasperated, "Eish, of course you can do it *justice.*"

The vote of confidence makes him smile. "I've never been to that part of America," he points out.

Shaking her head but giving him a fond look, she says, "If you already know you're going to take the job, tell me right now and save us both the time."

His pride tells him to hold off on making his decision. Then again, he's already made the decision, so it would just be holding off on telling her. "Get back to them and tell them I'll do it. When do I need to leave?"

Chapter Twenty-Five

OF COURSE Rob's email doesn't get a response. He didn't really expect one. He just hoped. But it's been weeks of hoping. And weeks of silence. His friends have had it with his hoping.

Case in point, Jaxon is pushing a beer across the table at him in that aggressive way that suggests, *I need to get you drunk so you stop moping* more than *fun night out with your BFF!* "Thanks," Rob says, swallowing a quarter of it in one gulp.

"Wings are coming," Jaxon says. He rubs a hand over his fade and leans back in his chair. "You hear back from him?"

Sometimes Rob isn't sure he should have told Jaxon about Percy, but if he hadn't spilled his guts within days of getting home, Jaxon would've figured it out, anyway. They've been friends since freshman year of high school, Rob the new kid trying to fit in, Jaxon the quiet loner who always had a book and who'd given up on fitting in years ago.

"No," Rob sighs. "I should probably move on, right?"

"You should've moved on weeks ago." Jaxon sips primly at his beer. "Just go on Grindr. Have a rebound hookup. Or three."

Rob groans, folds his arms on the table, and drops his head onto them. "I'm so sick of Grindr. It's so much effort and for what?"

"Orgasms."

Rob raises his head and his right hand. "I've got this for all my orgasm needs."

Making a face, Jaxon says, "Please don't tell me about your whacking technique."

"You asked for it."

"*Wow*, victim blaming!"

Rob laughs, which makes Jaxon look relieved. Yeah, he probably hasn't laughed much since coming back from South Africa. It's lucky Jaxon still wants to hang out with him, considering what a drag he's been.

Surreptitiously, he checks his phone. Just, you know. In case.

It would be weird if he got a response from Percy now, though. It's late in South Africa. Six hours ahead—that makes it eleven at night. Not exactly prime emailing-back-your-ex time.

With another sigh, Rob gulps his beer. Lovelorn thoughts notwithstanding, he really needs it. Beer just tastes better when it's hot, that's scientific fact. July in Atlanta's always hot and uncomfortable, but the last few days have been especially unbearable. People always think he's used to it when they find out he's from Hawai'i, but Oahu is mild in comparison. Plus, he spent four years freezing his butt off in Wisconsin.

Point is, the air outside feels thick enough to swim in. Their regular Friday night bar has the AC turned up to vent-rattling full blast, but every time the door opens, a wave of heat rolls through the place.

Jaxon eyes Rob beadily. "Put the phone away."

Guiltily, Rob jams it back in his pocket. "Sorry. I know. I *know*," he adds when Jaxon looks dubious. "It's just…. Jax, this guy. He was really special. And I blew it."

Jaxon shrugs. "Yeah, you kind of did, but if you ask me, if he was as special as you think he was, you could've talked it out."

"He wasn't in the greatest place."

"He'd email you back."

Scowling, Rob says, "It's almost like you want me to shut up about him." It's not fair, and the hurt expression on Jaxon's face makes Rob feel like a prick. With a sigh, Rob says, "Sorry. I mean, if you *did* want me to shut up about him, that would be understandable. I know I haven't been any fun to hang out with."

"You have a broken heart. It happens. You were there for me through the Beau Breakup."

This time, Rob scowls for a different reason. "*Beau.* Nothing but hate." Not only is Jaxon's ex a jerk, he also took their dog in the breakup—the dog whom Jaxon picked out and Beau didn't even want in the first place. "Not to diminish my own situation, but I'm kind of surprised you're comparing your two-year relationship with my two-week one."

"I can tell it was…." Jaxon pauses, clearly considering his words. "Intense. Anyway, I totally believe people can fall in love in two weeks."

"I never said I was in love with him," Rob protests unconvincingly.

"But," Jaxon says, then has to stop talking when their wings get delivered—classic buffalo for Rob, mango habanero for Jaxon. Which is insane. Rob's sweating just sitting here; there's no way he's going to eat food that will make him sweat more.

They both ask for refills on their beer, and when the waiter leaves, Jaxon finally finishes, "Just because you fell in love doesn't mean you should keep torturing yourself over him. If he's gonna let you get away, that's his loss."

"Aw." Rob puts a hand over his heart and bats his eyelashes, which makes Jaxon threaten to throw a mango habanero wing at him. He's touched, though, for real.

"Did he even say anything about your article?" Obviously, Rob's silence says everything, because Jaxon sighs. "Not cool."

"He's dealing with a lot," Rob says. Again. And more weakly this time. It *isn't* cool. Percy's agent was really nice about the piece, though. Very complimentary. She said he was talented and that Percy was lucky to have found someone who understood him so well.

Which had been a sucker punch from halfway across the world, but also a weird kind of relief. He hadn't been crazy about the connection between them, about the two of them getting each other on a level that Rob hasn't experienced maybe ever.

He thought about asking how Percy was doing, but Eunice probably wouldn't have told him. Not his business, as Percy's made abundantly clear.

Aaaand that makes him want to thunk his head down on the table again.

"We should go clubbing," Jaxon declares.

"You hate clubbing."

"Yeah, but you need to have some fun. I remember how restorative clubs were after Beau broke up with me." Jaxon finishes off a wing. "Nothing like a hot, drunk guy grinding all up on you to make you feel better."

"Maybe," Rob says reluctantly. "Honestly, Jax, I'd rather just play *Smash Brothers* or something. I feel...." *Raw*, his brain supplies, but it feels dramatic to say it out loud, no matter how true it is. It feels like his ribs have been bent backward, cracking into splinters, and his heart and lungs have to function exposed and inches from bone shards. This is how it's felt for a month. He's been miserable over Percy for longer than he and Percy were actually together.

He looks at his phone again, unable to help it. No email, but the date catches his eye for the millionth time today. His exposed heart scrapes itself over a broken rib. All day, he's been trying to forget that this was the day Percy was supposed to arrive. The Cape Town to ATL flight lands early in the morning after a brutal fifteen-and-a-half-hour red eye going west, so they'd be wrapping their first day up. Maybe they'd even be here, having Friday-night drinks with Jaxon. Or maybe Percy would have crashed hours ago, and they'd be tangled together in Rob's bed. And Rob would be holding Percy's warm body to his, a knee between Percy's legs and their hands clasped while Percy slept, and that would be so perfect that Rob wants to cry.

Jaxon watches him. "Yeah, you don't really look like you can handle a club tonight."

Rob fiddles with the leather bracelet wrapped three times around his wrist. At home, he wears it all the time, but he didn't bring it to South Africa, figuring extraneous jewelry wasn't very safari. Percy's piercings and hair jewelry proved him wrong on that.

Percy. Fuck. Every damn thought leads back to Percy, and Rob's caught between wishing it didn't and longing for it to be a good thing. Every thought leading back to Percy and Rob counting down the minutes until they can touch each other again.

His throat aches and his eyes sting. "Actually, Jax, I think I'm just gonna head home. I'm a mess, sorry."

"Yeah, your *Smash Brothers* game would probably suffer." The words are teasing, but Jaxon's tone is sad. "You know I'm always here for you, babe, right? Like, you need to talk, or not talk, or you want a wingman, or to get blackout drunk while I'm responsibly sober and keep you from making bad decisions, you tell me."

Which. Shit. Goddammit. Now Rob really *is* going to cry. "Thanks, man. What would I do without you?"

With a smile, Jaxon says, "I don't know if anyone else knows which liquors you definitely can't mix, so you'd probably have puked a lot more over the years."

Rob's laugh is kind of snotty, but at least it's a laugh. "Such a beautiful friendship."

They finish their wings and their beers, settle up the bill, and head outside. Even with the heat, groups of friends and couples throng the Old Fourth Ward's streets. Showing the neighborhood to Percy would have been an awesome way to spend a day if he was here now.

But he's not, and Rob really has to get over him. Stop imagining what it would be like to be here with him. Stop imagining how he might react to everything, what restaurants he'd like.

Rob and Jaxon reach the Atlanta Beltline, the biking and walking trail that runs from Midtown to Reynoldstown. As Jaxon unlocks his bike from the rack, he asks, "You want to walk for a while?"

Shaking his head, Rob says, "Nah. You better get home to the new kitty."

Though Jaxon doesn't look convinced, he straps his helmet on and gives Rob a hug. When he hops on his bike and rides off, Rob waves, then slumps against the bike rack. Maybe he should get a cat too. Getting Lily really helped Jaxon through his breakup with his ex. Except, no. Rob travels too much for a pet. Also, he and Percy were barely a thing.

He sighs and kicks a tuft of grass. Maybe he'll take a walk after all. As the sun gets lower, it's starting to cool off, and being surrounded by people while not needing to interact with any of them might do him some good.

Chapter Twenty-Six

Percy pinches his arm for the fifth time in the last ten minutes and struggles to contain a yawn. It's not quite seven in the evening and he's determined to fight his exhaustion and jet lag until at least nine. It means he's been up for… er… all right, well, his brain isn't quite up for the math at the minute, but a long time. His flight left Cape Town at nine thirty last night and arrived in Atlanta, Georgia, at seven thirty this morning. Normally he can sleep on planes, but knowing he was going to get in touch with Rob and hope to speak to him? Sleep wasn't an option.

After he arrived, he met with the Explore Georgia people, who couldn't seem to stop thanking him and telling him what huge fans they were of his work. Percy has a feeling that after their previous photographer dropped the job, they frantically googled "nature photographers"—and he came up because he's been in the news.

It's fine. The job won't be challenging, but he'll get them some fantastic photos.

More importantly, he's now in the same city as Rob.

So far, he hasn't done anything about that. His meeting with Explore Georgia was over by lunchtime, at which point he dithered over whether he should call or text Rob. A text seemed better. Or safer, at least.

Now it's nearly seven o'clock and he still hasn't texted, though he *has* had several lattes at the quirky coffee shop he found as he wandered Atlanta's Old Fourth Ward. Google said the neighborhood was trendy, which was good enough for him in his exhausted, jittery state.

Percy lets his head flop back over the back of his patio chair. City sounds wash over him—traffic and car horns, bass thumping from passing cars, the whirr of air conditioner compressors. It's absurdly hot, but it doesn't seem to be keeping anyone inside. Google wasn't wrong about this being a trendy area. As afternoon ticked into evening, more and more people came out to throng the bars and restaurants.

Maybe Rob is one of them. Maybe he's on a date. It's Friday night and he's single. Who wouldn't want to go on a date with Rob? Gorgeous, funny, kind Rob, who anyone would be lucky to go out with.

So why does Percy keep stalling? He took this job specifically because it would bring him in close proximity to Rob. He took this job specifically so he would have an excuse to see Rob. To apologize to him. And maybe, if he's very, *very* lucky, to give their relationship a second try. It's more of a first try, really. Percy's not sure if before counted as a relationship when he ended things less than twenty-four hours after they started.

In all seriousness, the question *Why does he keep stalling?* is an easy one. This is one he's gone over in therapy. Rather a lot. Rather every-third-session a lot, in fact (which is more than it may sound like, because he's been going to therapy four days a week for the past month). He stalls because if he keeps being *almost* ready to do something difficult and emotionally vulnerable, then he hasn't yet been rejected.

Dr. Mente usually asks him why he's so convinced he'll be rejected, and Percy usually follows that up with dodging the question. Because he's been rejected. Because he wants love. Because he doesn't want to be hurt. Because who wants to be rejected?

One of the staff comes outside to wipe down tables. "Still doing okay?" she asks.

"Yes, thanks." He sucks at his iced latte to avoid having to talk anymore, and she moves off.

What if Rob doesn't actually want to hear from him? What if Percy texts him, and he sits here holding his phone like an idiot, tapping it to keep the screen lit, while he waits for a reply that's never going to arrive? After all, Percy didn't respond to Rob's email. That was a perfect, golden chance to make contact, and Percy just… didn't. Instead, he got on a plane and flew across the world.

To sit. To sit at a coffee shop and not text the man he came here to see.

He puts down the iced latte and grabs his phone off the table, devoting all his concentration into not freaking out about what he's going to do. He's not even going to think about what he's doing. His hands are simply picking up his phone and going to WhatsApp, and he's not thinking not thinking *not thinking* about what name he's pulling up or how Rob will probably block him, or maybe send him a message first to tell him what a rubbish person Percy is, and how he's happy they didn't end up in a relationship. Bullet dodged, there! Eat shit, de Villiers.

The inspired, sharply intelligent message he's managed to type so far consists of: *Hi Rob*

Sure to win hearts and minds!

Percy presses his thumbs against his phone screen, squeezing as hard as he can, until his skin looks bloodless and dull.

This is a mistake. He'll fuck it up if he messages Rob. This whole thing was a mistake. He shouldn't have come here, though actually he's sort of excited about the job now, because the part of the state he's going to does look quite pretty, but he didn't come here for that *really*, did he? *Let's be honest, Percy, that job was just the excuse you needed to get on that plane.*

His thumb slips across the screen, and suddenly his phone is doing something—something that looks alarmingly like making a call.

"No no no no," he breathes, searching for the end call button.

The screen changes from black to pixelated color. "Percy?" comes Rob's voice from the speaker.

And then. Then. There he is. Rob Hale, as gorgeous as ever, even with the unflattering angles of a video call. Percy makes a strangled sound, then forces himself to say, "Hi."

He's quite sure he looks like a deer caught in headlights. It's not the impression he wanted to make.

Rob looks befuddled, but not unhappy. "Percy," he says again, a statement this time, like he can't quite believe it. "Percy, you're… I never heard back from you. My email, I mean. You didn't respond. I didn't think you were going to."

"No, I—writing back didn't seem enough, I…." *Got on a plane and flew here to see you.* "Um, is this a good time? I can call later."

"No, no, it's fine! This is a good time. Anyway, it's late for you—midnight, right?" Rob glances around, apparently unaware how devastating that offhand observation was. The fact that he knows the time difference and would think of that is the kind of care Percy doesn't deserve from Rob Hale, not after the way he treated him.

"Well, yeah, five hours, but—"

"Hold on, I'm just gonna duck into this coffee place; it'll be quieter."

The wrought iron gate of Percy's coffee shop squeals as someone pushes it open. Percy glances up and freezes.

It's Rob.

Rob is standing stock-still too. The gate bumps against his thigh as it swings closed.

"Perce?" Rob asks, a waver in his voice as though he's afraid he's hallucinating.

Percy opens his mouth, but nothing comes out because his throat has suddenly become as tight as his fingers clenched around his phone. Texting was supposed to give him time to work out the right words to give him the best chance to win Rob back. Right now there are no words. Not one. But Rob's here, so Percy had better find some now now.

"I was trying to text you" is what comes out of his mouth.

Brilliant.

A ghost of a smile appears on Rob's face as he approaches Percy's table. "You have to tap the little paper airplane symbol after you type something for that."

"So that's what I was doing wrong," Percy quips right back. It's so easy, like the past month and a half didn't happen—like Percy didn't freak out and dump Rob at the Departures drop-off.

Rob huffs a little laugh, comes close enough to Percy's table that he could reach out a hand to touch it and stops. "Are you really here?" he asks. "I'm not losing it, am I?"

Percy pushes back his chair with a loud concrete scrape and stands. His legs feel like they're made of wet cardboard and his heart is beating way too fast. Jet lag, caffeine, and nerves, which now strikes him as an awful combination for this conversation.

"I got here this morning," he says. His entire body prickles with the need to touch Rob, but he can't, and it's all his fault.

The coffee shop's door opens and a group of laughing teenagers come through. Rob glances at them, then back to Percy. There's a question in his eyes, and a gleam of wounded hope.

And Percy could stall and dither and waffle and tell himself he doesn't want to have this conversation where some teenagers can livestream his possible humiliation and devastation, but this is exactly what he's been working on in therapy. Sometimes you need to risk rejection.

Also, this is America, and no one cares about him or his father here.

"I'm sorry," Percy says. "The way I treated you at the airport was terrible. And I'm ashamed, and I was… I was so scared you'd never want to speak to me again, and that's why I never got in contact with you. It's a terrible excuse. Not an excuse, I mean… I'm not trying to justify why I've acted the way I've done. Just, that's the reason, and as long as I didn't say anything to you, I could still imagine that maybe you wouldn't laugh in my face and block me, but once I'd done it, that would be it, and I'd have used my one chance, and—"

"Percy." Rob leans on the table, his hands splayed and strong arms bracing himself. He's wearing a leather wrap bracelet around one wrist and the sleeves of his T-shirt hug his biceps. "Do you want to take a walk?"

"Yes." The word is out of his mouth before he has a chance to register the question. A question isn't forgiveness, but it also isn't rejection.

They leave the coffee shop. Percy still feels shaky. Adrenaline has probably been added to the mix of jet lag, caffeine, and nerves. It keeps his throat locked up tight as they walk slowly, side by side, along the street. Their shoulders bump, then their wrists, and Percy wants to ask Rob to just say something, to just put him out of his misery. If they're over because Percy was a prick, he just needs to hear it. He's spent a month avoiding a situation where he might, but now he can't stand not knowing.

"So you got my email," Rob finally says.

It takes a second for Percy to swallow past the lump in his throat. "Yeah."

Out of the corner of his eye, Percy sees a muscle in Rob's jaw ticking. Finally, Rob says, "It's been kind of killing me that you didn't respond."

There's no hope of swallowing the lump in his throat, now. "I didn't know how to write what I wanted to say."

"You could've tried."

Yeah. He could've. Percy's eyes sting. "I'm sorry."

Rob shakes his head and stops walking, turning so they're facing each other. They're standing in front of an apartment building and a brewpub, and the noise of conversation and laughter floats on the hot, humid air. "Are you here because you want to give us another shot? Is that what this is? Because if you're just here to, like, apologize, because you feel bad or whatever, and you need me to absolve you or forgive you or something, I don't know if I can do that. I really…. That plane ride sucked, you know? I like you so much, it's stupid. I can't stop thinking about you, and… I don't… fuck. I don't even know." He rakes his hand through his hair.

"You still like me?" Percy asks.

The hurt on Rob's face and the way he looks at the ground, dark hair falling over his forehead in waves, makes Percy want to kill whoever put that expression there, even though he knows full well it was himself. "Can't make myself stop," Rob replies.

There's something in Percy's chest struggling to get out. Something frantic and scrabbling, all skittering claws and sharp teeth. "I want to give us another shot," he blurts. "Yes. God, yes, that's why I—yes. I'm here to beg you to take me back. I mean, I'm prepared to beg. If that's what it takes. I will. Down on my knees, the whole shebang."

That flicker-fast hint of amusement reappears on Rob's face. "Slow down. You don't have to get on your knees unless I take you back."

They stare at each other, Rob's eyes catching the fading summer sun and turning umber and gold. Then he cracks a smile, and Percy's smile follows, and Percy says again, "I'm sorry. I'm so sorry. I was awful to you."

"I shouldn't have kept it from you once I found out there was a hit piece about you online." Rob's expression grows serious again. "You were right to be upset about that."

"I didn't have to be as upset as I was. We could've talked about it."

"Well… yeah." Rob takes a deep breath. "But we're talking about it now."

Percy's heart thrums at his wrists and his throat. "It's something worth talking about, then?"

There's a light touch at his fingertips, a whisper of skin against skin. "It's worth it to me." Rob's fingers slip between Percy's but don't close. "If it's worth it to you."

All Percy can do is laugh and curl his fingers around Rob's, holding tight to his hand. "I flew halfway around the world. Of course it's worth it to me."

Rob tugs him closer, and then his strong arms wrap Percy up. Percy hugs him back fiercely. Someone's heart is pounding, but it doesn't matter whose. "Where are you staying?" Rob murmurs into Percy's neck.

"Um." He has to think about that for a moment. These sorts of hotels blur together in his mind, especially when he's been awake for thirty-six hours. "The Marriott downtown."

"You wanna come back to my place to talk?"

Percy doesn't care if "talking" is thinly veiled code for sex or actual talking. Ever since Rob walked away from him at the airport, he's missed both, but the worst loss of all was the severing of the connection between them. The intimacy Percy feels with Rob is unlike anything he's felt with anyone else, and once he threw it away, he understood just how rare and priceless it was.

"Yeah," Percy says. "Yeah, I'd love that."

Chapter Twenty-Seven

Rob doesn't do his safest driving on the way home. But how is he supposed to stop looking at Percy to make sure he's really there? That this is actually happening? How *is* this happening? In his wildest fantasies, he never imagined Percy would *show up.* Here. In Atlanta. Looking for Rob, because he wants to apologize. Because he still wants to be together.

If this is a dream, Rob hopes he never wakes up. If he's in the Matrix, he's happy to stay hooked up to the feeding tubes. As long as he can keep living this life where Percy's sitting next to him in his car while they drive up 85.

Jax texts that he got home while Rob's driving, which his car automatically reads out loud. "Jaxon is my best friend," Rob reminds Percy, because—well, because this is all suddenly information that's relevant to Percy. All of Rob's friends, his home, his city, his favorite spots. They've gone from things Percy would never know about to things he's *going* to know about.

Rob doesn't reply to Jaxon because it feels a little weird to be all *Guess what, Percy didn't just EMAIL back, he showed up!!* and take the chance that Jaxon will respond with something Percy isn't meant to hear.

When they arrive at Rob's house, Rob has to take a moment just to look at Percy in the passenger seat. The sun is skimming the tops of the trees now, and rich summer light dapples over Percy's face as the leaves of the big oak next to the driveway whisper against each other in the slight breeze.

"What?" Percy asks, but he doesn't sound nervous. There's something different about him. Something more solid. Like he has his feet planted more firmly, like he's realized he's strong enough to stand and fight.

It's making Rob even more crazy about him, but his invitation to talk was sincere. Talking has to come first. They didn't talk enough before and look what happened.

Rob shakes his head and smiles. "Nothing. Just—still wrapping my head around the fact that you're here."

A bright smile cracks Percy's face. "Me too, honestly."

With a quick, light touch to the back of Percy's hand, Rob opens his door. "C'mon, let me show you around hale o Hale." At Percy's bemused look, he chuckles. "'Hale' means house in Hawaiian."

Percy looks like he's suppressing either laughter or a groan, and both would be totally fair. "Do you use that on everyone you invite home?"

"Only the ones I invite home to talk," Rob says very seriously. His emotions have been a roller coaster over the past few hours, but now he's quickly climbing above the clouds, giddiness rising through him.

They ascend the crumbling concrete steps to the front door. The lawn is both overgrown and scraggly, and all his attempts at gardening have failed. There's a sad azalea next to the door that hangs on year after year and even manages to bloom each June. It still has some orange flowers clinging to its branches now, despite Rob's total neglect of it.

"This is pretty," Percy says, fingering one of the azalea's leaves.

"Probably could be prettier," Rob says, turning the key in the lock.

"I'll look up how to take care of it," Percy says vaguely as he follows Rob inside. Something happy squirms in Rob's stomach.

His house isn't company ready and definitely isn't boyfriend ready. Or guy who was your boyfriend and hopefully is going to be your boyfriend again. There's a pile of shirts on one end of the sofa, which Rob now can't remember if they're dirty or clean. Dirty dishes are piled in the sink and have started colonizing the counter. There's a pizza box he meant to throw out last night, and now the place smells like pizza crust and grease-saturated cardboard.

Rob freezes just inside. Shit. "I, uh," he says. Jesus, this is humiliating. Percy brought him to this beautiful, meticulously kept apartment in Cape Town, one of the most gorgeous cities Rob has ever been to. Rob, in turn, brought Percy to a dirty house in a very meh suburb of Atlanta.

When he looks at Percy, wincing, he's met with an expression on Percy's face that looks awfully like… joy? That can't be right, but Percy says a little breathlessly, "This is your house."

"Embarrassingly, yeah." Rob kicks an empty Amazon box behind a shoe rack. "Sorry for the mess."

Percy touches his wrist. "I showed up out of nowhere. You don't have to apologize."

"Your place was clean when you brought me back there."

"That's because I'm mentally ill, Rob, not because I'm innately a neater person than you."

Rob surveys his living room and kitchen again. "No, I think you're probably an innately neater person than me."

The fact that Percy just makes a noise is charitable. Rob spends a minute pointlessly tidying before he realizes it's a lost cause. He grabs the clothes off the sofa and dumps them inside his bedroom.

Fleetingly, he thinks maybe that's just kicking the can, because what if they move their conversation into the bedroom? Except—no. As much as Rob has missed fucking Percy, it feels too soon to jump into bed with him tonight. Rob needs a minute. Their relationship needs a minute.

When he comes back out to the living room, Percy is still standing by the door, and Rob feels like he's failing the Southern hospitality test, even if he isn't Southern by birth. His parents wouldn't be too impressed with his housekeeping either, both because they're Hawaiian and because they're parents.

Actually, Jesus, he needs to call his parents. His mom keeps making him food because she can tell something's wrong, but he's been really vague about what. Should he take Percy to meet his parents?

WOW, he needs to slow his roll. If he doesn't want to fuck Percy tonight, he definitely doesn't need to be thinking about introducing Percy to his parents.

"You can sit down," Rob says. His voice comes out kind of squeaky. It's crazy nerve-wracking having Percy in his house. Was Percy this nervous when he brought Rob home? "Can I get you something? Despite appearances to the contrary, I actually have more in my refrigerator than beer and a jar of pickles."

Hopefully.

"Some water, maybe?" Percy rubs his face. Even though Rob's been looking at him practically nonstop since they ran into each other at the coffee place, this is the first time he's really *looked* at Percy. The guy looks exhausted. His eyes are puffy and bloodshot, shadowed by dark circles. There's a wanness to his skin, and he's scruffy the way he was when they were in the bush.

"Water coming right up." Rob moves to the kitchen, which is only separated from the living room by a counter. As he fills a glass of water from the fridge door, he asks, "What about food? Are you hungry?"

"No, that's okay. My body clock is too fucked to eat proper meals the day I land."

When Rob brings the water out, Percy's settling into the sofa. It's surreal to see him sitting there. The beads and wires in his twists glint in the light of Rob's Target lamp. The silhouette of his bun in front of the living room mini-blinds feels like a work of art. *Beautiful man on IKEA sofa, 2020s.* Or maybe that's just Percy.

Rob sits down, leaving an amount of space between them that he tries really hard not to second-guess. Percy gulps down the water in a few swallows.

As Rob watches his throat move, he reminds himself sternly that they're not fucking tonight.

"You really flew in today?" Rob asks. Now that they're sitting here, he doesn't know how to begin their Serious Conversation. All his brain can do is squeal at him that Percy! Is here! Percy's here! In his house!

"Yeah." Percy peers into the glass like he expects more water to materialize, so Rob gets him more.

"So you landed this morning? How long have you been awake?"

"I haven't had enough sleep in two days to work that out."

Percy drinks half of his second glass of water as Rob settles next to him again. There's probably nothing subtle about the way Rob's watching his throat move, but whatever. It's not exactly a mystery that Rob's attracted to Percy. "When I got back from Cape Town, I crashed by noon," Rob says.

With a tiny flinch, Percy says, "That's not surprising, all things considered."

"Guess not." Rob picks at a loose thread on one of the sofa pillows. "So… yeah. Talking. We should do that."

Percy glances at him and smiles hesitantly. "I thought you'd have a lot you wanted to say to me. Possibly to shout at me."

"Don't like shouting," Rob murmurs. It seems to almost baffle Percy, so Rob files that information away. In some ways, it's the first thing Rob's learned about Percy's childhood. "And I mean, I did. I wanted to ask you what I did wrong, and why it was so bad. But then I figured it out. Then I wanted to apologize and promise I'd never do anything like that again. Then I thought, I have no idea what things are like for you, so how can I make that promise?"

"I didn't tell you what things are like for me," Percy says. "Not really."

"No," Rob agrees. "You didn't."

They're both silent for a minute. Percy takes another sip of water. "After you left, I started going to therapy. I got prescribed some medication. It's… helping. It's not perfect, but it's easier for me to… take a step back, I suppose?"

"That's awesome," Rob says. Impulsively, he takes Percy's hand. "Seriously. That's really good."

Hopefully he's not coming off as patronizing. Percy squeezes his hand back, so he'll take that as a good sign. "I was on meds years ago, but I got it into my head that I needed to suffer for my art. Or something rubbish like that." His thumb rubs along Rob's in that absentminded way that's like a shorthand for intimacy. "Anyway, I realized in therapy that I've never talked to you about my father."

That throws Rob for a loop. "I thought you didn't want to talk about him."

"No, I didn't. Not at all. I still don't." Percy's expression gets fierce and angry. "What he did makes me sick. But it's…." He waves a hand vaguely. "It's defining my life right now. *Our* relationship has been all wrapped up in my father stealing from the South African government. I never would have even met you without that happening, but I was trying to separate the two, and… I'm not making very much sense, am I?"

"I think I get what you're saying." Rob turns Percy's hand over, still holding it, and traces patterns in his palm with his other hand. "You were trying to compartmentalize and things got…."

"Away from me," Percy supplies. His gaze follows the path of Rob's finger on his palm. "They didn't stay neatly in the boxes I wanted them to, and it was overwhelming. And terrifying. And I think that I put you in a bit of a box too? You were so kind and good at listening. I said I didn't want to talk about my family, and you didn't ask me about my family. You did everything I asked when we were in the bush—"

Rob shakes his head. "That's not exactly true. I followed you that evening. You told me to stay by the fire? And you, well."

"Freaked out."

Definitely not the words Rob would have chosen.

Percy scrubs at his scruffy chin. "That's my point, though. You put a toe out of step with the way I expected you to act, and I couldn't handle it. I just—I don't know." His teeth click as he clamps his mouth shut. His face reddens. "I'm probably talking too much."

"No, talking is good. Talking is why we're here." Or maybe *not* talking is why they're there. Rob tries not to sound needy as he asks, "So if I didn't stay in the box you thought I fit into, do you actually, you know… like me?"

Percy's head snaps up so fast that it cracks. "*Like* you? Rob, I l—" His eyes get wide and his voice cuts off. After a second, he finishes. "Ja, of course I like you."

And yeah, maybe Rob should have trusted Percy to figure that out before he came here. This is a different Percy than the man from Cape Town. This is a Percy who's… talking. Opening up. Who seems surer of himself. This is a Percy who isn't just confident in his creative and professional abilities, but in his personal choices.

It makes Rob so happy to see that he's afraid the feeling might suffocate him. "Just making sure."

"If the whole flying here to try to win you back wasn't convincing enough?" Percy's mouth quirks into a smile.

"Hey, you probably have a lot of miles." Rob bumps his shoulder against Percy's, and neither of them pull away. The warm press of contact feels like an acknowledgment of something. Like forgiveness and fresh starts and, maybe, a promise.

He takes a breath. "I know you're going through a really hard time, and you're dealing with stuff that I have no frame of reference for. And you have every right to feel shitty about all of it, and to be overwhelmed sometimes. Honestly, I don't actually know how you hold it together as much as you do."

Meeting Rob's eyes, Percy says, "But?" He looks scared and vulnerable, a flash of the Percy from when things fell apart in Cape Town.

Rob covers Percy's hand with his. "If I do the wrong thing, or I act like an asshole, just give us a chance to talk through it?"

"Yes," Percy says fiercely. "Of course. What happened in Cape Town—I won't ever do that to you again. We'll talk and we'll work things out."

"Unless we can't, I guess," Rob says out of a possibly misguided sense that he should acknowledge that they aren't proposing marriage to each other.

"Right, unless we can't." Percy's shoulder presses against Rob's harder. "But we've worked things out now?"

Words aren't up to the task of telling Percy what Rob wants to tell him. Instead, he turns to face Percy, puts both hands on his scruffy chin, and leans forward to kiss him.

It's a soft kiss, an I-forgive-you kiss. An I-want-to-try-again kiss.

An I-probably-love-you kiss, for all Rob just acknowledged the possibility that they might not work out. If he has anything to say about it, they're working out. This time, they're going to do it right.

With a quiet sigh, Percy curls his fingers around the back of Rob's neck. They sink into his hair and press into his scalp, four points of light on his skin that race like lightning straight to his chest and illuminate his heart like a theater marquee. When Percy kisses Rob back, all that light sparkles through the rest of his body, through all his veins and nerves to seethe under his skin. He thought he knew how much he missed the feeling of Percy's lips on his. Now that it's happening, he realizes if he'd let himself miss it as much as he should have, he wouldn't have been able to function for the lack of it.

Percy's lips, even chapped and dry from plane air, are soft and warm and perfect. He kisses Rob like he's holding back a surge of feeling, like when the time is right, he's going to let it all loose and Rob won't know what hit him.

Fuck, Rob's here for it. When the time's right, yeah. He's going to make sure Percy lets go.

They break apart but keep their hands on each other. Percy's dark, liquid eyes look so full of feeling that Rob wants to brush them closed and kiss his eyelids. His chest swells again with stifling, overwhelming emotion. He's never felt this tenderness before, not for anyone. It's new and scary and wonderful.

Percy yawns.

It's not a little yawn, either. Nothing demure about it. His jaw opens so wide he almost looks like one of those videos of a snake trying to eat something that's ten times bigger than it. It is easily one of the least sexy things he's ever seen Percy do.

With a laugh, he wraps his arms around Percy, pulling him into a tight hug. Percy lets out a surprised yelp, then hugs Rob back hard. "I'm so glad you're here," Rob mumbles against Percy's neck. "So glad. But you're obviously exhausted. Let me drive you back to your hotel. What does your day look like tomorrow?"

Percy does some combination of sagging and curling into Rob. Tenderness surges in Rob's chest again. "I have to get a rental car so I can drive to someplace called Ellijay? I have a room at a Best Western there tomorrow."

"I'm gonna assume you didn't break some other guy's heart up in Ellijay who you have to apologize to?" When Percy's spine stiffens, Rob wants to thump himself on the forehead. "Sorry, baby. Bad joke."

"Terms of endearment again," Percy says, sounding pleased.

"Uh-huh." Tracing the wing of Percy's shoulder blade, Rob asks, "Seriously, though, what's in Ellijay? Isn't that one of those touristy mountain towns?"

With another yawn, Percy says, "Yeah. I took a job with Explore Georgia just in case you didn't want to see me and I needed to save face."

The idea of Percy working for Explore Georgia kind of cracks him up, but he doesn't laugh in case Percy takes it the wrong way. "Well, if you're going into the mountains, it'll be pretty." His heart sinks, though, because it means he won't see Percy until he gets back from working.

Percy's fingers find the edge of Rob's rib cage and follow it to his chest. "Want to come?"

And just like that, his heart is fluttering again. "Really?"

"Of course really." Percy pauses. "They aren't putting me up anywhere nice. The Explore Georgia people. And I know it's not exactly a safari—"

"What time do I need to be ready to go tomorrow?" Rob interrupts.

Instead of answering right away, Percy straightens to look Rob in the eyes. His gaze is exhausted but soft. Content? Certainly more content than Rob's seen him since they were in the bush. Maybe more content than he's ever seen Percy.

Percy makes a tiny noise and touches his fingers to Rob's lips. "Nine. Text me your address. I'll pick you up."

Rob kisses Percy's fingers, then Percy's mouth.

And then they spend some time making up for the past month and a half apart. They have a lot of kissing to catch up with.

Part Five: North Georgia Mountains

Chapter Twenty-Eight

Inviting Rob along on the shoot was an impulsive decision, but Percy doesn't regret it for a second. He takes an Uber downtown to his hotel to save Rob the drive (Rob insists he doesn't mind, but Percy remains firm) and barely stays awake through his nightly routine.

The next thing he knows, his alarm is going off, and he's thrashing upright under sheets and a duvet that he has no memory of crawling under last night. Actually, for a second, he has no memories at all, but then the previous day comes rushing back. He has to lie back down and take a moment, because—Rob. *Rob.* Rob still wants to be with him, and they're going to spend the next several days together.

He makes himself get out of bed, takes his meds, brushes his teeth, showers, and spends too much time choosing what to wear from his limited wardrobe, especially considering he'll be spending the day in a car and possibly doing a little hiking—it all depends on what catches his eye along the way.

Looking his best for Rob outweighs all logical considerations, though. Ideally, Percy will be treated to that hungry look Rob always got in his eyes when Percy wore something tight. He's missed that.

Finally, he settles on skinny chinos, cuffed at the ankles, and a pink T-shirt that makes his biceps look good. He does a little maintenance on his twists before tying them into a bun. Then it's off to the car rental place in the already thick-aired Atlanta morning. Once he has the car, he texts Rob to let him know he's on his way, immediately getting a series of happy emojis back. And a few trees, which makes Percy smile like an idiot.

In the syrupy morning light, Rob's house looks even homier than it did last night. It was obvious that Rob was a little… maybe not embarrassed, but definitely conscious of the difference in the way they live. It's probably unavoidable. It's always been unavoidable at home. There's been a period with everyone he's ever brought home, whether friend, boyfriend, or hookup, where things are weird. Percy's rich; most of the people in his life aren't.

Rob's townhouse is genuinely charming, though. The big tree by the driveway shades the front lawn. There are garden beds that have been neglected but look like they could be easily tamed. Whatever's growing in the bed around the mailbox (so American!) is buzzing with fat bumblebees.

The house itself is well-kept. It's built into a hillside, so the lawn slopes up, and is painted a sky blue that reminds Percy of Bo-Kaap. It's a brighter color than he expects from American suburban houses.

Percy climbs the concrete steps, running his hand along the white-painted wood railing, but before he can ring the doorbell, the door flies open.

"Hi!" Rob exclaims breathlessly. There's a duffel bag slung across his chest and his hair is damp, like he just got out of the shower. It curls around his ears when it's wet, which sucker punches Percy. He hadn't realized he'd noticed such a thing, but now all he can think about is how much he missed seeing it.

"I made some coffee if you want it?" Rob reaches for something in the house and brandishes a travel thermos at Percy. There's a peach emoji on it.

"Thanks." Percy takes it and rotates it so Rob can see the peach. "Is this meant to be topical, since I'm working for the state, or is it sexual innuendo?"

Rob's easy, crooked smile makes Percy's knees weak. "Can't it be both?"

That's a nice thought. Percy's not sure how slow Rob wants to take things. Whatever he wants, Percy will respect. If he needs more time before they start fucking again, Percy will give it to him. Percy gets it. The way he broke Rob's trust, it's no surprise he needs a little time. It's probably good for Percy, too, even if he *is* really horny.

They stand there looking at each other, then both start speaking at the same time. Percy motions for Rob to go first, and Rob asks, "Do you need to use the bathroom or anything before we get on the road?"

"No, I'm okay."

"What were you going to say?"

"No, nothing, just if you're ready to go or need a few more minutes."

Rob shakes his head. "No, I'm ready to go." He snorts, sounding somewhere between amused and exasperated, and leans forward to kiss Percy lightly. The softness and gentleness of it wraps gauzily around Percy and he puts his hands to Rob's chest.

Standing in the doorway kissing could easily turn into an all-morning activity, so Percy reluctantly breaks it after a minute. "Can we do more of that later?"

In answer, Rob plants a kiss on the side of Percy's neck and huffs into his skin, "We're definitely doing more of that later."

They put Rob's duffel in the trunk with Percy's backpack and get on the road. The car, Toyota-Camry-or-similar, is sort of terrifying to drive around Atlanta. Percy feels much too low to the ground and like a massive 4x4 or bakkie is going to roll right over him. Hopefully it will be better in the mountains. He feels ridiculous being nervous about driving, but Rob doesn't make fun of him when he drives significantly slower than everyone else.

If nothing else, there's less traffic once they leave the sprawling Atlanta metropolitan area. The big box stores and fast-casual restaurants give way to long, straight sections of motorway with tall, dense trees on either side. Sometimes they're completely covered in leafy vines, so they don't look like individual trees at all, but just one rippling carpet of green towering like mountains.

The motorway—no, freeway, that's what they call it in America—eventually turns to a highway with traffic signals. They drive through small towns while the terrain becomes more rolling, hills rising in the distance.

They stop at a Waffle House for brunch. Everything is sticky, from the floor to the table to the menus. Even the cutlery, somehow, is sticky, but it's worth it because the food is horrifically delicious. Horrifically unhealthy, too, Percy's sure. But he's embracing the American South while he's here. Especially when he can tell how happy Rob is that Percy likes Waffle House.

"It's a Southern institution," Rob says. "When we first moved here, I thought it was gross."

"Because of the stickiness?" Percy guesses.

"Yeah. I mean, I guess it's still pretty gross. But that peanut butter chip waffle, man"—he kisses his fingers—"fucking amazing."

He looks *so* happy, a big grin on his face and eyes bright and brown, and Percy wants to pull him into a hug even though they're in the middle of the parking lot. At the last second, he stops. In Atlanta, there were rainbow flags and bumper stickers on people's cars that made it obvious there were plenty of here-and-queer people. Percy hasn't seen any since they left the suburbs.

It makes the back of his neck prickle with the awareness of how out in the open they are. Not that Percy hasn't been places where it's unsafe to be gay. He most certainly has. But he's never been in them with a romantic partner.

And he looks very gay right now, doesn't he?

When they're back in the car and driving up the highway again, Percy asks bluntly, "Do we need to not act like a couple in public while we're here?"

There's a flash of giddiness on Rob's face—that would be the fact that Percy called them a couple, and it does something to Percy's insides too—that fades to uncertainty. "Oh. I don't know, actually. Was someone looking at us weird at Waffle House?"

"No, no. I mean, I don't think so?" It had actually struck Percy that their server might be queer, herself. "But I just don't want to invite negative attention."

Before Percy was even done speaking, Rob was on his phone. "Okay well, can't find anything about Ellijay, but Blue Ridge apparently has a big queer community? Oh! Yeah, I've totally been to this place! Oh my god, this town is so cute, Perce. We should go if we have time."

It's quite literally impossible for Percy to not reach over to brush his fingers through Rob's hair, just to feel the warmth of his skin. Every single one of Rob's smiles feels like a gift. Percy wants to be worthy of them. "I bet I could ring the Explore Georgia people to get our hotel reservation switched to Blue Ridge."

They come to a traffic signal and stop, so Percy unlocks his phone to find their number. Rob's practically bouncing in the passenger seat as Percy rings and gets the whole thing taken care of within ten minutes. By the time they're driving through the next small town, they've forwarded him the confirmation email.

It's the same hotel chain, so still nothing special, but Rob's excitement is infectious. Plus, Percy will feel better if it's a queer-friendly place. He doesn't think he can keep himself from touching Rob in public, and he shouldn't have to. An extra bonus? No one gives a toss about him here. He's a nobody.

Once they're in the mountains, Percy starts looking for photo opportunities. He gets off the highway to take smaller winding roads.

The area's beauty rewards him. The roads are serpentine and twist through glades, following clear streams burbling around mossy rocks.

Mountains rise around them, their slopes thick with tall, ancient-looking trees. Oak spread over their heads, their branches and leaves a green bower. The air smells fresh and clean, with a tendril of loaminess that gives it a tinge of wildness. Every time they get out of the car, birdsong fills the forest around them.

They drive over the greatest bridge, stone arched with moss and lichen clinging to the masonry. The sun's hitting the water and the bridge just right, making the green of the moss look extra green and the background warm. Percy drops the ISO and ratchets the aperture up, hoping he can get a long exposure shot of the water. The daylight might still be too bright, but he's got some really nice shots by trying despite conventional wisdom.

After the water, he tries to capture the movement of the light dappling through the leaves, the play of sun and shadow and the way the shafts of light have a heft and solidity as they cut through to the forest floor.

They move on only to stop a few minutes later for more photos, then repeat the process again another ten minutes after that. It's only after the daylight starts fading to dusty lavender gloaming that Percy realizes anyone would be sick of him by now. He should have warned Rob what coming on a work trip would entail, even though…. Well, he supposes Rob has already been on a work trip with him.

But "I love watching you work" is what Rob says, and Percy has to take a moment.

They're about to get back in the car, but a fierce rush of feeling rips through Percy and he has to stop. Stop, catch his breath, try not to push Rob up against the door and kiss the hell out of him. Rob said he wants to take it slow. Percy will just keep reminding himself. He doesn't want to fuck this up again, because he cares about Rob too much.

As they get back in the car, Percy can't stop himself from laying a hand over Rob's. Rob turns his hand over and interlaces their fingers.

Even though it isn't safe driving, they hold hands for the rest of the drive, as the mountain road twists around boulders and ancient trees and rockfall, following the course of the clear, cold water. Percy sneaks as many glances at Rob as he can, wishing he could capture this moment in a photo while knowing he never could.

Rob looks gilt, limned in honeyed sunset light. That fierce rushing feeling is still filling Percy up, until he feels like he might burst with it.

It's love, isn't it? This aching tenderness, this feeling that he never wants to go another day not speaking to Rob, not having him in his life. This certainty that all he wants is to make Rob smile, to see him happy.

If it's not love, Percy doesn't know what love is.

There's a frantic part of his brain that overdrives straight into panic—and then a fuzz of well-adjustedness blankets it before it can go further. This is okay. It's scary, but it's okay.

The scared part of his brain tells him it's *not* okay, that he acted badly and what right does he have to love Rob? Does he expect Rob to love him *back*? Who would love Percy back when his father is a criminal?

Except Rob's sitting here in the car with him, and their hands are intertwined. That's enough for Percy to shush the scared part of his brain, to comfort it that maybe, maybe, maybe it's okay for Percy to have something nice. Maybe he doesn't expect Rob to love him back, but he doesn't think it's impossible, either.

Chapter Twenty-Nine

"I HAVE THE confirmation email right here," Percy says for the third time. The front desk clerk at the motel looks about two-thirds less sympathetic than she did the first time Percy said so. She's one of those people who looks like her family has lived in these mountains for generations. Rob's always been a little afraid of the type.

"Sorry, honey." She doesn't sound that sorry anymore. "Someone double-booked you on accident. Nothing I can do about it."

"You really don't have a single vacant room?" Percy asks, though he sounds nearly worn down.

Rob's leg is jittery. He feels bad for suggesting they stay in Blue Ridge instead of Ellijay. Everything was all set for Percy in Ellijay, but something went wrong with the motel reservation switch, because there's no record that Explore Georgia ever called this place. Now Percy's going to have to get Explore Georgia on the phone and get them to switch the reservation back to the original place in Ellijay. Ugh.

This is why Rob hates being responsible for stuff. He took some initiative and look where it got them—fighting to get a room in a Comfort Inn that frankly looks like it's seen better days. The lobby is pure 2003, which was such an aesthetic wasteland that Rob can't even put his finger on how he's picking up on those vibes.

"You can try one of the B and Bs," the clerk is saying.

"Thanks," Percy sighs before turning around and joining Rob. They walk back outside into the parking lot, which is daylight-bright under tall, buzzing lights. Moths cast huge shadows as they flit through the blocks of light. "I'll see if I can get our original room back," Percy says, but he doesn't sound hopeful.

His contacts at Explore Georgia don't answer. After trying them a few times, he calls the Ellijay Comfort Inn and explains the situation. They, too, are completely booked. Rob can hear the person on the other end of the line tell Percy that they had a cancellation earlier in the day, but they'd just given that room to someone.

"Sorry," Rob says miserably when Percy puts his phone away.

Percy's brow furrows. "Sorry about what?"

"For suggesting we stay here." Rob turns away so he doesn't have to see the exasperation on Percy's face. God, he hates when he does stuff like this. He doesn't make good spur-of-the-moment decisions. Something always goes awry. Of *course* there's some event at the water park in Blue Ridge this weekend, and Rob should have checked before he got them switching reservations around.

"I don't think you did suggest we stay here?" Percy comes up behind him. "That was me."

"Well, I brought up Blue Ridge."

"You were being nice." Percy sounds genuinely confused and not annoyed, so Rob turns back around.

Percy doesn't look mad, and suddenly Rob feels stupid. Why would Percy be mad at him? It's not like Rob purposefully inconvenienced them. Taking a deep breath, Rob asks, "So what do we do now?"

Smiling, Percy says, "Well, there has to be somewhere to stay in this town, yeah?"

And, duh, Rob grabbed one of the tourist brochures in the motel lobby. At the back of it is a list of B&Bs and boutique hotels. It takes a few calls, but they finally find one with a vacancy.

"See? Problem solved." Percy looks around, then darts in to kiss Rob on the mouth, a there-and-gone kiss that Rob barely has time to react to. Maybe Percy's still concerned about homophobia, even though there are Pride flags all over. Granted, Georgia doesn't always present itself that positively to a foreign audience. Percy definitely isn't the first non-American to be worried about violence in the South.

As they get in the car to drive over to the B&B—Misty Mountain View Lodge—Rob says, "How do you stay so calm about not having a place to stay?"

"Because I'm normally such a head case, you mean?" Percy sounds tired.

"What? No!" Shit. Rob's making this worse somehow. Percy made it better, and now Rob's making it bad again. "No, I mean because it's stressful finding out you don't have a place to stay when you thought you did."

"Oh." Percy shrugs. "That's happened to me loads of times. There's always *somewhere* to stay, even if it's sleeping in the back seat of a car."

The GPS guides them out of town. Rob tries not to be freaked out by the absolute darkness. Did they accidentally book a room at the *Misery* cabin? "I'm not very good at spontaneity, I guess," he says.

Glancing over at him, Percy says, "You handled me spontaneously showing up pretty well."

Which makes Rob's chest feel all warm and gooey. "You spontaneously showing up was way better than losing our motel room."

"High praise."

Rob laughs and feels better. Percy really isn't mad at him, or even annoyed. They might still be headed to the *Misery* cabin, but Rob won't worry about it until they meet their number one fan.

Misty Mountain View Lodge isn't the *Misery* cabin. It's a gorgeous boutique hotel, its small lobby done up in warmly colored hardwood. There are survey maps all over the walls, along with survey and mapmaking tools. Compasses hang from the ceiling on varied lengths of chain, glinting brassily in the light coming off the Edison bulbs in the room's light fixtures.

It's quirky and fancy, and when Rob hears the price of the Weathervane Room for the night, he almost faints. Percy produces a credit card without blinking and hands it over.

"You have to let me pay you back for half," Rob says once they're walking up the stairs, keys hanging from both their hands. The idea of all that money makes him vaguely ill. Half of that rate is still more than his budget can handle, especially when he knows he's going to have to get his furnace fixed before winter. It went out in February and he just lived with it, but god, he really doesn't want to have to do that again come November.

Percy just makes a noise. When they reach the top floor, he puts the key in the lock and says, "It's fine, really. If the tourism people won't reimburse me, it's, well. It's not like I can't afford it." He winces. "I don't want it to be a thing. The money."

"Does it usually turn into a thing for you?" Rob asks. He feels a bit called out. Percy's money didn't seem like an affront in South Africa, but for some reason, now that they're on Rob's home turf, he's getting all proud and chauvinistic about it.

The door creaks open. Percy flips the lights on, and Rob makes a stupid *guh* sound. The room is beautiful. It smells like leather, spice, woodsmoke, and money. The walls and floor are the same warm wood from the lobby, but thick, sumptuous rugs cover the floor. A fireplace dominates one wall. A low fire is burning, crackling quietly. The staff must have come up here and lit it when Percy called and asked if they had a room available.

Picture windows take up another wall. In the morning, they're going to have an amazing view of the mountains. True to the name of the room, there are several weathervanes mounted throughout, including on one of the bedposts.

The bed is enormous. A thick duvet covers it. The color reminds Rob of the smoky purple-blue the Blue Ridge Mountains turn as the daylight fades.

The bathroom has an enormous shower and a jacuzzi, because of course it does. Next to the crackling fireplace, a small round table is set with a vase containing a single rose, an ice bucket, a bottle of sparkling wine, and two glasses.

As he goes to check the wine label, it occurs to him that Percy never answered his question. He turns to find Percy still standing by the door, both of their duffels at his feet as he fingers the small weathervane on the knee wall dividing the entry from the rest of the room. Rob's going to take that as a definite *yes*, money usually turns into a thing in Percy's relationships. Obviously he wants to know more, like who makes it a thing—though it's hard to imagine Percy being the one to do that. Even though Percy's the kind of rich that means money's just invisible, Rob can't ever see him turning money into an issue between him and whoever he's dating.

"I won't make it a thing," Rob promises. "This room is way too sexy."

Percy laughs—mission accomplished. "I think this is the honeymoon suite."

"Oh yeah?" Rob's interest, and libido, is officially piqued. "Trying to seduce me already, de Villiers?"

"Ohmygod no!" Percy's face goes red. "I mean—not that I'd—I *would*, but. You said." Somehow his face gets redder. "You said we should take it slow."

"Yeah." Rob wants to interview Past Rob to figure out exactly what he was thinking. Percy looks really good today. Rob noticed immediately this morning, but he's appreciating it again now. His pink T-shirt makes his skin glow, and his chinos hug his thighs and ass.

Rob's blood hums. They're alone. They're alone in this very expensive, very luxurious, very let's-fuck-all-day hotel room. Turns out Rob can come to terms with being given expensive things pretty quickly when they come with the possibility of sex. "Should we open the wine?"

Percy blinks. His eyes flick over Rob, head to toe, and his tongue darts out to wet his bottom lip. *So* not fair. Rob's going to have to pop the cork on this bottle, but now all he can think about is Percy's mouth. Percy's lips. Percy's tongue. The last time they had sex was that hot, wet mouth on Rob's cock. It would be a lie if he said he hadn't jacked off to the memory a number of times in the past month.

"Are we going to do wine and the hot tub…?" Percy asks faintly. His voice is a little rough.

"Well, it would be a shame to let all of this go to waste, right?" Rob pops the cork, only having to think a little harder about how to do it, and pours the sparkling wine.

It takes three strides to cross the room to Percy. Their fingers brush as Rob hands off the other glass. Bubbles stream from the bottom of the flute to the surface, making veins of glitter in the honeyed gold of the wine. Percy clinks his glass against Rob's and says softly, "To second chances. And taking it slow. If that's what you still want."

He gulps his wine quickly, the bob of his Adam's apple making it easy to follow the mouthful down his throat. Rob takes a sip of his wine too. It's really good.

The bottom of his glass clinks as he sets it on the knee wall, and Percy's does the same when Rob takes it from him to put it aside. "Screw taking it slow," Rob says.

"Oh, thank god," Percy breathes—then pulls Rob in as Rob lunges for him.

The way Percy moans as Rob pushes him against the door makes him ache with need. God god god he missed Percy so much, everything about him. The way he's so beautifully responsive during sex started to seem like a fantasy, but no, here he is, arching into Rob and panting already, hot breath in Rob's mouth that he swallows greedily.

Fingers grab Rob's hair, tugging with a sweet, sexy sting. Rob digs his grip into Percy's hips, pinning him in place, but Percy's hand spreads over his back, mapping its way across Rob's spine and shoulders and every muscle straining to get closer, has him pinned in place just as much. Rob's hard as hell already.

"Started to think I made up how good you feel," Rob groans on a breath. His hands skim up Percy's sides, catching the French tuck on his shirt to tug it from his pants. The heat of Percy's skin scorches through him.

Percy makes a noise and moves his hand down, down, down to grab Rob's ass, which he squeezes. Hard. "God," he breathes. "Me too."

They lose themselves to kissing again, mouths on mouths, mouths on jaws and throats, Rob sucking at Percy's neck and Percy scraping lips and teeth along Rob's stubble. All the while they're rutting against each other, hips and hard cocks grinding together, and Rob's flying and oh-so-heavy at the same time. His desire is sending his brain spiraling around stars while it weighs his body down.

He wants to drag Percy down and get so much closer. Just skin and spit and sweat, hands and mouths and cocks. He wants to get horizontal and tangled up, and to not know where one of them ends and the other begins.

Rob traces the shell of Percy's ear with his tongue. "Can I take you to bed?" His own breath makes everything more damp, but Percy's skin is dewy with sweat already. Rob licks it and swallows his taste, wanting more.

"I thought you'd never ask," Percy says. One of his legs is wrapped around Rob's thigh. Rob hitches it up and grabs the other, sliding his hands under Percy's perfect round ass. Muscles flex in his hands and Percy rides up and down, his ass bumping against Rob's dick in a sweet simulation of the real thing.

And god, Percy feels good in his arms. Heavy and muscular, the weight of him filling Rob's senses, his legs hooked around Rob's waist and his heels digging into the divot at the base of Rob's spine. Pulling, pushing, grinding them together.

When Rob gets them both to the bed, Percy drops flat on his back and yanks Rob down by his undone belt. Rob groans and happily covers Percy's body with his, shoving Percy's button-up off his shoulders.

God. *Shoulders.* Chest hair and pecs and Percy's nipples pebbling under his tongue while Percy's body writhes under Rob. They wrestle for a different position and Percy ends up on top, where he pushes Rob's arms over his head. As he squeezes and bites and licks his way down one of Rob's flexed arms, Rob asks, "What do you want, baby?"

Percy brushes his nose along the taut, extended muscle around Rob's armpit before burying his face there. Rob lets out a moan at the warm, slick wet of Percy slowly lapping him up. "Sweet fucking Christ." Rob's voice is turning into a sex-graveled rasp. "Fuck, Perce. That's hot."

Hands shove his jeans over his hips—right, those aren't off yet, and they really should be. Rob helps Percy strip him while Percy feasts on him. But now Percy's the one with too many clothes on: half-undone pants, the waistband of his underwear pushed down but not far enough. The velvet head of Percy's dick is poking out, and Rob swipes a finger over it, smearing the liquid dripping from the slit.

Percy jolts and sucks in a breath, stilling. "Wait—wait." He pushes himself up and looks down at Rob, face flushed and sweaty, hairline damp and hair stuck to his skin. His throat bobs with a sharp swallow and he laughs a little. "Almost just embarrassed myself."

"Mm, yeah. I want to see that." Rob inches Percy's underwear down, freeing his cock. And there it is, long and just the right amount of thick, fat head wet from Rob's fingers smearing pre-cum over it.

"Not yet." Percy lowers his body so they're pressed together again. Their mouths find each other's again. The taste of Rob's sweat on Percy's tongue is somehow one of the filthiest things he's ever experienced, and it turns him on so bad that he starts rocking harder against Percy. "Not yet," Percy repeats. He catches Rob's lip in his teeth and tugs gently before he asks, "Will you fuck me?"

Easiest question Rob's ever answered. He'd do anything Percy wanted.

"Baby, I'll spend all night fucking you through this mattress if you want me to." Rob closes his fist around Percy's cock and strokes slowly. Percy whines and grinds down into Rob, and Rob tightens his grip as he slows his movement. Percy is hot and so heavy in his hand.

They get the rest of their clothes off, and Percy produces condoms and lube from his bag. "So I guess you didn't buy me wanting to take it slow," Rob laughs.

Percy tosses the box and the bottle and Rob catches them on his chest. "Just being an optimist," he says. His eyes rake over Rob, sprawled on the bed and cracking open the box of condoms. "I've been wanting this for a long time."

"So no pressure." Rob rolls on the condom and strokes himself a few times while Percy's gaze eats him up. Warm liquid pleasure makes its sluggish way through his veins, pooling under his skin.

"No pressure," Percy echoes, but his tone is reassuring.

Which is… nice. Rob doesn't get in his head about sex, exactly. But topping makes him feel responsible. Like, he's in charge of this encounter, and it's up to him to make it good for both of them. But being with Percy doesn't give him that feeling. Percy is right here with him, sharing completely in the give-and-take of pleasure.

He reaches for Percy with one hand while he fumbles the lube with the other. Percy smirks and returns to bed, crawling up Rob's body as he drags kisses from dick to collarbone. Muscles flex and work under Rob's hand, and Percy is so smooth and warm. Rob could touch and touch and never get enough.

Percy sits up, knees bracketing Rob's hips, and slicks a finger with lube. Holding Rob's eyes, he reaches back. And even though Rob can't see him pushing a finger into himself, he can tell the moment it happens from the way Percy's eyelids flutter and his lips part.

Pure filthy lust surges through Rob. "Yeah, open yourself up for me, baby," he moans, any trepidation about topping forgotten. The way Percy fucks himself on his own finger—fingers—makes sweat bead on Rob's skin. God, he's too much—too beautiful, lean and graceful, each line and plane of his body cut from light.

Their cocks bump together as Percy moves. Without meaning to, Rob's moving with him, hips jerking up as he looks for friction. He needs to be inside Percy. Like now. Like three minutes ago.

Percy's arm twists and his chin tilts up as he lets out a low moan. "Need this to be you."

"Yes. Fuck. *Please.*" Rob drips lube directly from the bottle onto his dick. As he coats himself, Percy watches, eyes dark and blown wide with desire. Rob feels like the sexiest guy alive, and he wants to earn it. When Percy pulls his fingers from himself, wet and glistening, Rob grabs his wrist and guides them to his mouth.

Percy runs his slick fingers over Rob's lips first before Rob takes them into his mouth. And oh, fuck. The taste. Rob hasn't forgotten the way Percy tastes, but that musk sliding over his tongue is so much better in reality than memory.

After he sucks Percy's fingers clean, he asks, "Stay right there? I want to see you just like this."

For a second, he thinks he said the wrong thing. Percy goes still, looking down at Rob with his mouth open like he knows he should say something but can't find the words.

"Only if you want." Rob runs his palms up Percy's legs and settles them on Percy's hips.

"Only if I *want*, he says." Percy grabs both of their cocks and jacks them together slowly. The sound of his hand moving around them is wet and dirty. Rob fucks up into his hand, because how can he not?

"I wanna watch you ride me so bad." Rob's going to fucking lose it. This is too much for a guy who's been jerking off to fantasies for a month.

Percy takes pity on him and rises higher on his knees, shuffling forward. This is not, in Rob's experience, a maneuver that looks sexy, and the little grin and huff of laughter that Percy shoots Rob's way says Percy knows it too. Laughing during sex, though? Maybe the sexiest thing.

Then Percy sinks down on Rob, and Rob's mind whites out.

It takes more willpower than he knew he had not to thrust up into Percy's tight, hot ass. He's trembling, hips twitching as he sweats. Percy's chin drops to his chest. His hips rock, cock bobbing with each movement, as he seats himself.

His tight ass touches Rob's balls and his head drops back as he lets out a full-throated moan. Rob pushes into him and that makes Percy scrabble to find one of Rob's hands. "You're so gorgeous," Rob whispers.

He can't even put words to how gorgeous Percy is. Firelight turns his skin to precious metal, copper and bronze flecked with the gold flakes of his freckles. His eyes are an ink spill, endless pools, and god, Rob's falling back on clichés. But—

Oh.

Percy moves, fucking himself on Rob's cock, and even coming up with clichés is too much.

They move together, sweat and gasping nonsense, skin slapping against skin and the hot, tight slide deep into Percy's body. Milky-white fluid drips from Percy's cock onto Rob's stomach as it bobs there, thick and so, so fucking hard. The whiteout sex blaze in Rob's brain says everything about Percy is the sexiest thing ever, and *stays hard while getting fucked* goes on the list.

Rob is fast careening toward oblivion, a tight, building need through not just his hips and gut, but every part of his body. Closing his fist around Percy's cock, he growls, "Come on, baby. Fuck yourself harder. Wanna see you come all over me—"

"Jesus, Rob." Percy's voice comes out halfway between a sob and a whine. "Fuck *me* harder if you want to see me come."

Even through the haze of impending orgasm, Rob laughs. "Bossy."

"Very. Now fuck me so I can't walk tomorrow."

Rob obliges, his hips surging up into hard, punishing thrusts. Percy meets him thrust for thrust, moaning with complete abandon.

It shatters Rob's control. Pleasure rushes him, slamming into him like a Pipeline wave. He thinks he yells. He definitely grabs Percy's hips in a bruising hold, pumping into him over and over as his orgasm throbs out of him.

Percy shudders, tenses, and cries out. His cock goes steel-hard in Rob's hand before it pulses. He shoots all over Rob, painting his abs and pecs with cum. When Rob thinks he's done, he lazily thrusts up one more time as he strokes Percy, and it coaxes another spurt that drips down Rob's fingers.

With a groan, Percy pulls himself off Rob and collapses on top of him. Which one of them reaches for the other? Unclear—all Rob knows, all that matters, is that they're kissing, a kiss that starts wild and desperate but softens and slows to tenderness.

The fire crackles and burns lower and they don't move. Arms and legs twine together. Warm skin presses against warm skin, and Rob loses the sense of where one of them begins and the other ends, just like he wanted. And he can't remember ever feeling this way before, this sense of perfect belonging, like they're meant to go together, body and soul.

He's pretty sure he's in love with Percy, and it's the opposite of taking things slow—but it's not something he can help. It just is.

Chapter Thirty

THREE WEEKS later, Percy is still in America. He's still, to be precise, in Georgia. To be more precise, he's in Atlanta. No prizes for guessing—he's been staying with Rob.

Staying may not be the right word to describe it. They settled into patterns of domesticity startlingly quickly. They cook together; they share chores. Percy wonders what you call a person who's in the country on an O-1 visa (a person of extraordinary ability; that's him) when he's trimming back the azaleas on his boyfriend's front steps.

Lucky. That's what Percy calls himself. Stupendously, ridiculously fucking lucky, to get to call Rob his boyfriend. Of all the billions of people in the world, somehow Percy and Rob met. Born on the other side of the world, raised in different countries, only coming into contact through a series of decisions and events that could so easily never have happened. If Rob hadn't seen Percy's Namib-Naukluft photo. If Percy's father hadn't got caught. If Percy hadn't taken a chance on a no-name travel writer. If if if.

The one person, the only person, who's ever felt like home to Percy, and a billion trillion paths lead to them not meeting.

Or maybe it's the opposite. Maybe every path, every choice and branching possibility that makes up their lives, would have always led them to find each other.

Anyway. The azaleas look a lot better now.

Mostly he trimmed them in the early mornings or evenings because Atlanta is shockingly hot. Percy's sense of seasonality has to be recalibrated from the southern to northern hemisphere, but even so, things don't compute. August in Cape Town is winter, with spring on the horizon; August in northern Europe is the winding-down of summer, crisp mornings and woodsmoke hanging in the air as the temperature inches toward autumn.

August in Atlanta is beating sun, heat shimmer on asphalt, humidity, and sweat. Any body part that gathers sweat turns to a swamp. When Percy works outside, his armpits and balls should be cordoned off as biohazards.

There's something to be said for when Rob comes home from his in-office days, though, and his shirt is sticking to his back while he gives off the sharp, masculine smell of honest sweat.

Today is one of Rob's in-office days, and Percy is eagerly awaiting his arrival home. He thumbs through the email that just came in, reading it for the fourth time while a smile creeps over his face. This is good. He's really sure this is good. The email itself, that's unquestionably good. But Percy's also pretty sure it's good for Rob and him.

When the sound of a car in the driveway finally arrives, Percy goes to the window to peek out. Rob gets out of his Camry and bounds up the concrete steps. He beams when he opens the door and finds Percy there, says, "Hey, babe!" and pulls Percy into an easy embrace.

Percy kisses him fiercely. "Fancy going out for dinner tonight?"

Rob wriggles closer in Percy's arms, looking so besotted that Percy's breath feels snatched away. "Special occasion?"

"Maybe." When Rob makes his eyes big and bats his eyelashes, Percy relents. A pair of warm brown eyes with those dark eyelashes are Percy's weakness, and Rob knows it. The joke might be on him, though, because in fact, *all* of Rob is Percy's weakness. "I heard back from Kayla."

"Explore Georgia Kayla?"

"Ja." Percy stops. Rob waits. Percy presses his lips together.

"Perrrrrce." Rob makes a face that's probably supposed to be consternation and impatience but mostly just looks cute. "What did she say?"

Percy rocks up onto the balls of his feet, then back down, managing to keep his mouth shut. He really, *really* wants to save this news for dinner, but Rob's looking at him like that. Though, Rob's also sweaty, so maybe Percy can distract him with sex? The way they're pressed together is distracting Percy with the idea of sex, at least, so it only feels fair if both of them are burdened with the same travails.

"I'd tell you, but my mouth is about to be too full to talk." Percy nudges Rob toward the bedroom. Rob's eyes drop to Percy's lips, so Percy licks them slowly.

They end up mutually distracted, and mutually with their mouths full, locked together on Rob's bed as they suck each other off at the same time. Afterward, Percy sprawls back against the headboard with Rob snuggled up to his chest, tracing circles on his stomach. Percy can't stop watching him. There's a tenderness in his ribs, aching with how much he wants to keep this forever.

Rob yawns. "Gonna tell me yet?"

Dropping a kiss on Rob's head, Percy says, "They want me for the entire project."

"Percy!" Rob throws himself on Percy, the weight of him knocking Percy's breath from his body. His own helpless laughter takes care of the rest of it. "I knew they would! I *knew* it!"

They're kissing again, fiercely and happily, Rob's hands cradling Percy's head, and Rob's murmuring nonsense between kisses.

Maybe not nonsense. Pre-therapy Percy would have called it nonsense. Therapied and properly medicated Percy thinks it might just be the sorts of things you say to someone you love and believe in when they've had good news.

"They love the photos I've sent them of the Georgia mountains," Percy says, eventually. "Kayla said they've been trying to work out how to ask me to do the photos for the rest of the website revamp. They thought they'd need a perfect pitch to entice me to hang around."

Little does Kayla know that the perfect pitch is lying on top of Percy right now, hip bones pressed against Percy's in the kind of discomfort you want to bottle up because it means you have something real and physical. Like celestial bodies distorting space-time with their mass, the dig of Rob's hips into his makes this feel permanent. Stars catching each other in their gravity, the sweep of a thunderstorm across savanna.

Rob buries his face in the crook of Percy's neck to kiss a line from collarbone to jawline. "This is amazing. We're definitely going out to dinner."

And in that moment, Percy feels such a surge of feeling, such all-encompassing happiness and rightness, that he has to say, "I love you."

Rob's head pops up, his eyes wide. They catch the afternoon light streaming through the windows, making little amber flecks glow. Maybe he's not going to say the words back to Percy, but that's okay. Percy just needed to say them.

There's softness in Rob's eyes. He puts a hand over Percy's chest, right over Percy's heart. "I love you too."

"You do?" Percy blurts, because even if it's okay if Rob doesn't say it back, he obviously would still really, really like to hear it.

With a laugh, Rob kisses Percy on the forehead, then the mouth. "Yeah. God, yes. Are you kidding?"

Percy hugs him instead of answering. No, of course he's not kidding, and Rob probably knows that, but it doesn't need to be said, because—because everything is going right. Everything is so good.

"I've been starting to freak out about your visa," Rob admits. "It's only for three months. I didn't want to think about you leaving."

There are so many things to think about, and thank god saying goodbye soon isn't one of them anymore. Explore Georgia will extend the visa, but he'll have to get a car, find a place to live. A project like this will take at least a year—more likely longer. And he can't just move in with Rob... right?

He would if Rob wanted to. Here he goes again, head over heels, ready to go all in with the man he's currently convinced is his soul mate. But it feels different this time. It really does. The way Rob's looking at him—has anyone ever looked at Percy like that, with that intoxicating mix of wonder and tenderness?

It's different. Percy messed up and almost destroyed what they have. He's not going to do that again. Open communication from here on out. Once things are a bit more firmed up, Percy will broach the topic.

"Now I won't have to leave," Percy says. "Not for a while, at least. Who knows, maybe I can keep finding jobs in the States indefinitely. There's no limit on how long my visa can get extended."

Rob looks weirdly troubled by that. "You've never just worked in one place, though. Would you really be happy with that?"

"Well, it's a big country. There's loads of places to shoot." Percy's heart gives a nervous flutter. A minute ago, Rob was happy and excited. Why does he seem the opposite now?

A smile returns to Rob's face, but it's not as ebullient as before. "I just don't want you to get bored. Or like, uproot your life for me."

A cold little ball of ice and emptiness forms in Percy's chest. "Rob, I just told you I love you."

Now Rob looks, alarmingly, like he might cry. "I know! I know. God, Perce, I love you too. You don't even... I mean, I think I've been in love with you since pretty much the moment I saw you. I just don't want you to hate me for holding you back."

The lizard part of Percy's brain wants to demand if Rob even wants him to take the job. His higher cognitive functions make him pause and take a breath, consider where Rob's concern is coming from and whether there's any reason to believe that Rob secretly doesn't want him to stay.

"I'd never get resentful of you because of my choice to stay here." Percy chooses his next words carefully. "Yeah, I wouldn't take this job if not for you. But that doesn't mean it's boring or that it's beneath me or something. I'm *lucky* to be able to be able to pick and choose what I do so I can be near you."

Rob's Adam's apple jags as he swallows hard, and he leans down to kiss Percy softly. The icy clump in Percy's chest dissolves into the banked heat of the kiss. Open communication got put to the test quickly, but look at that! They came through it.

"Do you still want to go out for dinner?" Percy asks.

Rob kisses him again, this time more soundly. "Yeah! Yeah, of course. It's amazing news. Sorry for being weird. I want you to stay. Obviously. That's obvious, isn't it?" He bites his lip. "I just want you to be happy."

"I'm happy." Percy puts his hands on Rob's face. "I'm with you."

If he had to, he'd start all over again with his photography. He'd work his way up from the bottom if it meant he could stay close to Rob. Photography has been his life for years, but it's never meant more to him than the possibility of a future with someone.

And this, the possibility of a soul-shaking, forever kind of love that Percy's always wanted? He'd take pictures for the tourism agency in every state in this country for that.

THEY GO to a posh restaurant several suburbs over and get tipsy off cocktails in the bar before their fashionably late dinner reservation. They Ubered here so they can be as celebratory as they want, which Percy is taking advantage of. The restaurant is one of those trendy places with an open kitchen so you can stare at the chefs as they work. The tables are butcher block, there's exposed brick and ductwork, and sound bounces off every hard surface in the place, which is *every* surface in the place.

It's the kind of place you go because you want to be extravagant, and that's what Percy and Rob are doing.

After dinner, they walk across the street to get ice cream. The night air is warm and heavy, but not so stifling with the sun gone. Cricketsong thrums through the air while frogs chirp in a different time signature.

This night is like a mirror image of the last time they had a nice dinner and got ice cream. Rob's last night in Cape Town, when Percy got recorded and had a panic attack. Now here they are, celebrating that Percy isn't leaving instead of trying to make the best of an impending parting.

It's a good night, maybe even kind of a perfect night. They're drunk and happy and in love, and the fuzzy warmth of the evening buzzes through Percy's veins. Rob holds tight to Percy's hand, and when they walk to a nearby park, they stand next to the lake and kiss slowly.

Rob's breath puffs warm and intimate on Percy's face. "I love you so much," he says. "So much, Percy. I can't believe you're staying. I can't believe you'd do that for me."

Leaning their foreheads together, Percy says, "For us." The world tips and spins like a fair ride and Percy's giddier than any fair ride could ever make him. "This is the best thing in my life. You're the best thing."

Rob makes a sound deep in his chest, and then his arms are around Percy, holding him close. Percy wraps him up in return and closes his eyes. Cars whoosh by on the nearby road, and water laps quietly at the shore of the lake, and the night is warm, but Rob's body is warmer.

Things are good. Percy's happiness swells inside his chest until he feels like he's leaking light. Things are more than good. They might just be perfect.

Chapter Thirty-One

THERE ARE a truly absurd number of notifications on Percy's lock screen the next morning. He blinks blearily—too many cocktails—trying to make sense of the jumble from different apps.

Has Kayla emailed him back? He sent her a message last night with his official acceptance of the new contract. It would be nice if they could get the visa stuff started so Percy can work on all the practicalities. It will be better for his peace of mind if he knows definitively how long his visa will allow him to stay in the country. It will be better for talking to Rob about it too.

Rob grunts in his sleep and Percy twists to look over his shoulder, unable to keep the smile from his face. It's a huge feeling, seeing someone sleeping next to you and realizing you want to keep waking up next to them for the rest of your life. Percy feels like he's known for a while, but it still spreads through him now, slow and sweet like honey.

This thing with Rob—it's forever, isn't it? They haven't known each other long, but Percy feels settled. Like coming home from a party you don't really want to be at and finally relaxing, or sleeping in your own bed when you get back from a trip. Rob feels like *home*.

The barriers to being together hardly even feel like barriers. Yes, their home countries are on opposites sides of the world. Yes, they're citizens of different nations. They'll figure it out. They'll take whatever steps they need to so they can be together. Percy simply can't conceive of a universe where they don't.

A piece of Rob's hair lays across his face and it takes everything in Percy not to move it. He'll wake up Rob if he does, and Rob deserves the lie-in after getting up yesterday to drive to work. And there's something nice about being able to let Rob sleep. The urgency that comes with a long-distance relationship, the desperation to seize every single moment to be together, doesn't apply anymore.

He can't resist leaning closer to Rob to breathe him in, the fabric softener scent of the sheet and comforter and the natural musk of his skin. It's a good start to the morning.

Still smiling, Percy turns back to his phone. There's a WhatsApp message from Eunice telling him to call and another from Katli asking if he's okay and telling him to call if he needs to.

Unease prickles at him. Something's happened. Was it here? Was there some tragedy last night the two of them were completely oblivious to? Or is something wrong at home?

He unlocks his phone, almost afraid to investigate further. His thoughts go to his mother. His mother who he's not spoken to in months. What if something happened to her? What if she had a heart attack, or was in a car accident, or got some kind of awful diagnosis?

There's a text message, which rattles him further. No one regular-texts him. Stomach churning, he opens it.

It's from Ma. *Hello Percy please ring me Love Ma*

A faintly hysterical laugh pings around his chest and climbs halfway up his throat. Ma has always been horrible at texting. For some reason, part of him expected her to change in the months it's been since they've spoken. But no, same old lack of punctuation and treating a text like a letter.

He must have gotten out of bed because suddenly he's standing outside on Rob's back patio in nothing but his boxer briefs. The air is heavy already despite the early hour. His skin grows damp with humidity and sweat that won't evaporate.

It's seven in the morning here, which means it's one in the afternoon in South Africa. This text arrived hours ago while Percy blissfully slept the night away in Rob's arms.

His heart pounds and his chest feels tight. Maybe he'd be able to breathe if he went inside where the air isn't so dense with moisture—but no, he doesn't want to wake Rob. And if this is bad, he'll want a moment to himself. He loves Rob, but he's still him, and needing a moment to compose himself is a foundational part of his personality.

He forces himself to make the call and holds his phone up to his ear, hardly able to hear the ringing over the thundering of his own heart.

There's a click, the sound of breathing. "Percy," Ma says. "Oh patat, you rang."

It's the first time he's heard her voice since that day she defended his father. His mouth is so dry he has to swallow a few times before he can make words come out. "Hey, Ma."

For a second, there's nothing but the sound of her breathing on the line. She sounds—maybe—like she's struggling too. There's a lump in Percy's throat, but if she asks, he'll say it must be the connection.

"How are you, babatjie?" she asks.

"I'm, uh." His head spins. He was so bad the last time they spoke. It feels not quite like another life, but something adjacent. That version of Percy couldn't fathom standing in his underwear on his boyfriend's patio in America. That version of Percy was so lost in dark storm clouds that he couldn't fathom ever finding his way to the sun again.

"I'm good," he says. "I'm good."

"You sound good."

"Do I?" That hysterical laughter threatens again. He thinks he sounds tight and wound-up. It's certainly how he feels. "Ma, is something wrong? Why did you want me to call?"

Another silence. He thinks he hears birdsong on her end, so she must be outside. It's easy to imagine her sitting on one of the cushioned deck chairs next to the pool, surrounded by the kind of luxury that most people in South Africa will never come anywhere near. Luxury that was stolen from the people of South Africa because of his father's crimes.

The familiar rage burns through Percy, but he's also just… tired. He's so tired of being angry about this. He's so tired of this touching everything in his life and souring it.

"Can't we just talk for a minute?" Ma asks, a plaintive note to her voice.

A jay lands in one of the big live oaks that shades Rob's backyard. Its feathers flash bright cobalt blue in the morning sun and it lets out a warbling call. Percy wants a photo of it, the slant of the sun illuminating its startlingly bold coloring, the pop of the crest on its head, the intelligence in its black eyes as it regards him.

Another jay lands on the same branch, and the two birds have an exchange of soft warbles before they fly off.

"What do you want to talk about?" Percy asks, watching the birds spread their wings against the hazy blue of the morning. "Maybe how Pa was stealing aid money?"

"Percy—"

"That was money for ill people," he goes on, a remorselessness in his tone that he doesn't quite recognize. He can't remember if they've ever actually talked about this, or if Ma only said, *We need to support your father.* "It was aid money for people with HIV. Do you know how easily I could have been one of the people who needed that money? Colored and queer? Wager you'd have cared if it was me instead of a load of faceless, nameless people."

His voice is raised. He takes a shaky breath. "I don't know how to talk about anything else with you right now."

He can hear Ma breathing, so he knows she hasn't hung up on him. If she did, he wouldn't blame her. Maybe he would. He thought he'd used up all his anger on this, that all he had left was the sick, empty nausea of guilt and an inescapable certainty that he's complicit.

"No," she finally says, sounding as tired as he feels. "No, I don't suppose you do."

"Why did you want me to call, Ma?" Percy asks.

The birds, he remembers idly, are called blue jays. Smart and social. Corvids. He wonders if the two he saw were a pair. That would have been a nice photo, too, the two of them together with Spanish moss draped around them and sun dappling through the leaves.

"I needed to talk to you about your father." Ma pauses and Percy hears a thousand terrible scenarios in the silence. He's dead, he's been murdered, he's sick, he's gone and Percy never got to tell him what a monstrous thing he did, never got to do anything more than stare in mute shock as his father transformed into a criminal before his eyes.

And as angry as he is, it's still Pa. He's still Percy's father, and it's complicated and messy and stratified with hurt amidst the veins of love.

"What about him?" Percy asks, mouth suddenly dry.

"The trial date has been moved up."

"What?" Percy grabs for the back of a patio chair. It's already warm from the early sun and ambient air temperature. "But it's not—it was supposed to be months from now." Or—a month? He's spent so long pushing it out of his mind. The date was originally set for the beginning of October. It's nearly September now. Time has seemed to stop these past few months because of Rob, and Percy forgot to take into account that it didn't stop for anyone else.

"Next week," Ma says, ignoring his *what* in favor of answering the unspoken question that matters more: *when.* "I thought… I *hoped* you'd come by the house."

Head reeling, Percy replies, "I'm not even in the country."

But he's already making plans, thinking of how quickly he can get home. Same-day tickets are a thing of the past—at least he thinks so? He's never tried. He's never had a situation that necessitated a same-day ticket. Tomorrow, then. If he flies out tomorrow, he'll be in Cape Town by Friday evening.

Dimly, he hears his mother ask, "Where are you now, babatjie?"

"The States." Will Rob come with him? Not that Percy can expect that. He'll ask but not expect. It would just be nice, that's all. If Rob were there with him. Percy has no idea what he's going to face back in South Africa, but it will all be easier with Rob at his side.

"A job?" Ma asks.

"Ja. A job, and…." Actually, no. He's not doing this over the phone. He's not telling his mother about how he met the love of his life and fucked it up and got help and is building something now, something good and maybe a little fragile but worth it. "Next week, they're holding the trial? Why so soon? Why would they move it up?"

"I don't know." Now Percy hears the strain in Ma's voice, sitting alongside the weariness. "The lawyer doesn't tell me why, only what's happened. I feel like I was the last to know, Percy. It was already on the news just after he told me. I just"—her voice drops to a hoarse whisper—"this would all be easier if you were here."

"Nothing will make it easier," he says.

"It would be easier if I wasn't alone."

He clenches his fist. "You didn't have to be alone. You could have…."

Disavowed Pa entirely, like Percy had done? Ma isn't that kind of person.

There's a silence. Then Ma says, each meticulous word picked out like tiles in a mosaic, "It would be easier if I didn't have to be alone with the guilt and the grief. It would be easier if I hadn't lost my son at the same time I lost my husband."

Fok. Fok fokken *fok.* "You defended him."

"What do you want me to do? He's my husband. You're not the only one allowed to have complicated feelings about things, patat."

The pet name—sweet potato—takes the sting out of the words, even if they still lodge in Percy's ribs. Has he considered how Ma must feel? Caught between the bonds of family and the plain, stark knowledge that Pa did something awful? And Percy…. Percy ran away because he couldn't handle it. Couldn't handle hearing about it, much less talking about it.

Is this who he is? Someone who thinks he's the only one who gets to feel bad about things? Someone who expects everyone else to view everything as black and white, while only he has the right to nuance?

"I'm coming home," he says. "First flight I can get. I probably won't get in until Friday evening."

A sharp intake of breath from Ma, something that might be a sob. Percy hates himself for making his mother cry, because at heart he's a good South African boy. "Okay, Perce," she says softly. "Okay. Thank you."

There are a million things he wants to say, starting with *Please don't cry. I'm sorry* is in there somewhere. "I'll ring when I'm back. Okay, Mama?"

"I'll see you soon." Her voice still sounds thick, which makes Percy swallow convulsively. But he's doing what he can. Ma needs him, so he's going to her.

The patio door slides open with a plasticky clatter just as Percy disconnects. He turns to face Rob, who's tugging up his boxer briefs. "Everything okay, babe?" he asks, a notch between his eyebrows.

Percy forgets he's not wearing anything but underwear and goes to slip his phone into his pocket, barely catching it when there's obviously no pocket to hold it. The urge to stuff his problems away and hoard them all to himself rushes to the tip of his tongue. But he takes a deep breath, willing his voice to come out normally. "No. Um. No, not really."

The notch in Rob's forehead deepens and he comes forward, arms going around Percy instantly. "What's up?"

"Oh god." Percy lets his head drop so he can rest his forehead against Rob's shoulder. From that position, he explains everything. What he knows, at least. His father's expedited trial date, his mother's request for him to return home. Through it all, a need grows inside him, starting at a whisper and increasing in volume until it's a siren screaming in his brain.

"What are you gonna do?" Rob asks. His arms are still tight around Percy. One of his hands is rubbing up and down Percy's spine. Against all odds, Percy finds his shoulders unknotting a little. Just Rob's presence makes everything better. Percy didn't think another person could ever have that power. Then he met Rob.

"I'm going back," Percy says. By this time, his face is turned into Rob's neck. Rob smells like bed and home. "I have to. She sounded so—I just have to."

"Yeah, yeah. Of course." Rob holds him tighter. "When are you leaving?"

"Well, tomorrow, I guess. I don't think I can get a ticket for today. I don't think airlines do that anymore?"

Abruptly, Rob steps back, holding Percy's shoulders. There's a happy smile on his face. "I can get you on a flight today! I mean, my dad can. I'll call him right now; I bet there are still seats available. He can totally get a standby ticket for you; Delta pilot, remember?"

"Will you come with me?" Percy blurts. It's not what he meant to say. He meant to say *Thank you.* Probably. Or maybe that was exactly what he meant to say, because the siren that's been wailing in his mind abruptly quiets.

Rob makes things better. He wants Rob with him through this.

The smile on Rob's face falters. "Come with you?"

Percy nods and reaches up to hook his fingers around Rob's wrists. "It will just. Um." Why did this have to be so hard to say? Why did it have to be so difficult to ask for help? To articulate that he needs things from other people, to actually *say it out loud* and not expect them to intuit it?

He promised himself, and Rob, that he'd be better. He promised he'd tell Rob things. With a deep breath, he presses on, "It will be… better. Easier. For me. You make things that way. Better, I mean. You make it so I can get through the really hard stuff."

Rob looks a shade lighter, and the smile has fallen completely from his face. He doesn't say anything. Maybe Percy wasn't clear.

"I sort of need you, I think." Percy swallows hard, trying to clear the lump from his throat. "To be there, I mean. But if you can't, I…. Well, if you can't, you can't. I know it's last minute. Stupid last minute."

"Yeah, I just…." Rob's mouth opens and closes soundlessly for a few seconds, and Percy's heart plummets somewhere into the region of the Earth's mantle. "I'm not sure. With work, you know. I have a piece I'm supposed to send in tomorrow."

Percy waits to hear if there's more. There's not. Rob looks anguished.

"Oh," Percy says. Then, "No. I understand. Of course."

"I'm gonna call my dad," Rob says. He won't meet Percy's eyes. Percy wishes he would. It's not in him right now to articulate the soup of thoughts in his brain, but he could at least try to tell Rob with his eyes that it's okay. He really does understand. This is a lot to ask. Too much to ask, really. Even if they'd known each other for more than a few months, it's a milly thing to ask. *Get on a fifteen-hour flight with me today because I have to deal with the thing I've been trying to not deal with for months, and it would be comforting if you were with me.*

Okay, so. Maybe it's not the craziest thing.

Rob's shoulders hunch and he turns away. The screen door clatters shut behind him. In a minute, Percy hears him on the phone talking to his dad.

He needs to pack. He needs to let Kayla at Explore Georgia know he won't be able to work on the project for… for… a while. A week? A few weeks? Maybe he needs to plan on working on the project while he's in South Africa.

He needs to make sure his meds and his passport and his visa and supporting evidence are all in order. If Rob's dad is able to get him on the Cape Town flight today, it leaves in the afternoon. There are things to do.

All Percy does, though, is sit down on the plastic chair on the patio. He puts his head in his hands.

In the distance, the blue jays call to each other.

Part Six: ATL

Chapter Thirty-Two

Rob offered to drive Percy to the airport but Percy demurred, which leaves Rob sitting in his house alone, sick to his stomach and knowing he messed up.

Dad came through, of course. Got Percy on that flight to Cape Town this afternoon, with his only condition being that Rob brings Percy to dinner at his parents' once Percy is back. He was kind of joking, kind of not. His parents know about Percy, but they haven't met him yet. After Rob's spectacular plane crash of a failure this morning—real TWA Flight 800 levels of disaster—he's not sure they ever will.

God. He fucked up so bad.

It's just. When Percy said he needed him, all Rob could think was, *But this is so huge, and what if I mess up?* Like sitting in the exit row of an airplane. He can read the safety card all he wants, and he can be totally capable of lifting fifty pounds over his head. What if, when the moment comes and everyone is counting on him, he does the wrong thing? What if he lets everyone down and they all die?

In that moment that Percy said *I need you*, it didn't occur to Rob that life is full of exit rows and people counting on you. Percy was already counting on him, and Rob showed that he can't be relied upon.

His stomach churns and he buries his face in his hands. The *I have a piece due* excuse was true, but come on. He can churn that out in a couple hours. "Six Places to Relax and Reconnect." It's the kind of stuff he writes in his sleep, a listicle that will probably show up as an ad somewhere with links to airlines and luggage companies.

Rob checks the time. It's just after noon. Percy boards his flight at six. What does that say, that Percy bounced and headed to the airport hours earlier than he needed to? It says he's probably reevaluating their relationship in light of Rob's complete and utter emotional cowardice.

He sent Percy off, alone, to face the thing that's haunted him for months. And what's worse, he did it after Percy was brave enough to say he needed Rob to be there with him.

"My piece should be called 'Six Ways to Ruin the Best Thing in Your Life,'" he says to the empty house. Or the wishful-thinking sequel that he doesn't know how to write: "Six Ways to Fix the Relationship You Ruined."

Yeah right. One: show your boyfriend you actually are capable of being there for him. What's he going to do, show up at the airport and tell Percy he was stupid and made a giant mistake?

The thought crystallizes within Rob. That… is a thing he can do. He can still get on that plane with Percy and be the person his boyfriend needs. ATL can be a good place in their relationship—one of the stars in the constellation of them.

Suddenly, Rob knows what he's going to do. He jumps up, and then he sits down, and then he stops and thinks. Percy flew across the world to apologize to Rob. Rob can do better than just driving to the airport.

He stares into the distance, thinking, before he grabs his laptop off the side table.

Then he opens it up and starts to write.

Chapter Thirty-Three

"We'll begin general boarding for Cape Town in a few minutes. At this time, we'd like to offer anyone who needs a few extra minutes on the jetway to board."

Pre-boarding flashes up on the television screens around the departure lounge. Percy picks at one corner of his passport. He's never felt this nauseating combination of both desperately wanting to get on a plane and wanting to run in the opposite direction. Everything is unsettled and swirling around him: Pa's trial getting moved up, reconciling with Ma, and… whatever's going to happen with Rob.

Percy's still in shock about it. He keeps half-turning to say something to Rob, or just to grab his hand to ground himself, before he remembers Rob isn't here on the flimsiest of reasons.

Maybe it was all too fast. Too soon. Maybe this is it for them, even though Percy's entire body aches at the thought. He's always fallen hard and fast, but it's never felt like this when he contemplated it being over—like he's amputating part of himself, something vital that will leave him only half a person when it's gone.

He feels stupid. And hurt. And not ready to give up, even though he probably should. Katli would probably tell him he should. He talked to her—and Eunice—during the interminable afternoon he's spent puttering around Atlanta International Airport. Didn't tell them what had happened with Rob, because… well, it's not as though much actually happened.

It's just—he got it in his head that the secret was open communication. And he did open communication. He was vulnerable and admitted he needed Rob there. And Rob still said no.

Maybe it's the same as what Ma said to him earlier. *You're not the only one allowed to have complicated feelings about things.* He's not the only one with baggage. He's not the only one who cocks things up and makes mistakes. He can't fix everything just because he fixes himself, because he's not everything that's wrong in life.

Open communication can only take you so far. If you don't want the same things as another person, if you're not willing to take hits for them, no amount of communication can ever bridge that gap. It doesn't make either him or Rob bad people; it just makes them not right for each other.

Percy's throat closes. The problem is, Rob felt so right for him. Percy was so sure, and now it's crumbling again.

The PA system clicks. *"At this time, we'd like to welcome passengers seated in first class to board. Rows one through nine, you're welcome to board now."*

Percy starts. That's him. He clutches his passport to his chest and looks down at the black, glaring blank screen of his phone, which is perched on his knee. He should text Rob. Despite the gaping fissures in Percy's heart, they haven't actually broken up.

Before he can go over it a million more times in his head, he dashes off a quick text—*Boarding now, text you when we land*—and pockets his phone. He stands and slings his bag over his shoulder. It contains his laptop, his camera, and his medication. Everything else is either at Rob's house or Percy's flat in Cape Town. He hasn't brought anything because he doesn't know where he'll end up. All he knows is that his heart is in those two places, but that he'd have gone anywhere for Rob.

He queues to board. Just before he reaches the gate agent, he's filled with an overwhelming certainty that Rob's going to surprise him with a grand romantic gesture and cranes his head to look over his shoulder.

All he sees are the low ceilings and utilitarian gray carpet of the airport terminal. The stream of people going to and from their gates flows swiftly in the center of the walkway and slows to eddies along the edges. There's one of those ubiquitous airport shops selling device cables for everyone who forgot theirs; next to it is a bookstore for people who forgot something to read.

No Rob. No grand gesture. No indication at all that Percy still has a boyfriend instead of an ex.

An older white man in a pith helmet standing behind Percy gives him a disapproving look. "You're next," the man says impatiently.

"Sorry," Percy says. Not half as sorry as he is that there's no last-minute, miraculous appearance by Rob.

The gate agent scans his boarding pass and Percy walks down the jetway, feeling heavy. Of course Rob didn't make a last-minute appearance. Rob made it clear he wasn't willing to come along to South Africa.

There's a queue to get on the plane at the end of the jetway—someone's standing in the aisle struggling to get a nearly full-size suitcase into the overhead bin. Pith Helmet's footsteps thump on the jetway and Percy prepares himself for another impatient comment.

A voice behind him says, "Six Places to Fall in Love, by Rob Hale."

Percy's brain hiccups and his heart jolts into his throat. He turns around. There, behind him, is—a miracle.

Rob stands there, breathing heavily, his passport clutched in one hand and his phone in the other. He's disheveled and sweaty, his hair flyaway and a line of damp down the center of his T-shirt.

He's the best thing Percy has ever seen.

Before the gears of Percy's brain can start turning to make words—any words, even a bald statement of the obvious like *You're here*—Rob speaks again, holding his phone up to read from it. "Number one: the South African bush. By some wild turn of fate, you get chosen to spend a week in the company of your favorite photographer, whom you also, possibly, happen to have a bit of a crush on. You learn that he's smart, and interesting, and that he has a sense of humor and a smile like sunshine in winter."

Percy's heart does something stupid.

"Number two: a safari camp. Dinner by torchlight while the Milky Way arcs overhead, and you can't do anything but fall further for a man you can't believe you just met."

They're starting to draw a crowd. A couple flight attendants have stepped out of the plane into the jetway, and the passengers in front of Percy have all turned around. Normally Percy would despise being stared at, because normally it's because of who he is.

It might as well just be the two of them standing in the jetway, though, from the way Rob holds Percy's eyes. "Number three," Rob goes on, "Cape Town. It's a beautiful city you can't help but fall in love with, and you see all the sights. But the one thing that Cape Town will always be to you is sitting in a garden at sunset, watching gulls drift on thermals against the pink and orange of the sky as you hold hands with a beautiful, amazing, complicated man. And you know you can't possibly let him go, even though it's going to be hard to hang on to this thing you have between you."

Rob's eyes have taken on a shine and he has to stop to clear his throat. There's a lump in Percy's throat too, but something is expanding in his chest—something all wings and sky and the scatter of stars at night.

"God, can you have your romantic moment off to the side so the rest of us can sit down?" someone grumbles from behind Rob.

Pith Helmet rounds on them. "Let the man finish, for god's sake!" He pats Rob on the shoulder. "Go on, son, finish proposing."

The urge to cry flips itself to laughter, and Percy has to clap a hand over his mouth. Laughing in the middle of Rob's romantic gesture would be a truly shit move. Except Rob's eyes are bright with laughter now, too, and he says, "I can read you the rest on the plane. If you want."

There's worlds in that *if you want*. Percy takes a breath and says, "What's number six?"

The hitch in Rob's throat makes Percy ache—ache and then reach for Rob's hand, determined to hold it even though Rob's still holding his passport. "Number six." Rob puts away his phone and interlaces his fingers with Percy's. "Hartsfield-Jackson Atlanta International Airport, where you say I love you, and I'm sorry, and I'll sit in any exit row with you." His fingers squeeze Percy's tight. "I never want to let you down again, Perce. I was a scared idiot this morning, but I'll be there when you need me. Or when you want me. I'll go anywhere with you. I'm sorry I made you doubt that."

"Rob," Percy says. "What I need right now is for you to kiss me."

Rob's eyes get so bright that they have to be flecked with gold and amber—nothing else could catch the light like that. "That's easy," he says.

Except as usual, Percy can't wait, and he hauls Rob in for a crashing, messy kiss. It's a kiss that strides into Percy's rib cage and doesn't leave room for anything else, pouring itself into every empty space inside him until he's full up with a sharp, glowing happiness. Rob tastes like coffee and copper, and his lips are rough, like he's been chewing them, but they're soft, too, and they feel like home.

The sound of applause makes them break apart. Percy's face is hot, but he's smiling so wide his face hurts. Rob's fingers slide up the back of Percy's neck to cup his head. As they lean their foreheads together, Rob murmurs, "That wasn't a marriage proposal, just to be clear. Not that I don't—I mean, you know. First things first, win back the most amazing man I've ever met."

Percy wraps his arms around Rob and breathes him in, the scent of him and the warmth of his breath against Percy's face feeling like the greatest, most perfect intimacy. Like lying side by side in a tent under the stars, or standing under towering trees where it's nothing but the two of you and the sound of leaves rustling in the sunlight.

He kisses Rob once more. "Well, we have to leave something for later."

Epilogue

One year later

THE EXPERIENCE of spending ninety minutes in a prison waiting room probably isn't going in Rob's travel blog, but there's nowhere he'd rather be.

Okay, so. Maybe kind of an exaggeration. There are definitely places he'd rather be, but the *reason* he's here is a good one, and you couldn't drag him away. Wild horses and all that. Not when Percy's been making himself sick over this visit for the past month. No way was Rob not joining him for his visit back to South Africa. And no way was Rob not going with Percy to the minimum-security prison where his father is serving his sentence.

Rob is the only person who's remained in the waiting room. Everyone else arrives, checks in, and takes a seat until they're escorted to the visitation area. Rob asked Percy if he wanted him to go with back there, and Percy closed his eyes, said "Yes," then immediately added, "No, not really. I have to do this on my own."

The door opens and Rob whips his head toward it, just like he's done every time for the past ninety minutes. This time, he's rewarded—it's Percy. Rob is on his feet without thinking and crossing the room to his fiancé. Before he's said a word, he's wrapping an arm around Percy's waist and pulling him close. His lips brush Percy's cheek, stubbornly stubbly even though his ma suggested he shave.

"You okay?" Rob murmurs.

"I've been better," Percy replies.

Despite his words, he doesn't sound so bad. Considering he threw up last night at the peak of an anxiety attack, Rob's surprised.

Rob takes his hand. Percy squeezes it hard. "Where to now?"

They'd joked last night that since the prison was so close to Stellenbosch and wine country, they should do one of those tram wine tours after the visit, maybe look for a wedding venue. The reality, of course, is that Percy looks gray and exhausted and definitely not in the mood for a tram wine tour with a bunch of tourists—let alone wedding planning.

"Home," Percy says, rubbing the heel of his hand over his face. "We can still get drunk on wine, though."

Rob gives Percy's hand another squeeze and fishes the keys to Percy's truck out of his pocket. It seemed like a good idea for him to drive to the prison and back, considering Percy's nerves. His medication is really good and keeps him level most of the time, but a day like this would put a strain on even the most mentally healthy person.

As they leave the prison facility, they have to show their passports at the security gate. Then they're out. Mountains rise on one side of the road, brown with hints of green. The Cape Winelands sort of resemble Italy if you don't look too close, but then you realize the trees look different, and the vegetation isn't right, and the rocks look so much more ancient.

Rob's been learning about fynbos, both because Percy gets so passionate about it and because he's genuinely interested. While Percy unwinds in the passenger seat, Rob quizzes himself on the trees and shrubs they're passing. When Percy's ready to unpack the visit with his father, he'll say something. Until then, Rob's going to identify trees and concentrate on driving stick, which still requires more concentration than driving an automatic.

He decided to take the slightly longer and slower route through Stellenbosch because it's a nicer drive. As Rob navigates through Stellenbosch, a university town that can't get enough of its own hipster whimsy, Percy breaks his silence. "You're getting really good at driving stick."

Throwing a grin Percy's way, Rob says, "Must be my teacher. He was really good. Though I'm kind of surprised I learned anything, since I was pretty busy checking him out. And thinking about driving another kind of stick."

A hint of a smile twitches at Percy's lips. "I hope not. Those were all practical lessons; you were supposed to be watching the road."

At a stoplight, Rob reaches over to touch Percy's knee. "You want to grab dinner anywhere on the way home?"

Percy shakes his head. "Let's order in."

They're on the other side of Stellenbosch, heading back into the vineyards and mountains, before Percy speaks again. "He was so... normal."

Rob glances over. His role in this conversation is simply to facilitate—to allow Percy to process his feelings by verbalizing them. Yeah, he's been to a therapy session or two with Percy, one of them specifically to prepare for this day. "Normal?" he prompts.

Of course, Percy was in those sessions too, and the look he gives Rob is wry. "Yeah. Like… I was visiting the house or something. Like I'd come back from a shoot somewhere and had gone round to say hello." He lapses into silence for a mile or so. "I told him to stop pretending he wasn't in prison. And he"—Percy's face twists—"he said, 'Pretending I'm not in prison is the only way I can get through this.'"

"Oof."

"So I said if it's so easy for him to pretend he's not in prison, maybe he needs to be moved to a higher-security facility."

Rob and Percy have had a lot of conversations about how this visit would go. Percy has imagined countless arguments, cutting one-liners, and shattering speeches. For a while, he swore he'd never visit his father in prison, but somewhere along the line, he changed his mind. Maybe it's because according to Percy's ma, his father keeps asking for him. Maybe it's just something he finally felt ready to do.

But Rob doesn't remember Percy envisioning that his father would act like nothing was wrong. "He didn't seem like he was being, like… abused or anything, right?" Rob asks.

"No, nothing like that. I think he just…." Percy makes a frustrated noise. "He says he's sorry. You know? Like during the trial, when he was so contrite and begging for the country's forgiveness. He says the right things, but then he wants to pretend he's at some kind of… I don't know. Men's retreat or something. Like he's going to golf tomorrow or have an exorbitant lunch with the CEO of Anglo American."

Percy stares out the window. They're passing a particularly pretty section of mountains. Misty clouds crown the very tops, tendrils of fog trickling down the sides. There are vineyards stretching out on either side of them, grapevines laid in neat rows, rolling with the contours of the valley.

Sometimes Rob is amazed that this is the same country where he watched a rhino and her calf drink from a river and came face-to-face with a cheetah. Which is a really American conceit. Other countries are big too. Other countries have their own sea to shining sea, their own multitudes. It doesn't even require size—he's from Oahu, for god's sake, where the windward and leeward sides of the island are worlds apart.

"Are you glad you visited?" Rob hazards. *He* is, regardless of what Percy says. Percy needed this, whether it was closure or the start of something new between him and his father. Plus, it's a visit to South Africa. Percy's in the US for at least another two years, so any reason for him to get home has merit in Rob's book. They haven't set a date for the wedding yet, only decided that they want it to be here.

Percy's forehead thunks against the window before he looks over at Rob. "I'm glad I tried. I think? At least, I'm glad he's exactly the person I was afraid he was. Not *glad*. I—" He makes a frustrated sound. "I'm *vindicated*. I think that's as close as I can get to describing it."

They drive another mile or two in silence. Then Percy says, "And sad. Vindicated and sad. It doesn't make very much sense."

"It makes sense." Rob signals a turn. "Okay, maybe it doesn't. But maybe it doesn't have to?"

Warm fingers cover Rob's on the steering wheel for a fleeting moment. After a year, Rob knows every inch of Percy's hands: the bitten nails, the calluses from his camera, the scar across two knuckles from a schoolyard fistfight.

"Maybe not," Percy concedes. Then: "At least one thing does."

Rob hooks his fingers into Percy's. "Chinese for dinner. Definitely."

Percy snorts with undignified, purifying laughter.

When they get back to Cape Town, Rob has to let Percy park the truck in his apartment building's garage after he stalls it three times. Once it's safely in its berth, they go inside and open a bottle of wine to drink in the garden.

The bird feeders are all newly filled as of this morning, and as the two of them press close on the canopied loveseat, birds flit around the garden. Cape white-eyes and canaries flutter around while lemon doves coo from the surrounding trees, occasionally making forays to the ground to peck for seeds in the grass. A jewel-bright malachite kingfisher alights on a stalk of long grass before darting away again.

Percy lets out an excited squeak and taps Rob's knee with one hand while he points at the hummingbird feeder with the other. Not a hummingbird feeder in South Africa—here they have sunbirds and sugarbirds. Percy's been trying to tempt one to his garden but hasn't had any luck—until now.

The sunbird feeder sits in the middle of a fynbos garden, which Percy planted the previous March during their last visit to the Cape. He pays a service that specializes in fynbos to take care of his gardens and indoor plants (they fill the birdfeeders too), which he says is extravagant but a worthwhile use of money, considering most of the fynbos biome is endangered.

The proteas are just starting to flower, and a sunbird is sitting on the feeder hook, looking between the feeder and the flowers. Rob holds his breath, afraid to breathe in case he scares it away. Percy doesn't have his camera, which is probably killing him on one hand, but also making him happy he can appreciate the sighting without the distraction of trying to capture it.

The sunbird's feathers flash in the angled afternoon sunlight, iridescent blue-green-purple on its head and breast band, while its breast is a bright, searing orange, the same color as the sun as it sets across the ocean. Its curved bill and button-black eye make it look very judgy, which is a dumb observation Rob's going to keep to himself. Well. For now.

They watch as the bird cocks its head before it hops down to investigate the proteas. It nuzzles its bill into the flowers for a minute, then flies back up to the feeder. There, it drinks its fill of sugar water.

It turns around, regards the two of them watching in rapt silence, and flies away in a rustle of feathers. It looks like a piece of costume jewelry taking flight, bright and flashing.

Percy lets out his breath in a whoosh of air. A smile breaks out over his face. "Did you see?" he asks excitedly.

Rob can't stop himself from kissing Percy swiftly. "I saw," he confirms.

"Wow," Percy exhales. "I'll consider that a reward rendered for character growth."

"Definitely." Rob wraps his arm around Percy and pulls them tight together. Percy leans his head against Rob's. "I'm super proud of you. You know that, right? Visiting your dad after everything… facing that when you could have just walked away…. That's amazing. *You're* amazing. I'm proud of you, and I really hope you're proud of yourself too."

Percy puts his hand over Rob's where it sits on his own hip, and Rob opens his fingers so Percy can slide his between the gaps. "I'm telling myself I should be proud. That's a victory for now."

Turning his head to kiss Percy's cheek, Rob says, "Gotta take the wins."

There's a minute or two of comfortable, companionable silence. Percy takes both their wine glasses to set them aside on a table. He swings a leg over Rob and straddles his lap so they're facing each other, the warm press of Percy's body against his making Rob feel like he has a flock of those sunbirds inside him.

"Hey," Percy says.

"Hey yourself," Rob replies.

Percy puts his hands on either side of Rob's face and holds them there, camera calluses resting on Rob's cheekbones, fingertips alighting on his pulse point. His inky eyes regard Rob before a smile tugs at his lips. "You know what?" he asks. "I don't think I ever thanked you for applying to come on that photo safari with me."

Rob laughs his dumb seal-bark laugh, and it's so loud that a bunch of doves take panicked flight. Percy grins and kisses him, lips warm and soft.

"Anytime," Rob says.

Acknowledgments

This book wouldn't exist without covid-19, a Botswana airstrip losing its clearance to land international flights, and a last-minute scramble by our travel agent to book my wife and me into a new safari camp on a trip to South Africa that the pandemic had already delayed by a year. Thanks are in order to Katie at Travel Beyond for sending us to Marakele National Park and the Waterberg. I fell in love with that last minute safari camp and the region, and this book is a tribute to a place that feels like home to me now.

To the wonderful guides we've had, who are the most knowledgeable, personable, and quick-thinking people I've ever met; thank you for sharing your knowledge and entertaining my sometimes puzzling questions. Timba, Marco, and especially Frinette—I couldn't have written this book without the time you spent with me. Thank you also to the entire staff at Marataba.

Thank you to Anke for the beta read, and huge thanks to Amber for the sensitivity read. As always, the Dreamspinner team makes the process of turning a manuscript into a published book so smooth. Thank you so much to my editors, the art department, marketing team, and everyone else who has a hand in the process!

My little panther, Isabella, kept me company while I wrote, going all the way back to that very first (unpublished) novel sixteen years ago. I'll never have the words to express how much you mean to me, little cat.

Finally, thank you to my wife, Laura, who reads the first drafts and is always game for an adventure.

Keep reading for an excerpt from
Strangers to Husbands
by Lee Pini!

Chapter One

Lewis is drunk off his ass when he decides riding the mechanical bull is an awesome idea. After finding his pockets disappointingly empty of cash, he gets Stacy—also super fucking drunk—to spot him ten bucks.

When he gets back, some guy is handing over a ten to the operator. Lewis leans his elbows on the railing to wait his turn, and the guy looks over and meets his eyes.

Lewis's stomach swoops, and it's not just the six shots of tequila he chased the pitcher of beer with. The guy has this beautiful head of auburn hair, curly and thick, gorgeous cheekbones, longish, pointy nose, a sharp chin, and an even sharper smile. He's T-A-L-L, taller than Lewis, all legs in tight black skinny jeans. Jesus fuck it should be illegal for someone to walk around with a bulge like that.

The guy smiles slowly and says something to the operator, who shrugs and nods. "Wanna join me, cowboy?" Tall, Dark, and Gorgeous drawls to Lewis.

"Um," Lewis says. The guy unsteadily crosses the crash pad to the bull and puts one foot in the stirrup. Lewis's eyes go straight to his ass.

Damn. He is tooootally not a one-night stand kind of guy because he believes in LOVE, that's L-O-V-E Love. Or wait, no? He doesn't, not anymore. Love is dead! Love is dead, so he should blow this guy in the bathroom.

Hot Mystery Man's shimmery black tank pulls taut across his chest. Muscles in his forearm pop as he holds the pommel on the bull's saddle. The divots of his collarbone look like the perfect place for Lewis to put his tongue.

Does he want to join? Um, *yeah* he wants to join. He wants to join so bad he trips over his feet as he stumbles across the crash pad.

"How's that going to work, though?" Like he cares about anything except getting closer to this man.

The guy's gaze travels from Lewis's head to his feet and back up, lingering at his hips, his chest, his shoulders, and his mouth. Heat floods Lewis. His jeans tighten as his cock stirs.

"You'll know what to do once we start." The guy swings into the saddle and pats what little space is left beside him.

Yeah! He will, totally. He will, and—oh shit. Lewis knows he shouldn't ogle but he gets an eyeful of what's between the guy's legs, and. Nnnng. That is. He is. Okay they're in a western bar so the joke is *right there* but—

Okay. Fine. Yeah. The guy is well hung. And Lewis's mouth is literally watering.

If he was sober, he'd wait his turn. But he's not sober. He is not at allll sober. So he climbs on and finds himself basically in his new friend's lap, Lewis facing forward and the man facing backward. The heat of his legs pressing into Lewis's brings the stomach swooping back.

"Shouldn't we face the same way?" Lewis asks.

Up close, he can see Mystery Man's blue eyes and a thick scatter of freckles that start on his cheekbones and spill down his neck. How far down do they go?

The guy's smile gets wicked, and he leans forward. His lips brush Lewis's ear. And then it's all hot breath and gravel as the guy says in a low, dirty voice, "I like to look at men when they're giving me a good, hard ride."

"Fuck," Lewis breathes.

The guy draws back, looking ridiculously pleased with himself. And ridiculously drunk.

Lewis puts his hands on the guy's knees, and at his nod, slides his palms up his thighs to his waist. The man arches into his touch, and his body is warm and firm and Jesus—will Stacy be cool if he bails on the bachelorette party to take this gorgeous man back to his hotel room?

The mechanical bull starts rocking slowly, swinging in a gentle circle, and Lewis absolutely cannot tear his eyes away from the way the man moves. His hips roll, all fluid sex on legs, and one of his arms loops around Lewis's back as he shifts closer. He slides into Lewis's lap, and they're moving against each other, grinding their hips, and Lewis is so hard it hurts.

There's a rope overhead, and the guy pulls himself up with it. Lewis gets a view of his abs and treasure trail, and he wants to put his mouth there and lick and suck his way down, down, down—

His mouth waters. The guy's legs hook around his back, and he rubs his hard cock against Lewis's stomach.

Lewis can't breathe.

There's a shrill whistle and a couple catcalls. Without looking, Lewis knows it's the bachelorette party. A small, slightly more sober part of his mind informs him he's never going to hear the end of this—he's basically fornicating on a mechanical bull in the middle of a honky-tonk during his best friend's bachelorette party.

But as Lewis pushes the guy down to the bull's neck and ghosts his lips over the man's jaw with its prickle of stubble, it's pretty hard to care.

He smells like gin and rose; spice and wood; *sweat*, and Lewis has never wanted to take someone to bed so bad in his entire life.

The bull slows and stops. Lewis is still on top of the man. Their faces are inches apart. The man's freckles are like stars. Lewis's pulse pounds in his fingertips and in his crotch. His skin is on fire.

"Lew!" Stacy yells. "Who's your friend?"

The guy grins, and where before he was all sultry and sexy, now he looks a little shy, a little giddy, like maybe he can't believe he just did that. It's adorable.

Lewis grins back. "I think I should probably ask your name?"

"Tad," the man says, biting his lip and watching Lewis's mouth.

Lewis shifts off him as Stacy's friends keep whooping. "I'm Lewis. And I would really, *really* love to buy you a drink, Tad."

"I would really, really love if you bought me a drink," Tad replies. He slides to the ground and helps Lewis down, and the two of them stumble into each other's arms, crash pad undulating beneath their feet.

Lewis laughs and leans into him, Tad's arm goes around his waist, and before Lewis knows it, they're jammed together at the bar, doing shots. "Aren't you here with someone?" Lewis asks.

"My brother and his friends." Tad flaps a hand. "They're not *here*. I left them at some casino."

"You left them to come ride a mechanical bull?"

"I left them because they're boring."

"What about me? Am I boring?"

Tad's hair falls in curly wisps over his forehead. He has the clearest, prettiest blue eyes Lewis has ever seen. "I don't think you're boring. You're like, the least boring person I've ever met."

Leaning into him, Lewis says in his ear, "I don't think you're boring, either." He trails a finger along the line of freckles on Tad's neck, down to where they disappear under the neckline of his tank. "I like these," he adds, because it seems really important for Tad to know.

"Really?" Tad sounds awed.

"Mm-hm." Lewis leans in. It's easy to dip his head to Tad's neck, because Tad is taller than him. He kisses the spot where the freckles spill onto Tad's collarbone and disappear under his clothes.

It's happening, isn't it? Finally. Love at first sight *is* real. Take that, Jonah! And Diego, and Liam, and Jayden, and every other ex-boyfriend who ground him down and made him doubt true love was out there waiting for him. The rom-coms and Disney movies he loves are right, after all! Because his stomach's fluttering and his heart's pounding and every inch of his skin has this buzz pulling him toward Tad.

Sure, Lewis is drunk right now—really, really drunk—but Tad is definitely a person Lewis falls in love-at-first-sight with.

Tequila seems like it will make him fall even more in love with Tad, so he gets another one of those. And so does Tad, and the night turns to a hazy blur of dancing and singing along to Garth Brooks and Dolly Parton and Carrie Underwood. Tad yells to Stacy at one point, "I'm sorry I didn't get you a gift!"

Stacy yells back, "I'm just really happy you're here, Chad!"

"It's Tad!"

Slinging an arm around Lewis's neck, Stacy pulls him in for a sloppy kiss on the cheek and shouts over the music, "Lewis loooooves you, I can tell! Maybe someday you guys will get married! Lewis, I really want us both to be married."

Goddddd Lewis wants to get married so bad. Ahhhh it would be *amazing*. Stace is getting married, which he is like, *so* happy about! They can both be married to the loves of their lives, which Lewis is now like 99 percent sure Tad is. Stacy will marry Alang, and Lewis will marry Tad, and everyone will live happily ever after.

Tad presses into his side. He laughs and nuzzles his face into Lewis's. "We'll have a long engagement."

Which is like the funniest thing Lewis has ever heard, and now he knows he's in love-at-first-sight with Tad.

They leave the bar, and—stuff happens? Stuff must happen, because Lewis is having a blast, he's having so much fun; his hand is in Tad's, he's kissing Tad, and there's champagne. It's the best night Lewis can remember having in forever, even if he already can't remember most of it.

DESERT SUN on his eyelids wakes Lewis. His mouth is gummy, his stomach is sour, and his eyes are sandy. Something is twisted around his legs. Hotel sheets? Hotel sheets. The air conditioner is blowing on him, which is when Lewis realizes he's super naked.

He rolls over, groaning—and discovers he's also super not alone.

But hey, if you're going to wake up in bed with a man you've only known for twelve hours, it might as well be the most beautiful man you've ever seen.

The most beautiful man Lewis has ever seen opens his eyes groggily. His hair is in curly snarls on the pillow. A flash of hot memory scorches through Lewis's body—his fingers twisted in that hair, a warm, wet mouth on his cock.

Mr. Beautiful, He-Of-The-Best-BJ-Lewis-Is-Pretty-Sure-He's-Ever-Had, stretches, and Lewis's eyes track down and back up his body. He's lean and gorgeous, rangy strength, legs for days, *very* nice cock currently providing a nice display of morning wood. The freckles are all over his body. Lewis vaguely remembers trying to kiss all of them before getting distracted by the aforementioned very nice cock.

Lewis hopes his breath isn't toxic. "Hey."

Looking sated and wrecked, Mr. Beautiful says, "Hi."

What are you supposed to say in the morning to the gorgeous guy you drunkenly hooked up with?

"It's Tad, right?"

Which isn't his best effort, but he's rewarded with a bright, beautiful smile. "Yeah. Lewis?"

Well, Lewis doesn't remember a whole lot else about last night, but at least they remember each other's names.

He extends a hand for a handshake. "Lewis Mancini-Sommer."

Tad's smile gets a little crooked and a lot mischievous, and Lewis's heart swoops. "You don't do this very often, do you, Lewis Mancini-Sommer?"

"Dry hump a stranger on a mechanical bull and then hook up with him? Not really."

Tad laughs. It's hoarse, but—it's such a nice laugh. Sounds out of practice. His hand slides into Lewis's and they shake, which is when Lewis realizes there's definitely cum caked in the creases of his palms. Like. Kind of a lot.

"I don't," Lewis says. "I mean, obviously not the mechanical bull stuff. But… yeah, the like, drunk hooking up."

There's a sad little twist to Tad's mouth for a second and he pulls the sheet up to his waist. Maybe Lewis is still drunk, but the sight of Tad being unhappy makes him want to fix it. "Hey, um. Is there, like. Anything you want to… do? Like breakfast? Or, I don't know, coffee?"

Or sex? Because Lewis is leaving Vegas today and obviously never going to see Tad again. So… sex?

Tad's eyes flick to Lewis's. "Can we do each other?" He bites his lip. "Sorry! God. I'm actually usually not like this, like, at all. Slutting it up isn't really my thing. I mean, it's fine if it *is* your thing, like, no slut-shaming! I'm just, like, not that way. Usually. I was last night I guess? Sorry, I just—I was here with my brother and his friends, and they make me feel invisible, and—wow, did I really just ask if you want to fuck and talk about my brother in the same breath…?"

That's a lot of words that Lewis's brain can't really process, not after the ones at the very beginning. "I think we should do each other." He slides a hand over Tad's stomach and up to his chest. His stomach is just defined enough, but still soft. His pecs, on the other hand, are hard and warm, and Lewis has a faint memory of sucking Tad's nipples and him really, *really* liking that.

So he brushes a thumb over one. Tad's eyes close and he breathes in hard, and Lewis rolls on top of him. Tad grabs his hand and brings it to his mouth, then stops. His eyes widen.

"You're married?" he demands.

"What?" Lewis laughs. "Um, no."

Tad jabs a finger at one of Lewis's. "You're wearing a wedding ring. Why would you be wearing a wedding ring if you weren't married?"

"I'm not—" But Lewis's eyes flick to his own hand, and—

He is. He *is* wearing a wedding ring. He's wearing a rose gold band (gay, wow) with a viney, scrolling pattern.

"What the fuck?" Lewis asks, looking at Tad, even though Tad's made it pretty clear the existence of the wedding ring was unknown to him until this moment.

"I don't sleep with married men," Tad says in the same tone you might say *I don't sleep with serial killers.*

"I'm not married!" Lewis repeats. Tad rakes a hand through his hair and starts to get out of bed, but Lewis grabs his wrist. "Um, hey, excuse me, Mr. I-Don't-Sleep-With-Married-Men? What's that on your hand?"

"What's *what* on my—" Tad looks at his left hand. There's a ring there.

Tad stares. "What the hell?"

"Fuck if I know," Lewis says. "I don't know where mine came from, either."

Their eyes meet. Lewis's mouth goes dry, and Tad scooches back into bed with him, holding out his hand until it bumps against Lewis's.

Tad's is also rose gold, with the same pattern of vines and flowers.

The rings match.

The rings. Fucking. *Match.*

"Do you remember what we did last night?" Tad asks slowly.

"Well." Lewis looks at him meaningfully. "I remember doing a lot of things."

Tad's face colors. "Before that."

"Um." Lewis is saved from answering by his phone buzzing. He dives for it and opens the text from Stacy.

"Oh," he says. "Fuck."

I found this in my purse??? Stacy's text says. Beneath it is a photo of a marriage certificate. Lewis can only see four pertinent words on it: Lewis Mancini-Sommer… and Thaddeus Pierce.

Scan the QR Code
Below to Order!

LEE PINI is a queer author who has been writing since they could pick up a pencil. They have lived in England, Northern Ireland, and Florida, and currently live in their home state of Minnesota with their wife and cat. Lee studied archaeology at the graduate level but currently uses their degree primarily to chuckle knowingly at classics memes. When they aren't at their day job or writing, they're reading vociferously, listening to music, enjoying nature, or nerding out. Their dream is for someone to one day write fan fiction about their characters.

Connect with Lee:

Website: www.leepini.com

Instagram: @leepiniwriting

Bluesky: @leepini.bsky.social

Facebook: http://www.facebook.com/lee.pini.is.writing

Follow me on BookBub

When We Finally Kiss Good Night

LEE PINI

Camp Bay Lake Holiday: Book 1

Jake lost his Christmas spirit when his husband left him on December 26. This year, when a friend offers him her reservation at a resort in Florida, he jumps at the chance to get away. No snow, no Christmas trees, no problems.

Except the resort does a Christmas Golf Cart parade every year, and Alex, the man in the neighboring cabin, wants Jake's help with his.

Jake just wants to be left alone… until he spies Alex's design. Maybe working together won't be so bad. Can an unexpected friendship reawaken more than Jake's holiday spirit?

SCAN THE QR CODE
BELOW TO ORDER!

As Long As You
Love Me So
LEE PINI

Camp Bay Lake Holiday: Book 2

Theo Stirling, a shy electrician at Camp Bay Lake Resort, has been secretly in love with his best friend and coworker, Adi Rodriguez, for years. Little does he know, Adi—a bubbly front desk worker and grad student—feels the same way about Theo. Neither has been brave enough to confess their feelings, but this Christmas, they both plan to use the resort's Golf Cart Parade as the perfect moment for a grand gesture.

Just when everything seems to be falling into place, Adi's sister is in a car accident, and he has to miss the parade. Determined not to lose his chance, Theo brings the holiday magic—and his heartfelt confession—directly to Adi and his family, proving that love is worth the wait.

A heartwarming rom-com about friendship, family, and the courage to take a leap, "As Long As You Love Me So" is full of holiday joy, humor, and romance.

SCAN THE QR CODE BELOW TO ORDER!

Good at
People
Lee Pini

In a last-ditch effort to finish a manuscript, Thomas Kovacs packs up his teenage daughter, Alexis, and relocates to a small town in northern England. Things have been strained between them for months, but the closer Thomas gets to the end of his book, the more distant Alexis becomes.

Krishna Singh came to Corbridge to open a bookstore and start a family. After two years, his business is thriving. His family? Well, he hasn't gotten around to that yet. Actually, he hasn't even dated. The closest he gets is bonding over books and music with an American teenager who comes into his shop.

When it turns out the teenager's dad is none other than Krishna's favorite author, he wastes no time in getting to know Thomas. But attempts at something more go about as well as Thomas's writing, or his relationship with Alexis. Can Krishna convince Thomas that they all deserve a happy-ever-after?

SCAN THE QR CODE
BELOW TO ORDER!

The Boyfriend Fix

LEE PINI

Renowned surgeon Ben McNatt is up for the job of his dreams, and when he gets it, he'll be the youngest chief of neurosurgery in his hospital's history. His success rate is flawless, but his perceived lack of compassion is hurting his chances. He's always viewed relationships as a distraction, but a loving partner might change his colleagues' ideas about his heartlessness. He'll do whatever it takes for this promotion—even pretend to date. The natural choice for his fake boyfriend is the cute guy at the coffee shop.

Jamie Anderson is in student loan debt up to his eyeballs. He has three roommates, and not in a quirky found-family way. He works sixty hours a week as a barista, and his boss won't stop hitting on him. He's even given up on love. He makes do with fantasies about the hot doctor that comes in for coffee every day like clockwork.

A fake relationship might solve Jamie's handsy boss problem too. And there's no way it will lead to real feelings when that's the last thing either of them wants.

So why are they having so much trouble convincing themselves they aren't falling for each other?

SCAN THE QR CODE
BELOW TO ORDER!